PRAISE FOR THE AUTHOR

Writing as M

For *Gon*

'[A] stunningly accomplished debut . . . deserves to shoot to the top of the best-seller lists. I read it in a single sitting.'

Daily Mail

'A full-bodied police procedural thriller from start to finish – with a whirlwind plot and sensational sub-stories, it's a real binge-read kind of book.'

Stylist

'A clever but all too believable crime thriller that's right on the money when it comes to creepy, twisted plots.'

Fabulous magazine

'A tense thriller that kept us guessing.'

Heat

'I couldn't put it down. Every single character in *Gone Astray* has a strong and unique emotional story to tell.'

Rachel Abbott, author of *Only the Innocent*

'I read it in one sitting.'

Erin Kelly, author of *He Said/She Said*

For *Wrong Place*

'Gripping.'

Sun

'Cleverly plotted.'

Daily Express

'Full of twists and turns.'

Good Housekeeping

'I loved it . . . A brilliant, compelling read.'
Debbie Howells, author of *The Bones of You*

'Gritty, no-nonsense.'

Red

'This all-too-believable thriller is full of plot twists.'

Essentials

'A gripping debut novel.'

Bella

'[A] compelling, twisty debut crime novel.'

Dead Good Books

For *False Witness*

'Gripping, thought-provoking and expertly plotted – a cracking read.'

Katerina Diamond, bestselling author of *The Teacher*

THE
SEVEN

THE
SEVEN

ROBYN DELVEY

Text copyright © 2025 by Robyn Delvey
All rights reserved.

Published by Thomas & Mercer, Seattle

www.apub.com

Amazon, the Amazon logo, and Thomas & Mercer are trademarks of Amazon.com, Inc., or its affiliates.

ISBN-13: 9781662521935
eISBN: 9781662521928

Cover design by Dan Mogford
Cover image: © Wild Carpathians © Ivan Kovbasniuk © nattapon sukjit98 © faestock / Shutterstock

Printed in the United States of America

For Rory

Prologue

MADELEINE

THEN

21 April, 11.33 a.m.

Madeleine Farmer was on the verge of throwing up. The stench was unbearable. Sour and cloying, it spread like poisonous gas from the centre of the theatre, where the sound and light desks were located. For a few hours now, the area had become a makeshift restroom. The waist-high screens that usually concealed the technical desks from the audience were all that separated users from public view – but it was either go there or soil themselves where they sat.

Trying not to breathe through her nose, Madeleine distracted herself from the foul smell by trying to regain the feeling in her feet. They'd been strapped into high-heeled sandals for almost sixteen hours and were numb. She flexed the muscles in her legs – stretched out in front of her and encased in four thousand dollars' worth of Versace silk – but still the pins and needles didn't ease. She couldn't risk moving any more than that though, because Nye had ordered everyone to sit still and be quiet or else. The last person who'd defied his instructions was still convulsing in the corner.

She grew teary again but blinked quickly to stop herself crying. Emotion was like catnip for Nye and his followers, and showing any fear or distress ran the risk of triggering further violent outbursts. So instead of crying, she counted backwards from a hundred like her therapist had taught her, her body trembling with the effort of trying to calm down.

Eventually – mercifully – her distress began to abate, and around the fifty-four mark she exhaled, grateful that neither Nye nor any of the bastards doing his bidding had seen her distress. The time to cry and break and process would be later, once they were out of this hellhole and safe. For now, her focus had to be on staying calm and staying alive.

Another half-hour passed in silence, until a lone voice rang out. Madeleine looked up, startled. They'd been sitting so quietly that the interruption rattled her, spiking the adrenaline already coursing through her. She wasn't the only one. Others looked up fearfully too. Was something about to start up again? Or had the cops finally done what they should have hours ago and stormed the building? Madeleine didn't understand what was taking them so long. She was aware the British police didn't carry guns like the cops back home in LA, but the delay in rescuing them made no sense. As far as she could tell, there wasn't even a negotiation going on. What were the authorities so scared of? This wasn't like the last time, when Nye had hundreds of people helping him barricade in. She'd counted twenty people inside the theatre alongside him, tops.

But that lone voice was simply someone on the other side of the auditorium needing the toilet. Nausea rose in her again. There were functioning bathrooms in the foyer, but they weren't allowed to use them after Nye had realised that taking the guests out one at a time diluted his group's presence in the auditorium. Two male guests had already tried to take advantage, attempting to take out one young woman on her own. Both men had been badly beaten

2

by her male companions for their trouble. After that the foyer was declared out of bounds, and the group set up the toilet area by the console desks under Nye's instructions.

Patrick Nye. If she hadn't seen him with her own eyes, she'd never have believed it. The infamous cult leader everyone thought had been killed trying to escape the FBI was back from the dead. God only knew how he'd ended up in London, but here he was, living, breathing and holding them hostage while still spouting the same bullshit theories about wealth and greed that had led to his 'demise' in the first place. If she wasn't so scared of what he might do, she'd tell him everything he stood for was a joke. She'd heard more convincing arguments that Santa Claus existed.

But she felt powerless in his presence. Her status as the world's highest-paid actress counted for nothing. Not that it was in her nature to milk it – stars who pulled that 'don't you know who I am?' crap revolted her – but Nye didn't care who she was as an individual. He didn't care about any of them. They were simply his means to an end.

The guest needing the toilet was Samuel, Dame Cynthia's dear assistant. He looked like he'd aged decades in the few hours since they were all sitting on the top table together, his devastation clear to see. None of this was his fault, but she knew he'd blame himself regardless. He'd planned tonight's event with Dame Cynthia's grandson, Matthew, and between them they'd convinced many film-industry names, Madeleine included, to fly to London to celebrate her career. A career now forever tainted by what Nye was putting her guests through.

As Samuel drew level with her, another voice rang out – this time from behind the double doors that led into the foyer. Madeleine and Samuel locked gazes, their expressions mirroring their mutual terror. Then the doors burst open and one of Nye's followers came running in, without the rifle he'd previously been holding. He was still wearing the all-white waiter's uniform he'd acquired to infiltrate the event and the front of his shirt was speck-led with someone else's blood.

'They've escaped,' the man yelled, clearly panicked. 'I couldn't stop them. They got out and the police are outside.'

Madeleine's heart pounded at the thought of rescue, and she scrambled to her feet using the wall behind her for support, ripping her gown in her haste. It was over, they were saved. Others rose to their feet too, patently thinking the same, and a swell of chatter now filled the previously silent auditorium. Nye's followers grew agitated seeing the guests mobilise, shouting at them to sit down again, but the man himself, gazing down at the auditorium from the stage, seemed unperturbed.

'The guests will walk out first,' he said, raising his voice above the clamour. 'We will follow them.'

Relief spread through the theatre, but Nye's followers looked bewildered. The one Madeleine had heard the others refer to as 'Snow White' on account of his pure-white hair – an ironic nick-name, given the particularly vicious streak he'd displayed – rushed up to him.

'You promised we'd get out of this alive,' he cried. 'If we go out there now, they'll shoot us.'

'No, they won't,' said Nye calmly. 'Trust me.'

He had them line up next to the doors. Relieved though she was that freedom was imminent, instinct told Madeleine to hang back where it might be safer. She hid herself within the crowd next to Samuel, but Nye sought her out anyway, shoving people aside to reach her. He forcibly grabbed her arm so she couldn't pull away; he had the cold, flat eyes of a shark. 'You're going first, Ms Farmer,' he said. 'The public will want to see the most famous person here up close.'

Madeleine knew there was no point fighting him this close to escaping. She walked to the front as instructed. When Nye gave the word she stepped into the foyer, trembling with apprehension.

Sunlight streamed through the floor-to-ceiling windows at the front of the theatre, blurring her vision after the dimness of the windowless auditorium. But as she blinked furiously to adjust, she could also see the windows were lit up with flashing blue lights and there was a police cordon in the street outside. Dozens of officers were poised behind it, guns raised. Her face crumpled. Salvation was a few metres away. Now, finally, she could cry.

The rest of the hostages filed out of the auditorium behind her but were soon jostling for space in the much smaller foyer. Madeleine didn't know whether to keep going until they were outside so she looked over her shoulder to search out Nye for his next instruction, fearful of what might happen if she proceeded incorrectly.

She couldn't make him out among the swell of people though. Then, with a start, she realised she couldn't see any of them. She looked wildly from side to side, but there was no sign. Nye and his followers had disappeared.

'They're gone,' she shrieked. 'Oh my God, they're gone.'

Her yell stirred the crowd and people began to shove past her to reach the exit first, tripping over themselves and each other in the process. Madeleine, unsteady on her heels, fell backwards on to the floor. She tried to get up, but someone's foot landed heavily on her stomach, forcing her back down again. Then someone else trod on her, then another, one foot after the next as she howled in agony. Just as she was on the point of passing out, the crowd suddenly stopped surging forward. Someone reached down and tried to pull Madeleine up, which made her scream again, her abdomen burning as though it had been ripped open. Then, over the commotion, she heard a woman near her say, 'Why won't the doors open?'

Seconds later the first bomb went off.

FIFTEEN MONTHS LATER

Chapter One

EVE

Now

Eve Wren paid scant attention to the squalling rain coming down at an angle, holding her umbrella tight and low in her left hand as she hurried through the crowds of commuters walking to work. With her right hand she scrolled the article on her phone, her frown deepening as each new paragraph revealed itself. By the time she'd reached the last line, her Monday morning outlook had gone from fairly middling to angry and despondent.

Crossing at the next junction, she stuffed her phone back into her bag, wishing she hadn't bothered to check it at all. Until this morning she'd managed to push the article's impending publication from her mind, until a reminder notification she'd forgotten to delete pinged just as she was emerging from St James's Park Tube station for the last part of her commute.

The article, posted on a popular legal affairs website, was a run-down of London's best new female criminal defence solicitors under thirty, and Eve was supposed to be on the list. She'd been nominated for the accolade by her managing partner at a respected City law firm, and the website had got as far as interviewing her and even taking her photograph – until her unexpected sacking saw her dropped from the article's line-up. Worse still, it wasn't even her mistake that got her fired.

She'd been preparing a case for court when she'd spotted that a senior partner – also her line manager – had made a serious error that could have resulted in the client having grounds to sue them for a failure to advise. Eve pointed out the mistake, but her colleague refused to admit it was his or rectify it, so she went over his head to report it to the managing partner. She was protecting the client and the firm. Instead, doing the right thing blew up in her face. The managing partner took her colleague's side, agreeing that the error must've been Eve's in the first place. That she was trying to pass the buck. Because she'd been there less than two years, they were legally able to dismiss her without cause.

To add insult to injury, the website then asked the managing partner to put someone else forward to replace her in the article. So it was her colleague's name and beaming smile Eve had just seen where hers should've been.

Rounding the corner into the next street, she grumpily side-stepped a fellow commuter fighting in vain to keep her own umbrella from turning inside out. The woman's mid-length tea dress and flat sandals, normal attire for July, were both soaked through by the unseasonal downpour. She glanced up as Eve passed, taking in her black trouser suit and block-heeled courts that were as comfortable to walk in as trainers, then looked away to resume her battle against the elements.

Eve didn't do summery, not even when it was heatwave temperatures, and despite the dress code at the Crown Prosecution Service, where she now worked, being more relaxed than at her previous employer. She'd joked to friends that the Capri trouser suit – a designer, look-how-well-you're-doing splurge – would be her armour against self-doubt when she moved from the Midlands to London. Since being sacked and joining the CPS, she'd worn it almost every day, alternating with a couple of high-street copycats in different neutrals when it needed dry-cleaning.

Five minutes later she arrived at the CPS headquarters at Petty France, a building in Victoria notable for its hulking Brutalist design. The London South division where she worked was on the second floor and had an open-plan layout.

She hadn't even made it to her desk when a co-worker called Ashley, stationed by one of the windows, called out to her. Eve tensed. Not long after she'd joined the CPS, she'd stupidly confided in the older woman about her sacking over a post-work glass of wine – only for Ashley to blab to the entire office the next day. Since then, Eve had tried to give her a wide berth, but it wasn't easy when they were on the same team.

She was mortified everyone in the division knew she'd been sacked. She'd built a stellar reputation as a criminal defence solicitor on the West Midlands court circuit before a headhunter had approached her about the City job, but now it felt like she was back on the bottom rung and having to prove herself all over again. The scrutiny of her colleagues – particularly Ashley, who sniped about the need for accuracy whenever Eve was within earshot – unsettled her.

But at least her bosses weren't on her back constantly. In her interview for the position, she'd tried to fudge the reason for her departure from the City firm, saying the environment hadn't suited her. But she had been compelled to admit what had happened when the interviewing panel said they'd be seeking a reference. Their reaction to the truth surprised her though. The panel appeared to believe Eve's account and decided the experience of uncovering her former colleague's error made her a great candidate for reviewing cases. She was grateful for the second chance, but the confidence that had got her headhunted to come to London in the first place remained shaken.

Ashley called out her name again. Knowing she couldn't keep ignoring her, Eve pasted on a smile. 'Morning. What's up?'

'Beverly wants to see you. She's not happy about something.' Ashley, on the other hand, sounded positively gleeful.

Eve looked over at their line manager's glass-walled office. Beverly was at her desk and beckoning furiously. Whatever she wanted to see Eve about wouldn't wait.

'You must've done something really bad to put her in such a foul mood,' Ashley added smugly.

Alarmed, Eve dumped her bag on her desk and hurried across the room. She entered Beverly's office with a polite hello and her stomach in a knot. Her contract was in its third month, but she still didn't feel as though she and her boss were at the 'how was your weekend?' stage of familiarity. Nor did Beverly, evidently, launching straight into work.

'Sit down,' she ordered. Then, after a moment's pause – which felt like an age to Eve – she declared, 'We have a problem with a case.'

Eve sat ramrod straight while the knot turned to jelly. Different office, different boss, but the same preamble that had ended with the words 'you'll get two months' severance pay'. She racked her brains trying to think what she might've done wrong. Her caseload included reviewing the evidence for an armed robbery in Hatton Garden in which a jeweller had been shot and paralysed. Just last week Beverly had praised her pre-trial preparation.

'What's the issue?' Eve asked, trying to sound calm. It looked as though being left out of that article wasn't the worst thing to happen to her today.

Beverly reacted like she hadn't heard the question. She looked exhausted, like she hadn't slept a wink. She wasn't making eye contact either, her gaze trained on her computer screen, index finger tapping rhythmically on her keyboard. Eve wished she could see what she was reading. Was it a letter terminating her contract?

'I'm pulling you off the Tindal case,' said Beverly.

Tindal was the surname of the accused in the Hatton Garden case. Eve's throat went dry, but she forced herself to ask. 'Have I done something wrong?'

Beverly shook her head. A few white flecks took flight from her greying bob.

'Not at all. Quite the opposite, in fact. You're being redeployed to work on another case for the next few weeks.'

Eve didn't relax her stiff pose, but her heart thundered in her chest with relief. The echo of that other conversation in that other office faded to white noise. 'Which case?' she asked briskly.

'The Novus Theatre bombing.'

Finally, her composure faltered. 'Really?' she asked, shocked.

'Yes.'

'You're moving me on to the Novus case?'

'That's what I said.' A faint smile played on Beverly's lips. 'Unless you don't want to?'

'But . . . but the trial's already started,' Eve stuttered.

'I know it has, which means we're up against the clock now, playing catch-up. Or rather you are, Eve.'

Chapter Two

Fifteen months previously, forty-three people were killed when two home-made bombs detonated inside the Novus Theatre in the East London district of Stepney. Two dozen more were injured, some life-changingly so. That death toll alone would've made it headline news across the globe, but the nature of the event guaranteed that it was – a black-tie dinner to celebrate the illustrious career of three-time Oscar-winning actress Dame Cynthia Seymour on her home soil. The majority of the deceased invited to attend on 20 April worked in the film industry and more than a third of the hundred and twenty guests had flown in specially from the States to attend the event. Twenty-three of them never made it home.

Then there was Patrick Nye, the mastermind behind the bombing. Not quite the household name Dame Cynthia was – but not far off it.

Californian-born Nye had gained notoriety in the early 2000s as the founder of a non-religious movement called The Decorous. He established the movement to protest against what he called 'the excesses of celebrity corrupting society' and singled out the film industry in particular for its 'slavish devotion to creating obscene wealth and its sexualisation of young people'. Nye had his followers picket studios, movie sets and every premiere and awards show, and pretty soon became as famous as the people he despised.

The Decorous attracted thousands of followers worldwide, with sub-factions springing up in the UK, Europe and Australia. A select few were invited to give up their jobs, homes and families to live with Nye at his compound in the small resort town of Carpinteria, an hour's drive up the coast from LA. Whatever money they had they put straight into Nye's pocket to fund his cause, quickly amassing him a small fortune. His live-in followers included a TV sitcom actress and an NBA all-star shooting guard.

Nye denied accusations he was heading a cult, yet The Decorous bore all the hallmarks, right down to Nye positioning himself as the kind of enigmatic leader the word 'charismatic' was invented for. Tall, sandy-haired and softly spoken, he commanded attention and unwavering devotion from his followers.

Then the FBI received a tip-off from a former Decorous member that Nye was plotting to take his cause to the next level. He'd amassed an arsenal of weapons with the intention of hijacking a film premiere at Hollywood's iconic Grauman's Chinese Theatre, which at the time was newly renovated after being acquired by two studios, Warner Bros. and Paramount Pictures.

Believing the intel to be sound, the FBI carried out a dawn raid on the compound. Nye and his followers fought back, Waco style, until on day three he abandoned them and fled through an underground tunnel, before pitching himself off a nearby cliff into the churning waves of the Pacific Ocean to evade arrest. Although his body was never recovered, he was later declared legally dead, presumed drowned.

Yet Nye was very much alive when he and his newly acquired followers entered the Novus Theatre last April and proceeded to humiliate and torture Dame Cynthia's guests to mark the resurrection of both himself and the Decorous movement. Now he and six others were standing trial at the Old Bailey charged with carrying out the bombing and orchestrating the sit-in that had precipitated it. With the evidence stacked against them including scores of eye-witness accounts and even live footage broadcast from inside the theatre, it was little wonder legal commentators were calling it one of the most 'bang to rights' cases in the history of British justice.

The accused – collectively branded The Seven by the media – had other ideas though and pleaded not guilty to each and every charge of murder, conspiracy to commit murder and conspiracy to cause an explosion. They were invoking 'loss of control' as their defence, arguing they had been provoked by the actions of others. In other words, by virtue of who they were and the greed and iniquity they represented, the guests at the Novus Theatre had brought it upon themselves.

No one expected the defence to fly. But in exercising their right to a free and fair trial, The Seven were ensuring that every pernicious, horrifying detail of what had happened that night became public record. Nye didn't want his crimes paraphrased at a sentencing hearing – he wanted the world to know he couldn't be stopped. Two decades after his first attempt to hijack a celebrity event was thwarted, he and his followers had finally brought the rich and famous to their knees.

'What do you need me to do?' Eve asked, excited but mystified why she'd be selected for the case. There were advocates at the CPS with more experience than her and who'd worked there longer. Why her?

'Have you seen this?'

Beverly had a copy of that morning's *Guardian* on her desk, and she pointed to it. Even upside-down Eve could easily read the banner headline on the front page:

RAPE TRIAL COLLAPSES AFTER CRUCIAL EVIDENCE IS LOST

'The defendant was acquitted because the DO mislaid a statement from a witness who swore they saw the accused elsewhere at the same time he was meant to be attacking the victim,' said Beverly. 'Defence pushed for a dismissal and got it.'

It wasn't a case Eve was familiar with, but she understood the ramifications. Disclosure officers were serving police officers, but the outcome would reflect poorly on the CPS as well. Too many cases recently had collapsed at trial stage due to misplaced evidence, and the pressure to stop the rot was being felt from the Director of Public Prosecutions – head of the CPS – at the top of the chain, right down to Crown advocates like Eve, whose job it was to review case evidence submitted by the police.

'The same DO was on Novus in its early stages,' said Beverly. 'Last night the Attorney General ordered an urgent review of any evidence he handled.'

Eve blanched. The intervention of the government's chief legal adviser underlined the seriousness of the situation: if this DO had also failed in his duty on Novus, it could force a retrial and would feed into Patrick Nye's narrative that he and his followers were disruptors of the Establishment.

'Logistically we can't halt the trial now that it's started, so the review will have to be done in tandem, and bloody quickly,' Beverly added.

Eve knew this wasn't unusual: case evidence was often reviewed as a trial proceeded. But the sheer magnitude of Novus made it a daunting prospect.

'One of our most senior advocates, John Horner, has been on Novus since day one and he's already reviewing all the evidence this DO put into disclosure both for us and the defence. We don't expect him to find any problems because he was thorough in the first place and the defence has been all over the disclosure like a rash too, and they've not flagged anything.' Beverly grimaced, which

17

made her look even more worn out. 'It's the unused evidence this DO oversaw that kept me awake most of last night.'

'Unused evidence' was the term used to describe anything that came to light during the course of the investigation deemed not important enough to be presented in court. There was a variety of reasons why such evidence might not be chosen, including that it would simply be a waste of everyone's time hearing it, such as a statement taken from a bystander witness who had seen the aftermath of the incident but nothing particularly crucial. But it was material that still needed to be gathered by the police to show that every line of inquiry had been pursued. Unused evidence still needed to be collated and entered into the system by disclosure officers in order that the CPS and defence teams knew it existed. The hard copies often ended up dumped in boxes in a corner of some incident room, gathering dust.

'With Sol's approval, your sole remit is to review all the unused evidence this DO handled. It's currently stored at Lewisham station.'

Solomon 'Sol' Archer was the DPP. That he even knew who Eve was came as a surprise.

'There shouldn't be much – it sounds like the officer was moved off the investigation pretty early on. I spoke to the SIO this morning, DCS Strutton, and he's adamant the disclosure process has been rigorous throughout, but this' – Beverly jabbed the newspaper headline with her finger – 'means we have to be sure. If this DO overlooked anything we need to know before the trial goes any further. The OIC is a DS Lees and he'll be your other contact at Lewisham.'

OIC stood for officer in charge. It was the OIC's job to ensure all lines of inquiry had been pursued in an investigation, and they were also responsible for appointing DOs to report to them. Eve imagined DS Lees had had a sleepless night too after yesterday's case collapsed.

'Why was the DO moved off the case?' she asked.

'No idea, and it's not important. Reviewing the unused material is your only concern right now.'

'Would finding something really make a difference at this stage?' Eve wondered aloud. 'What's being heard in court will surely be enough to secure their convictions.'

It helped that she'd followed Novus since day one. Her interest was naturally piqued by the complex legal aspects of the case, but she was also fascinated by the human angle and what had compelled Nye to plan and carry out an atrocity on such a huge scale.

Beverly answered her with a look that could wither a houseplant. 'You know that, and I know that, and the jury should see that, but that doesn't stop an awful lot of people wanting us to cock it up,' she added. 'Sol's had hourly calls from the AG over the weekend about making sure we don't, which means I've been getting the same from him.'

Now Beverly's exhaustion made sense. Eve watched her silently as she picked up her takeaway coffee cup, slurped a mouthful then set it down again. 'Right. Any questions?'

Eve sat up straight again, lengthening her spine the way she'd learned in her Pilates class in the hope it projected confidence. She needed to show she could do this.

'I do have one,' she said. 'Why me? There are advocates far more experienced who could do this.'

Her boss nodded. 'True, but Sol agreed that we need someone who has a fresh perspective and the mentality of a fine-tooth comb. Someone not jaded, in other words. Plus, in the short time you've been with us you've shown yourself to be a hard worker with an impressive memory for detail.'

Eve wondered how the rest of the division would take her being assigned this one. She knew Ashley wouldn't react well to being leapfrogged by her in the pecking order. She'd watch her like a hawk even more, the thought of which made Eve's stomach knot again. She couldn't afford to lose this job. Another dismissal would be the death knell for her working in London. She'd have to return home, tail between her legs, broke and humiliated. Eve gulped down a breath to steady herself. She couldn't mess up, simple as that.

'The review needs someone like you,' Beverly added. 'So, are you in?'

Eve was flattered by Beverly's appraisal of her, but doubt clouded her mind again. What if she made the wrong call on a piece of evidence? She knew she'd been right to speak out about the mistake she'd spotted at her old firm, but it had still got her sacked. Then a little voice in her head reminded her that the media was already calling Novus the trial of the century. She'd be mad to decline. If Beverly and the DPP thought she could handle the review, maybe she should believe it too. She allowed herself a cautious smile.

'I take it from your expression that's a yes?'

'Yes, I'm in. It's an amazing opportunity. Thank you.'

'Don't get carried away,' said Beverly, smiling too. 'It's mostly grunt work, going over files.'

She stood up to signal their meeting was at an end. 'You need to get to court. Horner will meet you there and he'll run you through everything his end when there's a break; he knows the ins and outs better than anyone. If you're lucky, you might also get to catch a bit of Madeleine Farmer on the stand. She's on the list to give evidence today.'

Eve tried not to appear eager, but it was hopeless. Madeleine Farmer had been the world's highest-paid actress before Novus. She hadn't been seen in public since that night and had given only one media interview, over the phone, in which she'd confirmed that she'd sustained severe injuries in the blasts but wouldn't elaborate beyond that. Her testimony was bound to be riveting.

'One last thing,' said Beverly. 'The review needs to be done as quickly as possible, so you might want to reschedule any plans for the next two weeks at least. You can take time in lieu once it's over.'

Eve was more than happy to clear her calendar. She had a train ticket booked to go home to Shropshire on Saturday morning for an overnight stay, and this was the excuse she'd been looking for to get out of going. Anything to put off telling her family that she no longer worked where they thought she did.

Chapter Three

John Horner had the harried air of someone whose ordered life had been turned upside down and he wasn't quite sure which part to right first. Briefed ahead by Beverly, he was waiting for Eve inside the main door of the Central Criminal Court, shifting impatiently from foot to foot. He was in his fifties, with longish, floppy grey hair and large-framed glasses that made his eyes appear owlish. As they shook hands Eve caught a trace of mustiness leaching from his navy suit and clocked the sheen of sweat on his forehead. He was thrumming with tension and standing there with him – inside the nation's most hallowed courthouse, better known as the Old Bailey – she felt the stirrings of it too.

'Beverly speaks highly of you,' he said. 'How are you finding the CPS so far?'

'I'm enjoying the variety of the work, but a case this big is something else,' she admitted. 'I'm keen to get started.'

'Glad to hear it. First, I need to brief you though. Court's not in session yet and there's a room we can use to talk. Follow me.'

Beverly had emailed ahead to clear Eve to use the designated entry lane for counsel while the trial continued. Horner walked as briskly as he talked, leaving her no time to take in their surroundings as they crossed beneath the Grand Hall's spectacular glass-domed ceiling. She'd been to the Bailey only a handful of times before – since moving to London, she learned those in legal circles rarely applied the 'Old' – and that was while studying for her law degree in Bristol. London itself was not a familiar destination; home for Eve was a small town in Shropshire, in a terraced house she'd lived in with her parents, two younger brothers and an older sister. Her dad was the sole wage earner for their family growing up and considered trips to the capital far too costly to contemplate, so they never went.

The building they hurried through housed the Bailey's oldest courtrooms and its most iconic: Courtroom Number One, where many of the nation's most notorious killers had been tried for their crimes. Due to the number of defendants involved, however, The Seven's trial was being heard in Courtroom Number Two, which had been renovated some time ago to become a high-security venue, and was more spacious as a result.

Eventually Horner stopped outside an unmarked door, no sign to proclaim its purpose, and entered a code on the keypad for them to enter. Eve went in first, expecting the room to be empty, but was surprised to find two men already seated behind a small table, both suited, both sour-faced.

'This is Eve Wren,' Horner told them. 'She's going to be reviewing the unused material for us. Eve, this is DCS Seth Strutton, the SIO on Novus, and DS Gary Lees, OIC.'

Neither detective rose from their seat, and their handshakes were perfunctory. Detective Chief Superintendent Strutton, the senior investigating officer, was mid-forties at a push and had short, tightly coiled dark curls barely touched by grey, olive skin and thick eyebrows that made his eyes appear permanently narrowed. Fair-haired Lees was a younger, paler imitation, with skin so white it was almost translucent, his cheeks mapped with wispy blue veins.

Taking a vacant chair across from them, Eve felt unnerved as they continued to glower at her. Then she gave herself a little shake.

Since when did she get nervous dealing with the police? She'd had countless meetings with detectives when representing defendants and had never felt out of her depth in any of them.

Meeting their stares head on, Eve waited for one of them to speak. Both men appeared tightly wound, as though the meeting was holding them up from being somewhere far more important. Strutton cleared his throat.

'Just so you know, this case is watertight.'

Horner winced and Eve knew why. It was a bullish statement for Strutton to make considering the reason they were meeting was because the sloppy effort of the case's original DO had caused another trial to collapse. But she wasn't going to say that out loud. Instead, she acknowledged that the evidence amassed against The Seven was substantial.

'It is,' said Strutton, nodding, 'but just because we gathered plenty of evidence doesn't mean corners were cut.'

His accent was Estuary English, with an absence of aitches and the distinct twang that came with being raised in East London by East Londoners who came from a long line of East Londoners.

Horner held his hands up placatingly, showing reddened palms to match his flushed face. 'No one says they have been.'

Suddenly Eve understood. Strutton was angry because he believed their eleventh-hour review cast doubt on his investigation. He bore the mood of an officer who had lived and breathed the case for months, most likely sacrificing his physical health, mental state and possibly personal relationships along the way. And now, when the finishing line was finally in sight, the CPS was telling him they needed confirmation it had been done properly.

'My remit is simply to look at the unused material this particular DO dealt with,' she said. 'It should be straightforward.'

Strutton nodded, but Eve could tell he still wasn't happy. She sympathised a fraction, because she knew what it was like to have your judgement called into question. But that didn't mean he'd get a free pass. Eve needed to do a good job on this review because at some point she wanted to return to defending private clients, and a decent reference from the CPS was essential if she wanted prospective employers to overlook her now chequered history.

'You're right, it should be straightforward. The DO was only on the case for a couple of weeks. He didn't get through much,' said Lees. 'But in the unlikely event you do find something, you bring it to me.'

When Eve didn't respond a pause filled the room, thickening the atmosphere. Any disclosure anomalies were usually raised with the OIC, but Eve had her own chain of command to adhere to. Was it her place to say that though? Thankfully Horner answered for her.

'Eve comes to me first with anything she finds, then we'll pass it on. Standard review procedure.'

Strutton looked as though he was on the verge of arguing otherwise, then nodded curtly in Eve's direction. 'The files are being sorted out for you at the nick and will be ready this afternoon,' he said, the edge in his voice betraying his annoyance.

'I don't want anyone else touching them,' said Eve.

Strutton's face mottled. 'What the fuck is that supposed to mean?' he barked. 'You do know who you're talking to, right?'

Eve held her nerve. He knew exactly why none of his officers should go anywhere near the evidence; she shouldn't have to explain it to him. Did he really think being aggressive would make her more compliant? She had so much to prove with this review – both to herself and to others – that being cowed by him wasn't an option.

'No one but me should handle the material until my review is done,' she said coolly, her gaze staying locked on his.

Strutton appeared to bite back a response. He got to his feet, buttoning his suit jacket as he did so. 'Ask for me personally when you get to the station.'

He was almost at the door, Lees in his slipstream, when Strutton suddenly turned and put his palms flat on the table so he could stoop down to eyeball her.

'There's something you should know about this case, Ms Wren. In all my years with the Met, I've never worked on one with so much incriminating evidence. We've got fucking truckloads of it,' he said. 'But we can't just lock them up and throw away the key, because that bastard Patrick Nye wants his fifteen minutes again. He's forcing those poor survivors to take the stand and relive the worst moments of their lives so the media can churn it out with clickbait headlines for the public to pick over like vultures.' Strutton trembled as he spoke, the toll of the case imprinted on every furious word spilling from his mouth. 'It's a fucking travesty but that's the justice system as it stands; they're entitled to their day in court. But once they've had it, they are going away for the rest of their lives, no parole. So, let's not balls this up, okay?'

Eve took her cue from Horner and said nothing. Strutton took her silence as a challenge.

'I'm not joking,' he said, his face darkening in anger. 'Their guilt is beyond doubt and I'm not having you swan in and tell me we've fucked it up.'

Eve couldn't keep quiet any longer. 'Let's hope you haven't then.'

This time Horner didn't wince. Instead, he caught Eve's eye and grinned.

Chapter Four

LUKE

Now

Standing across the street from the Novus, Luke Bishop saw nothing of the splendour that had greeted him when he'd arrived at the theatre on that gloriously warm evening last April. In his mind's eye, however, he could still picture the pristine red carpet that had swept them inside, the incessant flash of photographers' bulbs that never failed to make his eyes smart, and hear the shouts of fans who'd come to catch a glimpse of their favourite stars and maybe even get a selfie or an autograph if they were obliging enough. Such glamour, such pomp . . . and then carnage.

He became lost for a moment in the awful, hideous memory of it – acrid smell of the explosives finding their target, the smoke that billowed and blinded him, the blood and tissue of others that soaked his suit – until the sound of a digger firing up jolted him back to the present. He watched as the driver manoeuvred its bucket to shovel a pile of rubble. The theatre was a demolition site now, and what was left of it was being slowly and painstakingly razed to the ground.

Luke had seen the plans for the memorial to the victims that would take its place, but he still couldn't envisage what it would look like as he stared across at the site, no matter how hard he tried. All he could see were the broken bodies of the dead, among them Sebastian, his partner and the man he'd been planning to spend the rest of his life with.

Knowing he'd reached his limit of remembering for today, Luke turned up the collar of his jacket to keep out the drizzle and forced himself to keep walking. Five streets away was a no-frills café that served mugs of tea the shade of brick and sandwiches made from white bread only. Anyone who requested wholemeal or a panini was given short shrift. Luke headed there.

When he arrived, the café's shopfront window was steamed up so he couldn't see who was inside, but as he pushed open the door, bell tinkling, Ruby greeted him cheerily. 'Hello, Luke, darling. Get yourself in quick and out of the wet. So much for it being summer, eh?' When he reached the counter, she lowered her voice. 'You're the last to arrive. The others are in the back already.'

'Can I have a tea to take through?'

'Course you can.' She beamed. 'On the house.' It remained a source of immense pride that she'd succeeded in educating him, a Canadian interloper, on the joys of tea drinking.

The café was warm and clammy, so Luke shed his jacket while he waited for her to make his drink. Ruby eyed him up and down, lips pinching.

'How about I make you a bacon sandwich as well?'

'No, thanks, I'm not hungry.'

'Darling, you need to eat,' she said reprovingly, but not unkindly.

Luke knew why she was worried: he'd become too thin for his six-foot-three frame and looked ill. But he had no appetite these days. For food, for life, for work, for anything.

'How's Jimi?' he asked, deflecting her concern.

Ruby's expression greyed. 'Today's one of his not-good days.'

Jimi was her son. He'd been working in the foyer bar at the Novus Theatre on the night of the bombing, his waiting experience at his mum's café helping him land the job. Only twenty years old, he – along with the other theatre employees – had been ushered into the main auditorium when the siege began. But when the bombs went off Jimi had been outside with Luke, after they'd managed to flee the building. Jimi's colleagues from the bar weren't so lucky. They died from their injuries and he remained wracked with survivor's guilt, blaming himself for leaving them behind. In turn, Luke felt a crushing responsibility for him now, because he was the one who'd persuaded Jimi to make a run for it.

'Hopefully seeing us all will help,' he said, accepting the mug of tea Ruby slid across the counter.

'He's nervous about going on the stand.'

Luke glanced over both shoulders to check out the other patrons. They were all regulars, but it didn't hurt to be sure. Ruby was the only person outside their group who knew about these meetings, and they all wanted to keep it that way. This was their sanctuary, the only place where they could let their guard down and speak freely about what they had gone through that night. The thought of the press finding out terrified them.

'I think we all are. The police keep telling us it's a sure thing and they'll be convicted. But who knows, really?'

Ruby scratched the side of her head, something Jimi told Luke she did when she was stressed. Since April last year, she'd worn away a patch the size of two fifty-pence pieces, but you couldn't tell: her artificially bright blonde hair was meticulously styled in waves to cover it, and she hid her anxiety behind a smile enhanced by vivid berry-red lipstick. She was sixty-two now – she had been in her early forties and contentedly unwed when a short-lived affair with a musician had given her Jimi – and she was still a strikingly attractive woman, that Sebastian definitely would've called 'beauty queen level'—

Luke gripped the edge of the counter as grief took an unheralded aim at his guts, doubling him over. This stage of mourning was far worse than what he'd experienced in the first few days and weeks after the bombing. The stealth punches that hit him out of nowhere were much harder to absorb than the continuous anguish his grief had been at the start. Each punch winded his weakened spirit and broke his heart all over again.

Ruby stopped scratching and grabbed his hand over the counter. 'Oh, Luke,' she said, her eyes swimming with tears. She knew.

Exhaling deeply to compose himself, Luke thanked her for the tea then carried the mug through a door separating the café from the rear of the building marked by a 'Staff Only' sign. He followed the narrow corridor until he reached a doorway on the left hidden behind a thick brown curtain, a home-made security measure Ruby hung up to protect the privacy of what went on in the room. He reached behind the material, which smelled faintly of mothballs, and rapped loudly with his knuckles. 'It's me, Luke.'

The door opened inwards, and the curtain shifted to reveal Samuel. Luke was pleased to see him and said so as they hugged. Samuel had missed the two previous gatherings because he had needed another operation. He'd been hit in the lower legs by shrapnel and had undergone three operations so far, including a skin graft. His advancing age made his rehabilitation a slower process. But while he hadn't regained his former sprightliness, he looked well, Luke noted, his limp less pronounced than the last time they saw each other.

Luke stepped into the room. As usual, the chairs were arranged in a circle. Jimi was slumped in the one closest to the door, his vacant expression confirming that he was struggling today. Next to him was Hilary, who'd travelled down from Scotland the night before; she couldn't make every meeting but came as often as she could. She rose from her chair to hug Luke, and he clung to her as though his life depended on it. She was the eldest member of the group after Samuel and its most pragmatic, and it was her solidness and stoicism they all clung to when their emotions became too much. Then, fanning out, were Annie, Richard, Samuel and finally Horatio, the man without whom they might have never found each other.

Horatio Moser was the assistant manager of the Novus Theatre. Six months ago, he had approached some of the others while they attended a support centre set up by the police for the survivors of the bombings and their families. An ebullient man who lived alone, the professional counselling he'd been offered wasn't helping, so he'd thought it might be an idea to start their own group where they could share their experiences and try to make sense of what they'd been through, together. The others had jumped at the suggestion, as had Luke and Jimi, who met him a couple of weeks later outside the Old Bailey following The Seven's plea hearing.

The about-turn The Seven performed that day had stunned everyone. The survivors, the victims' families, the CPS, the police, the media. Luke had been assured by his witness support officer that the hearing was a formality, that there wouldn't be a trial because the defendants had indicated to their legal team that they would be pleading guilty. Once those pleas were entered, there would be another adjournment while reports were prepared ahead of sentencing. But Patrick Nye – Luke couldn't even think of his name without rage swilling inside him – had a surprise up his sleeve. When that first 'not guilty' came out of his mouth, Luke, in the public gallery with Jimi next to him, had thought he might faint. Then Jimi had stood up and started yelling at the dock and the judge had told them he'd need to leave the court if he couldn't restrain himself. The two of them had left together.

It was as they stumbled out into the street outside – Luke blinded by tears and Jimi howling at the injustice – that Horatio intercepted them and told them about his group. They already knew him because, besides being one of Jimi's bosses at the theatre, he'd aided their escape before the bombs went off. Horatio was already in the foyer after they fought their way out of the auditorium, before Nye intercepted them all. In an act of selflessness Luke would never forget, Horatio had surrendered himself to the cult leader in order to let the others flee.

Once Horatio had explained what the group meetings involved, Luke and Jimi had readily agreed to join. Jimi then suggested they use the café's back room for their meetings. They needed space and privacy and Ruby's could give them both.

They'd all lost someone that night in April. For Horatio, in his forties and a father figure lacking children of his own, it was the employees he managed and the workplace he loved in the country he'd adopted as his own. Jimi lost his mates. For Richard, it was his fiancée, the woman he'd turned his life upside down to be with. Annie lost her father, the acclaimed film director Ellison Moran – she'd only stepped in to be his plus one that night because her mother was laid up with flu – while Hilary's husband, a screenwriter, was the forty-first victim to be formally identified. Then there was Samuel, Dame Cynthia Seymour's personal assistant for thirty years, who'd moved from his native Paris to live in LA with her, then relocated to London five years ago when she wanted to come home. Beyond retirement age himself now, he remained in service to her grandson, Matthew, at the house in Hampstead he'd inherited after the bombing, helping him to tie up the loose ends of her life.

And Luke had lost Sebastian, the love of his life.

'I wonder how Madeleine's doing,' said Hilary, after Luke had completed his circle of hellos and sat down.

Annie pointed to her phone. 'I've been following the updates on Twitter. She's not started yet.'

Madeleine Farmer had attended one meeting at the café following her initial release from hospital after Samuel, who'd met her many times due to her friendship with Cynthia, reached out to her. The next day she'd returned to the States to receive further treatment for her facial injuries – which Luke could tell were severe even under the swathe of bandages – and the damage to her pelvis that required her at that point to use a wheelchair. However, from back home in LA, she continued to join them via speakerphone, no matter the time difference.

Outsiders might presume the inclusion of such a huge star in the group would skew the dynamic, but the bombing had stripped them of their differences. It didn't matter who was wealthy, who was famous, what colour their skin was, what religion, gender or belief they ascribed to – when they entered Ruby's café and went behind the curtain they were all the same. They were just people trying to wrap their minds around the enormity and horror of their collective experience.

'I'm being called to give evidence the week after next,' said Luke. 'I got a call confirming it this morning.'

The others stared at him, conflicting emotions moulding their expressions. They were all due to take the stand and dreading it, but at the same time they wanted it done and over. Luke being called was something to pity – but also to envy.

Horatio, assuming once more his position as their unofficial leader, leaned forward in his chair. 'Do you feel ready?'

'Yes, no. I don't know.' Tears pricked Luke's eyes. 'I don't know how I can speak publicly about Sebastian without completely losing it.'

'Talk it through now, with us,' Hilary suggested. 'Imagine you're giving evidence and the barrister's just asked you to describe you and Sebastian arriving at the event. How would you answer?'

The rest of the group – bar Jimi, who was still staring into space – nodded encouragingly. They weren't breaking any witness rules by talking about their experiences. Hilary had checked with a family friend who was a solicitor. The statements they gave to the police right after the bombing, when the incident was still fresh in their minds, were what the prosecution would refer to when they were on the stand. Anything they'd learned of since, from what they'd read or from talking to others, would be disregarded as hearsay.

'That's a good idea,' said Richard. 'Treat this as a rehearsal, mate.'

Richard was a British television actor, and a successful one at that. Before the bombing, his last role had been playing the baddie in a Marvel spin-off series. Yet he was almost unrecognisable now from the well-built, swarthy fifty-something actor he used to be, everything about him folded in by trauma and loss.

'It's like learning lines,' he continued. 'If you go over what happened now, with us, in our safe space, you'll be better equipped to remember everything when you're in court without getting upset.'

Slowly, Luke nodded. Then he set the mug of tea down by the side of his chair and folded his hands in his lap to hide that he was trembling.

'Do you know what's the biggest irony of me being there that night?'

The others stayed silent, watching him intently.

'Sebastian didn't want me to go. I forced him to take me, and he died because of it.'

Chapter Five

LUKE

Then

20 April, 7.46 p.m.

Luke stifled a yawn. His flight had landed at Heathrow just ninety minutes before the event was due to start, and from the airport he'd been whisked straight to a hotel, where he'd had precisely eight minutes to change before being ushered out the door again. Arriving at the venue, it had taken just one sip of champagne for jetlag to hit him square in the face, and now he was struggling to keep his eyes open, while Sebastian was deep in conversation with the guest on his other side. Luke recognised the man as a producer of several Best Picture Oscar nominees.

He didn't have the energy to engage in whatever they were discussing and slumped back in his chair. Already he was thinking he'd made a mistake in pushing for this trip. Sebastian had been less than enthusiastic when he said he wanted to come, which he should have taken as a sign, plus friends thought Luke was crazy to travel to London just for a long weekend – two flights total-ling almost twenty hours in four days – because it would change nothing. And they were right. Once again, he'd been relegated to the role of Sebastian's childhood best friend while reporters on the red carpet clamoured for confirmation that Sebastian was dating his latest female co-star, with Sebastian saying nothing to dispel the rumours. Smarting, Luke reached for his glass and downed it in one.

The producer suddenly waved a hand in front of Luke's face to get his attention. Older than them both by a few decades, the man had the sharp, pinched and slightly waxy look of someone familiar with a plastic surgeon's scalpel.

'Sebastian tells me you're Canadian.'

Luke nodded. 'I am.'

'We shoot a lot in Vancouver. Do you know it?'

Luke felt Sebastian tense beside him. He took a breath and trotted out the go-to lie, rolling it off his tongue with practised ease.

'Not much. I'm from Calgary, but I grew up in the States—'

'We've been friends since junior high,' Sebastian butted in.

Now it was Luke's turn to stiffen. Their 'best buddies' routine was the cover story Sebastian's publicist had concocted to dispel rumours about his sexuality and Luke had regretted going along with ever since. And while it was true that he wasn't from Vancouver originally, he lived and worked there now as a lighting technician on the very shoots the producer was talking about.

It was through work that he and Sebastian had met six years previously, on the set of a TV pilot. But his boyfriend always implored him never to mention his profession at industry events to avoid undermining the backstory. Sometimes, though, Luke got so damn tired of lying that he just wanted to say, 'You know what? We're actually a couple.' But he knew if he ever did say it, that would be the end of them. Sebastian apparently knew plenty of other marquee male actors hiding their sexuality because they'd been warned that coming out would harm their image, and he wasn't going to risk his.

'What do you do?' the producer asked.

'I'm between jobs.' That wasn't a lie: Luke was waiting for his next project to start in a month's time, a six-part drama for Peacock.

The producer lost interest upon hearing Luke wasn't anyone of importance and turned to the person on his right.

'Nice talking to you too,' Luke muttered.

'Don't be rude,' said Sebastian, leaning towards Luke so the producer couldn't hear.

'Me be rude? Try telling your new friend that.'

'What is wrong with you tonight? You could at least try pretending you're happy to be here.'

'I'll leave the acting to you,' said Luke grimly.

'What's that supposed to mean?'

Luke levelled his gaze at his partner, taking in the dark, wavy hair he loved to weave his fingers through and the blue eyes that could still floor him even after all this time. Life would be so much easier if he didn't love him so much.

Sebastian had been an unknown when they met, and moved to Vancouver when the TV pilot that brought them together was green lit as a continuing series called *Breakneck*. Although still dating under the radar at Sebastian's insistence, Vancouver had afforded them a level of privacy they wouldn't have got in LA. Then three years into their relationship, Sebastian landed the lead in a Netflix premium drama, and everything changed. He made the cover of *Variety*, was nominated for an Emmy, and the studios came knocking with movie roles. He returned to LA, while Luke remained in Canada for his work, and that was when their relationship became something to be conducted entirely behind closed doors.

'It doesn't matter.' Luke sighed, and Sebastian hitched an eyebrow waiting for him to answer. 'I didn't fly all this way to fight with you.'

'Good. But you still need to cheer up. This is supposed to be our date night.'

'Why bother calling it that when we're not allowed to tell anyone we're dating?'

'Don't be such a bitch,' Sebastian hit back. 'I hate it when you get like this.'

'I'm just tired, okay,' said Luke testily. 'I was at the airport at five this morning and you know I can't sleep on planes.' He hated flying and would spend the entire duration of each journey as tense as a coiled spring, refusing to take anything to knock him out because he wanted to keep his wits about him in case of the kind of emergency that stopped him relaxing in the first place.

'It was your idea to come,' said Sebastian harshly, his voice still low.

'I thought it would be a nice thing for us to attend together.'

'An early-bird dinner in Stepney? Not my idea of a good time.' Sebastian was only at the event as a favour to his manager, Jim, while he was shooting in London: Jim worked for the same agency as Dame Cynthia's manager in LA and had called Sebastian to say they were having trouble filling the tables.

'This is Stepney?' asked Luke, who hadn't bothered to check their destination in the rush to get there. 'I've never heard of it. Which part of London is it?'

'East, but not the cool part.'

'It's a good turnout, though.'

'It is, now, after pressure was applied.'

Luke gazed up at the ceiling, from which hung the most glittering chandelier he'd ever seen. It hurt his eyes to look at it, but not as much as the scarlet velvet walls surrounding them or the scarlet carpet beneath their feet.

'Why this place?'

'This is, apparently, the theatre where Cynthia made her acting debut as a teenager,' said Sebastian. 'It's just been renovated after years of being left to rot. I swear it still smells of mould.'

'I'm not sure she remembers it, judging by the look on her face,' said Luke.

They both turned to study the guest of honour, whose table was at the front of the room next to the stage. She was sitting between two men and appeared lost; her slight frame was dwarfed by their broad ones. She was still beautiful, with delicate features and pearl-grey hair swept back from her face, and she was wearing a diamond choker that looked so heavy around her throat Luke wondered if she could breathe, let alone eat her food and swallow.

'How old is she?' he asked Sebastian.

'Almost ninety, apparently. She looks good though. I should ask for the name of her surgeon.'

'Who's the cute guy on her left?' asked Luke, fixing his stare on the man. Very blond and in his early thirties like Luke, he had cheekbones you could slice steak on.

Sebastian looked annoyed. 'That's her grandson. Don't get any ideas.'

'He's Saul Seymour's son?'

'Yep, that's him.'

The Seymour family history was part of Hollywood folklore. Saul Seymour was Cynthia's only child and had been making his own way as an actor when he got in with a crowd that inhaled hard drugs as readily as air. He died of an overdose in New York in 1993. Ten months later, his distraught wife, Annika, a Swedish model, committed suicide by jumping from their high-rise apartment, leaving behind their toddler son to be raised by Cynthia.

From across the room, Luke observed Matthew tenderly taking his grandmother's champagne glass from her when her shaky hand threatened to cause a spillage and thought again how cute he was.

'Tonight was the grandson's idea,' said Sebastian. He picked up a thick, cream card detailing the evening's itinerary that had been left by each place setting and quoted from it. 'An evening of tributes to one of Hollywood's original superstars.' He pulled a face. 'It sounds more like a wake than a celebration.'

◆ ◆ ◆

Sebastian fell into conversation with the producer again. So, feeling bored, Luke excused himself to use the restroom. Sebastian didn't look up as he left the table, which may have been unintentional but was more likely a deliberate slight because Luke had checked out another man. He sighed. It was going to be a long night.

Feeling light-headed from the combination of alcohol and jet-lag, he locked himself inside a cubicle and lowered the toilet lid so he could sit down and close his eyes for a moment. Almost instantly he began to drift into sleep, until the next thing he knew he was being jolted awake by the sound of two men arguing furiously right outside his cubicle. He went to get up, but one of the voices suddenly rose in volume.

'But I don't want to handle a fucking gun.'

'Keep your voice down,' the other voice hissed.

They were male and their accents British, but with a twang Luke guessed might be regional. He took both men to be fairly young.

'I don't want any part of this. I'm going home.'

Luke heard scuffling, then a dull thud followed by a yelp of pain. He was on his feet now, his heart racing and his hand on the lock, ready to slide it back.

'What'd you do that for?' asked the first voice. 'That hurt.'

'Because you're being a dick,' whispered the other one furiously. 'Look, you just need to hold it for a bit. It's just to keep them in line, put the frighteners on.'

Luke was shocked. What the hell? He tried to peer between the door and the cubicle frame, but the gap was too tiny. He wasn't about to confront them though, not if they were armed. He had a pretty good idea of the damage a bullet could do at close range. His hand went to his pocket to retrieve his phone and summon help, but then he remembered – every guest had been asked to hand in their cell phone as a condition of entry, in addition to their bags being searched and their persons given a thorough going-over with hand-held scanners.

Before he could consider another plan of action, the tone of the conversation changed, and both voices reached a normal volume.

'Mate, I'm just pulling your leg.'

That was the voice of the second man. The first joined in, laughing, although his voice was shaky. 'You had me there for a second.'

Luke was confused. Talking like they had a firearm was just a joke? It didn't sound funny to him.

Slowly he slid back the lock and walked out. He washed his hands in one of the basins, keeping his gaze raised just enough to be able to surreptitiously glance at the two men in the mirror above it. Both were white with dark brown hair. The older one was in his twenties, the other in his late teens at most. He had a smattering of freckles across the bridge of his nose that looked as though they'd been pencilled on. Luke could see a family resemblance between them.

Both watched him watching them.

'Having a good night?' the older one asked. Luke tagged his voice as the second one he'd heard in the stall.

'Yes, thanks. You?'

'Nah, we're working.'

Engaging him in conversation allowed Luke to turn round and fully take them in. Both men were dressed pristinely in all-white waiter's uniforms.

'We need to get back.' The younger one nudged his companion fretfully. 'Patrick will do his nut if he catches us slacking. Enjoy the rest of your evening,' he said politely to Luke.

'Thank you.'

The older one snickered as they walked out together, the rest-room door swinging closed behind them.

Luke left it for a few moments then followed them out, a feeling of unease settling in the pit of his stomach. It really hadn't sounded like a joke to him.

Why would a waiter at a black-tie event teeming with security talk about needing a gun?

Chapter Six

LUKE

Now

As Luke started to cry, Horatio gripped his hand. Recalling his last moments with Sebastian inside the theatre had crushed him. The rest of the group looked on sympathetically.

'It's okay,' said Horatio soothingly. 'Let it out.'

It was the unspoken if-onlys that had overwhelmed Luke. If only he'd confronted the men he'd overheard in the restroom that night. If only he'd raised the alarm immediately. If only he hadn't returned to his table and got into another fight with Sebastian – a rerun of his refusal to acknowledge Luke as his partner – so that when the siege began, they would not have been so annoyed with each other.

The moment Patrick Nye and his followers had swept into the theatre was the last time they'd spoken. Somewhere between the shouting, the screams and the first killing, they'd been separated. Luke had been put in a group that was marched to the back of the theatre, while Sebastian was paraded onstage with some of the other, more famous guests.

Luke felt no embarrassment at breaking down though, and he knew the others wouldn't find it awkward either – they had all cried with abandon many times since their group first came together. Eventually, when he was spent, Horatio let go of his hand.

'Better?' he asked him.

Luke nodded. The release helped.

'Thank you.' He smiled weakly at the others. 'Now I know what not to say on the stand.'

They all nodded, except Jimi, who was still staring into space. Luke wondered what horrors his mind was replaying today. The two of them had run back into the theatre after the first bomb had gone off to see if they could help with the casualties, and the scene that confronted them was like something out of a war zone. The entire foyer was awash with bodies and blood. It was this mental snapshot that haunted Luke every single night just as he was going to sleep.

'We all experienced moments we'd rather not relive in court,' said Horatio darkly. 'But relive them we must, in the interests of justice.'

Horatio hadn't shared much about what had happened to him after he'd surrendered to Nye, other than to say the retribution hadn't lasted long because once Luke and Jimi had escaped, the Decorous leader had primed the bombs to explode. It pained Luke that Horatio had suffered because they were freed.

'Is your family coming over to support you?' Annie asked Luke.

'I haven't been able to let them know I've been called to give evidence yet.' Luke checked his watch. 'It's eleven here, so four in the morning in Calgary. I'll call them later, but I know my mom will make the trip. She said she would.'

Luke's family wanted the trial to be over as much as he did, because they assumed he would return to Canada for good once it was done. They were struggling to understand why he hadn't gone back home already. He was dreading telling them that he had no plans to leave London at all, because it was where he felt closest to Sebastian now; the last place they'd been together. He couldn't imagine relinquishing that sense of comfort. At some point he planned to look for work, but for now he was content to live off his savings and the rental money he got from letting out his apartment in Vancouver. He needed to heal before he could think about joining real life again.

Hilary turned to Samuel. 'How's Matthew doing?'

'I wish I knew,' said the old man morosely. 'He's still carrying on as though it never happened. I keep trying to talk to him about staging a memorial for Cynthia, but he won't entertain it. She deserves one, though, after that awful funeral.'

The service had been basic to say the least. Barely lasting twenty minutes in the smallest room at the crematorium, there was no music and only a handful of mourners were invited to attend. Luke wasn't one of them, but Samuel was, and he'd told them how pitiful it had been. It was not the send-off Dame Cynthia would have wanted.

'I don't understand Matthew's attitude to the bombing,' said Annie. 'It's not like any of us blame him; he couldn't have predicted what was going to happen. Do you think he blames himself and that's why he's being like this?'

'I don't believe he does,' Samuel replied wretchedly. 'His attitude is simply that it's done and we must all move on.'

'Losing his parents at such a young age may have desensitised him to loss,' said Hilary. 'Although it still wouldn't hurt him to condemn what happened.'

Matthew's refusal to make any kind of public statement after the attack had surprised everyone. The first and only time he would speak publicly about it would be at the trial.

Richard cleared his throat. 'Speaking of families, I have a favour to ask of you all.'

He sounded nervous and the others looked at him expectantly. Even Jimi was roused from his stupor.

'It's Faye. She's really not herself, and it's affecting the children. With your permission, I'd like to bring her along to the next meeting.'

Luke wasn't alone in being surprised by Richard's request. Hilary's eyebrows shot up her forehead, while Horatio offered a wry smile and Annie quipped that she hadn't seen that one coming. Richard smiled, easing the tension.

'No, I imagine you didn't. But, well, a lot's happened, and I'm really worried about her.'

Faye was Richard's ex-wife. She'd also been at the Novus Theatre on the night of the bombings – in fact, it was the first time the two of them had been in the same room since their very acrimonious and very public divorce.

The others knew all about Faye, both from what Richard had told them and also from what had been published in the media about their break-up. In her fifties, and British-born like him, before having their children she'd been a wardrobe assistant on film sets. One of her first jobs had been on a costume drama starring Dame Cynthia, where the two women became friends. Faye continued to assist on many other projects with her, which was why she'd been invited to the event. Richard, to Faye's consternation, was invited because, on the many occasions they'd socialised together, Cynthia had taken a shine to him. She liked to joke she was sizing him up to be husband number four.

Richard and Faye had been married for nineteen years when he left her for a model called Liberty, who he'd been having an affair with. Their divorce was so ugly that it filled the gossip columns for the best part of a year. It turned out Richard had secretly lawyered up in the months before leaving and had hidden enough assets to make it seem as though he was worth a fraction of his real wealth when the divorce went through. He did set aside enough money to provide for the children for the years they'd still be in education, but Faye had been lucky to hang on to their house in Dulwich, South London. Then he sat back and did nothing while Liberty trashed Faye on social media and called her a parasite who wanted to bleed him dry.

In the months that the support group had been meeting, however, Richard had repeatedly acknowledged how despicably he'd behaved towards his ex-wife.

'I can't believe I treated her like that. I swear I'm not that man any more,' he'd told them several times.

They believed him. None of them was the same person they had been before Novus. They were all irrevocably altered by the events of last April.

Luke asked Richard if he'd told Faye about the group. If he had, he would have broken their unwritten agreement to maintain its secrecy.

'No, I haven't said a word,' he said, shaking his head for emphasis. 'I was waiting until I'd spoken to everyone.'

Like Luke, Richard had felt compelled to stay in London. He'd tried to fly back to LA, where he and Liberty had lived together, but had suffered a panic attack at the airport when he tried to board the plane. The same thing happened when he tried a second and third time, so Faye suggested he stay with her and their children while he underwent therapy, and because he felt bonded to his ex-wife by their shared experience he agreed. A year later he was still there, living in the guest room.

'Where does Faye think you are when you're here?' asked Horatio.

'At the gym.'

'Not being funny, mate, but hasn't she noticed you're not very fit?' Jimi piped up, his first contribution to today's discussion.

There was a moment's pause, then peals of laughter broke out. Even Luke, who only a moment ago had been sobbing, hooted.

Richard patted his untoned stomach with a grin. 'I don't know what you mean. There's a six-pack under this shirt.'

'Packet of biscuits, more like,' Jimi deadpanned, to more laughter.

It had taken the group a while to let themselves see the funny side of things, their guilt making them believe that to do so was a sign they didn't care about everyone they'd lost. Then one day Horatio did an impromptu and brilliantly camp impression of Dame Cynthia in her best-known role, when she played a gloriously verbose chorus girl who catches the eye of the President. Suddenly they were falling about in mirth and the impasse was broken. These days there were as many laughs in their meetings as there were tears.

'So, can I bring Faye along?'

Richard directed the question at Horatio, a reflex, because he was the person who'd set up the group. But it was still a collective decision. Annie answered first.

'I'd be happy for her to join us. I know how much coming here has helped me, so if it can do the same for her, great.'

Hilary, Samuel and Horatio echoed her sentiment, while Jimi nodded his agreement. Only Luke hesitated, which Richard noticed.

'If you're worried about her fitting in, don't,' he said. 'Faye gets along with everyone.'

Luke hoped that was true. The group meant everything to him now, it was all that kept him going, and he trusted his new friends implicitly. He'd told them things he'd never shared with anyone, and he would never stop being grateful to Horatio for bringing them all together. The thought of Faye changing the dynamic scared him, but he could see he was outvoted.

'I'm not worried,' he lied. 'Tell her she's welcome.'

Chapter Seven

EVE

Now

The scale of the bombing, combined with the fame of the victims, meant there had been blanket media coverage for weeks afterwards. The minute-by-minute updates did slow eventually to occasional articles and recapping news reels, but with the trial now underway the coverage had again ramped up to near-hysterical levels. Eve and Horner had to push through the scrum of reporters lining up for the allocated press seats on their way into the courtroom. With so many vying to get inside, some would be relegated to an overspill room to watch the proceedings live-streamed.

It was Horner's suggestion that Eve stayed to watch the start of Madeleine Farmer's evidence. Eve was itching to get started on the review but they both agreed DCS Strutton needed time to cool down, and that they should honour his request for Eve to wait until after lunch to arrive at Lewisham Police Station. During the discussion they'd had after the two detectives had left, Horner made it clear she needed to keep them on side. But he'd also assured her that her parting comment to Strutton was justified.

'DCS Strutton is a brilliant officer, one of the Met's best. It's why he was chosen to head up such a huge and complicated investigation in the first place. I understand that this review bothers him – he just wants to do right by the victims and the survivors,' Horner had said. 'That doesn't mean he can order you about and it's good you're not prepared to take any crap from him. I can't stand all that bloody good cop, bad cop posturing, so you let me know if he starts interfering with your work in any way.'

Relief surged through her, making her tremble. What a welcome change to have a colleague watch her back instead of stabbing it. She knew from that moment she and Horner were going to get on.

As CPS advocates, they were entitled to sit directly behind 'counsel's row', the name given to the courtroom's front benches where both prosecution and defence KCs sat. Their route to their seats took them past the dock, allowing Eve to finally come face to face with the accused.

It was unnerving to see The Seven in the flesh. So much had been written about them, and their photographs had been published so frequently in the media, that each was now as recognisable to Eve as the celebrities they'd targeted that night. Yet seeing them together in the dock, police officers bookmarking both ends of it, she was struck by how normal they appeared. Well, all except Nye.

The youngest was eighteen. Cal Morgan, from Stockport. Lived at home with his parents. Had a younger sister, Caitlyn, and an older brother, Brendan. Prior to Novus, Cal was studying to sit his A levels, for which he was predicted to get two As and a B. He spent his spare time either gaming in his bedroom or skateboarding in the park with his friends. He joined The Decorous after Brendan became obsessed with Nye's teachings about the need to rebalance the distribution of wealth in society. The Morgans' parents were minimum-wage earners and couldn't afford the time or expense required to learn new skills to further themselves, so the family had become stuck in the poverty trap. Both brothers resented their parents for not having money like their friends' parents did.

It was Nye's claim that governments deliberately kept people poor to keep them in jobs no one else wanted to do that had triggered Brendan to start blaming the rich and famous for stoking financial inequality. His resentment spiralling, he joined The Decorous because he wanted to fight back in every sense, then persuaded Cal to sign up too. Brendan had died in the bombing, along with eight other followers.

Second youngest was Millie Tinkler, twenty and from Macclesfield. Dropped out of school at fifteen after two years of non-attendance, sacked from a succession of low-paid jobs since, the most recent working on the till at a convenience store. She'd discovered The Decorous after watching a 2008 documentary about Nye on YouTube and was taken in by his teachings in the same way Brendan Morgan had been. Her parents disowned her after her arrest.

Brian Woolmore was forty-two and divorced. He was nick-named 'Snow White' by the others due to his prematurely white hair, which during the siege fell below his shoulders and was tied back in a ponytail. Now, for the trial, he'd cut it brutally short. Woolmore had been a senior supervisor at one of the largest manufacturing plants in the Midlands and his colleagues were stunned to learn of his involvement. They said he'd never mentioned The Decorous, or Nye, much less revealed he was a fanatical follower. For Woolmore, it was Nye's message that people couldn't afford to be impotent in the fight for financial equality that had drawn him to the cause. He told the police he was 'sick and tired of rich liberals trying to dictate what I should think, say and support' and was driven to take a stand on behalf of ordinary people like him.

Mark Cleaver, from Guildford in Surrey, was from day one pegged by the media as the anomaly among The Seven due to his previous convictions. Two for assaulting his wife, one for racially abusing a neighbour. Four children by three different women, including the wife he'd attacked, and he was still only twenty-five. He had consistently refused to say where and when he'd first heard of The Decorous and Patrick Nye. The police's theory, however – based on talking to Cleaver's friends and associates – was that he didn't understand what he was signing up to but liked the idea of holding a room full of 'rich tossers' to account.

Edwin Barker was the second oldest after Nye. Fifty-five and from West London, he'd quit his job in DIY retail and moved in with his elderly mum to care for her after his dad died. Barker, who had been engaged to be married in his twenties, until his fiancée called it off the night before the wedding, had joined The Decorous the first time round, back in 1999. He fervently subscribed to Nye's belief that the rich and famous had no right to dictate to the rest of society what mattered to them, and in recent years had spent his free time trolling celebrities on social media using various fake accounts. When his mum died, Barker sold her house and bought a derelict hotel on Bournemouth seafront. It was there he set up a new UK sub-group for The Decorous, which eventually attracted the attention of Patrick Nye online. Alongside multiple murder charges, Barker faced a separate charge of sexually assaulting Madeleine Farmer.

Then there was Jenna Sandwell. Halfway through a sociology degree at Durham University after achieving four straight A*s in the sixth form of an independent school near Norwich. The middle of three children from an affluent household, both parents earning six figures, she discovered The Decorous after a classmate at university referenced it in an essay. She quickly became obsessed with Nye, reading and watching everything ever produced about him. For her, it was less about the cause, more about the man. Sandwell was being held responsible for the siege escalating into the bloodbath it became when she allegedly killed the first hostage for sport.

On paper, the followers were an unorthodox group who, under any other circumstances, probably wouldn't have given each other the time of day. But in the dock they appeared united, staring resolutely ahead and dressed all in matching navy.

Finally, Eve's gaze fell upon Patrick Nye. He was dressed head to toe in white. Suit, tie, shirt. His sandy hair, now streaked with silver, had grown to collar-length since his police mugshot was taken. He looked younger than his fifty-five years and, though it pained her to acknowledge it, he was attractive. Nye caught her gaze and stared back with such intensity that she shivered. He didn't look like the benign advocate for upholding morals he claimed to be. He looked evil.

She had read up on why Nye had set up The Decorous and its origins could be traced back to his childhood. Nye was born in California, near San Diego, and put up for adoption as a baby. His adoptive parents were a wealthy couple from Ohio, and he lived an uneventful suburban life in Cleveland until his early teens, when he happened upon a newspaper interview with Susan 'Sadie' Atkins, a follower of the infamous cult leader Charles Manson. Atkins, along with Manson and three others, had been convicted of carrying out the 1969 Tate–LaBianca murders in Los Angeles, in which six people were slaughtered during a two-night killing spree. One of the victims was actress Sharon Tate, wife of film director Roman Polanski. She was eight months pregnant when Atkins stabbed her to death.

The article detailed Atkins renouncing her crimes since becoming a born-again Christian while in prison, but what caught Nye's attention was the line about how she'd had a one-year-old son who was taken into care and put up for adoption after her arrest.

Atkins' son was born in California in October 1968 – the exact same month, year and location as Nye. It was a coincidence – Nye knew his birth mother was an unmarried teenager forced to give him up by her Methodist preacher father – but he *wished* he had been Atkins' son. Being born into the Manson Family, as they were known, was a damn sight more interesting than his birth story. From the moment he read that article, Nye wanted to know everything there was to know about the cult. In particular, he was fascinated by how Manson had managed to position himself as a leader who had others do his bidding – he wasn't even present when his followers carried out the Tate–LaBianca murders, even though he was convicted of the crimes. The brutality of the murders also excited Nye. The victims had wealth and power but there wasn't a thing they could do to stop themselves being killed.

Nye soon knew the Manson Family history inside out, and not a day went by when he didn't reference it in some way, much to the alarm of his adoptive parents. So, when he was approaching seventeen and announced he wanted to study at the University of Southern California in LA, they desperately tried to dissuade him, fearful that returning to his home state and the city where the Tate–LaBianca murders took place would only escalate his obsession. Nye's mind was made up though. He was going back.

His adoptive parents had one last desperate trick up their sleeves to try to get through to him, however. Unless he applied to go to college elsewhere, they told him, they would withdraw their financial support.

Nye was incandescent. His college fund amounted to tens of thousands of dollars – without that money, he couldn't afford to go. But they dug their heels in and refused to relent until – after a violent row during which he'd throttled his dad and left him choking for air – Nye left home and hitched a ride to LA. Using what little savings he had, he found somewhere cheap to rent in Van

Nuys then bounced between dead-end jobs to try to save money. Yet despite his best efforts, college remained a financial impossibility. By the time he was twenty, Nye had turned to petty crime to survive, starting with scamming a neighbour.

Being deprived of money by two people he didn't get to choose to be his family was the catalyst for him establishing The Decorous. He wanted to create his own movement with his own devoted following, but unlike the Manson Family's Helter Skelter race war, The Decorous' cause would be money. Nye and his followers would stop rich people like his adoptive parents using their wealth to control the less fortunate – and like the Manson Family they would do whatever it took. Nye's planned attack on Grauman's would make the Tate–LaBianca murders look small fry.

Then the tip-off to the FBI ruined everything.

For twenty years, while in hiding, Nye had burned with the humiliation of being stopped from fulfilling his ambition to hold the rich and famous accountable. He wanted to show the world that Patrick Nye was not the failure history had recorded him to be – and he had achieved that last year inside the Novus Theatre by getting his message to violently hit home forty-three times over.

Chapter Eight

Lead counsel for the prosecution was Darius Philbin KC, a veteran of multi-defendant cases. Eve could see straight away why he'd been picked for this one: toweringly tall, with soft brown-grey hair tucked beneath his wig, he radiated the calm but emphatic authority required to conduct a trial as complex as the one against Novus.

There was no time for a formal introduction though. The moment Eve and Horner slid into their seats directly behind Philbin and his junior, Lacey Cartwright, the clerk asked everyone to rise for His Honour Allardyce Ritchie. The judge – another man with experience of multi-defendant trials – entered the courtroom and sat down with a brisk swish of robe and a near-imperceptible nod of his head.

Philbin stayed on his feet while everyone else followed the judge in sitting down. Then, when the room had stilled, he cleared this throat.

'With your Lordship's leave I call Madeleine Farmer,' he said in a strident tone.

Everyone turned expectantly towards the courtroom door, Eve among them, as it swung open to allow one of the world's most famous women to enter.

Madeleine paused for a moment on the threshold. Several people in the public gallery audibly gasped, and Eve could barely contain her own shock. Madeleine's injuries were far worse than any online speculation had suggested. Her left eye was covered by a patch made from the same colour and material as the fitted purple pantsuit she was wearing. But there was no hiding the rope-like scars that tentacled across both sides of her face, or the burns that lividly marked her chin and throat and appeared to continue below the neckline of her shirt.

Madeleine acted as though she hadn't noticed the court's reaction, and slowly walked to the witness stand, supporting herself on a black cane. When the dock came into view she stared resolutely ahead, sparing herself the smirks from Jenna Sandwell and Millie Tinkler as she passed them. Nye leaned forward impassively in his seat as though wanting a better look. Finally, Madeleine reached the witness stand and turned to face the courtroom straight on, her chin jutted in defiance.

Philbin waited patiently while she was sworn in, thanked her for coming to court, then asked her to state her name for the record. Her voice was clear and strong, carrying easily to all corners of the room.

'Madeleine Blake Farmer.'

Placed right in front of the witness box was the seating plan for the gala. The diagram, mounted on stiff card and propped up on an easel, was an old-fashioned touch when so much evidence was now relayed on screens via a presentation system known as Clickshare. Perhaps the prosecution wanted to remind the jury of the old-fashioned glamour of the gala. Philbin drew Madeleine's attention to it.

'Can you please tell the court where you were seated on the evening of April twentieth last year.'

Madeleine squared her shoulders and looked directly at the jury, who appeared mesmerised by her presence. Eve felt a deep tug of admiration for the woman, once one of the most famous faces in the world and now rendered virtually unrecognisable by her injuries. Yet even though Madeleine no longer commanded the biggest fees in Hollywood, she was still a star performer.

'I was on table one.'

◆ ◆ ◆

Her testimony was methodical, unhurried, and utterly heartbreaking.

Philbin opened his questioning by cataloguing the injuries Madeleine had sustained. As Eve rightly surmised, the scorch burns continued down her torso and stomach, only stopping at her upper thighs, and while her dark brunette hair might appear lustrous, it was a wig she'd had custom-made to cover her scalded scalp. But the most shocking moment came when Madeleine disclosed what was hidden behind the eye patch.

'There's nothing there. I got hit in the face by shrapnel and my eye was so badly damaged it had to be removed.'

Her delivery continued to remain admirably steady as she revealed she needed the cane to walk, because her pelvis had been crushed when she fell to the ground right before the explosion and was trampled underfoot. Such was the severity of the injury her doctors were unsure if she would walk again. She'd defied those odds, she told the jury, but she would never be able to conceive naturally.

Then Philbin asked her what her injuries meant for her career.

'Oh, I'm done. I'm thirty-one and I'll never act on-screen again,' she said, her voice catching for the first time. 'The studios and production companies I've worked with before haven't said it outright, but I know. My agent and manager aren't saying it, but they know, too. An industry that rates image as high as talent, if not higher, can't accommodate an actor with my disfigurements, however inclusive it claims to be. I mean, I can still work, but I'll be limited to voiceovers.' She paused, swallowing hard. 'They took everything from me that night.'

Eve could see the impact Madeleine's testimony was having. Several members of the jury, men and women, appeared to be blinking back tears. The reporters in the press box were equally sombre and, glancing skywards, Eve could see that many of those watching from the public gallery at the top of the courtroom were also ashen. Only The Seven seemed unmoved. Nye was watching Madeleine as intensely as he'd stared at Eve, but the corners of his mouth were curled into a smile.

Philbin spent the next ten minutes establishing Madeleine's reason for attending the Stepney event. At the age of fourteen, she had been cast as Dame Cynthia's granddaughter in a low-budget drama called *Constancy*. It was her first big screen role and the success of the film took everyone by surprise: *Constancy* swept the board during award season, with Madeleine becoming the third-youngest actor ever to win the Oscar for Best Supporting Actress. Dame Cynthia was nominated again in the lead category (but lost out to Meryl).

Whenever their paths had crossed afterwards, the two women had greeted each other with genuine affection.

'I adored her. She might have had a reputation for being aloof and a snob, but she showed me nothing but kindness,' said Madeleine touchingly.

Their friendship had been truly cemented around a decade after *Constancy* came out, when Madeleine accepted the lead role in an ill-conceived romantic comedy that saw her career stumble and her box office status wane. She sought counsel from the older woman about what roles she should be seeking, and they began to meet for dinner at Dame Cynthia's home whenever Madeleine was in LA. When she was asked to fly to London to attend the event in

April and deliver a speech in her friend's honour, she had accepted without hesitation, clearing her schedule to do so.

'But that speech never happened, did it, Ms Farmer?' said Philbin.

'No.'

'Please tell the court why it didn't happen.'

'You really need to ask?' she deadpanned, which earned her an admonishment from the judge. Chastened, she told the jury, 'My speech didn't happen because they killed Marty, and all hell broke loose.'

'You're referring to Mr Martin Coel, known to his friends as Marty,' said Philbin.

'I am,' Madeleine confirmed.

'Can you describe what happened to him?'

Madeleine's chin dropped and Eve could see she was fighting to maintain her composure.

'It was terrible. They slaughtered him like an animal.' Her voice trembled. 'The poor guy didn't stand a chance.'

Chapter Nine

MADELEINE

THEN

20 April, 8.33 p.m.

The Novus Theatre had been a small-scale, vaudeville-style venue when Dame Cynthia Seymour made her stage debut there as a seventeen-year-old in 1951. Then named the Regal, it was one of the few buildings in the Stepney area not damaged by bombing raids in the Blitz. It survived as a theatre until the seventies, when it was bought by a consortium who turned it into a bingo hall. By the late nineties, the bingo had moved out and the building fell into disrepair until, in 2018, a group of theatre lovers led by Dame Cynthia's grandson, Matthew, raised the finances to restore it, replicating the sumptuous red-velveted grandeur of its heyday and rebranding it Novus, Latin for 'new'.

As in its heyday, the Novus wasn't a theatre in the traditional sense. There were no uniform rows of seats stacked backwards from the stage, no balcony and circle seats overlooking it. Instead, circular tables of six lined both sides of the auditorium and filled a sunken area in the middle of the room. There was a stage at the front, but it was narrow and this meant that productions tended to be on a smaller scale.

The pandemic had delayed the renovation, but also created an opportunity of fortuitous timing: when the theatre was finally finished, Cynthia's ninetieth birthday was fast approaching, so what better way to mark that milestone and the theatre's reopening night than with a dinner celebrating the two.

Madeleine Farmer was learning all this from the man seated next to her, a Hollywood legend in his own right. Martin 'Marty' Coel was one of the most prolific stunt performers ever to work in the industry, racking up world records for his daring feats. He was also a history buff. 'I love how everything in London has a story behind it,' he'd told Madeleine as he regaled her with the theatre's past.

Marty was the stunt driver responsible for one of Cynthia's most talked-about scenes. It was in the 1955 film, *Johnny Speed*, when she and actor Larry Nelson had embarked on a car chase that started – and continued – with her character straddling his character's lap as he drove. Considered highly risqué and thrilling for its time, Marty had stood in for Nelson for parts of the filming. It was rumoured he and Cynthia became lovers promptly afterwards, with their affair outlasting two of her three marriages.

True or not – and Madeleine didn't dare pry – Marty and Cynthia were still friends fifty-odd years later. Matthew had invited him to share his recollection of filming that famous scene with tonight's audience, alongside a roll call of other industry names paying tribute to her, including Madeleine, who was giving the closing toast. Marty, now in his late eighties like Cynthia, said he was surprised he'd been asked. He was now exhibiting the kind of nerves she wouldn't expect from a man who'd made a living throwing himself off buildings and escaping from burning cars.

'You all set?' she asked him, nodding at the stack of index cards next to his plate setting.

'I guess. I'm not used to talking in front of so many fancy folks,' he said.

It was a high-calibre turnout, Madeleine conceded, but intimate by industry standards, with only a hundred and twenty guests. The size of the venue wouldn't allow for more, but according to Matthew, when he'd called to invite her, there had been no question of them holding the celebration anywhere else. Full circle, he called it.

'You'll be great,' she said to Marty. 'You've got such an interesting story to share, people will be hanging off every word of it.'

His reply was drowned out by a booming, disembodied voice announcing that the evening's proceedings were about to begin. There were to be four speeches first, including Marty's, then a break for dinner to be served, during which clips of Cynthia's most memorable performances would be played on screens set up around the room. Then more speeches, with Madeleine's last, until Cynthia took the stage to make a final one of her own. The event would draw to a close at around ten thirty – early by most standards, but necessary when your guest of honour was weeks away from turning ninety and needed her rest.

The opening three speeches went smoothly and were given by Cynthia's long-time manager Gerry Shah, Demetri Miller, a former studio head whose wife was sitting to Madeleine's right, and Priscilla Dalton, a venerated film critic. All of these drew laughter and applause from the audience. Then it was Marty's turn. Madeleine felt nervous for him as the spotlight tracked his path to the edge of the stage. There he was greeted by a 'walker', a young woman in a black dress whose job was to escort the speakers up the steps to the podium.

Madeleine watched as, instead of steering him gently in the right direction, the young woman forcibly grabbed Marty's elbow and whispered something in his ear. Then she shoved Marty forwards up the stairs and the elderly man, now deathly pale, stumbled, prompting a chorus of disconcerted voices to ripple around the room. Why was the walker being so rough with him?

Reaching the podium, Marty faltered, and the microphone picked up his voice. He was saying, 'Who are you? What do you want?'

The walker, who had dishevelled blonde hair that looked as though it hadn't been near shampoo for weeks, ignored him entirely and leaned forward to speak into the microphone. Each word was enunciated clearly and slowly.

'Every one of you is privileged, greedy scum and you will pay for the damage you are wreaking on our society.' She turned to Marty, a rictus grin splitting her face. 'Starting with you, sir.'

Gasps of shock and indignation reverberated around the room, but there were also chimes of laughter. 'This is a stunt, right?' the ex-studio head's wife said to Madeleine. Marty did stunts; this must be a set-up.

'He didn't mention anything about it,' Madeleine replied doubtfully. Marty was in excellent shape for his age, but could he really pull off a performance that involved prolonged physicality?

That was when the walker raised her hand and Madeleine caught a glint of steel. Time seemed to stop. She watched, horror-struck, as the knife was dragged across Marty's throat, spraying arcs of blood across those seated nearest to the stage.

There was a scream, followed by another, then another. By the time the fourth scream echoed, Marty Coel was dead.

Chapter Ten

EVE

Now

Eve took an instant dislike to the defence KC, a bombastic show-boater named Peter Cheney. He had already interrupted Madeleine half a dozen times to object to her 'straying into embellishment' and now appeared poised to do so again, after Philbin asked the actress to describe Jenna Sandwell's demeanour before and after she killed Marty Coel.

'She looked like she enjoyed it.'

Jenna Sandwell – sitting with her fellow defendants – hadn't stopped grinning since Madeleine entered the witness box. On hearing the comment, she began to giggle loudly, triggering murmuring in the public gallery.

This prompted Madeleine to glance towards the dock for the first time since entering the courtroom, and as she did there was no denying the shudder that ran through her. The Seven were responsible for her scars, both visible and hidden, and Eve could only imagine what it must feel like to be confronted by them again.

'Can you describe her expression?' Philbin asked Madeleine, more forcefully.

Sandwell's giggles subsided, but she continued grinning.

'She looked manic, like she was high on something.'

Cheney was on his feet again. 'Objection. The witness is speculating about the state of mind of my client.'

'No, the witness is describing how she looked to her in that moment,' argued Philbin. 'She's not saying she was under the influence, just that she appeared to be.'

Justice Ritchie contemplated for a moment. 'I'm going to allow it. Overruled.'

Philbin nodded at Madeleine. 'Please continue, Ms Farmer.'

'That was it, really. She appeared manic.'

'In a happy way, or angry?'

'Oh, definitely happy. She was smiling and laughing. That's what I mean by manic. She looked like she was enjoying everyone watching her.'

Sandwell let out a peal of laughter from the dock. Tinkler joined in. Then Nye, sitting at the other end, leaned forward in his seat and turned his head to look at them. The stare he gave the two young women chilled Eve to the bone. They instantly quietened, the smiles slipping from their faces.

'Was Mr Coel able to do anything to defend himself or prevent the attack?' asked Philbin.

Madeleine's composure finally slipped. She began to quiver as though she'd been blasted with cold air. Her right hand clenched over her left, causing her knuckles to blanch.

'No, it happened too quickly,' she said. 'He clutched his throat for maybe a second, then he was gone.'

'Gone?'

'Sorry, I mean he died. He lost so much blood so quickly.' Madeleine sounded angry now. 'Then that bitch let his body drop to the floor like she was discarding trash.'

Cheney objected to Madeleine's namecalling, but the damage was done. Eve didn't need to be a body-language expert to see whose side the jury was on. They were all pulling for Madeleine, and for poor Marty Coel.

Eve felt the same. The testimony was so affecting that she instinctively wanted to fold inwards to shy away from its horror. But she forced herself to sit tall and listen. The victims deserved her and the court's undivided attention.

'How did the other defendants react?' asked Philbin.

'There was a lot of screaming and shouting from the audience, people were getting out of their seats and running for the door, but I do remember one of them, a young man in a waiter's uniform, running up on the stage and yelling in her face.' She motioned to Sandwell. 'He was saying it wasn't how it was supposed to go, that it was too early. I didn't wait to see her reaction; I left my table like everyone else.'

'Is that young man sitting in the dock today?'

'No, he's not.'

'That remark, "It was too early", makes it sound as though Mr Coel's murder was planned, but just not at that particular point in the evening,' said Philbin.

Cheney objected again, this time on the grounds that the prosecution counsel was leading the witness. The judge sustained, but Eve could see Philbin was unruffled. He'd got across his point about premeditation to the jury, planting the seed that whatever The Seven might claim in court about loss of control triggering the violence, their actual behaviour on the night suggested otherwise – starting with Jenna Sandwell's murder of Marty Coel.

Eve left court as it recessed for lunch. Madeleine had yet to reach the part of her testimony where she would have to recount how she'd been dragged away from the other guests and taken backstage by Edwin Barker. As the victim of an alleged sexual assault, Madeleine was entitled to anonymity for this part of the trial but had waived her right, Horner told Eve as they crossed the Great Hall. She had been a leading voice in the Hollywood #MeToo movement, supporting women who'd come forward to share their experiences, so she didn't want to shy away from making sure her evidence was heard. Eve's admiration for the woman had no limits.

Horner walked Eve outside, ostensibly to give her a pep talk before she headed to Lewisham, but also to discuss what they'd just heard.

'I don't know how Cheney is going to argue loss of control with a straight face,' said Eve. 'Everything points to them having planned to take lives that night, from the weapons they carried, to the bombs they planted, to killing Marty in cold blood.'

'If they offer any defence – at this stage we still don't know if they will – I expect it'll be the bigger picture. I've read Nye's statements and he's claiming his followers were provoked because they entered the Novus to start a peaceful dialogue with the guests about the negative impact wealth and greed have on society and young people in particular, but the hostile reaction they received is what turned the situation violent.'

Eve scoffed. 'The jury won't believe that. They were armed. There was nothing peaceful about their intention that night.'

'All it takes is for one or two jurors to believe Nye's claim that they armed themselves for protection. All it takes is one or two jurors to share the mindset that the distribution of wealth in society is skewed towards the rich, especially if they themselves are affected by the poverty divide. We tell juries they must only consider the evidence put before them when making their decision, but we know personal prejudices can taint their judgement.'

'I was watching the jury listen to Madeleine and they looked like they believed her account of Marty Coel's death. He did nothing to provoke Sandwell into attacking him.'

Horner nodded. 'Sandwell is the biggest obstacle to The Seven arguing their case convincingly. Nye apparently didn't want her to stand trial with the rest of them because her murdering Marty makes it harder to maintain the loss of control defence. But it seems someone pointed out to him that The Seven collectively dancing to the same tune is far preferable to them having separate barristers. It mitigates any chance one of them might suddenly turn round and claim they've been coerced, which is what Cal Morgan initially told an officer after he was arrested,' said Horner. 'Cheney acting for them all is a clever tactic.'

Outside the Bailey, they stopped for a moment to observe a smattering of Decorous supporters who had gathered across the street. All dressed in navy, some waved placards spelling out 'Free The Seven' and 'Money Is Evil'.

'I'm not sure they even know what they're supporting,' said Horner.

'What do you mean?'

'There's a school of thought that Nye doesn't give a rat's arse about the film industry making billions and corrupting society, and never did. A lot of people think it was just one big con so he could make his own fortune, starting with the millennium bug and his so-called great global reset.' He threw Eve a sidelong glance. 'Do you know about that?'

'I've read a bit about how Nye got started, but nothing about it being a con.'

Horner glanced at his watch. 'Let's grab a coffee before you go and I'll fill you in. You need to know this.'

◆　◆　◆

They found a Costa in the next street and settled down at a window seat with their order. Horner launched straight in to detailing Nye's background.

'The same time Nye was founding The Decorous in 1996, the media had started to report that a global computer meltdown might happen on December thirty-first, 1999, because systems couldn't recognise the sequence 00 in standard coding,' said Horner. 'It meant when the clock turned to 2000 at midnight on New Year's Eve, all hell could break loose. It became known as Y2K, or the millennium bug.

'Nye saw it as an opportunity. He seized upon people's hysteria that, worst-case scenario, the banks would collapse, we wouldn't be able to access our money, and everyone would turn on each other. There would be looting, civil unrest, people killing each other in the streets. So Nye started spinning the bug as a positive, saying that, actually, it would herald a great global reset, a moment in history when societal values would turn away from the greed and consumerism of the nineties in favour of a more profound and selfless way of living.'

Eve was puzzled why that would make Nye a con artist. His so-called reset sounded very much in keeping with the Decorous cause. But she kept quiet, keen to hear what else Horner had to say.

'Nye quickly gained a following because he preyed on people's insecurities that we'd become too dependent on computers and banks and stock markets,' Horner continued. 'People signed up for The Decorous in droves and were happy to comply with its main principle of sharing wealth equally—'

'Which meant turning over their assets to Nye,' Eve finished for him.

'Exactly. Cults are about control. With the millennium bug, Nye had found a way to control his followers; a fear to exploit. When the FBI went through his records after he supposedly died, they found his followers had collectively signed almost twenty million dollars over to him. Quite a chunk of that change was used to finance The Decorous' protests, buy weapons and keep the compound running, but the rest was supposedly redistributed to the poor – but there's no record of where that money went. The assumption is he must've stashed it somewhere to live off in the event of needing to disappear.'

'Is that why people assume he's a scammer?'

Horner nodded. 'Nye told his followers what they wanted to hear, and he was rewarded handsomely for it before he disappeared. There are plenty who now think he only set up the cult to get rich himself.'

'Do the police still not know where he was for twenty years?'

'No, and he's not saying. All we can be sure of is that he arrived in the UK about eighteen months before Novus on a false passport and, at some point, he linked up with the other defendants to begin plotting the attack.'

After his arrest, it emerged that Nye and his new band of followers had been holed up in Edwin Barker's derelict hotel on the Bournemouth seafront. It was a far cry from the sun-drenched balmy shores of California.

'This time The Decorous wasn't about money, though, was it?' asked Eve, even though she already knew the answer. But she wanted to hear Horner's take on it because, with the exception of DCS Strutton, he probably knew more about the case than anyone else.

'No, it wasn't. Nye spun the same line to his new followers that the world was even more overdue a reset, and that was why they had to take a stand against the rich and famous. But it was obvious to any impartial observer that the Novus attack was about him getting revenge. Nye might deny it, but the footage proves it.'

One of Nye's followers had filmed inside the Novus and uploaded the footage to social media while the siege was underway. It had been speculated since that Nye was unaware the filming was happening, because he could be seen in the background telling another follower that 'every asshole who wrote me off as a has-been is going to have to take me seriously now'. His comment flew in the face of his claim that his motive for hijacking Dame Cynthia's event was honourable.

Until the footage was uploaded, no one outside the theatre had an inkling there was such a dangerous situation brewing inside. All attendees had been made to give up their phones when they arrived and the only people who could potentially have communicated with the outside world were the theatre workers and the catering staff serving meals already prepared off site, but they also had their devices removed and were rounded up and frogmarched into the auditorium to wait it out with the VIPs as soon as the siege kicked off. The footage ran on social media around the same time the event was due to finish and cars were lining up in the street outside to take everyone home.

Listening to Horner, Eve realised there was still a lot about the case she didn't know and felt a sudden stab of panic thinking about the review. 'I haven't read anywhere that Cal Morgan initially claimed he'd been coerced,' she said.

'Well, he did, and there was even talk he might plead guilty and accept a lesser sentence in return for giving evidence against Nye. But then he changed his mind and went along with the others. Obviously, his conflicting statements will be put to him if he takes the box, but we are expecting him to blame the police for putting words in his mouth during that first interview.'

Eve's experience in criminal defence meant she could guess what had prompted Cal's change of heart. 'He must've been persuaded by Nye or someone else that they have a good chance with the loss of control defence,' she said. 'But I just can't see that cutting through to the jury.'

'No, I don't think it will either. But I'm also not a betting man. Nye still has a hugely devoted following – you only have to go online to see how many supporters he has,' said Horner. 'There are multiple websites extolling his virtue and plenty of the people behind them aren't even Decorous members. They're just ordinary people who think he's right about the poverty divide. For all we know, some of the jurors might be just as like-minded.'

Eve was again struck by the magnitude of the case – and her task specifically. It wasn't only going to be her bosses and colleagues watching to see if she did a good job: if the review became public knowledge, Nye's supporters and detractors would have something to say about it too.

'Is there anything specific I should be looking out for in the review?' she asked Horner anxiously.

'No, there isn't. But you know what to look for, so just trust your judgement. And I meant what I said in our meeting with Strutton and Lees: if you find anything that looks out of place, you come to me first, not them. They're going to be looking over your shoulder throughout,' Horner warned, 'so be ready for that. Every scrap of paper you look at, they're going to want a gander too. Don't be afraid to tell them to back off if they start to get in the way of you doing your job.'

He hesitated for a moment. 'I know you had a rough ride with your last job, but Beverly says you're the best new advocate she's worked with in years, so clean slate, okay? None of that matters now.'

She squirmed. He knew she'd been sacked. He must've heard it along with the rest of the division when her co-worker Ashley blabbed.

'For what it's worth, you did the right thing. I'd have gone over his head too,' Horner added. 'Sacking you for it was bloody unfair.'

Eve managed a hoarse 'thank you' then looked away, embarrassed. But Horner ducked his head to force her to make eye contact again, peering at her through his oversized glasses.

'I mean it,' he said kindly. 'It was a shitty thing that partner did, trying to offload his mistake on to you. But you've got two choices as I see it. You can either let it continue to undermine you, or you can chalk it up as experience and move on.'

Eve decided to be honest. There was something about Horner that made her feel at ease, like she didn't have to pretend to be brash and assertive around him in the way that was expected of her by the men at the City firm. 'I am trying to put it behind me. But it has knocked my confidence a bit,' she said.

'I'm not surprised.' He crossed his arms, head tilted to one side. 'I haven't got time to hand-hold you through this review, so if you need to bring something to my attention and I'm not available, or you think I've not listened to you, take it further.'

'What?'

'You heard me. You have my permission to go over my head. Talk to Beverly if you need to.'

Eve found herself smiling. 'Seriously?'

'Yes. This isn't the kind of case where we can allow egos to get in the way of doing our jobs. You'll have enough of that when you get to Lewisham.'

Chapter Eleven

The quickest way to Lewisham Police Station was on the Thameslink from Cannon Street. The squalling rain from that morning had given way to thick grey cloud, but the unseasonably low temperature hadn't disappeared with it, and Eve shivered in her suit as she made her way along Ludgate Hill to Cannon Street. She was by the barrier and fishing in her bag for her contactless bank card when her phone pinged twice in quick succession. The first message was from her sister, Emma, wanting to know what time Eve's train was getting in on Saturday morning so she could collect her from the station. Eve closed the message down immediately, knowing she'd have to let her family know she wasn't coming any time soon.

The second was from her flatmate, Leah, saying she'd be at home that evening, and did Eve fancy sharing a takeaway and wine? Leah was a junior doctor at St Bart's Hospital, near their flat in Old Street, and was currently in the middle of an A&E rotation that meant she was doing crazy hours. Tonight would be a rare evening at home for her.

Another text followed, seconds later. *My shout*, it read.

Eve was immediately grateful. This wouldn't be the first time Leah had paid for a meal in the last three months. She knew Eve's funds were tight after the huge drop in salary that came with being sacked from a City firm. Eve was also frantically trying to build up a buffer in case the CPS job didn't work out. Leah didn't want her to have to move out and return to Shropshire any more than she did, so for the time being was happy to cover Eve's share for treats like takeout.

Eve messaged back thanking her, but added she might not be back until after eight because of work. Leah replied with a thumbs-up.

Half an hour later, Eve arrived at Lewisham, which held the honour of being the largest purpose-built police station in Europe. It even had a stable block to accommodate some of the Met's equine law enforcers. DCS Strutton came to collect her from reception himself. He could have sent an underling, but Eve recognised the gesture for what it was: he wanted to be seen walking her through the station, him leading the way, to make it clear to anyone who might be harbouring doubts that he was still in charge.

The incident room for Novus was still operational in the south block. Strutton led Eve there in silence, the only sound as they walked coming from her heels clicking conspicuously against the hard floors. She toyed with trying to strike up a conversation but was pretty certain it would be one-sided and quickly decided it wasn't worth it.

The incident room was a decent size, but smaller than she'd imagined it would be. Maybe it had been scaled down from the start of the investigation when the team would have had hundreds of witnesses to interview and thousands of pieces of evidence to collate. None of the desks were occupied this afternoon though, which she found odd.

'You don't have any officers working in here?' she asked Strutton.

'Not right now.'

He didn't seem prepared to elaborate, so Eve had no idea if this set-up was typical or not. She suspected not, and that the room had been cleared for her arrival. Silent again, Strutton stalked off towards the rear of the incident room. Eve followed and saw a door to the left marked 'Storage'.

'Everything you need to review is in here,' he said.

Strutton opened the door, then stood aside so she could peer past him. It was a narrow, windowless space, more a corridor than a room, with a low ceiling and an overhead fluorescent tube light so bright it could burn a person's retinas. Most of the space was taken up by cardboard boxes that were stacked haphazardly. There wasn't time to count them, but Eve guessed there were around ten in total.

'I had them moved in here this morning,' said Strutton gruffly. 'We had to separate out what DC Colgan had worked on.'

'DC Colgan was the DO?'

'Yes.' Strutton gestured towards the stack. 'This is all the unused evidence we think he dealt with.'

'Think?'

'Well, some he might not have. I thought it was better to err on the side of caution and give you everything. I thought you'd prefer that.'

Was the helpfulness a sign of him thawing? It was on the tip of Eve's tongue to ask him why Colgan had left the Novus investigation, when Strutton announced he would leave her to it. She held up a hand to stop him.

'Hang on a minute. Where am I meant to work?'

Strutton hooked his thumb towards the boxes. 'In there.'

'I can't work in a cupboard,' she said, half laughing. 'I need a desk and a chair and access to COPA, CJSM and Cellebrite.'

COPA stood for Case Overview and Preparation Application and was a two-way interface application used to collate all disclosure; it could be accessed by both the police and CPS. CJSM was the Criminal Justice Secure eMail used for secure message transmissions and Cellebrite was used for digital intelligence gathering, such as phone records. Eve had no idea what was awaiting her in the boxes, but she needed access to all three, for cross-referencing. Yet Strutton was now looking at her as though she'd asked him to sprout another head.

'You want an office?'

'I want a decent working space. I'm not just flicking through a bit of paperwork and that's it, the review's done. I need to be thorough.' Eve paused. 'You need me to be thorough.'

Strutton's cold glare could crack glass. 'Meaning?'

'If the defence decides to file for a dismissal on the grounds of inadequate disclosure, it's not going to be on my head,' she said, now emboldened by Horner's reassurance and his comment about not letting ego get in the way. 'Everyone's expecting the trial to be straightforward because of the volume of evidence gathered against The Seven, but if it collapses on a technicality because something was left in unused that shouldn't have been, who do you think they'll blame? Me? The rest of the CPS? No, it'll be the police, or rather you, the SIO, the person ultimately responsible for the slap-dash DO. Given the Met's currently in special measures, I'm not sure that's something you want to take a risk on.'

Strutton bristled. 'He wasn't slapdash.'

'My presence suggests otherwise,' said Eve. 'Look, I'm not here to pick a fight. I'm here to do the task I've been assigned to do, and I want to do it well.'

'Do you regret switching sides?' Strutton asked suddenly.

'Sorry?'

'You used to defend. Do you miss it?'

Someone had been doing their homework, Eve realised with a start. What else did he know about her?

'Um, no,' she replied, flustered he'd read up on her. 'Joining the CPS was an opportunity I couldn't turn down.'

'That's a politician's answer.'

That made her laugh, but Strutton's expression remained blank.

'I hadn't thought about switching sides, but then the job came up and it sounded interesting and I'm enjoying it. I'd like to keep it too,' she added pointedly.

Strutton regarded her for a moment, then he slowly nodded. 'I'll have you set up with everything you need. We'll have to move these boxes again though.'

'No, you won't,' said Eve, setting her bag on the floor and shrugging off her coat. 'Show me where to take them and I'll shift them myself.'

For that, she finally got a smile.

Her allocated office wasn't much bigger than the cupboard, but it did have a desk, a chair, a fully functioning computer and natural light. It was on the same floor as the incident room but down a long corridor, and it took her half an hour to lug all the boxes to it. Strutton did offer to help again, but she declined, not wanting to appear hypocritical when she'd made a fuss earlier on about the evidence not being touched by anyone but her.

By the time she'd deposited the last box inside the office and set it down she was ravenous. She hadn't eaten since breakfast and now her stomach was gurgling in protest. Strutton had said to find him in the incident room if she needed anything, so after grabbing her coat and bag, Eve returned there, and found him at a bank of desks in the middle of the room along with a handful of other officers, an even split of male and female.

DS Lees was among them, and when he saw Eve he smiled smugly and called out, 'Found anything yet?'

She knew he was trying to get a rise out of her, so she ignored him and told Strutton she was going out to get a coffee. The security pass she'd been issued with at reception allowed her to swipe in and out at will, but to her surprise Strutton got to his feet and said he'd come too.

'The coffee here is shit, there's a place round the corner that's better,' he said. 'I need the toilet first, wait for me here.'

Eve did as she was told, although she moved away from Lees to wait by the door. That was when she caught sight of it; the wall to the left of the door, out of her line of sight when they'd come in earlier, was covered with headshots. Four rows in all. Most were in colour, but a few were black and white. Eve recognised exactly who the photographs featured and without counting she knew there would be forty-three images in total.

The thirty-four victims of the Novus bombing, plus the nine Decorous followers who died alongside them.

Taking in the images one by one, a lump formed in Eve's throat. She was appalled that anyone would try to argue that the victims deserved to die by virtue of how much money they had. Using that rationale, how on earth did Nye justify slaughtering the theatre and catering staff too?

The youngest victim was sixteen and on an unpaid internship. As Eve's gaze fell upon the girl's picture, she couldn't stop the lump forming in her throat and she had to swallow hard to dislodge it. Getting upset wouldn't help the victims now – she needed to stay focused on the review and ensure justice was served for them.

Strutton came back into the incident room, saw what she was staring at and stopped in his tracks, his expression twisting in a way Eve couldn't read. Then, without preamble, he turned to her and said he was sorry.

'What for?'

'Being rude and giving you a hard time. They' – he nodded towards the gallery of headshots – 'are the reason I get so wound up. If you saw the state those bastards left them in, what their families are being put through . . .' His gaze dropped towards the floor and Eve saw he was struggling to maintain his composure. She stayed mute, knowing nothing she said would be of comfort. The vast weight of his responsibility as SIO was his alone to bear.

Then Lees joined them, his mobile against his ear.

'Boss, there's been an update from court. The judge adjourned early for the day because Madeleine Farmer couldn't continue.'

'Is she okay?' Strutton asked.

'She is now, but it sounds like she went to pieces on the stand.'

Strutton's fists balled as he swore. 'Bastards. Fucking not guilty pleas.' He looked at Eve, and then at the wall. 'This is why they can't get away with it.'

Lees slunk silently back to his desk, which made Eve suspect this wasn't the first time he'd witnessed such a reaction from Strutton. Taking her cue from the OIC, she waited quietly until she could see Strutton had collected himself. When it looked as though he had, she asked if he still wanted to get a coffee.

'Yes, but let's get a takeout and bring it back so you can get started,' he said gruffly. 'The quicker you get the review done and this trial ends, the better.'

Chapter Twelve

Eve spent the rest of the afternoon opening every box to get some sense of what she was dealing with. As was often the way with unused material, there was no system to how the boxes had been packed and so she found various statements mixed in with unrelated crime scene photographs and expert reports. She thought about trying to stack them into piles, but there wasn't enough space in the tiny office. So, after making a rough list of what was in each one, she decided to methodically work through each box at a time, starting with one that contained statements from Cal Morgan's sixth-form tutor and teachers.

The press reports about Cal Morgan having been a good student were not an exaggeration; they all had nothing but nice things to say about him and were shocked by his involvement in one of the worst atrocities ever carried out on British soil.

Before she read the statements in detail, Eve set up her own file on COPA to record the material each box contained. She also decided to record a handwritten document on one of the yellow legal pads she always kept stowed in her bag. It made the process slightly more laborious, but she liked the reassurance of knowing she had a back-up system.

At 7.30 she decided to head home and start afresh early the next morning. She was hungry, tired and in truth a bit overwhelmed by the turn her day had taken. She needed to offload about it and she knew her flatmate would be happy to listen, because Leah was the only one in Eve's small circle of friends in the capital who knew she was working at the CPS. Eve knew Leah didn't fully understand her reasons for not telling people she'd been sacked, but she didn't judge her for it either, knowing herself that the reality of moving to London in your twenties for work rarely matched the idealised notion you had carried around in your head beforehand. Leah, who hailed from Cardiff, had joined St Bart's four months before the global pandemic struck and so her introduction to emergency medicine in the capital had been stressful, exhausting and traumatic. They hadn't known each other then – Eve had moved in only six months ago, responding to Leah's ad on SpareRoom.com after having to downgrade from the one-bed flat her old City firm salary had enabled her to rent.

The journey to Old Street took less than forty-five minutes. Their flat was in a modern block with shops beneath it, including a Co-op, so Eve ducked inside and bought a discounted bottle of white wine before heading upstairs. Eve let herself in, and Leah shouted out hello from the open-plan lounge next to the hallway, where she was watching TV. 'There's wine in the fridge, and I've ordered a curry,' she added, voice still raised.

Eve's mouth watered on cue. She hadn't eaten since she and Strutton had gone to the coffee shop around the corner from the police station and she'd bought takeaway lattes for them both and a cheese salad roll for her.

'You read my mind, you star,' she hollered back, hanging her suit jacket at the end of a row of coat hooks screwed to the wall. She kicked her shoes off and left them in the pile of footwear accumulated on the floor beneath it. 'Do you need a top-up?'

'I'm good at the moment, thanks.'

Eve went into the kitchen, deposited the new bottle in the fridge and helped herself to a glass of chilled white from the one already opened, savouring the sensation of that first delicious sip. Then she headed back into the lounge. It was a decent-sized space, with two sofas placed at a ninety-degree angle in front of the television and a dining table and chairs and shelving to one side. Leah, dressed in a T-shirt and sweats, was stretched out on one of the sofas, her phone in one hand and a glass of wine in the other. Eve flopped down on the opposite sofa.

'Tough day?' she asked.

'Relentless.' Leah sighed. 'Six-hour waiting time, and it's not even the weekend. You can imagine what they were like by the time they got to me.'

Eve didn't need to imagine because Leah had come home many times complaining of how she'd been shouted at and abused by patients irate at having had to wait so long to be seen. As though, somehow, she was personally at fault.

'But you know what, I'm off now for three days and I don't want to talk or even think about work,' said Leah, raising her glass with a grin. '*Love Island*'s on in a bit, and that's about as cerebral as I can manage tonight.'

Eve tilted her glass towards her flatmate. 'Amen to that.'

'How was your day?'

'Eventful. I've been moved on to another case to do an urgent review.' Eve swallowed a mouthful of drink. 'It's the Novus Theatre trial, actually.'

Leah's eyes widened and she sat up quickly, almost spilling her wine. 'No way. That's such a big deal, Eve. I was just reading about it when you came in. Did you hear what happened in court with Madeleine Farmer?'

'Yes, I was with the police in the Novus incident room when I heard. I also saw her give evidence this morning.'

Leah was impressed. 'Really? You saw her in the flesh? Tell me everything!'

Eve gave Leah a potted rundown of her morning, from arriving at work to suddenly be told she was being redeployed, to being in court at the Bailey when Madeleine took the stand.

'Is it true she's lost an eye?' asked Leah.

'That's what she said. She was wearing a patch, but you can see that side of her face is heavily scarred.'

'God, the poor woman. Can you imagine being that stunningly beautiful and then that happening to you?'

Eve didn't consider herself particularly attractive. Of the two of them, Leah was the better-looking, with thick, straight, naturally blonde hair and a slim, toned body she never bothered exercising because being on her feet all day in A&E did it for her. Eve had dark brown hair, cut to her shoulders, with an annoying kink that always rebelled against any attempt at styling, and she needed thrice-weekly Pilates classes and long runs to offset her love of wine and junk food. Yet even though she ranked herself fairly average in looks, she'd still be devastated to be robbed of hers in the way Madeleine Farmer had.

'It was so impressive how she held it together,' said Eve. 'When she walked in everyone was staring at her, but she acted like she just didn't care.'

'She's a great actress,' said Leah sagely. 'So, what are you doing on the case if the trial's already started?'

Eve explained what her review involved and how quickly it needed to be done. 'It's just for a couple of weeks, but it's great experience for me and could lead to something really good.'

'I'm so pleased for you.' Leah beamed. 'They must think highly of you to put you on the case – maybe you can relax now about not losing this job as well?'

'I guess.' Eve wished she could, but just thinking about the review made her pulse spike. 'You won't see much of me for the next couple of weeks. I need to put in some serious hours to get it done. I'll be here on Saturday now, but I still won't be able to do lunch.'

She'd already told Leah she was going to Shropshire for the weekend and wouldn't be around for a get-together her flatmate had organised with some friends.

'Isn't it your parents' big anniversary?' asked Leah.

'Yes, it's their thirtieth. But I have to work,' replied Eve uncomfortably, aware of where the conversation was headed. Leah made no secret of thinking that Eve was wrong not to tell her parents about her career shift.

'Won't they be upset? What will you tell them?'

'That I'm sorry, but I have to work.'

'But they still don't know what kind of work you're doing, Eve. If you told them it was for the biggest trial of the decade, they'd be happy for you.'

'Yeah, but the first thing they'll ask is why I didn't tell them sooner about being sacked. I can't face the interrogation. I will tell them, soon, but not yet. I can't deal with it right now.'

'Coward,' said Leah, grinning.

'I know. It would actually be easier if they weren't so bloody lovely. But I put them through so much shit to take that job I can't bear to see their faces when I tell them I lost it. Or Nick's. I can just imagine the told-you-so's.'

'Is he going to the party?'

'Yep. Mum wanted to invite him. He's still an important part of the family, apparently.'

Leah pulled a face that reflected Eve's discomfort. Nick was Eve's ex-fiancé, who she'd left when she moved to London. Despite what she'd pretended at the time, it wasn't an awful, gut-wrenching decision. She adored Nick but knew there was a part of her that had been settling for security rather than love. He was kind, dependable and he made her happy, but in the end the thrill of moving to the capital was a bigger draw than he was. The wedding had been a year away when she'd called it off, with the venue already booked and her dress bought. The latter was now stored in the box room at her parents' house, gathering dust, and was another reason not to go back there at the weekend, because that was the room she usually slept in when she stayed over.

'You could use his being invited as an excuse,' Leah suggested. 'Say you've decided it would be too weird to see him.'

Eve shook her head. 'But that wouldn't be true, and I don't want to hurt his feelings. We're fine when we see each other. We still get on.'

'Then be honest and tell them you're working for the CPS and you're on the Novus case. You can't let it drag on much longer—'

Eve, not wanting another lecture, was relieved when the door buzzer signalled their takeaway had arrived.

Later that night, slumped in her bed with a belly full of chicken dopiaza and onion pakora and a fuzzy head due to the wine, she had a quick scroll through Nick's IG to see what he'd been up to. He looked happy in the few latest pictures he'd posted – no sign of a new girlfriend though – and she was pleased about that. He was a nice guy and he deserved to be happy. She knew she hadn't been the right person to do that for him, however.

She shut down his page, then clicked on a news website. Every report relayed the same details. Darius Philbin had begun quizzing Madeleine about what happened to her when the defendants had split the guests into groups, and she'd been put in one guarded by Edwin Barker. At the mention of his name, Madeleine began hyperventilating, leading to a full-blown panic attack that saw her eventually black out for a minute or so.

According to the reports, while this was happening supporters of The Seven in the public gallery laughed and jeered. Eve snapped the lid of her laptop shut. If she was appalled to read of such callousness, she could only imagine how poor Madeleine must've felt in the face of it.

Chapter Thirteen

MADELEINE

Now

It was nearing midnight, but the bars and restaurants of Marylebone High Street continued to thrum with laughter and conversation. Madeleine, in the apartment she had rented above a pizzeria that sent delicious smells wafting through the cracks in the doors and floors, didn't mind the noise. She welcomed it. It distracted her from the silence, and that was a good thing, because being alone with her thoughts was too dangerous. If she let silence in, it took her to the darkest of places, to the line that once crossed she knew she'd never return from. A line she'd toed many times since last April.

Each time she'd come close, when her despair was screaming at her to cross that final threshold, the sounds of life continuing outside – traffic, music, conversation, birds in chorus – had dragged her back. The sound of the streets was why she was staying here during the trial, and not in a penthouse suite on the top floor of a Park Lane hotel, where the soundproofing was so efficient the only noise she could have heard at night was her own breathing. Only when the trial was done and The Seven were behind bars did she plan to let the silence envelop her for good.

With sleep a long way off and only accessible by throwing down pills, Madeleine, barefoot in pyjamas and holding on to the wall for support, hobbled into the Shaker-style kitchen. It was another upside of the rental. Painted cupboards meant there was no surface reflection. Her assistant, Gina, had also requested every mirror be removed from the apartment when she made the booking, including the one in the bathroom. The owner was resistant at first, until Gina offered to pay triple the nightly fee for his cooperation, and even the cost of having the bathroom refitted if the tiles were damaged during the mirror's removal. The owner hadn't been told Madeleine was the renter – Gina was practised in making sure her employer's name was never anywhere on a booking – but she wondered, after all the publicity today, whether he might now work it out.

She felt another surge of anger as she poured herself a glass of water from the fridge dispenser. She was so pissed that she hadn't been able to hold it together in court. She'd spent weeks going over her evidence, making sure she was able to articulate everything the prosecution wanted the jury to hear, but the mere mention of Barker's name had sent her into a tailspin. She was also angry that, once she had come round and been helped down from the stand, she'd glanced over at Barker in the dock. She had promised herself that she wouldn't look at him the entire time she was in court, but his presence had the pull of a magnet, forcing her head to turn against her will. To her fury, he was laughing at her, just like he had when she'd begged him not to hurt her that night.

Tomorrow she'd be stronger. Tomorrow she wouldn't give him the satisfaction.

Madeleine carried her glass back into the lounge, re-treading the same path, holding on to the wall for support. It had been years since she'd stayed somewhere so small with a square footage still in the hundreds. It reminded her a lot of the condo her parents had rented for them to stay in when the family first moved to Los Angeles from Arizona, when Madeleine's dreams of becoming an actress were just that. It was one of the happiest times of her life, despite living hand to mouth off her dad's meagre salary as a car-wash attendant and the tips her mom made waiting tables. All their money went on Madeleine's acting classes, and trying to keep their ageing car on the road so they could drive their daughter to and from auditions. Yet despite the hardship, Madeleine had never felt so full of hope or optimism. The world had been hers to conquer back then.

The TV was on, showing a Hulu drama set in the near future and starring a friend of hers. The sofa looked inviting, but Madeleine sat down on a hard-backed chair near the window instead, knowing she would struggle to get up from the deep cushions without assistance. Gina had offered to stay with her, but she'd said no, and instead paid for a hotel for her close by. Difficult though it was to do certain tasks unaided, Madeleine was tired of being manhandled, whether it was Gina helping her in and out of cars, physios manipulating her hips and pelvis to support her rehabilitation, or her stylist getting her dressed for court. She knew their intentions were good, but it did nothing to quell her fear that people saw her as some kind of helpless freak now. Also, if Gina had stayed, Madeleine wouldn't have felt comfortable removing her wig and eye patch in front of her, and the best part of every day now was the moment when she could discard them both.

Tonight, her wig was already on its mannequin's head on the chest of drawers in the bedroom. It was the best money could buy; real hair, handmade by a Parisian wig maker whose work had featured at New York Fashion Week, styled and dyed to look exactly like the hair Madeleine had lost. Yet lovely though it looked, it still felt artificial and heavy, like she was walking around wearing a borrowed bicycle helmet.

Gingerly, she lifted the patch that covered the space where her left eye used to be. The shrapnel that had hit her in the face had also severely torn the surrounding socket tissue, making it tricky for a prosthetic eye to be fitted. Not impossible, but the ocularist said she needed to undergo another operation first, possibly two, with skin grafts. In the meantime, she'd been fitted with a conformer: a small device that slotted beneath her eyelid to keep its rounded shape and which could be removed for cleaning. The ocularist was adamant he could help her and that the prosthetic eye would appear natural when they could eventually get it fitted, but she wasn't sure she could bear it. She'd already endured so much pain.

She didn't know what her eye socket looked like now. She'd had only one fleeting glimpse of it since the bombing, a few days later while she was still in the hospital. She'd insisted, and a nurse had given her a hand mirror of her own. In her horror she'd thrown it to the floor and smashed it. The nurse had accepted her apology and offer to replace it with good grace.

Madeleine knew how the socket felt. Not from touch – she couldn't bring herself to touch the left side of her face at all now, even though all her specialists said it wouldn't cause any harm to do so. Instead she paid for a private nurse to come a few times a week to remove and clean the conformer so she didn't have to.

She knew how it felt from sensation. To her astonishment, there had been a couple of occasions when her eye had not only felt intact again, but she was also sure she could see things. Her ocularist had confirmed that, much like phantom limb syndrome, where patients who'd lost a leg felt an itching sensation where their foot used to be, it was possible for people who'd lost an eye to still have the perception of sight, and even imagine seeing colours, lights and shapes. Madeleine wasn't sure what was worse: knowing she'd lost her eye or her brain tricking her into thinking she hadn't.

Then there was the depth misjudgement and imbalance caused by her functioning right eye missing its partner, which made her dizzy and clumsy. That, coupled with the chronic pain she'd been warned might never abate, had degenerated her once fit body into something woefully frail and incomplete. A body that would never bear a child, might never walk fully unaided and would never appear on-screen again.

Her anxiety beginning to bubble, Madeleine turned up the volume on the television as a distraction. Every day she fought hard not to let silence draw her to the line, knowing she needed to see out the trial. But every day she wished Barker had killed her when he had the chance.

Chapter Fourteen

MADELEINE

Then

20 April, 8.42 p.m.

The air was thick with screams and panic. A young man dressed all in white rushed on to the stage and began yelling at Marty's killer, who was now laughing as she stood over the body. When Madeleine saw he was carrying some kind of rifle, she jumped to her feet, her chair toppling backwards on to the floor in her haste to escape. Struggling to catch her breath, she found herself swept along by the crush of the crowd, everyone desperate to distance themselves from poor Marty lying dead on the stage, blood still spilling from his throat. She knew even then that the terror in his eyes as the blade dug into his throat would stay with her for ever.

Another guest pushed her roughly in the stampede towards the exit, the momentum ejecting Madeleine from the heaving mass like a fish flipping out of a shoal. The pressure of being hemmed in from all sides now eased, she looked back to the table and was shocked to see Cynthia hadn't moved from her seat. Her ashen-faced grandson, Matthew, and Samuel, Cynthia's personal assistant, were imploring her to stand up, but the guest of honour was frozen in horror, her stare trained on the stage. The woman with the knife had disappeared, and now a couple of guests were on the stage trying to help Marty. Madeleine watched as the man in white raised his rifle to force them back. He was then joined by an older man, wearing head-to-toe navy, also carrying a rifle of some description. Who were these people?

For a moment Madeleine was torn. Instinct told her to run, but she couldn't leave Cynthia. Still shaking, she headed back to the table.

'Gran, we've got to get out of here,' Matthew was saying, standing behind Cynthia and cupping his hands gently around her shoulders.

'But what about my Marty?' the elderly woman answered. 'Look, he's hurt. We must help him.'

Madeleine forced herself to check the stage, but she didn't need to look twice to see that Marty was beyond help, his lips rapidly turning blue.

'He's going to be okay,' she said, hating herself for lying but knowing it was necessary if they wanted to get Cynthia to safety. 'The paramedics are on their way, and they'll take good care of him.'

Matthew shot her a grateful look. 'Madeleine's right, Gran. We should wait outside for them to arrive.'

Cynthia finally conceded and slowly got to her feet. She moved at a glacial pace though, and Madeleine had to bite her lip to stop herself from yelling at the poor woman to go faster. It wouldn't have mattered anyway; when the four of them finally reached the rear doors of the auditorium, they were blocked by a group armed with guns. Madeleine counted eight of them, five men, three women. A few were dressed as waiters, but the rest were wearing plain navy trousers and matching sweatshirts. They had made no attempt to obscure their faces, so she doubted their intention was robbery.

Surely if they were here to steal from them, they wouldn't want to be recognised afterwards?

There was a growing clamour as the guests demanded to be let out. The group ignored them and kept their weapons raised. Madeleine shuddered. Why wouldn't they let anyone leave? What did they want?

The tumult grew louder until a gunshot rang out from the stage and the screams started again. A man with long white hair drawn back in a messy ponytail, also dressed in navy, had fired a handgun into the ceiling. Madeleine shook violently as the weapon discharged again but resisted the temptation to dive under the nearest table, where she would be hidden by the thick white cloth draped over it. She couldn't abandon Cynthia to these people.

Suddenly a man's voice boomed over the loudspeakers. It wasn't the same announcer who had earlier invited guests to take their seats ahead of the event starting. This was someone much younger.

'EVERYONE STAY STILL,' the voice boomed.

Madeleine did as she was told. In her peripheral vision and looking straight ahead, she could see that people had stilled like she had. It was like the weirdest game of freeze dance she'd ever participated in.

Then, from the crowd, a male guest in a tux stepped forward. He held himself with poise and authority and Madeleine recognised him as the British director Ellison Moran. He'd won a slew of awards over the years for gritty feature films known as kitchen-sink dramas.

'This is nonsense,' Ellison said, his tone commanding. 'You need to let us out of here now.'

'Dad, don't,' rang out a young woman's voice from further back in the crowd.

Madeleine couldn't see where Ellison's daughter was, but she knew she was right: he shouldn't antagonise them. Three of the men had now moved from the door to stand in front of Ellison with their guns raised.

'Let us go,' he repeated firmly.

The ponytailed man who had fired into the ceiling climbed down from the stage and passed through the tables. When he came into Madeleine's scope of vision, she took a long, hard look at him, wanting to commit his description to memory. He was tall and lean, but his shoulders were also broad, suggesting he worked out, and his face was defined by a prominently hooked nose. Close up, he looked younger than his snow-white hair implied, mid-forties at the most. Around his waist he wore a utility belt with a smartphone pouch and a holster that housed a small handgun.

He stopped barely inches from Ellison, so they were almost toe to toe. The director didn't flinch and stared the gunman down.

'You people aren't going nowhere,' said the gunman. He spoke languidly and surprisingly without rancour. He sounded British, with a trace of an accent that Madeleine couldn't place.

'What do you want with us?' asked Ellison. 'Why did your accomplice kill that poor man?'

His imperious tone was not well received.

'I'd get down off your high horse if I were you, mate,' the man spat. 'Like you even know what the meaning of the word "poor" is. You're all the same. Filthy rich and polluting our society with your woke shit. Fucking liberals.'

Ellison frowned. 'Is that what this is? A protest against liberalism?'

The man smirked. 'All in good time.' Then he took a step back from Ellison to address the room, his voice slow and sonorous.

'Everyone needs to go back to their seat. That's the seats you were in before, not somewhere else. No talking.'

Madeleine could see the hesitancy in people's expressions – what if this was a trick to shoot them where they sat? The gunman rolled his eyes.

'Are you all deaf or what? Come on, move it!'

Slowly, almost as one, the crowd began to inch forward. Madeleine was almost back at her table when a hand grabbed her upper arm roughly.

'Not you, sweetheart.'

Madeleine's legs gave way in terror as the man pulled her forward towards the stage, where Marty's body still lay. She screamed and tried to pull away, but the man was too strong, and the thin soles of her strappy sandals couldn't get purchase on the carpet. Then a heel snagged on the rear hem of her gown, causing her to trip over it, but he still wouldn't relent. He just kept dragging her forward until she was on the stage, facing the horrified faces of the other guests, who must've thought, as she did, that they were going to kill her too. Such was her terror that she couldn't even cry. She simply stood there, too scared to even blink, let alone move, as though she'd been encased in ice.

Then, from the wings, another man emerged. In his early fifties, with longish, sandy hair slicked back off his face. Unlike all the others in their navy attire, he was dressed in a loose-fitting white V-neck sweater and white trousers with sharp creases down the front. His shoes were also plain white. As he came closer, Madeleine frowned. His face was familiar, but she couldn't place him. Unlike the others, he wasn't armed, and if she had met him under any other circumstances, she might have said he had a kind face. Certainly, he was smiling as he approached. He said nothing when he reached her side, though, but instead gave the nod to the one with the ponytail to readjust the microphone stand until it was level with his mouth. Then he began to address the crowd.

'My name is Patrick Nye,' he said, in a disturbingly amiable tone, 'and we are The Decorous.'

There were gasps from the crowd. A voice cried out, 'Patrick Nye is dead!'

Madeleine knew where she recognised him from now. The cult leader. Wasn't he supposed to be dead? She'd been a kid of about eleven when the raid on his headquarters made the news.

'The cops said you drowned,' she blurted out.

He ignored her and continued to address the crowd. 'You've all gotten so much greedier since I was last among you,' he said, like a disappointed parent chiding a naughty child. 'Lining your pockets with billions of dollars while you pollute our children's minds with your immorality.' He suddenly looked down at Marty's body, as though he'd only just noticed it. His expression darkened and he put his hand over the microphone so the audience couldn't hear.

'Who the fuck did this?'

'Jenna, sir,' said the one with the ponytail. 'We warned you she was disturbed.'

'No, this is your failure. You were meant to watch her.'

His delivery was composed, but Madeleine could see he was thrumming with anger. So could the one with the ponytail, who for all his macho posturing with the audience now quailed as Nye's stare bore into him.

'No more killing the hostages until I say so.'

Then Nye snapped to and returned to the microphone.

'We don't want to hurt anyone else, so I suggest you do as you're told. Failure to comply will not end well for you.'

Madeleine began to tremble, which Nye noticed.

'No need to panic, you're just here to be my assistant,' he said.

'Wh-h-why me?' she stuttered.

'You're the most famous person in this room,' he said simply. 'I need you to help me sort everyone into groups.'

Bewildered, she stared at him. 'What?'

'You're going to be separated into groups now,' he announced into the microphone. 'Madeleine here is going to rank you in order of how famous you are.'

His gaze fixed on Madeleine's then, and she saw that his intention to keep them there was deadly serious. But surely someone would realise what was going on and call the police?

'Oh, and in case you're wondering,' he said to the audience, as though he'd read her mind, 'help is not coming. We've locked down the building. No one is getting in or out, and we have smashed all your cell phones to pieces.'

On cue, another man emerged from the wings, this one dressed in a catering uniform. He was holding a large plastic crate and on reaching the front of the stage he tipped out its contents, scattering the broken fragments of dozens of cell phones across the floorboards. Then slowly he raised his eyes to Madeleine and stared as though he was trying to bore through her skin. Nye followed his gaze and chuckled.

'We're not here for that, Barker. Don't go getting any ideas.'

But Madeleine could tell from Barker's expression that it was already too late.

Chapter Fifteen

EVE

Now

Eve woke up an hour before her alarm was due to go off, too wired to sleep and eager to get to Lewisham as early as possible. Once showered and dressed, she tiptoed out of the flat so as not to wake Leah, who on her day off needed to catch up on sleep.

She bought coffee and a bagel at a concession next to Old Street station, then caught the Tube to Bank to catch the DLR to Lewisham. She spent the latter part of her journey above ground, scrolling more news reports about Madeleine's testimony being cut short. The actress's distress at giving evidence wasn't conveyed only by words though. Someone had also managed to catch a picture of her leaving the Old Bailey by a back exit. It was long lens, and only a profile shot, but the side exposed to the camera was Madeleine's left – the side most severely injured – and the accompanying head-lines reflected the shock that Eve had felt in court when she first saw her. Eve wondered if today would be any easier for Madeleine on the stand, but she doubted it.

There was also a new interview doing the rounds with one of Nye's more ardent followers, Lisanne Durand. She was thirteen when her parents – Lily and Ramon – had taken her from their native France to live in Nye's compound, drawn by his idealisation of creating a society where children didn't grow up impoverished or corrupted by wealth. Her parents had long renounced all association with The Decorous, but Lisanne had remained steadfastly loyal, never believing Nye was dead and crowing in triumph when he re-emerged after twenty years in hiding.

The interview – in which Lisanne nauseatingly gushed about how thoughtful Nye was in waving to her every day from the dock – mentioned she wasn't the only devoted female follower staying in London for the duration of the trial. Joan Beck, Nye's girlfriend at the time of his apparent death, had also flown in from the States. She had been prosecuted as a ringleader at the compound and served twelve years in federal prison.

Intriguingly, the article said Joan wasn't attending the trial itself because she had an undisclosed chronic health condition. Eve made a note to ask Strutton about Joan and where things stood between her and Nye twenty years on.

Eve arrived at Lewisham just before seven-thirty. Predictably, the incident room was empty at that hour. She spent a moment lingering in front of the wall of headshots, better able to take them in without Strutton or Lees watching her.

Of the forty-three victims whose images were on the wall, thirty-four had been guests at the event, some more VIP than others. The most notable casualty was the guest of honour herself, Dame Cynthia Seymour, although she died not from blast injuries or from being shot or stabbed – as some of the guests had been during the siege – but from a stroke that was almost certainly stress induced. The other high-profile victims included actors, a director, producers, screenwriters and a former studio head and his wife. The remaining victims were theatre and catering staff. The youngest was sixteen and an intern, a girl named Saffron whose job it had been to help collect all the cell phones from the guests as they entered the Novus. She had been tasked with stashing the devices in security pouches that could only be unsealed using a unique magnet. Within moments of the siege beginning, the pouches were reopened by Nye and his men and the phones smashed to pieces, so there was no possibility of anyone getting hold of theirs again and summoning the police.

Strutton's wall of headshots did not tell the full story of that night, however. It didn't account for the living victims, the dozens who survived but were maimed when the bombs went off, some seriously so, like Madeleine Farmer. Eve knew at least two of them – one a guest, the other a theatre employee – had suffered degrees of brain damage from being crushed beneath masonry when the foyer collapsed in on them. Then there were those who'd survived unscathed – the handful who managed to escape from the theatre right before the explosions and those who were shielded from the blast by the bodies of others. Physically these two groups appeared unharmed, but their psychological injuries ran deep and would for a long time to come, if not for ever. Their photographs might not be on any wall that Eve was aware of, but there was no doubt they equally deserved justice for what they'd been put through.

Resolute, she headed out of the incident room and along the corridor to the office she'd been assigned. Last night she'd locked the door behind her and taken the key home for safekeeping, but when she went to open it now, she found that the office was already open. Eve paused for a moment in the doorway. Nothing seemed out of place from what she could see, but she was still unnerved. She'd made it clear to Strutton that the evidence wasn't to be touched by anyone but her, so there was no reason for anyone to enter the room when she was absent. Why would he or anyone in his team ignore that request? Then her gaze fell on the wastepaper bin in which she'd deposited her sandwich wrapper and takeout coffee cup the day before. It had been emptied, suggesting a cleaner must've unlocked the door and had forgotten to lock it again afterwards. She allowed herself a relieved smile for jumping to conclusions, but as she slipped off her jacket and settled herself behind the desk, the idea that someone had been in the room still niggled at her. She made a mental note to ask the station's facilities manager to let the cleaning staff know her cubbyhole was out of bounds for the foreseeable.

◆ ◆ ◆

In an active case, unused material fell into three categories: statements or evidence that pointed to the credibility of the victim or witness; records of communications involving the defendant, victim and witnesses; and third-party material such as health records, forensic science reports and Social Services files. Cal Morgan's school reports, which Eve had read yesterday, fell into the latter.

The second box in her review contained material relating to the post-mortems of the victims who had died as a result of the explosions, specifically transcripts of the pathologist's voice-recorded notes. Eve could see why the transcripts weren't being used in court – it was unlikely the defence would dispute the causes of death in these instances, so there was no need to take up time presenting them in court as evidence. She checked COPA to confirm that the pathology reports for the six people murdered separately by Nye's followers during the siege – the deaths most likely to be contested – had been revealed to the CPS and disclosed to the defence, and indeed they had been.

Eve was meticulously checking the transcripts for any anomalies when John Horner called at eleven, during a recess. She'd spoken to him briefly yesterday evening to confirm she was up and running at Lewisham and that she was ploughing through each box in order. He was calling in case she had anything she needed to run past him before court resumed.

'No, everything seems in order so far,' she said. 'There are corresponding MG6 forms for everything I've reviewed so far.'

'Have you got to any phone records yet?'

'I haven't.'

'Make sure you've got plenty of coffee on hand when you get to them.' Horner chuckled.

Eve knew what he meant. Mobile phone records could run to thousands of spreadsheets, downloaded on to Cellebrite. Reading through them was a tedious, eye-straining task, but one that was absolutely necessary.

'How's it going in court?' she asked.

'Not great. Madeleine Farmer's back in the witness box this morning, but she kicked off during Cheney's cross-examination and is refusing to answer his questions. She told the judge she's already said everything the jury needs to hear from her, and she isn't prepared to go through it again. She's trying to leave.'

'How's that gone down with His Honour?'

'His restraint so far has been admirable, but you can tell he's getting close to holding her in contempt. That's why Philbin forced a recess.'

'I can see why she's had enough. I read what happened after I left yesterday,' said Eve. 'It must've been so hard for her, having to relive it while everyone gawped at her injuries.'

'You know that's not how it works though. She's compelled to take the stand and answer questions from both sides,' Horner replied. 'But yes, from a moral perspective it looks pretty awful that we're forcing the poor woman to keep going over what happened to her. Philbin and Cheney are in chambers with the judge, arguing about how to proceed. Philbin wants to release her; Cheney wants to continue.'

'Why was she called in the first place? Prosecution witnesses are usually only compelled to take the stand if the defendant disputes their evidence. There are plenty of other guests who could've given the same testimony she did about what went on inside the theatre.' Eve paused. 'Or was it because everyone wanted a star witness in the literal sense?'

Horner sounded annoyed by the insinuation that Madeleine was being used. 'She was called because Barker denies sexual assault and, as the law stands, he's entitled to question her account.'

There it was again. *Entitlement*. It was at the heart of this case in so many ways. In the eyes of The Seven and their dead accomplices, the guests at the Novus Theatre reeked with entitlement because of their wealth and status and they wanted to hold them to account. Yet now they were determined to exercise their own entitlement by having their day in court. Eve doubted they recognised the irony.

'Madeleine annoyed the jury by the end though. You could tell they thought she was grandstanding.'

'She was upset,' said Eve. 'Surely they won't hold that against her?'

'Her threatening to storm out might be all they'll remember of her testimony now, rather than what she recalled about the siege, which was incredibly compelling. It's making Philbin question the order of who we put on the stand. We're bringing forward some of the theatre employees to remind the jury that ordinary people were involved too, that it wasn't just rich celebrities.'

'I don't think Madeleine getting upset will stop the jury from returning a guilty verdict though,' Eve ventured. 'They can see what she's been through.'

'I don't think it will either, but we still don't how Cheney is going to present loss of control as their defence. In the meantime, we don't want the jury being swayed into thinking The Seven have a point about wealthy entitlement,' he said. 'I think Philbin's right about changing the order of witnesses. Okay, I should go back in now. Text me if anything comes up, I'll be checking my phone at the next break.'

Eve said she would, then got back to work. She quickly lost track of time, until eventually her back twinged and she realised she'd been hunched over reading documents for two hours straight. She stood up and went over to the window, where she had a view of the courtyard where the police horses were exercised. Looking down, she raised her arms to stretch them out.

'Yoga class, is it? All right for some.'

Eve jumped, then spun round. DS Lees was standing halfway between the doorway and her desk. He'd walked into the room without knocking.

'Can I help you with something?' she asked, ignoring his jibe.

'Just wondering how you were getting on.'

There was an undercurrent to the way Lees spoke to her that raised Eve's hackles, a snide tone he did little to disguise. As the OIC, he should be supporting her while she carried out the review, but she couldn't shake the feeling that he'd trip her up the first chance he got.

'I'm making progress.'

'Anything we should know about?'

'Nope, nothing. It's all been textbook so far. DC Colgan was very thorough with his MG forms.'

Lee stared at her, his pale blue eyes rendered near colourless by the sunlight streaming through the small window, yesterday's downpours now a soggy memory.

'How old are you?' he asked.

Eve was taken aback. 'Excuse me?'

'We've been trying to work out how old you are, because you seem young to be given a review this important. You haven't been at the CPS long either.'

'I'm twenty-eight, and I'm very good at my job, thanks,' said Eve waspishly. She really didn't like this man.

Lees walked over to the boxes, scanned the pile, then casually lifted the top flap of the one near the door, which Eve had been planning to get to last.

'Please don't touch that,' she said.

'Just making sure you haven't missed anything.'

'I thought you and DCS Strutton were confident nothing had been missed.'

Lees swung back around and eyed her up and down. 'You know, my missus had hair the same as yours, but she got some highlights done and now it looks so much better than that drab brown. You should think of getting some.'

Eve was furious but refused to stoop to his level by retaliating with an insult of her own, even though there was plenty she could say about the suit he'd clearly picked up from the floor to re-wear that morning, or the way his eyebrows met in the middle. Instead, she asked if there was anything else he wanted because she needed to get back to work.

He smirked. 'No, nothing for now. I'll pop back later.'

'Great,' she said, but they both knew she didn't mean it.

Chapter Sixteen

By Friday, Eve's back, neck and shoulders were in serious need of a deep-tissue massage. She'd neglected to take regular breaks from the screen and desk, the review absorbing every ounce of her concentration. She was making good progress though, the six completed boxes now pushed to one side of the office proof of that. That left four to go, which she planned to tackle over the weekend. She'd sought clearance to come into Lewisham out of office hours, and it had been approved.

She spent the morning reviewing some of the statements from first responders on the scene. They made for harrowing reading. These were experienced officers and paramedics used to dealing with all kinds of incidents and injuries, but what had confronted them at the bomb site that morning was beyond anything they'd seen before. More than once, Eve had to stop reading, her eyes swimming with tears triggered by the bleak testimony.

Despite the hard work and long hours, she was finding the review interesting and rewarding and it gave her second thoughts about her future. She'd been envisaging a return to private criminal defence work once her CPS contract was up, but now she wasn't so sure. She was finding it far more palatable being on the side of the victims than the low life she'd previously defended. She felt a sense of moral purpose she hadn't experienced once while working at the

City firm. If she stayed on at Petty France, she could reach Horner's or even Beverly's level if she worked hard and proved herself. She might not make the salary that had lured her to London in the first place, but it would still be decent enough.

Lunch was a sandwich on the go as she walked a stretch of the nearby River Ravensbourne, to get some fresh air. It felt good to escape her cubbyhole briefly, after seeing little but its four walls for over a week, but her stroll was short-lived. There was too much work to do.

Returning to her desk, she pushed aside the thought that she still hadn't told her parents she wasn't going home the next day for their anniversary. Her plan was to call them first thing in the morning and pretend she'd come down with food poisoning from a dodgy takeaway and couldn't travel. She took no pleasure in adding another lie to the web she'd spun for her family over the past few months, but she couldn't face the disappointment of her parents knowing she'd been sacked and was now working elsewhere, even if she was part of the Novus prosecution team. Once her career felt truly back on track, that was when she'd tell them the truth.

She should've known they'd catch up with her first though. Late in the afternoon, while she was checking something on COPA, a call came in on her mobile from a number she didn't recognise. Distracted, she failed to exercise her usual caution of letting it ring until the caller either hung up or left a voicemail.

The moment she heard the familiar voice at the other end her heart sank.

'Oh, so you are alive, then,' said her sister spikily. 'We were starting to think otherwise.'

Eve's hackles rose on cue. She was in no mood to deal with her eldest sibling, whose default setting was to be perennially disappointed in everything Eve did. Emma was a significant factor in why she hadn't told her parents about her employment hiccough;

she knew they'd be upset she had kept it from them and had been lying to them since, but Emma would be livid, and would react as though Eve had got sacked on purpose just to spite her.

'I'm sorry, I've been really busy,' she said. 'I can't really talk now either.'

It was a cowardly cop-out, but she didn't want to tell her sister she wouldn't be returning home for the weekend before she'd had a chance to give the excuse to her parents. Emma wasn't going to let her off the hook though.

'No, you can spare a minute to talk to me now. It's the least you can do when I've been doing all the running around for tomorrow . . .'

Eve listened while her sister let fly with her list of grievances about how she was doing everything for their parents' party while Eve swanned around London and their brother, Joe, was God-knows-where with his new girlfriend, who was not the same new girlfriend he had last month, FYI. Emma was calling from her workplace, hence the unknown number, and was talking in a fierce whisper so as not to be overheard. Eve pictured her sister hunched over the landline receiver, light brown hair fanning across her flaming cheeks. She was so worked up already Eve decided that telling her she was skipping the party would make little difference to how the conversation was going. Instead of making an excuse, she might as well be honest.

'Actually, about that,' she interrupted. 'I'm really sorry, but I won't be coming home tomorrow, now. I have to work.'

There was a short silence before Emma exploded like a geyser. 'You are fucking kidding me. No, Eve, no. Just no. That's not acceptable. You have to be there.'

'It's not my choice. I'm on this big case and I've got to work all weekend to get it done.'

'I don't give a shit. I don't care if you bloody well lose your job' – Eve winced at the irony – 'but you can't let Mum and Dad down again.'

And there it was. Emma's go-to insult, with added emphasis on the word 'again'. She believed Eve had let their parents down terribly by cancelling her wedding to Nick and causing them to lose the deposits they'd generously paid – even though Eve was incrementally paying back every penny they lost – and her sister was never going to let her forget it.

'I'll call them tonight to explain,' she said.

'Too right you will,' Emma snapped back. 'I'm not telling them. Wait – how long have you known about this?'

Eve decided to be honest again. 'I found out about the case on Monday. I've been snowed under since then. I was going to call.'

'Save it. I'm not interested. If you can't be bothered with us, I can't be bothered with you. Do whatever you want. I'm done.' The next thing Eve heard was the click of the call ending as her sister hung up.

As warring sisters, they'd had worse fights, but something about this one really stung. Eve felt bad she was going to miss her parents' party, but she knew that if she told them it was because she'd been seconded on to the Novus trial, they might understand and even be proud. But to tell them that would mean admitting she'd failed at her last job, and her pride stubbornly wasn't ready to do that. With a sigh she resumed working and tried to ignore the feeling that since leaving her hometown and moving to London, she'd never felt so distant from them.

Chapter Seventeen

FAYE

Now

The sound of breaking glass yanked Faye from her sleep with a start. What the hell was that? Then she heard Richard swear and the noise of fragments being swept up. She groggily turned her head to check the time, squinting at the clock on a shelf in the alcove. It was nearly noon. She'd slept through breakfast and the kids departing for their usual Saturday-morning activities. Why hadn't they woken her to say goodbye? Why hadn't Richard made them, or done it himself? The lambswool throw presently swaddling her up to the neck was his doing, and it irked that he'd left her to sleep on the sofa again. He knew the fabric made her skin itch.

Her gaze strayed to the empty wine glass on the coffee table, the dregs of a 1984 Merlot she'd downed alone last night now staining its bowl. With a groan, Faye turned her head to face the ceiling again and waited for today's hangover to viciously announce its arrival. It didn't disappoint, the thunderous headache that presented almost immediately matched by the soreness in her shoulders and lower back from sleeping so awkwardly on the sofa.

She lay there for a few minutes, knowing she should get up but putting it off because she couldn't face Richard busying about the kitchen, preparing the ingredients for the elaborate lunches he now liked to eat and getting under her feet while she forced down coffee. *The perfect stay-at-home husband*, she thought hollowly, except a few years too late for her. Where had all this effort and thoughtfulness been when they were married? It was like living with a stranger now, although that was probably just as well, because this set-up of him staying in his former matrimonial home wouldn't have worked with the old Richard, who was selfish, inconsiderate and disdainful of domesticity.

When she did eventually stumble into the kitchen-diner that stretched the width of the rear of the house, Richard greeted her like a long-lost friend he hadn't seen for decades. This sober effusiveness was another new trait for him and another new irritant for her.

'Hello, sleepyhead. Shall I put some coffee on?' he asked.

She managed a nod, then carried her empty wine glass over to the sink, gave it a quick rinse and downed two glasses of water in succession. Richard immediately appeared at her shoulder with a clean tumbler. He tried to take the wine glass from her, but she wouldn't let him.

'But it's dirty,' he said.

'So?'

The deliberate edge to her tone worked; he clearly thought twice about badgering her again and slunk back to the island, where he was filleting trout. Her stomach heaved at the sight and smell of it, and she quickly walked across to the slide-and-stack doors, pulling one open to gulp in some fresh air.

'I wouldn't do that. It's meant to rain again in a bit,' Richard called to her.

'I'm hot,' she said.

'That will be the booze sweats,' he said piously. 'You should have a shower.'

She knew he was right – her hair felt matted against her head and her skin was sticky and stale – but God, she didn't have the patience for him today. Why couldn't he bugger off and leave her alone? This wasn't even his house any more; he'd signed it over to her in their divorce. What had she been thinking, inviting him to stay? He could've stayed in a hotel or rented his own place. But she'd felt sorry for him that he was suffering panic attacks and agreed it was important he was close by for the children. Too old to need a babysitter, Olivia and Freddy had been getting ready to take themselves off to bed when the news began to filter through on their social media channels that the Novus was under siege. Family friends and relatives came to the house to support them through the night as they waited desperately for updates, but they'd been deeply affected by not knowing whether both their parents were alive or dead. Now, though, Richard staying with them was too much. He was too much.

You know why you let him stay, a small voice rang in Faye's ear. *It's because of what you did. Every excruciating minute of him living under your roof is how you say sorry, even if he has no idea that's what you're doing.*

Flustered, Faye shoved the thought from her mind and turned to find that Richard had stopped filleting and was watching her. His concern was visible, and she knew what was coming next, the words that were forming at the back of his throat. She was spiralling again. She mustn't push him away. Don't bring the shutters down and make them impenetrable. Talk to him. Think of the children. Let him help her heal. It was like a mantra for him, and Faye was sick of it.

For once, though, she was wrong. That wasn't what was on the tip of his tongue. 'I've been going to some meetings,' he suddenly blurted out. 'With some of the others.'

'What others?'

'Some of the other survivors. There's a group of us, just a handful of people, who've been meeting regularly. For support.' He hesitated. 'I've been talking to them about you, and they've said you can join us.'

Faye reared backwards in alarm. She couldn't possibly sit in a room with other survivors and pretend she was suffering like them. Richard misread her reaction though. He scurried out from behind the island and came over to her, bringing the piquant odour of raw fish with him.

'There's nothing to be scared of,' he said, taking hold of her hands. His touch was so familiar it made her ache, but the smell of raw fish was overpowering, and she pulled away, ignoring his look of hurt. 'The meetings are a safe space for us to talk about how we're feeling. We're getting together on Monday because Jimi, one of the others, found out late yesterday that he's being called to give evidence this week, when we thought it would be Luke next. Jimi's in a bit of a state about it and needs our support.' He wavered for a moment. 'The start of the trial has triggered all of us, and I think that's what's happening with you and why you're drinking so much. I really want you to come with me on Monday.'

Faye shook her head vehemently. 'I don't think so.'

'If you're worried about privacy, don't be. It's a small, exclusive group.' He leaned forward conspiratorially, as though they were somewhere other than the empty kitchen and could be overheard. 'Madeleine Farmer's in the group. She hasn't been to many of the meetings because she's usually in LA, but she's coming this time.'

There it was: a flash of the old Richard, the mid-range Hollywood actor who liked to hitch his star to even bigger ones.

Faye smiled faintly, which Richard took as her accepting his invitation.

'I haven't said yes,' she protested. 'It doesn't sound like my kind of thing.' Then, more forcibly, 'I don't want to talk about it. I want to forget it ever happened.'

Richard's face darkened. 'Well, I can't. I owe it to Liberty not to forget.'

But that's why I have to, thought Faye desperately. *I need to forget how she died. I need to be able to close my eyes and not see Liberty's face staring at me accusingly, reminding me of the choice I made that night. A choice I've had to make every day since: my family, or the truth.*

'I can't, Richard. I can't open up in front of complete strangers.'

His expression lifted. 'But they're not all strangers; Samuel's part of it, too,' he said jubilantly. 'You've known Samuel for years.'

Faye's heart sank. That made it even worse. She couldn't sit next to that darling man knowing what she knew and say nothing.

'I am not going,' she said decisively. 'Please stop asking me.'

But Richard wasn't going to relent. His expression hardened.

'If you don't want to do it for yourself, do it for the children. Your behaviour is damaging them,' he said forcefully. 'They were really upset this morning because of what you said to Freddy last night.'

Faye's mind was blank. She couldn't recall any conversation – she only remembered drinking. 'I didn't say anything.'

'Yes. You did. You told him he mustn't ever get married or "he'll end up fucking around like his piece-of-shit father",' said Richard, deploying air quotes to make his point.

The shame of not remembering she'd made such an appalling comment to her son crawled up Faye's spine and sat heavily on her shoulders.

'I – I'm sorry,' she faltered. 'I didn't mean—'

Richard cut her short. 'If you truly are sorry, you'll come to the meeting on Monday. You might not like the idea of it, but I really think it will help.'

Faye stared at him despairingly. He had no idea how wrong he was.

Chapter Eighteen

FAYE

Then

20 April, 9.11 p.m.

Faye had been doing a valiant job of remaining as invisible as humanly possible. When Marty was murdered, she held back from screaming. When everyone charged for the exit, she didn't run. When they were forced to return to their seats under the threat of gunfire, she slid into hers without a word. She did everything a compliant hostage should do until Madeleine Farmer was dragged up on to the stage.

It wasn't clear at first what was happening, until Patrick Nye strolled from the wings to introduce himself and what was already a frightening situation ratcheted to terrifying. Faye knew exactly who Nye was and what he stood for, because she'd been on film sets and at premieres disrupted by The Decorous. Like millions of other TV viewers, she'd stayed glued to the round-the-clock news coverage when the FBI raided his compound. The siege that followed back then showed what a dangerous man he had been, and it took only a few minutes of him speaking now to realise he hadn't changed.

After issuing instructions to Madeleine to separate the guests according to their fame, Nye had made it clear that he and his followers were in control. They had killed Marty and they would kill again if anyone stepped out of line. Faye could tell from their resolute expressions and the weapons they had in their possession that they meant every word.

Now Madeleine, openly crying, was picking guests out of the audience. Panic-stricken, Faye scanned the crowd for Richard. When she couldn't see him, she forced herself to look for a flash of gold instead. Liberty, the twenty-something bride-to-be, was wearing a gold silk sheath dress with spaghetti straps and – very obviously – no bra. Everyone had stared as she'd sashayed across the auditorium when they'd arrived earlier. Faye was the slimmest she'd been since having the kids – thank you, heartbreak diet – and was wearing her favourite vintage Chanel, but she'd felt dowdy and every one of her fifty-four years in comparison.

She had to know Richard was okay, though – and to warn him not to do anything stupid. Life too frequently imitated art for her ex-husband, and he would forget he was an actor and not an actual lawyer/doctor/Marvel baddie/whatever other role he was playing. He'd end up dispensing dodgy advice or squaring up to people in parking lots and bars if he thought they were having a go at him. She needed to dissuade him from thinking he could tackle these men because he once had a bit-part role as a hostage negotiator in a film starring Nicolas Cage.

Eventually she spotted them, a shimmer of gold giving away their position. They were seated to the left of the stage, a stone's throw from where Nye was watching Madeleine continue her task. Faye's pulse accelerated when she realised Richard and his fiancée would be separated; Liberty's credentials as a reality-TV-star-slash-model-slash-influencer would almost certainly place her lower on the pecking order than him.

The crowd sat stock still as Madeleine pointed at them one by one. Faye didn't know if she dared move to get to Richard's side before it was too late – would she be hurt if she tried?

Before she could do anything, it was Richard's turn. Singled out by Madeleine, he was now being directed to go to the right of the auditorium to wait with some others. Liberty tearfully clung to him, refusing to let him go, and Faye felt an unexpected stab of compassion for the clearly terrified young woman. Nye's followers were shouting at her to let go, while Richard, now standing, tried to prise her hands off, saying they should do what they were told, but Liberty held firm. The other guests on their table started to fidget in their seats, presumably fearful of being caught in the middle of the situation, which took a turn when Liberty started screaming.

As she did, Nye casually walked to the middle of the stage to take the knife from the girl who'd killed Marty Coel.

In an instant, Faye found herself winding through the tables, like an unseen force was propelling her forward. People were on their feet shouting and yelling and she clawed them out of the way until she reached the circle that had formed around Richard and Liberty. Without thinking, she plunged into the space next to them and placed her hands on top of Liberty's, which were still clinging to the sleeve of Richard's tux. Her former husband reacted with surprise to see Faye, but Liberty was crying so hard she didn't notice.

'It's okay,' said Faye loudly. 'Come with me. I'll look after you.'

She had no idea if these men would let that happen, but she had to try. If Liberty didn't let go of Richard they might kill her, like they had Marty. No matter their differences, no matter what Liberty had done to her, Faye couldn't let that happen. She still loved Richard too much to watch him suffer that kind of loss.

Liberty finally realised it was Faye holding her hands. 'You?'

Faye couldn't answer – she didn't quite understand it herself. But Richard, at last overcoming his shock, did it for her.

'Stay with Faye, honey, she'll look after you.'

Nye walked to the edge of the stage above them, slowly rotating the handle of the knife in his palm. The blade was slick with blood.

'You have to let Richard go,' Faye urged Liberty. 'They've already murdered one person. You can't be next.'

The warning hit home and Liberty at last released her grip. Marched by two of Nye's followers to the other side of the room, Richard looked back at Faye and mouthed 'thank you', then he shouted to Liberty that he loved her.

Chapter Nineteen

EVE

Now

The weekend passed in a blur of documents, snatched coffee breaks and very little sleep, until Eve couldn't believe it was Sunday afternoon already. Her progress was slower than it had been during the week, because she was dog-tired and her eyes were strained from staring at her monitor and small print for so long. But she wouldn't give up and go home until she was satisfied she'd got through as much of the review as possible before Monday morning came round.

This afternoon had been particularly hard going because she'd been looking over lists of phone records. The bulk of them belonged to family members of The Seven, bar Patrick Nye; DCS Strutton and his team had cast their net wide to find accomplices, and the known involvement of two brothers – Cal and Brendan Morgan – made it feasible that other relatives were party to the plan. Yet going through the corresponding MG forms entered by DC Colgan, Eve could see none of these records had yielded anything relevant that should be presented in court. The families of The Seven, bar Nye, either had no idea of what their loved ones had been planning until after their arrests, or they were incredibly careful to cover up that they did know, possibly using untraceable burner phones of their own, paid for with cash, to communicate.

Nye had no family to investigate. His adoptive parents were long dead, and he'd been their only child. The only known associates he'd been in contact with on a personal level were Lisanne Durand, his most ardent follower, and Joan Beck, his former girlfriend, both of whom he'd contacted one month before Novus. Despite exhaustive probing, no evidence was found to suggest either woman had known about his plans. It was a sore point for Durand, who had reacted angrily in interviews when it was put to her that Nye couldn't have thought much of her if he didn't use her for Novus and instead recruited newer, younger followers like Jenna Sandwell.

While ploughing through the files, Eve had learned that three unregistered mobile devices were recovered from inside the Novus Theatre by Crime Scene Investigators (CSI). Two of them, found in the backstage area, were traced to one of the defendants, Mark Cleaver, via his fingerprints. He admitted they were pay-as-you-go smartphones he'd used to keep in contact with his secret girlfriends, so his poor wife didn't find out he was cheating. It was almost comical – in the midst of a siege, he was still planning to sext? In the end, he only managed to send four messages to both women during the sixteen-hour period – with the exact same wording – but they were still so graphic Eve cringed reading them. DC Colgan had been right to set them aside.

The third unregistered burner was an old-fashioned flip-lid Motorola, which was found in a metal waste bin in the men's toilets in the foyer. The corresponding MG form said the string of texts found on it took the same tone as Cleaver's phone. Eve decided she wasn't in the mood to read any more smut tonight, so she set it aside to tackle first thing in the morning and picked up another report. This was a statement from a police officer who was among the first responders to arrive at the Novus not long after the footage filmed inside the theatre was uploaded to social media. The officer's statement detailed how he and colleagues set up a cordon to keep everyone back once it had become obvious they had a siege situation on their hands. Again, DC Colgan had been correct to leave it in the unused evidence pile.

By the time Eve looked up again, the sky's earlier bright blue had begun to bruise as dusk started to fall. She took that as her cue to delve into the bag of supplies she'd brought with her. There was a satisfying pop as she cracked open a can of pre-mixed gin and tonic and she also tore into a sharing bag of her favourite crisps, her rewards for making it through the weekend. It was nearly nine, so after a quick break she'd do one more hour, then call it a night.

While she ate and drank, she propped her feet up on the desk and pulled up Instagram on her phone, desperate for some mindless scrolling to counter all the reading she'd been doing. After liking a few images on her thread, she went on to her sister's feed to see if she'd put up any photographs from last night's party. She hadn't yet, and it was unlike her not to, so Eve imagined she was refraining from posting on purpose to annoy her. It had worked. She debated for a moment whether to look at Nick's grid – she didn't follow her former fiancé's account but stalked it regularly – then talked herself into it with another gulp of gin.

Nick had posted a picture from the party, and it winded Eve to see him happy and smiling alongside her mum and dad – him in the middle of them both with his arms slung around their shoulders. He looked like the son-in-law her parents had hoped he would be: loving and supportive. Sadness washed over her. It was only for their sakes she wished things could've been different, that she'd loved Nick enough to stay and marry him. Maybe if they'd had more of the kind of chemistry that kept Mark Cleaver sexting throughout the siege, they might have lasted. They'd tried it once, but Eve found it awkward and unnatural—

She sat bolt upright, her feet flying off the desk. Wiping her greasy fingers on her jeans, she scrabbled through the paperwork on her desk until she found the MG form relating to the pay-as-you-go phone found in the men's toilet waste bin in the Novus wreckage and reread it to make sure she hadn't misunderstood. She hadn't. According to DC Colgan's entry, the phone had no call history, no photos, no contacts – all it held was a string of one-word texts to and from the same unsaved number and those messages matched the tone of Mark Cleaver's to his girlfriends. Eve stared at that last sentence again, her mind bubbling with a singular thought. Her one and only awkward attempt at sexting Nick was mortifying to recall now, but Eve imagined their messages were standard in terms of content and length – unlike the ones on the burner phone. Who the hell sexted one word at a time?

Feeling more awake than she had in hours, she booted up Cellebrite, the system used by the Met for digital intelligence gathering, and found the corresponding data for the phone. The first message had been sent to the bin phone from another number.

'Here?'

Then whoever had the bin phone had replied with, 'Yes.'

'Starting?'

'Five.'

'Now?'

'Yes.'

And so on.

As Eve slowly went down the page, she could see this was nothing like a conversation between two sexually involved people, as the MG form had claimed, and a feeling of unease crept over her. Why had the police been so quick to lump it in with Mark Cleaver's phones? Not only were the messages on it nothing like sexting, but the pay-as-you-go mobile receiving and sending them was found in an integrated bin below the sink counter in the men's toilet, suggesting it was purposely dumped rather than accidentally dropped. Both the guests and all personnel working within the theatre that night relinquished their phones as a condition of entry, so where did this one come from? The obvious answer was that it belonged to another of The Seven, or to one of their accomplices who'd died when the bombs went off. But why hadn't its provenance been more thoroughly checked to confirm that?

Eve stared at the form until the words began to swim; exhaustion was finally getting the better of her. She made a note on her legal pad to re-check everything relating to the phone first thing in the morning, when she had a clearer head. Then, finally, she logged off and went home.

Chapter Twenty

LUKE

Now

Luke had endured another grim night ruptured by nightmares; seeing Sebastian's body being pulled from the bomb site. He gave up trying to sleep in the early hours, leaving his apartment at eight and walking aimlessly around for two hours until he could lose himself in the sounds and smells of Borough Market as it opened.

The market, near London Bridge, was one of his favourite places in the capital but not somewhere he had visited with Sebastian. He'd discovered it on a morning much like this when his nightmares had forced him from his bed and he'd found solace in walking the streets. While he'd stayed in London to feel closer to his late partner, it felt good to switch off occasionally and not be reminded of why he was there. At the market there was no memory of Sebastian that could haunt him.

He was ordering some Malaysian street food for breakfast when his phone buzzed. It was a message from Madeleine, sent to their private WhatsApp group.

Can we meet earlier than 4? Need to talk. Anyone free
at 12? Mx

Luke checked the time. It was only ten-thirty now. He answered that he was free. Within seconds, Annie, Richard, Samuel and Jimi replied with the same. Horatio's response took a little longer to ping, but he said he'd be there too. Only Hilary, back in Scotland and due to miss today's gathering anyway, sent a regretful no, adding that she missed them all. His phone pinged again.

Great! You guys are the best. Mx

He knew why Madeleine needed to offload. Her appearance in court had been rough on her, but the headlines that followed it were even rougher, with her behaviour on the stand prompting criticism and her appearance dissected in graphic detail. It had sent Jimi into a spiral about going to court tomorrow after he'd suddenly been bumped up the witness list, and Luke, relieved his appearance had been put back, had spent most of the weekend trying to calm his fears about it.

He'd never say it to the others, but in Luke's mind Madeleine had suffered the worst of anyone in their group. Their grief at losing their loved ones would lessen in time, like a shoelace gradually working loose, but she would always have to live with her injuries, not to mention the memory of what Barker did to her. Whatever else he might be claiming in court, it didn't take a genius to work out what had gone on when he'd brought Madeleine back with her hair in disarray, her gown ripped and her expression shellshocked. Patrick Nye had then made her sit alone, distressed and crying, while Luke and the other hostages could only watch in sympathy.

Like Jimi, the fallout from Madeleine's court appearance also made Luke nervous for what he'd face when it was his turn to give evidence. He was expecting a grilling about Brendan Morgan, the protestor who'd aided his and Jimi's escape along with three others. The police found it hard to comprehend that Brendan, described by many survivors as one of the chief instigators of the violence, had suddenly experienced a change of heart and had helped the very people he professed to despise. Yet Luke knew that was too simple an explanation.

Brendan didn't so much have a change of heart midway through the night as an epiphany. He hadn't thought about the impact their actions would have on actual, living people; it wasn't until he was inside the Novus Theatre and carrying out Nye's orders that the Decorous doctrine turned from abstract and half-baked to something real and harmful and he'd realised he wanted no part of it. At least that was what he had told Luke.

From the fraught, snatched conversations they'd had before he helped them escape, and everything he'd learned about him since, Luke strongly believed that Brendan and his brother Cal had been brainwashed by Nye. It was why Luke knew he couldn't in all conscience give evidence specifically against Cal when he was called to the stand. He refused to damn a teenage boy who'd clearly been groomed to commit violence, no matter what acts he was guilty of carrying out. He wanted the trial outcome for Cal to be one of rehabilitation and understanding, not condemnation and a lifetime behind bars.

But Luke couldn't tell a soul that was what he wanted, least of all anyone else in the group. He knew they wouldn't understand – not even Jimi, who Brendan had also helped escape. He dreaded what their reaction would be when he took the stand and spoke in Cal's defence – but that was still exactly what he planned to do.

Chapter Twenty-One

EVE

Now

Eve had looked at the data every which way since she'd arrived back at her desk that morning, less than twelve hours after she'd left it, but her conclusion remained the same: the texts received and sent on the burner phone found in the waste bin were nothing to do with sex. So why had the police entered them into evidence as such?

And if the messages weren't about sex, what were they about? One thing Eve was certain of, they were enough of an anomaly to flag up to John Horner. She texted asking him to ring back when there was a recess.

In dire need of caffeine, she decided to have a break and walk to the café round the corner to get another coffee. Exiting the police station on to the street, she pulled out her phone to check the time . . . and that was when it hit her.

Timestamps.

Racing back inside, Eve didn't slow down until she was back in her cubbyhole, door firmly shut behind her. She scrabbled to log into Cellebrite, fingers jabbing the wrong keys in her haste, and in due course pulled up the thread of texts yet again. This time, though, she focused not on their content but on when they were sent and received. Then, using information shared on COPA, she painstakingly checked the timings of the texts against the timeline of the siege.

After a few minutes Eve sat back in her chair, stunned. Her hunch had been right. The timings matched. These texts had been sent at regular intervals throughout the evening of 20 April and during the early hours and the morning of the twenty-first. In other words, throughout the entire sixteen hours the Novus Theatre was in lockdown.

The first text was sent to the burner phone at 7 p.m. – the same time guests started arriving at the theatre. Whoever had the burner had replied almost instantaneously: 'Yes.' The next text – 'Starting?' – was sent to the burner just before the speeches were due to start, but the timeline recorded on COPA revealed there had been a delay of five minutes because Dame Cynthia was slow in taking her seat. The 'Now?' text sent from the other phone to the burner and its 'Yes' response were traded moments before Marty Coel had his throat slit and the siege got underway.

Heart thumping, Eve re-checked the timings twice more against COPA. She hadn't misread anything: every key moment in the siege was precipitated by a text exchange on these two phones. Whoever had hold of the other number would text a question, then the burner phone would reply. It happened before Marty was dragged onstage; before Madeleine Farmer was made to split the guests into groups; before the next hostage was killed.

'Here?'
'Yes.'
'Starting?'
'Five.'
'Now?'
'Yes.'

'Next.'

'Done.'

'Another.'

'Yes.'

The last text on the thread was sent to the burner phone from the other number a mere ten minutes before the first bomb went off. It simply read, 'End.'

Eve cupped her chin in her hands as she stared at the monitor screen. It should've been picked up earlier that the texts corresponded with the siege's timeline. Instead, they'd somehow been dismissed as messages sent between lovers.

She reread the texts a few more times, her mind continuing to swirl. Nye had provided each of his accomplices with a modified device pre-loaded with an encrypted messaging app to protect their communications. The app was a replica of EncroChat, which had been favoured by organised crime gangs – and a few of Eve's former clients in the Midlands – until it was shut down in 2020 after a European-wide police operation. Ironically, EncroChat itself had been developed as a means for celebrities just like those attending the Novus to keep their communications safe following the UK's tabloid phone-hacking scandal, but it hadn't been long until criminals also realised its worth.

Eve decided the burner phone found in the men's restroom was most likely used by one of Nye's accomplices instead of a pre-loaded device, as a back-up. Cleaver was the likely candidate, given he already used burners to message his girlfriends. She got to work then, pulling up files on COPA until she found the one she was looking for. Once she'd clarified who'd used the burner, she could amend the MG form to reflect the evidence and strike out all mention of sexting.

The file listed the modified devices Nye had provided to every Decorous member who took part in the siege. Eve frowned.

According to this, a device was seized from each of The Seven when they were arrested and also from the bodies of their accomplices who perished. In other words, every hijacker dead or alive was found to have one in his or her possession. She checked Cellebrite again and her frown deepened. The corresponding data showed every device was in regular use on the night, with dozens of messages flying back and forth on the app. Baffled, Eve slumped back in her chair. If all the modified devices were working, why did one of them need to faff around with a burner as well? It clearly wasn't needed as a back-up. And who had been texting it? No other untraceable phones had been found in the aftermath of the bombing, so was it someone texting from outside?

Eve gasped as the pieces slotted together. What if there were more Decorous accomplices out there that the police had failed to identify – one using the burner phone and another one texting it? Had Strutton and his team been so focused on The Seven and the followers who died inside the theatre that they'd overlooked the possible involvement of others?

Fired up, Eve grabbed her own phone and rang Horner. The call went straight to voicemail, so she left a message saying she had something urgent to discuss with him and it couldn't wait. Then she sat back, slightly breathless, to reread the damning texts. The more she went over them, the more certain she was in her gut that she'd found something significant.

When an hour ticked by and Horner still hadn't replied, Eve decided to take an impromptu field trip to talk to him in person at the Bailey. She wouldn't be able to relax or focus on anything else until she ran her discovery past him.

She shoved the MG form for the burner phone into her bag, locked up the small office and headed out. It would take her half an hour or so to get to court.

She got as far as the downstairs reception when DCS Strutton appeared from nowhere. From his short, panting breaths and the flushed cheeks, Eve guessed he'd run to catch up with her.

'Where are you off to?' he asked, his face only centimetres from hers, hostility radiating from every pore.

Eve instinctively crossed her arms, putting a barrier between them.

'Well?' he demanded.

'Ah, I . . . well, I've been summoned back to Petty France.' It was the best excuse she could think of under pressure that sounded plausible.

'I thought this review was urgent?'

'It is, but I was on other cases before this and there's a query I have to deal with in person. I won't be long.'

Strutton's stare hardened, but he didn't say anything.

'I should get going,' she said, trying to sound relaxed. 'I'll be back later.'

He let her go, but Eve could sense him watching her as she left, tracking her departure from the building. She wasn't doing anything wrong, she told herself: Horner's orders were to share any discoveries she'd made with him before briefing Strutton or Lees. The lying didn't sit well though, because it fostered suspicion and she was meant to be working with the police, not against them. They both wanted the same thing, to ensure justice was served, and after seeing Strutton's reaction to the victims' headshots yesterday Eve understood his keen interest in what she was up to. Still, she was relieved to round the corner of the building and finally be out of range of his hooded stare.

Chapter Twenty-Two

Horner jumped out of his skin as Eve slid on to the bench next to him. Her arrival in court had coincided with a break in the proceedings: the jury had been sent out, the witness box and dock were both empty, and the prosecution and defence counsel were nowhere to be seen.

'What's going on?' she asked him.

'Never mind that,' Horner blustered. 'What are you doing here?'

'I did call first, but you obviously couldn't pick up,' she said. Then she lowered her voice. 'I've found something in the unused I think you need to see.'

'Couldn't it wait until later?'

'No. I came across it last night, went over it again this morning, and I'm still concerned,' she said firmly. 'I think an important line of inquiry has been missed.'

Horner looked shocked. 'Okay, but not in here. Let's go for a walk round the block. The session isn't due to resume for a while.'

Outside, they walked past the protestors demonstrating their support for The Seven. The crowd had swelled in size since last week and there were more placards being waved too. One featured a photo of the bombed-out Novus superimposed with dollar signs, its 'Kill the Rich' slogan proclaiming that Patrick Nye had the right idea.

'So, what have you found?' asked Horner.

Eve dragged her gaze away from the chanting and waving.

'I've been reviewing some phone records, including data for a burner phone that was recovered by CSIs from inside the men's restroom in the theatre foyer. The texts on it don't add up. Well, actually, they do, but that's the issue.'

Horner stopped in the middle of the pavement, forcing people to walk round them. 'I know the phone you're talking about. The retro Motorola. The police said there was nothing relevant about the data found on it.'

'That's what the MG form says,' said Eve, 'but I'm not so sure.'

She explained what the messages said and how innocuous they appeared on the face of it, but how the timestamps matched various incidents that had happened during the timeline of the siege.

'The police have lumped the phone in with the ones Mark Cleaver had on him during the siege to message his girlfriends, but there's nothing similarly graphic about these texts,' said Eve. 'It's a one-word conversation with no mention of sexual activity. And because of that, I think it warrants more investigation.'

Horner pondered for a moment. 'The police reckon the phone belonged to one of the elderly guests, because it was an original nineties model and older people are less likely to upgrade their devices.'

'The same could be said of dealers who don't want their phones easily traced,' Eve pointed out. She'd defended a few in her time.

'True, but the police's theory was that the guest somehow managed to dodge the security checks at the start, then ditched the phone before Nye's lot noticed they had it, when the restrooms were still in use,' he said.

'But that would mean the guest was sexting throughout the siege, according to the MG form and the timings,' said Eve. 'Not only do the messages not read like sexts, but no hostage was going to risk being caught by Nye and the others using their phone, whatever the subject. And if they did take that risk, surely they'd have texted for help?'

Horner's expression shifted and he exhaled noisily. 'Shit. You're right.'

'Yes,' said Eve emphatically. 'That's not all though. Initially I thought the burner phone must've been used by one of The Seven or their accomplices instead of a pre-loaded device. Nye was meticulous about everything else – it stands to reason he'd have contingency plans for communications, like if the app failed.'

'Except we know the app didn't stop working – we have all the data from it,' Horner finished for her.

'Exactly. Every hijacker had one of Nye's adapted devices on them, and they used them throughout the siege. So who had the burner instead, and who was texting on it?'

'The others using their devices doesn't make it conclusive there were more people involved, Eve,' Horner cautioned. 'The most likely explanation is one of them also texted on the burner as a back-up.'

'That would mean typing out everything twice. Who would bother doing that?' she challenged.

Horner thought for a moment. 'They were inside the theatre for sixteen hours and we know from the witness statements that for the most part they stood around guarding the hostages. There was plenty of time to compose two sets of messages, but let's not forget we're talking about one-word texts here. Easy to type and send.'

Eve had to concede his point, but she couldn't shake the uneasy feeling that the texts needed more investigation. If the CPS let it slide and it turned out there were other accomplices involved, she'd be the one in the firing line for not reviewing the evidence adequately. There would be no second chance this time. Just a one-way ticket back to Shropshire.

'What if the explanation isn't the most likely one?' she pressed. 'John, if there's even a tiny chance Nye had accomplices using burners who slipped through the net and are still at large, we have to push for a fresh investigation.'

'I do understand what you're saying, but the investigation into accomplices has already been exhaustive,' he said. 'The police checked links to every member of The Decorous. If there had been any others out there, they'd have found them.'

Eve didn't share his certainty. The fact they were having this conversation about the burner showed corners had been cut.

'Okay, so which of his accomplices do you think Nye favoured enough to give the back-up phone to?' she asked. 'Barker? Woolmore?'

Horner shook his head. 'Barker was too clueless to be given added responsibility, and Woolmore's role on the night was being Nye's attack dog. My money would be on one of the younger ones, like Sandwell or one of the Morgan brothers,' said Horner. 'But so we're clear, nothing else points to a new follower being involved. As I said, the police did an exhaustive search of The Decorous past and present, and the followers who were at the Novus were the only active members. Nye liked to think the group had the same clout as it did in the noughties but, in reality, it had fewer followers than a Girl Guide pack.'

But he didn't sound as sure now, so Eve stood her ground.

'We can't ignore what I've found though. Not now the trial's started.'

It would be a legal minefield if any new suspects were arrested now. On the one hand, it would weaken The Seven's loss of control defence, because the covertness would make it harder for them to argue that they'd been triggered into committing carnage. The downside, however, was the very real possibility that Nye could try to shift the blame on to the new suspects and get the trial halted. The victims' families and the survivors would be devastated if that happened.

Horner lifted the bridge of his glasses to pinch his nose, sighing heavily.

'Okay, here's what we'll do. You go back and review every file and scrap of paper you can find relating to the burner phone in the unused pile, just to be certain there isn't anything else that's been missed.'

'And if I find anything?'

'We tell the DPP and he takes it to the Attorney General, then all hell breaks loose,' said Horner heavily. 'We need to get this done quickly, Eve. The longer the trial goes on, the worse it could be.'

Eve nodded. 'Should I mention any of this to DCS Strutton and DS Lees?'

'No. Review the evidence first, then we'll worry about telling those two.'

Chapter Twenty-Three

By the time Eve turned back into Lewisham High Street and the police station loomed into view again, she'd been gone nearly three hours. She expected the length of her absence to be noted, but she wasn't expecting to find Strutton waiting for her in her office, swivelling impatiently back and forth on her chair.

'Where the hell have you been?' he snapped on seeing her.

Eve found the ambush irritating. She was happy to work with him to achieve their common aim of securing justice, but he wasn't her boss. He had no right to question her so aggressively.

'I told you,' she replied bluntly.

'Really? You went to Petty France? In that case, why were you just seen outside court?'

Eve stared at him. Had he followed her or had her followed?

'I guessed as much,' he responded gruffly when she didn't deny it. 'I won't ask why you lied about where you were going, but I won't be happy if you lie to me again now. What were you and John Horner discussing?'

Eve had no intention of telling him anything until Horner said to. But how was she going to get out of Strutton's interrogation? He was like a dog refusing to give up a chew toy.

'One of the other cases I'm working on involves a defendant he's previously prosecuted. He had some background information he thought might be useful,' she fibbed.

'It couldn't be done on the phone?'

Eve put her bag down on her desk in front of Strutton with a thump. 'I'm not sure it's any of your business.'

He suddenly switched gears. 'Why were you sacked from your last job?'

Eve knew this had been coming. Of course he had checked up on her. She decided to set him straight.

'I pointed out an error a senior colleague had made that could've cost the firm and he didn't like it. Then he twisted it so I was blamed for the mistake. Being sacked for something I didn't do was really shitty.'

Strutton had the decency to appear admonished. 'That must've been rough. Look, I don't mean to sound as though I'm having a go at you,' he said. 'Call me paranoid, but I thought you'd sneaked off to see Horner because you'd found something and you weren't telling me. I know he wants you to report to him, but I'd like to think you'd give us a heads-up first.'

Eve let the comment drop unanswered but made a mental note to tell Horner the excuse she'd invented in case Strutton asked him. 'Can I please have my desk back so I can get to work?'

Strutton swung himself out of the seat. 'Be my guest.'

He was almost in the corridor when Eve remembered there was something she wanted to ask him. 'Actually, before you go, can I ask you about Joan Beck? It's nothing to do with the review,' she added hastily. 'I'm just curious.'

He turned back. 'Go on.'

'It's about her not giving interviews. Lisanne Durand is never out of the media, but Joan hasn't ever spoken publicly. I wondered if you had a theory as to why.'

Strutton seemed to consider his response for a few moments. 'We didn't take a statement from her ourselves because she was in the States when Novus happened, but the FBI did, and they said it was a struggle getting her to open up about Nye and their time together. So maybe talking to the press is her idea of hell. Or maybe it's because she doesn't want to contemplate the questions they might ask. How much do you know about Patrick Nye? Before he went missing, I mean?'

'Only bits that I've read.'

'Well, what you won't have read, but which I was told by my FBI counterpart, is that Joan was under the impression Nye would take her with him when the compound was raided. They suspected it might happen at some point and had a plan in place. When the FBI questioned her last year after Novus, she finally admitted Nye had a rental lock-up near Faria Beach, which is just down the coast from Carpinteria. He'd stashed a fake passport there, tens of thousands of dollars in cash and the keys for a car that was parked nearby. We know he survived the jump into the Pacific, and the FBI's theory is he'd practised making it beforehand, and Joan might've too. It was an eighteen-metre drop, so not ridiculously high. Apparently, there is a way you can enter water from a height like that and not injure yourself.'

Eve was sceptical. 'How?'

'You need to go in feet first, toes pointed, and slightly lean backwards with your arms pressed tightly against your sides. Everything needs to be rigid, so you glide through the water's surface, rather than slam against it.' Strutton jammed his hands in his trouser pockets and leaned against the doorframe, his expression less intense than usual. 'So Nye made the jump and either let the current take him down towards Faria Beach or he got out further up the shore and completed the rest of the journey on foot. The FBI didn't consider the sea a viable escape route when they planned the raid, so it wasn't covered. No boats in the water, no agents on the beach. They now think he collected the money, passport and car and then escaped through a nearby national park.'

Eve was shocked. 'Joan kept the lock-up a secret all this time?'

'Her excuse was the FBI told her Nye was dead. There was no reason for her to disbelieve them and think he'd managed to get away, much less use their escape plan without her. He wouldn't do that to her, not the woman he loved.' Strutton rolled his eyes as he said it. 'Also, she was in custody so had no way of checking herself whether the lock-up had been cleared out.'

'I wonder how she feels now, knowing he did escape without her.'

'Apparently she doesn't care. She told the investigators he obviously did what he had to do and she forgave him for it, which is big of her,' Strutton growled. 'If she had told the FBI about the lock-up in the first place, they might've caught Nye, and he'd have been banged up, meaning the thirty-four Novus victims might still be alive.'

Eve noted he never included the Decorous followers who died in the death toll. They'd perished in the basement of the theatre after the second bomb went off. Nye and the others on trial were arrested fleeing the rear.

'What do you make of her being in London for the trial?'

He shrugged. 'Again, I couldn't give a shit. She claims she had no idea Nye was alive until she started receiving messages from him about a month before Novus. She thought it was someone trying to scam her, and her phone records back up her version that she never replied. Maybe she's here to see him one last time before he's sent down for life.'

'I read that she's not attending court though because of health issues. It's strange she's come all this way just to sit it out.'

Strutton's gaze strayed to the boxes stacked against the wall. 'Why the sudden interest in Joan Beck? Are you sure you haven't found something?'

'I'm just curious about her. Imagine waking up and finding out a person you were in a relationship with and thought was dead for twenty years is still alive. I wonder if she's here because she still has feelings for him. We know how blindly loyal his followers were.'

Eve saw Strutton eye her bare ring finger. It had taken her a while to get used to not wearing the diamond solitaire Nick had given her when he proposed, but now it felt normal. 'Would you stay loyal in her shoes?' he asked.

Eve shook her head. 'Not a chance. She spent twelve years in prison for him while he was on the run God knows where. I'd hate him if I were her.' She paused. 'Can I ask you something else?'

'If you want.'

'What do you think Nye hoped to gain from Novus in the long run? He can't have thought he'd get away with a Houdini act a second time and he must've known that if you storm a theatre and hold the guests hostage before blowing them up it's not going to end well for you.'

Strutton's jaw clenched. 'Nye's clammed up in every interview, so we haven't had it from the horse's mouth, but the case we've built against him points to him wanting to execute the plan he had twenty years ago to hijack a celebrity event. But he didn't get to carry out the attack on Grauman's in LA, and it enraged him.' The detective grew visibly angry himself. 'Until Novus, history had Nye down as a coward who'd died fleeing while his followers stayed to fight. Now he's going to be remembered as the cult leader who carried out one of the worst atrocities ever committed on British soil. The bastard finally finished what he'd started.'

Chapter Twenty-Four

FAYE

Now

Richard gave Faye little choice in the matter. He burst into the master bedroom they'd once shared without knocking to tell her the next meeting of his support group had been brought forward to that afternoon, at Madeleine Farmer's request no less, and they needed to leave in ten minutes. Faye was reading a book while lying on top of the covers, trying to relax away her malingering hangover. Richard paused to look her up and down.

'You might want to get changed first.'

'What's wrong with this?' she asked, defiantly pulling at the hem of her sweatshirt. Her jogging bottoms matched its sky-blue hue.

'It's covered in stains, Faye. I can count three different meals from this week alone on it.'

He said it as a joke, his tone light-hearted, and his face creased into a smile, but it still stung to know he was right. The tracksuit was stained – albeit only with splashes of last night's red wine and a drip of honey from some toast she'd just eaten – and she looked a mess. When had she stopped caring about her appearance? She used to be meticulous and neat, every outfit planned and coordinated, the wardrobe assistant in her refusing to let her leave the house unless each item had been pressed or steamed. Where had her pride gone?

Then, with a painful twist of anguish that almost winded her, she remembered: she'd abandoned it inside the Novus Theatre, at the very moment she'd sacrificed Liberty to save herself.

'I'll change,' she said, moving in an ungainly fashion to the side of the bed. 'But I need to shower first.'

'Best get a move on then. The others are expecting us. I've texted the kids to say we'll probably still be out when they get back from school.'

He spoke with the excited air of someone meeting friends for a social occasion, and Faye felt resentful. Richard had confessed yesterday that he'd been going to these meetings for months when she thought he'd been at the gym, and it was clear from how he said it that sharing his experience with the other survivors had been enormously beneficial. Why hadn't he asked her to join them sooner? Then it had dawned on her he'd been dealing with his intense grief over losing Liberty, and Faye being privy to that wouldn't have helped either of them.

One lightning-quick shower and some hastily applied make-up later and they were in Richard's Tesla and on their way to Stepney. It was the first time she'd been back in the area since the night of the siege, and it surprised her how apprehensive she felt. Nothing bad could happen to them now, but the closer they got, the more her stomach churned with nervous anticipation. By the time they entered the Rotherhithe Tunnel to cross beneath the Thames towards Limehouse, she was shaking. Richard seemed oblivious to her discomfort though, perhaps presuming it was down to her hangover, so while she fought to stay calm, he lectured her for the rest of the way to Stepney about giving up alcohol.

She was grateful when he chose a route that allowed them to avoid the Novus site – 'I never go that way if I can help it,' he said – but was taken aback when they pulled up in a narrow residential back street outside a corner café that had seen far better days, its once white facade yellowing as though nicotine-stained. Torn half-nets hung at the window and there was a letter missing from the signage, so it now read 'Caf'.

'You meet here?' she asked, unable to mask her surprise. 'Even Madeleine Farmer?'

'It's really nice inside,' said Richard defensively. 'It's owned by Ruby, Jimi's mum. And she's lovely too.'

As they got out of the car, another vehicle pulled up in the bay behind them. Faye recognised the burgundy Phantom Rolls-Royce as belonging to Cynthia and her breath caught in her throat to see it again after so long. She squinted to see who was driving but sunlight bouncing off the windscreen rendered the person behind the wheel a featureless outline. Her breath constricted even tighter when she saw Samuel climb out of the passenger side. He looked alarmingly frail, his clothes hanging off him, but when he saw Faye, his face lit up.

'My dear Faye, it's been too long,' he exulted, before pulling her into an embrace that could only be described as feather light. Samuel had never been particularly sturdy but now his physique was wasted and it shocked her how ill he seemed. She felt terribly guilty, knowing that since Cynthia's funeral service last year she'd been dodging his calls and messages. But Samuel didn't seem to be holding it against her.

'I was thrilled when Richard asked if you could join our little group,' he said, but was interrupted from going any further by the man himself, who urged them both to enter the café before anyone spotted them.

'What about—?' Faye gestured to the Phantom. The driver was still obscured by the sun's reflection on the windscreen.

'Oh, that's Roddy,' said Samuel. 'He doesn't come to the meetings, although I'm sure they would help him as much as I know they'll help you. I ask, but he always refuses. He either waits outside or drives around and comes back for me when I call him.'

Roddy was Cynthia's live-in carer and another Novus survivor.

'Why is he driving you around?' asked Faye, her unease growing.

'Matthew's kept him on. Insisted upon it. He thought I could use the help after my operations.' Samuel clutched Faye's hand and they slowly walked towards the café entrance.

Arriving at the threshold, she glanced over her shoulder. She still couldn't make out Roddy's face in the glare, but she sensed him watching them. 'It was Matthew's idea to keep him on?' she asked.

'Yes. Roddy was looking for a new position, but Matthew told him he wasn't going anywhere. He adores him as much as Cynthia did,' said Samuel. 'The three of us are rubbing along quite nicely, although at some point soon Matthew will sell the house. He's hardly ever in the country as it is.'

Matthew had inherited everything upon his grandmother's death, including the Greenhill Gardens mansion she'd owned for the past twenty years that backed on to Hampstead Heath and was worth at least £10 million. Faye had read some rather unsavoury newspaper stories about him spending with impunity since Cynthia's demise, which commentators seemed to think was in bad taste in light of what had happened to her.

'What will you do after it's sold?' asked Faye.

'Cynthia made sure I would be well looked after until it's my time too,' said Samuel, tears pricking his eyes. Then he gathered himself. 'Come, you must say hello to Ruby.'

They entered the café and Faye had to acknowledge Richard was right: the interior was lovely, inviting and clean, and Ruby greeted Faye like a long-lost friend. The woman's kindness made Faye tear up. Then Ruby turned to the two men, her expression becoming downcast.

'Madeleine's already here. She was the first to arrive, in a right old state. I got Jimi to sit with her, but he's not much better, knowing he's going on the stand this week.' Ruby swallowed hard. 'You need to prepare yourselves for when you see her. Her doctors have worked marvels, but—'

Faye blanched. Her being here was wrong. She shouldn't have come. She had no right to be here among these poor people, not after what she did. She grasped at Richard's sleeve. 'I'm sorry, I need to leave.'

'Don't be silly, Faye,' he said. 'You're among friends now.'

She shook her head and started to back away from him and Samuel, who looked equally perplexed. 'I'm sorry. I can't stay,' she said, her chest now heaving in panic.

'Faye, love—'

But Richard's entreaty was wasted: she was already at the door, bolting outside. She had no idea of her exact location, but she didn't care. She had to get away from the café, and from Stepney. She scurried up the street and was almost at the junction with the next one when she heard someone holler her name and made the mistake of turning round. Roddy had wound down the Phantom's window and was shouting after her.

'Faye, where are you going?'

She ignored him and continued her hasty path up the street, certain he wouldn't come after her because he was the only person alive who knew her secret – and why she was running away now.

Chapter Twenty-Five

FAYE

THEN

20 April, 11.42 p.m.

Faye couldn't see where Richard was because they'd dimmed the lights in the auditorium. When she'd arrived at the event, her reaction at seeing inside the theatre had been one of awe. Now, three hours into the siege, the same setting felt claustrophobic: its red velvet walls, carpets and fittings bleeding into one. It was like they'd been sealed inside a giant lined coffin.

The group she and Liberty were part of had been made to gather by the foot of the stage. There were tables nearby that could've accommodated the twenty or so people, but instead they had been forced to stack the chairs on top of one another and then sit on the floor next to them, a cruel taunt by their captors. They did make one concession for Cynthia's age – she was given an upended beer-bottle crate to sit on.

Faye was grateful to be with Cynthia; the three men who usually tended to her – Matthew, Samuel and Roddy – had been placed in other groups as an act of deliberate vindictiveness by Nye. It amused him to see how bewildered Cynthia was at none of them being there to assist her.

He'd given another brief speech earlier, after poor Madeleine Farmer had finished her egregious task of splitting them into groups. If they did as they were told – kept quiet and didn't move from where they'd been made to sit – no one else would get hurt. He gave no indication how long they'd be kept there or why he was holding them. Someone far braver than her had shouted up from the audience to ask him but was met with a look that could freeze water. The guest was then dragged from his seat and hauled onstage to be beaten by three of Nye's followers while he looked passively on.

The more hours that ticked by, the more fearful Faye grew, to the point where all she could think about was whether she'd live to see her children again. It pained her to think of Olivia and Freddy learning about the siege and being distressed that both their parents were caught up in it. She prayed their friends and extended family were rallying round to support and comfort them. And Liberty's relatives, too. Much as it pained Faye to admit it, Olivia and Freddy had grown to like Liberty and had accepted her with far more ease than Faye had anticipated – or secretly hoped – they would.

Liberty was sitting on the floor on the other side of Cynthia's crate. They'd spoken little since Faye had prised her away from Richard, and she suspected that, now her tears had abated, Liberty was cross with her for doing so. Liberty's gold slip dress was now covered by a dinner jacket one of the men in the group had given her, and she was talking quietly to a girl who couldn't be much older than Olivia, dressed in the black uniform of the Novus staff. The girl's cheeks glistened with tears, and it looked to Faye as though Liberty was trying to whisper words of comfort to her, letting her blonde hair fall in front of her face to obscure her moving lips. Their group had been screamed at and threatened by one of their armed captors for making too much noise so Liberty was right to be cautious.

Still, Faye found it nauseating to watch her rival showing compassion for another woman. She had shown Faye none whatsoever when she'd set her sights on Richard, even though she'd known Faye before becoming Richard's lover. Liberty had come into their lives when Faye employed her as their dog walker – a profession she noticed Liberty had quickly erased from her CV after she and Richard began officially dating – on the recommendation of a neighbour in the Holmby Hills enclave in LA where they'd been renting a house two summers ago while Richard was filming in the States. Faye had been too slow to notice that Liberty was only collecting their dog when she was out and Richard was home. It was only when, a few months down the line, another neighbour complained to Faye that their dog was making too much noise, barking in the yard of their home when he should've been out on a walk, that Faye realised Liberty had swapped one old hound for another – her husband. By the time she'd gathered the courage to confront Richard, he'd already set in motion his plan to leave her by hiding most of his assets.

Faye forced herself to swallow down the bitterness that still swelled whenever she thought about Richard and Liberty scheming behind her back. She couldn't dwell on that now, not when she needed to keep her wits about her. She reached forward and gently touched Cynthia's hands, which were lying limp in the old woman's lap. Her skin was ice-cold, the silk folds of her dress not thick enough to keep her warm, the dinner jacket draped around her by another kind man in their group proving inadequate too. It kept slipping off her frail shoulders and she didn't have the strength to pull it back into place herself without help.

Cynthia was dozing, slouched forward, when Faye touched her hands. She looked befuddled when her eyes opened and focused on her, sitting on the floor beside the beer crate.

'Whatever are you doing down there on that grubby floor, Faye?'

Cynthia's mellifluous voice belied her petiteness and as an actress trained to project it was loud as well. A couple of people sitting closest to them shot Faye an anxious look on hearing Cynthia boom. In a whisper Faye told her that she needed to talk quietly, but the woman's response was a strident, 'Whatever for?' followed by 'Where's Matthew gone? Why isn't he here? Why have they stopped serving dinner? I'm hungry.'

'Cynthia, please lower your voice,' said Faye, now regretting waking her up to check on her.

'Why? It's my event.'

More members of their group looked uncomfortable now, then Liberty hissed at Faye, 'Make her shut up or we'll all be in trouble.'

'Make her how?' she shot back. 'Shall I put my hand over her mouth or—'

Something hard suddenly rammed into the middle of Faye's back and she pitched forward. Too shocked to cry out, she turned to see the captor with the long white ponytail turning his rifle round in his hands – he must've used the butt to strike her.

'What did we tell you about talking?' he said.

Faye tried to reason with him. The others, Liberty included, shrank back, leaving her to it.

'I was just checking on Cynthia,' she said through clenched teeth, her back throbbing horribly. 'She's too frail to be kept here like this. Can you at least give her some water? And a proper chair?'

The man stared at her. His stark hair made him look older from a distance, but up close he was younger than Faye.

'What if it was your grandmother?' she added.

'Mine's dead,' he replied sharply. 'And she will be too if you don't shut her the fuck up.'

Nye must've noticed the altercation because he called down from the stage. 'Hey, Snow White, what's going on over there? Is the old dear causing trouble?'

To Faye's horror, Cynthia unsteadily rose to her feet. 'I will not be spoken to like that, least of all by an oaf like you. Now, where's my Matthew?'

Nye climbed down from the stairs and ambled over to them. 'Who?'

'Her grandson. He organised the event,' said Faye, nervous to be addressing the cult leader directly. 'It would be nice if you could let him sit with her. She's confused and upset, but he'll be able to keep her calm.'

Nye appraised Faye for a moment and her skin crawled as his eyes bored into hers. He was undeniably attractive for a man his age but there was something almost robotic about his intense presence. She'd never seen anyone stand so still – if she didn't know better, she'd think he wasn't breathing.

Finally, after what felt like an age, he spoke. His voice was even and flat.

'I know you. You're the one whose actor husband stiffed her in the divorce. You really didn't see that one coming, did you?'

Flooded with shame, Faye glanced in Liberty's direction, a snap, involuntarily reflex. Nye's gaze followed and the corners of his mouth tugged upwards. 'She's her, isn't she? Well. That's a fun twist.' He studied Liberty, who stared resolutely at the floor, and then looked back at Faye. 'This must hurt,' he said, 'having to sit with the woman he left you for.'

'If you must know, Faye insisted on taking care of Liberty when you awful people interrupted my celebration,' said Cynthia. 'She is a good person, unlike you.'

Faye was astounded by her friend's unexpected moment of clarity, but heart-sick too. It would actually be a small mercy if Cynthia's failing cognition spared her from what was going on, but it appeared she was more aware than any of them realised.

Nye turned on Cynthia. 'You don't think I'm a good person?' he said, an edge creeping into his voice. He turned to Snow White. 'Get me the grandson.'

Faye was terrified. What were they going to do to him? The gunman left and returned a few moments later, dragging Matthew along by his arm.

'Oh, Matthew,' exclaimed Cynthia upon seeing him. 'My darling boy.'

But as his grandmother reached out to embrace him, Matthew didn't move to hug her back. He stood ramrod straight, eyeballing Nye, his expression unwavering. It was unsettling to observe, and Faye prayed he wasn't about to do something stupid. Then Nye's hand went to his trouser pocket, and she recoiled, fearing he was about to draw a weapon. Yet he simply patted his hand on the front of his pocket, like he was checking for change.

'Got something you want to say to me?' he asked Matthew, who was still staring at him.

There was no hostility or aggression in Nye's tone though, or a sense he was readying to square up to Matthew – if anything, he sounded friendly.

Matthew's expression finally shifted. He turned his attention to his grandmother, but not before Faye saw him catch Nye's eye and give him the briefest of nods.

Chapter Twenty-Six

EVE

Now

Eve refocused her efforts on the burner phone, Horner's warning about the need for expedition ringing in her ears. She could almost feel the seconds galloping by and her panic started to rise. There weren't enough hours in the day for her to get everything done, and there could be no let-up in standards either. She had to be even more precise now, with so much at stake.

She called up the burner phone's data and for the umpteenth time reread the messages sent and received during the siege. She was pretty sure she could quote them verbatim now. It was only by scrolling right back that she noticed it wasn't the only conversation between the two phones downloaded to Cellebrite. Shock zipped through her. There were at least eight other occasions when the Motorola had traded texts with the other unknown number, stretching back across months. Why weren't any of them mentioned on the MG form? Spurred on, Eve peered intently at her monitor as she read an exchange in the December before the siege. They weren't single-word texts this time, but were still brief in content – 'You there?', 'On for Friday?' and so on.

Then one message in particular made her sit up. It was the first text sent in a conversation initiated by the burner phone in the September before the siege. It comprised just four words.

'Nye, need to talk.'

Right. So that established it wasn't Nye who had the Motorola during the siege and before, but he *had* been in possession of the other one – the unknown number. Exasperated, Eve made a note on her legal pad. These additional exchanges should have been recorded on the MG form by the disclosure officer, DC Colgan. No wonder he was facing a disciplinary for shoddy work over the rape-trial collapse.

Then she went back further – and that was when she stopped dead. Almost a year before the bombings, in May of that year, Nye had texted the burner phone a message so unambiguous in its context that Eve didn't need to read it twice.

'The others don't know about you and never will. Not even once we're inside the place. You have my word.'

She gasped. How could this have been missed? Nye had texted the burner phone a message that, unless she was reading it wrong, made it sound like they were being kept a secret from the other Decorous followers involved in seizing the Novus. Why? What was so special about the person who had the burner?

Eve sat back in her chair and forced herself to examine the message rationally, in the way she knew Horner would. Maybe it was something Nye said to everyone to get them on board initially, to make them think they'd be protected, or to make them feel as though they had his ear and were more important than the others. Maybe playing followers off against each other was some kind of cult initiation? But as she stared at her monitor, she couldn't ignore the question now gnawing at her: what if her initial gut instinct was right, and still no one knew anything about this person? Not only from the other followers, but also from the police during the investigation? It would go some way to explaining why they alone had a burner phone while the others were using the encrypted app.

Eve knew Horner needed to see this straight away. She thought about printing out the data from Cellebrite, but she was too impatient, and so used her phone to take a photo of the incriminating text before bundling the device into her bag along with her legal pad. Then she grabbed the key for the office door from her desk drawer, locked it behind her and set off for the Bailey again, her mind churning all the while over the implications of what she'd discovered.

Someone who Nye had promised to keep a secret from his other followers had been using the retro flip-lid Motorola during the siege. The police hadn't spotted the link because they hadn't thought to check the timestamps; they'd just lumped the device in with Mark Cleaver's two mobiles. If Eve was right – and it didn't feel like guesswork because the timings spoke for themselves – this someone had been on the ground and helping Nye inside the Novus Theatre that night. But who were they and, more to the point, how was Strutton going to take the news that his officers had overlooked potentially major evidence?

Court was already in session when Eve arrived, so she asked a clerk to fetch Horner from inside, explaining it was urgent. He was flustered when he came out, his face as pale as the off-white shirt he wore beneath his suit, but he wasn't annoyed to see her.

'Eve. I don't have long. What's up?'

Quickly she told him what she'd found. Then she showed him the photo on her phone of the text Nye had sent promising to keep the other person's identity a secret. He looked at it intently for a moment, then handed her phone back to her.

'It does look like one of The Decorous had the burner phone, but it's still not conclusive, Eve.'

'Nye's promise to keep them a secret means it can't be any of the ones we already know about. Only he was in touch with them.'

'That's not necessarily true, Eve,' said Horner. He peered again at the text. 'This was sent a full year before the siege. What's to say Nye didn't change his mind and tell the others about this person nearer the time? The burner could also have been used by more than one person – whoever had it during the siege might not be the same person who was texting back then. We shouldn't assume anything.'

Eve's face fell. He was right. There was no way of knowing if Nye had gone back on his word about keeping this person a secret or if the burner had changed hands. Then something occurred to her. 'There is a way we can find out which of them besides Nye had the phone,' she said excitedly.

'How?'

'Well, we could ask Forensics if the burner was dabbed for prints. The Seven had theirs taken when they were arrested, and the pathologist would've taken any from their accomplices who died in the blast. If Forensics shows us which one of them had the burner phone, it can stay in the unused pile but we'll correct the MG form to say who had it.'

Horner nodded thoughtfully. 'Good idea. I have a very good contact in Forensics I can check with. We don't have to go through the usual channels.'

'We're still not telling Strutton and Lees?' asked Eve, surprised.

'Technically we should. But given this is a police oversight I'm not sure how helpful that would be right now. I'd rather find out what we can about who had the burner phone before we let them know,' he said. 'It's still a long way from meeting the threshold.'

The threshold test that determined the relevance of a particular piece of evidence involved the CPS deciding whether it might reasonably undermine the prosecution's case or assist the case for the defendant. If it did either of those, it had to be disclosed with a view to being presented in court.

'Wouldn't it meet the threshold if Forensics found prints but couldn't match them to any of The Decorous known to be at the siege?' asked Eve.

'If that turns out to be the case, we've got a serious problem on our hands,' said Horner, lowering his voice to a gruff whisper. 'It means you've been right from the start about this and there's an accomplice still at large.'

'They could be planning another atrocity,' said Eve faintly, her stomach clenching in fear. 'This would be the perfect time to do it, when the world's attention is on the trial.'

Horner blanched. 'I know, that's what scares me too. We should pray the forensics come back confirming it's one of the others, Eve. If it comes up blank, that means The Seven should really be The Eight and there's another suspect missing from that dock.'

Chapter Twenty-Seven

Eve returned to Lewisham feeling at a loss. They'd left it that Horner would speak to his contact in Forensics, so there was nothing left to do but wait and hope the response came quickly. The idea of an eighth person still walking free was terrifying, and she couldn't help thinking that Horner was wrong to insist they didn't tell Strutton or Lees what the review had thrown up, so the police could be primed to act. But she didn't feel able to challenge him. Horner was the senior advocate and he wanted to proceed with caution, because too much of what they suspected was based on assumption. The only thing they could conclusively show, based on the data, was that Nye had been texting the burner. Eve had no choice but to go along with Horner's instructions – even though she feared that a delay in identifying who had used the burner could have devastating consequences.

She felt mentally drained when she finally got back to her desk. The relentless pace of the review was starting to take its toll, and she found herself wishing she could've slipped into the courtroom to sit down and watch the proceedings for a while. Her defence career had mostly involved her being an instructing solicitor for Crown court hearings, but sometimes she represented her clients at magistrates' level, and she'd relished those occasions where she could stand up and make a case. She was still doing that now, she reminded herself, just in a different way, and with a level of concentration that the teachers who had chided her in class for being a daydreamer would be astonished to see.

It felt like she'd only just sat down again when DS Lees poked his head round the door, saying he was heading home but had something to give her first. Eve braced for more snideness, but he was being straightforward for once.

'John Horner just called to say something came up in court this afternoon. He asked to pass on a message for you to meet him in half an hour for a debrief.'

Eve was thrown. 'Really? I only saw him a couple of hours ago. Why didn't he call me himself?'

'No idea.'

'Did he say where? Does he want me to go to Petty France?'

'No, he said to meet him at the French Horn, the pub round the corner from there. Here's the address.' Lees handed Eve a scrap of paper. 'Sounds like he wants to shout you a pint.'

'Thanks,' said Eve, taking the note. The message was a near-indecipherable scrawl, like a child had written it. She didn't ask Lees if it was his – she didn't want to set him off again.

The pub was half empty when she arrived – which was only natural on a midweek evening. She was late. Horner's deadline was too tight to meet even in the Uber she called to get there. But thankfully he must have been running behind too because he was nowhere to be seen. Eve ordered herself a glass of white wine – she figured they were, technically, off the clock now, so she didn't think he'd mind – and found a table near the rear. Fifteen minutes later he still hadn't arrived, so she sent him a text letting him know she was waiting in the pub, and would he like her to order him a drink?

Shortly afterwards Horner burst through the door, thrusting his phone towards her at arm's length like it was a toy rattle. The screen was open on her text.

'What's all this?' he asked, looming over the table at her. 'Why are you waiting for me here?'

Eve gaped at him. 'But you asked me to come and meet you.'

'No, I didn't.'

Her insides constricted. Lees had pranked her, and she'd fallen for it. The bastard. Didn't he have anything better to do than mess with her time?

'DS Lees gave me a message to say you wanted a debrief and that I should meet you here,' she said tightly.

'I left no such message.'

'He wrote down the name of the pub for me,' Eve said, regretting she'd left the Post-it on her desk. It was the only proof she had that she'd been conned.

'The plonker. He must've got his wires crossed.' Horner's gaze fell on Eve's half-drained glass of wine. 'Now I'm here I suppose a pint won't hurt. Same again?'

'Sure. Dry white wine, please.'

While Horner was at the bar, Eve rewound her conversation with Lees. He'd definitely made it sound as though he was passing on a direct message from Horner. He was probably in a pub himself now, pissing himself laughing that he'd managed to trick her. She felt embarrassed and infuriated in equal measure.

Eve had worked alongside men like Lees before. They'd deny point-blank they were bothered by a woman doing well at her job, or even being passed over for promotion in favour of one. But their resentment showed in the subtle, insidious put-downs they managed to drop into conversations, the jokes that were never funny, or by taking credit for work that wasn't theirs. They were emboldened by the knowledge that many women were reluctant to cause a fuss in the workplace, and Eve imagined that made Lees think he could pull a stunt like this with no consequences or comeback. Tempting though it was to give him hell, she knew ignoring him would be a far more effective reaction.

Horner returned to the table, setting down their drinks, and Eve made a concerted effort to push Lees from her mind. They discussed the burner phone briefly – Horner said he'd spoken to his contact in Forensics but didn't know when they'd get back to him.

'I can't push it too much because they haven't been working on the Novus case and they could get into trouble if they're caught poking around,' he said. 'But I know they'll give me an answer as soon as they can.'

'Soon' didn't feel anywhere near fast enough to Eve, but she refrained from saying so. Horner sipped his beer. 'I've been thinking about it, and I could be wrong about Barker not having been given the burner. He's the reason The Decorous started up again, and we know Nye trusts him.'

Eve was familiar with Barker's background. He had become a fan of Nye's first time round and was a card-carrying member of a Decorous sub-group in the UK. Everyone else had lost interest after Nye supposedly died, but Barker kept the flame alive, and he used the inheritance he got when his mum died nearly four years ago to buy the hotel in Bournemouth as a base to restart it.

'He set up a website to recruit new followers, and through that Nye got in touch, and the seeds for Novus were sown,' Horner added.

Eve shook her head. 'Who does that? Who waits until their mum dies and leaves them some money to blow up a room of famous people?'

'Someone in the thrall of a man who'd waited a long time to make his comeback,' said Horner darkly.

'I still find it hard to believe Nye never popped up on anyone's radar,' said Eve. 'Where was he for the twenty years he was missing?'

'No one knows. I think he probably slipped out of the US on his false passport to a country with no extradition agreement. Then it was a case of biding his time and waiting for the right moment to strike again. He needed people to help him, though, so he monitored online for any mentions of The Decorous, until Barker's website popped up.'

'How did he and Barker recruit the others?'

'Again, all online. People mindlessly scrolling, looking for meaning and kindred spirits, I suppose.'

Eve shuddered. Committing mass murder together wasn't her idea of friendship.

'We also have Barker's mum to thank for why they chose Dame Cynthia's celebration as their target,' Horner added.

Eve knew the backstory already, but let Horner repeat it anyway. He was clearly happy to oblige after a day sitting silently in court, when his conversations would have been reduced to a few whispered comments between him, Philbin and Lacey, the KC's junior. It was also a welcome distraction from worrying about the eighth person missing from the dock and what they might be plotting.

'Barker's mum, Glenys, was a huge fan of Dame Cynthia and had been since she was a young girl. She had all her films on DVD, was an active member of her fan club, and her most treasured possession was Dame Cynthia's autograph. Then Glenys Barker found out the Novus Theatre where her idol had made her acting debut was being renovated, and was to reopen with an event to mark Dame Cynthia's ninetieth. Even though she was in her eighties herself by then, Glenys was all set to go and wait outside with the other fans to watch Cynthia arrive. The carers who supported

Barker in looking after her said she talked about it incessantly, but a few weeks later she had a heart attack and died.'

'Do you think Barker would've still gone ahead if Glenys had been outside with the rest of the fans that night?'

'No, because she had to die for him to get the cash to pull it off,' said Horner.

'Nye must've thought all his Christmases had come at once when he made contact with Barker and realised how far he was willing to go in his name.'

'Nye masterminded it though, not Barker. Barker planted the idea about the event being a possible target for some kind of protest, but from the communications between them it was clear Nye was the one who worked out the logistics, and he also recruited the rest,' Horner explained. 'Once he was certain he could trust his new followers for the mission – that was his description of it, not mine – he provided each of them with the modified handsets for them to use the app on. The rest of the planning was easy after that.'

'Why?'

'The theatre's renovation required planning permission, so the floorplans were available to download to anyone who went on the local council's planning portal. They could work out all the building's weak spots,' said Horner. 'The Novus wasn't your typical A-list venue, either – it had no experience of staging any events, let alone a high-profile one.'

'Didn't Matthew Seymour hire event planners and security people who knew what they were doing, though?'

'Yes, but they were ineffective, to say the least. The Decorous had better expertise, specifically among the followers who were killed. One was a former squaddie who'd handled explosives in Afghanistan, and another had the hacking skills to override the building's alarm system. Nye also planted followers within the security and catering firms working at the event, so they had the upper hand there as well. Once the building was rigged to go up it was theirs to control.'

'The ones who had the technical skills were all killed in the explosions?'

'Yes. The group split into two to escape and their group ended up in the path of the second bomb, while they were trying to get out via the basement.'

Eve's mind began to race. 'Surely the one with experience of explosives would've known where the two bombs had been planted? Why didn't he avoid them? Doesn't it strike you as suspicious that the men who could've revealed exactly how Nye pulled it off all happened to perish on the night?'

'No, it doesn't,' said Horner, a note of irritation in his tone. 'Nye had no way of knowing when the siege was going to end or how. Once Brendan Morgan helped those four guests to escape, it was everyone for themselves. It could just as easily have been Nye who ended up in the path of the bombs.'

Chapter Twenty-Eight

Eve was annoyed that Horner had been quick to dismiss her question, but at least he seemed to sense it had rankled her.

'You did really well to work out the link between the texts and the siege timeline,' he said. 'I'm just saying that because there's been no other evidence to suggest anyone else was involved, I don't know where it will lead.'

Eve didn't answer and instead gulped down a mouthful of wine. She respected Horner but was starting to think his approach to getting to the bottom of the burner phone was too passive. Should she go above him and talk to Beverly, like he'd said she could? But if she did and it turned out the burner had been handled by one of the known accomplices, how would that look? She'd be the new advocate who had not only jumped to the wrong conclusion but had also tried to drop her senior colleague in it. That wasn't a path she was keen to re-tread after her sacking.

Horner was now talking about the witness who had given evidence earlier that day, theatre bar worker Jimi Regan.

'We were hoping for a bit more from him because he was one of the escapees helped by Brendan Morgan. But the poor lad was terrified and pretty much monosyllabic. It was like pulling teeth for Philbin,' said Horner. 'One of the other escapees, Luke Bishop, is up next week so hopefully he'll have more to say.'

'Perhaps Brendan had the burner phone,' said Eve. 'They escaped through the foyer, didn't they, so that could've been the moment when he ditched it in the men's restroom.'

'Could be,' agreed Horner. 'Hopefully we won't have to wait long to hear back from my mate in Forensics to find out if it was him.'

They talked about the ways in which the defence KC Peter Cheney might present the loss of control defence, none of which were particularly convincing. By the time they'd finished, Eve had drained her second glass and was feeling a bit tipsy as the alcohol sloshed inside her empty stomach.

'I should get going,' she said.

Horner nodded in agreement, then downed the dregs of his pint.

'Which Tube station do you need?' he asked, as they both stood to leave.

'Westminster. I live in Old Street so I can get the District or Circle to Monument then change for the Northern Line. You?'

'Same. I live out in Loughton and change at Monument for the Central Line. We used to live in Stockwell, but Lizzy – that's my wife – didn't want us to raise our kids there. She wanted somewhere a bit greener, with less gangs and drugs.'

'How many children do you have?' Eve asked as they left the pub and set off on the short walk to the station.

'Two. Boy and girl twins, in fact. Thirteen going on twenty-one. Drive me mad, but they're good kids. So why Old Street?'

'I had to move somewhere cheaper after I got sacked,' said Eve wryly, at which Horner smiled and replied that she might not think it yet, but she should consider it a lucky escape.

'The burnout at those City firms is ridiculous. No one can sustain eighty-, ninety-hour weeks for long. I've got friends I trained with who dropped out of practising law altogether because a firm like your old one worked them into the ground. That's not to say it's not tough at the CPS, and the courts' backlog is having a massive toll on our workload, the likes of which I've never seen before. But I like to think we still care about our staff's wellbeing.'

'How long have you worked for the CPS?' Eve asked.

'For too many years than I care to recall.'

The upper concourse at Westminster station was busy and noisy, the worst of it coming from a group of rambunctious rugby fans. Eve tried to tune them out because Horner was now telling her about when he'd worked on the appeal hearing of an infamous serial killer, and how it was the first time he understood what it meant to be in the presence of evil. It was fascinating to hear him describe it and again confirmed to her that a permanent career with the CPS could be good for her. The cases she worked on at the City firm were small fry compared to murder trials at the Old Bailey.

'The Novus is the biggest trial I've worked on,' Horner was saying. 'It's one of those once-in-a-career cases you might get put on if you're lucky.'

As one of the lucky ones, Eve knew she should feel grateful too. But her suspicions about the burner phone were overshadowing everything else.

'What do you think the public's reaction will be if there is an eighth accomplice missing from the dock?' she asked.

'I dread to think. The media will have a field day at the Met's expense though, that's guaranteed.' He cast her a sideways glance. 'Failing to investigate a lead that results in someone getting away scot-free is about as serious as it gets.'

They had reached the bank of escalators down to the platforms, with Horner walking ahead of her, when Eve became aware of someone coming up quickly behind them. She went to step aside, thinking the person must be in a rush to catch a train and wanted to get past them, but to her shock the person barrelled straight into her, sending her flying. She crashed sideways on to the floor, pain thudding through her hip. On hearing her cry out, Horner spun round.

'Are you okay?' he exclaimed. Then he glared at the man who'd knocked into her, who was dressed for the wet weather in a black waterproof jacket, the hood pulled up. 'You should watch where you're going, mate.'

Horner held his hand out to help Eve up, but the man had other ideas. He threw himself at Horner, who let out a yelp of alarm as the two of them collided. Horner's hand was yanked from Eve's and the blow knocked his feet out from under him. But when he reached out to steady himself there was nothing to grab hold of except thin air. Eve heaved herself off the floor to help, but was too slow. His face twisted in panic, Horner began to topple backwards down the escalator – with Eve's scream following him down.

Chapter Twenty-Nine

MADELEINE

Now

Meeting the others at Ruby's on Monday had done nothing to ease Madeleine's despondency. Instead, it dragged her further into the mire until, three days later, she was hovering fitfully somewhere between despair and rock bottom.

It wasn't the group's fault, she decided, it was Faye's. Her fleeing the café was all the others wanted to talk about. They went over and over it, trying to formulate a plan to help Richard to help Faye. Not one of them acknowledged it was Madeleine who'd called the meeting in the first place because she needed support after giving evidence. In the end she made an excuse and left. She was devastated when they didn't try to stop her.

It wasn't fair. Faye had Richard and their children, but Madeleine had no one she could truly count on – not even Gina, who was paid to be nice to her. Because she'd started acting so young, dropping out of high school before graduation and skipping college, all of Madeleine's friends worked in the entertainment industry, and the majority had shown themselves to be fair-weather since Novus, making excuses not to visit because they were busy getting on with their lives and careers. The ones who hadn't disappeared she wouldn't trust with her cat, let alone her most private thoughts. She had no siblings to lean on and her parents had adopted devout religious beliefs in recent years that put them at odds with their daughter's occupation. Her dad had even called her injuries a 'divine intervention' to set her on the path away from acting, conveniently overlooking that it was he and her mom who'd encouraged her pursuit of it in the first place, by selling up and moving to LA when she was a kid.

Madeleine poured herself another shot of Clase Azul Añejo tequila from the ceramic decanter she'd sent Gina out to buy from Selfridges Food Hall before dismissing her for the evening. No, the only person she could count on was herself – except she sucked at it. She should've explained to the others why she was upset instead of skulking off like she was in the wrong, and she should've stuck to her guns about not going back in the witness box.

Her throat burned from the sharp sting of alcohol as she knocked back the first shot. Then she lined up another and downed that in one too. Her plan for this evening wasn't to get a little drunk – it was to get so tanked that her recollection of giving evidence against Edwin Barker was obliterated. For now, though, her mind kept replaying it like a shaky movie reel.

The way the defence lawyer had dared to question her recollection of the assault was humiliating. He'd implied she'd somehow been mistaken about the way Barker had groped her. He'd asked, had she been made to undress? No, she hadn't. Well in that case, it was a misunderstanding on her part. Barker was merely helping her sit down in a dress that was so fitted it was, by her own admission, tricky to walk in.

Madeleine burned with rage as she recalled that particular comment, because even though it was true that the dress had been tight, she knew it wasn't why Barker had violated her. Cheney had also intimated it was convenient that no one else saw the 'alleged' assault, because it happened backstage, away from the others. She'd shouted at him then, saying that was the entire point – Barker had deliberately isolated her to carry out the assault so it would be her word against his. She'd yelled, how could anyone believe the word of a man who was standing trial for multiple murders?

Cheney had a rebuttal for that, like he had a rebuttal for everything: just because Barker was accused of those acts of violence didn't mean he was guilty of this one too. Madeleine had scoffed at him then, which earned her another telling-off from the judge. That was when she got down off the stand and refused to continue.

She downed another shot. She'd lost count of which number it was, but she was well on the way to achieving her aim of total intoxication, because when she tried to get up from her usual straight-backed chair she plopped straight back down. Giggling, she tried again, and this time managed to stay upright. She weaved unsteadily to the bathroom and noted that the tequila was doing a fine job of numbing the chronic pain that wracked her body from morning to night. For a brief moment she felt almost normal again.

Almost.

On her way back from the bathroom she decided to get something to eat from the kitchen. Give the tequila something to bounce off.

Giggling again, she was trying to toast some bread – unsuccessfully, because she failed to notice the toaster wasn't plugged in – when the intercom buzzed. At first she thought she was hearing things, and it was only when it buzzed again – more insistently the second time – that she grasped someone was at the door. Staggering from side to side, she went into the hallway and peered with her remaining eye at the intercom's tiny screen, then blinked a few times because the picture was fuzzier than normal. Eventually it came into focus and she saw Luke was standing outside the building. She jabbed the button to talk to him.

'Hey, Lukey, what are you doing here?' Her words slurred and she could smell a backdraught of tequila fumes on her breath.

'I came to see how you are. Can I come in?'

'Sure. Give me a minute, then I'll buzz you up.'

First, she retrieved her wig from the mannequin's head in the bedroom, along with her eye patch. Then, once she'd clumsily fitted both, it took a couple of attempts for her to activate the main door downstairs to allow Luke to enter the building, and a few more to fumble with the apartment door, which she kept double locked. By the time Luke was inside she was exhausted and needed to sit down. She gratefully let him help her back into the lounge and on to the sofa. As he laid his coat over the armchair next to it, she gestured for the tequila bottle and her shot glass on the table. 'Can you pass me that?'

'How many have you had already?' asked Luke, getting up to oblige her.

'Not nearly enough. Want one?'

He looked as though he was about to decline then changed his mind. 'Where are the glasses?'

'In the bureau.'

Luke found himself one to match hers, filled it, then raised it in a toast. Madeleine smiled sloppily. She liked Luke a lot. He was considerate, smart and funny. Sebastian had been a lucky man.

'Here's to getting justice,' said Luke.

Madeleine's smile slipped and she put the glass down on the table in front of them with a clank.

'What's wrong?' he asked.

'I really needed to talk on Monday, but you guys' – she circled her finger at him – 'were only concerned with Faye. Faye, Faye, Faye,' she said in a sing-song voice. 'You know, I was really upset.

I'd just been mauled on the stand in front of the whole world, and I really needed to offload, but oh no, it was all about her, and then when you finished talking about Faye, it was all about Jimi. I didn't get a chance.'

Luke looked pained. 'I'm sorry. We let you down. We got distracted when she ran off, and we let it take over the meeting. I'm here now if you want to talk.'

'Too late now,' Madeleine said huffily, flopping back against the sofa with an ease she hadn't experienced in months. Tequila really was better than all her pain meds combined.

'It isn't too late. I can stay and talk for as long as you need.'

'It's not that,' said Madeleine, locking her gaze on him and realising how blurred her vision had become. 'I'm just far too drunk now.'

Luke laughed loudly, throwing his head back. Madeleine joined in. It felt good to find something funny for once.

'Like, really, really blasted,' she added.

'In that case,' said Luke, reaching for the bottle, 'I've got some major catching up to do.'

Three shots for him later and another one for her, Madeleine remembered there was something she wanted to bring up, something that Luke had said in passing on Monday. She hadn't wanted to put him on the spot on their WhatsApp group and had been waiting until she saw him again in person to ask.

'Why did you say on Monday that you owe Brendan Morgan?'

'You mean when we were talking through the questions Jimi might be asked?'

'Yes. What did you mean?'

'Exactly what I said. Brendan got me out of there and I owe him for that.'

Madeleine was immediately outraged. 'How the hell can you defend that piece of shit? He was one of them! Of course he was a bad man.'

'He helped me and Jimi escape.'

'So? He still took part in the rest of it. Dozens of people were murdered, Luke, including your partner. You should be angry, not forgiving.'

'I am angry,' said Luke hotly. 'But I can also see how he was brainwashed by Nye. If it wasn't for that, he would never have got involved in an event like that.'

Madeleine shook her head in disgust. 'You're making excuses for a killer.'

'I'm not, I just think there are lessons to be learned from what happened.' He paused. 'Shouldn't the jury consider why an eighteen-year-old kid like his brother Cal is in the dock?'

'He's in the dock because he's a fucking murderer,' she snapped, fighting to keep her one eye open. God, she was drunk. 'That's all there is to it,' she said, angrily jabbing the sofa seat beside her for emphasis. 'I can't believe you're standing up for him.'

'It's more complicated than that,' said Luke. His voice sounded far away now, even though he was sitting right next to her.

'No, it's not,' she said, giving in and closing her eye. 'Look at me, Luke. Those men ruined me. How can you defend them for that?'

She passed out before he could reply.

Chapter Thirty

LUKE

Then

21 April, 1.06 a.m.

There were twenty of them in their huddle, a mixture of guests and theatre staff. Luke knew only one of them by name, Ellison Moran, the director who'd dared to confront their captors before the room was divided. He was nursing a split lip and bloodied nose after being punched for daring to demand better treatment for the elderly guests being made to sit on the floor. Luke privately wished he'd been put in another group though; if Ellison carried on railing against the people keeping them here, he might get them all hurt.

The auditorium was dark now, but the stage was illuminated. Four male captors walked up and down its edge, guns trained on the hostages below, while a few of the younger women brandished long knives and skipped and giggled through the auditorium like it was all a big joke to them. The body of the man whose throat was cut had been dragged into the wings, a long, dark smear of blood tracking its passage across the stage.

There were another two males standing guard over Luke's group. One had cropped hair, a thin, pinched face and forearms scored with rudimentary tattoos that looked self-inked. But he was a pussycat compared to his accomplice, who was one of the men Luke had overheard talking in the restroom before the event started. This second man was mean as all hell. He was the one who'd delivered the blow to Ellison's face and had also kicked two of the women in the group for moving too slowly for his liking, breaking one woman's ribs. He had screamed at the group too, unleashing a torrent of bizarre rhetoric about how the rich and famous were to blame for the evaporation of common, decent values and that everyone inside the Novus deserved what was coming to them, and he was a foot soldier for the greater good, until Nye, the ringleader, came over and said, 'Chill out, Brendan,' in the same mild manner a grandparent might chasten a child.

Embarrassed at being made to look silly, Brendan was stewing now, pacing up and down in front of them and aiming kicks at anyone who dared to stretch their legs. His expression was full of hate.

Luke was at the rear, next to the wall, so at least his back was supported. He could see how difficult it was for some of the others; many were sitting awkwardly, hands flat against the ground to prop themselves up, or knees up and chins resting on them. It had been hours since they'd assumed their positions and stiffness was starting to bite.

Next to Luke was a young man who was one of the Novus staff. His badge said his name was Jimi. He and the other theatre employees and catering staff had been ushered into the auditorium at gunpoint, hands on their heads, at the start of the takeover. Luke could tell Jimi was terrified. He hadn't stopped trembling since Brendan's rant, so whenever he caught his eye, Luke gave him what he hoped came across as a reassuring smile. Twice Jimi went to say something in response, but Luke shook his head. He didn't want

Brendan to catch them talking and for either of them to be beaten for it. He feared Jimi would come off worse. He looked so young and vulnerable.

Brendan had noticed, though. As soon as Jimi tried to whisper again he pounced, yanking the youngster roughly by the arm and causing him to fall sideways on to the carpet. He raised his fist above Jimi's cowering body, but Luke shouted at him to stop.

'Don't hurt him. It was my fault, not his. I was trying to get him to talk to me.'

Brendan let go of Jimi and turned like a cobra ready to strike. Luke sat up straight and pulled his shoulders back. Even without his regular gym-going, he was broader than Brendan and taller, too, and wanted to demonstrate that. Brendan might be armed, but Luke reckoned he had good odds of being able to overpower him.

The sizing trick worked. Brendan became less bullish once he'd appraised who he was dealing with, but he was still angry. 'We told you, no talking.'

'I was just checking he was okay. Jimi's diabetic, aren't you? Type one.'

Jimi's forehead displayed the beginnings of a frown until a loaded look from Luke sent it packing. 'Yeah, that's right. I'm not well,' he said, playing along with the lie. 'I need my medicine.'

There was a reason Luke had mentioned diabetes. He figured it was less likely someone else in the theatre would be T1 and have the necessary meds, compared to a condition like asthma, where an inhaler could be shared. He had a cousin who was T1, so he knew what it involved. He was also banking on Brendan not being aware.

'You'll have to wait,' said Brendan.

'But for how long?' Luke asked. 'I bet Jimi isn't the only person here with a condition that needs meds. What are you going to do when people start getting sick? Or don't you care?'

Luke knew he was pushing it, but he hoped that by engaging with Brendan he might begin to see them as real people and not merely a section of society he'd been brainwashed to hate.

'We'll deal with it when it happens,' said Brendan, but there was a perceptible lack of conviction in his tone.

'It might be too late for Jimi. If he goes into a hypo, he could die.'

'What's a hypo?' asked Brendan.

'It's when your blood glucose level crashes.'

'Can't we just give him some sweets to get it back up?'

Luke was impressed by Brendan's quick thinking, realising he shouldn't misjudge or underestimate him, or the others. Just because they came across as ignorant didn't mean they were.

'I guess. Do you have any candy on you?'

Brendan shook his head.

'What about some water?' said Ellison Moran, who had been listening intently to the exchange. 'People are getting thirsty.'

The director's interruption made Brendan's hackles rise, their previous altercation evidently still fresh in his mind. Unlike Luke, Ellison Moran had made no secret of his disdain for Brendan and the others holding them hostage.

'You won't be getting anything, Granddad. Sit still and shut the fuck up.'

Luke prayed Moran would do as he was told, but the director must've had a death wish because he got to his feet again. Brendan's hands clenched his rifle, causing Jimi to edge across the carpet so he was closer to Luke.

'He'll get himself killed,' he whispered.

Moran positioned himself in front of Brendan and launched into another tirade about the absurdity of what they were doing and how it was beyond a joke now and they needed to let them go. Brendan ordered him to sit down, and in a matter of seconds it descended into a screaming match of who could yell loudest. The escalation was frightening to witness, and Luke felt Jimi lean into him as though Luke might shield him from it.

Moments later, Jimi's fear was realised. The man with the long white ponytail came charging across the room and shoved Brendan out of the way. Then, putting one hand on Moran's shoulder and staring into his eyes, he plunged the knife he was holding in his other deep into the director's stomach.

◆　◆　◆

In the hour it took for Ellison Moran to slowly bleed to death, Jimi went to pieces, crying like a small child. Luke did everything he could to comfort him, but they had been made to sit two metres apart again and his efforts were reduced to the occasional whispered, 'It'll be over soon.'

But Jimi wasn't the only one to lose it. Brendan went from being stunned as he watched his accomplice coldly murder Moran to yelling the place down that this wasn't what he'd signed up for. He seemed genuinely horrified by the violence, which surprised Luke, because he was comfortable enough with kicking and hitting, and he'd been there when the old man was killed on the stage at the start.

Now he was slumped on a chair in front of their group, staring down at the director's body. His hands were slack on his rifle, which was balanced across his lap, and Luke, who was closest to him, was pretty sure that if he reached up to take the weapon from him, Brendan wouldn't put up a fight. The fire had gone from his eyes. Luke studied him for a few moments more, then leaned forward.

'Are you okay?'

Brendan didn't seem bothered by Luke talking. He didn't react at all, in fact. Luke asked him again, and this time the young man's eyes flickered in his direction. To Luke's surprise they were filled with tears.

'I didn't mean for him to die,' Brendan whispered.

'You have to stop this before anyone else dies,' said Luke, keeping his voice low and soft. 'You have a phone, don't you? Do the right thing. Call the police.'

Brendan shook his head. 'Can't.'

'But people are dying.'

'I know, and I'm sorry. But there's Cal.'

'Who's Cal?'

'My brother. He's over there.'

Luke followed Brendan's eyeline to the stage, where a teenage boy was standing, also armed, watching the audience. It was the same kid who'd been in the restroom with Brendan earlier, arguing about not wanting to use a gun. He looked at ease holding one now, though.

'How old is he?'

'Seventeen. It's my fault he's here,' said Brendan, blinking back fresh tears. 'I got him into this.'

'But whose fault is it that you're here?' asked Luke gently.

'What?'

'If you got Cal involved, who did the same with you? I mean, someone filled your head with their warped ideology. Was it the one you call Snow White, with the ponytail?'

Brendan shook his head. 'No.'

'Nye?'

'Yes.'

'How did you meet him?'

Brendan looked behind him nervously, as though he expected to catch Nye eavesdropping. Yet the size of the auditorium meant the groups were well spaced out, and Nye was currently nowhere to be seen.

'I can't say.'

'But he's the one in charge, right?'

'Yeah, I guess.'

'You guess?'

'I only met him a week ago.'

Luke wanted to press him further, but Brendan told him they needed to be quiet now. 'I don't want them to hurt you or your mate,' he whispered, nodding at Jimi, who had at last stopped crying and was listening to them. 'Here, give him this, it might help him.'

Brendan pulled something from his pocket and slipped it to Luke, who held it in his open palm for Jimi to see.

It was a strawberry-flavoured Starburst chew.

'Eat it,' Brendan urged Jimi. 'It'll stop you getting sick.'

For the first time in hours, Luke felt hope.

Chapter Thirty-One

EVE

Now

An amateur rugby player named Mikey saved Horner's life. He and his mates – the rowdy group Eve had tried to tune out on the station concourse – had stepped on to the escalator moments before Horner was pushed, and their collective bulk, with Mikey nearest the top, broke his fall. Had they not been in his way, he'd have likely plummeted all the way to the bottom. He did, however, receive a nasty blow to the back of the head as he tumbled against the moving metal staircase, and was semiconscious as he was loaded into the ambulance. But the paramedics told Eve his vital signs were otherwise strong.

They had insisted she be checked over too. On arrival at nearby St Thomas's, Horner was whisked off for a CT scan, while she was put in a cubicle in A&E for monitoring. She declined the sedative offered to her for the shock, knowing it wouldn't mix well with the two glasses of wine she'd had, and was eventually examined by a doctor who confirmed she hadn't sustained any injuries in the accident that warranted further treatment, but her hip might be bruised where she'd fallen on to her side.

She was certain it wasn't an accident. She and Horner had been deliberately pushed. She said the same to the two British Transport Police officers called to the scene. They'd wanted to take a statement there and then, but the paramedics insisted they get her to hospital first, so one of them handed Eve a business card with a number on it and told her to call it as soon as she felt able to.

She was discharged shortly before midnight. Back home, she managed a little sleep and now, the morning after, she couldn't stop raking over what had happened. Her mind kept replaying the horror of Horner tumbling backwards on a pin-sharp loop and her conclusion was always the same: if she'd reacted quicker, she might've been able to reach him and pull him back before he fell. Her failure to do so made her numb with regret. Thank God that Mikey and his eighteen-stone solidness had been there instead.

The transport police indicated at the scene that it was most likely a mugging gone wrong. Eve did not agree, because the assailant had made no attempt to grab her bag or demand cash from Horner. It had crossed her mind they might've inadvertently strayed into his path, and he'd barged into them because he was annoyed at being held up, but the way he'd stood over her as Horner tried to help her up made her dismiss that theory. Surely he'd have carried on walking if he was in a rush? Why pause like he did, then attack Horner too?

Eve's hip throbbed as she adjusted her position on the sofa, trying to get comfortable. She'd turned the breakfast news on to watch while she drank her coffee, but she wasn't paying attention. Her mind was too full of last night's incident.

Her next thought as she sipped her drink was that their assailant was mentally unwell. That was the theory Leah had favoured when she'd insisted on examining Eve herself last night after her discharge. Her diagnosis matched the A&E doctor's – Eve's hip would be sore for a while, but she was otherwise uninjured.

'It might've been someone having an episode and lashing out uncontrollably,' Leah had said. 'We often get patients like that coming in.'

But there was no sense he'd been out of control, Eve thought to herself. In fact, he'd seemed utterly composed in the seconds before he shoved Horner down the escalator. She shivered at the recollection and wished she wasn't on her own in the flat. Leah had got up early to catch a train to Oxford to see a friend on her day off, and the quiet in the flat was unnerving. Eve turned the telly up a fraction.

Eve had another theory about why she and Horner were targeted, one she didn't want to contemplate and hadn't shared with Leah but couldn't ignore. What if the assailant was something to do with the Novus trial? Horner was at court every day, so he was known to Nye's supporters as being a part of the prosecution team. He could've easily been followed by one of them from the CPS offices to the pub—

Suddenly she was gripped by an even greater fear. What if the assailant had eavesdropped on them discussing the burner phone and Eve's insistence that someone else might still be at large? What if he'd decided to take matters into his own hands to stop her and Horner digging further, because he knew about the eighth person and wanted to protect them – or even was him?

Heart hammering, Eve set her coffee cup down on the side table with a clatter and hobbled into the kitchen, where her phone was charging. Logic told her she needed to calm down and that the assault on them was opportunistic, like the police had said, but she couldn't let go of the feeling they had been specifically targeted because of who they were. That man had meant to seriously hurt them both.

She decided to call Beverly. It was almost eight and she'd been waiting until now to ring her, thinking any earlier might be too early. They'd exchanged messages late last night but had yet to talk.

But when she went to pick up her phone from the counter, she saw the business card given to her by the transport police lying next to it. On impulse she decided to call them first, her need for answers burning as intensely as her guilt that Horner had been hurt after coming to her rescue. They might have checked the CCTV at the station by now and have a zoomed-in image of the man she could look at. Calling them proved a futile exercise, however. The number on the card she'd been given was for the main switchboard and, while she had the name of the officers who had attended the scene, she was passed around until someone said they'd take her details and someone else would call her back.

Frustrated, she hung up and called Beverly's mobile. Her boss picked up on the first ring.

'How are you? I've been so worried,' she said.

'I'm alright. Is there any word on John's condition?'

'He's concussed, but he's going to be okay. I think they're keeping him in for observation for another day, just to be on the safe side. What exactly happened? Your texts last night didn't make much sense. You mentioned someone called Mikey?'

'Sorry, I was a bit out of it when I sent those,' said Eve. 'Mikey was one of the rugby fans who broke Horner's fall on the escalator. It's thanks to them he wasn't more seriously hurt.' The group, Eve was pleased to relay, weren't injured at all: her scream had alerted them to what was happening, and they'd managed to brace themselves against the impact as Horner had toppled towards them.

'It's unlike him to get so drunk that he lost his footing,' mused Beverly. 'What was the occasion?'

Eve frowned into the receiver. 'Who said he was drunk? He wasn't at all. He'd had one pint in the pub beforehand, and that was it. We were both pushed. This man came out of nowhere and shoved me to the ground and then he went for Horner as he tried to help me up.'

Beverly sounded shocked. 'That's not what the police report says. There's no mention of anyone else being there.'

'But that's what happened,' said Eve, exasperated. 'I told the officers when they got there. Why isn't it in the report?'

'It says you were unable to give a full statement at the time because you were in shock,' said Beverly. 'When you speak to them again you can set them straight.'

'I've tried, but I can't get through on the number they gave me,' said Eve hotly. 'They need to investigate it properly. If they check the CCTV they'll see. It was a man wearing an oversized waterproof jacket, all black. The hood was up, so I couldn't see his face clearly, but I remember he had blond hair. He pushed me to the ground first, then he pushed Horner down the escalator.'

'Why would anyone do that?'

Eve was torn. Should she tell her boss about the possibility of there being an eighth man or wait until she'd spoken to Horner about her theory? She didn't want to go running her mouth off and making a fool of herself, nor get him into trouble for sitting on the burner phone discovery. But when could she talk to him next if he was in hospital? Unsure what to do yet, she opted to say nothing.

'I don't know. He didn't say a word the entire time.' Eve shivered again. 'But it was like he'd followed us. It didn't feel like an accident.'

'Who else knew you'd be at that Tube station at that time though, or that you'd gone to the pub first?'

Eve froze. DS Lees. He knew. He had set it up for them to meet.

Beverly's voice rang down the line. 'Eve? Are you still there?'

'I . . . I am. I'm sorry. I'm just feeling a bit overwhelmed,' she said. She couldn't bring herself to mention Lees, knowing what a shitstorm it would unleash. She tried to think rationally. Yes, he knew they were in the pub, but how could he have known they'd be at Westminster station at that time? The fanatical Decorous supporter theory was far more likely.

'I'm not surprised you're shaken up. Based on what you've just told me, Horner's lucky he escaped with just a bump to the head. Don't feel you need to come into work today,' Beverly added. 'Someone from his team will be filling in at the Bailey until he's fit enough to return so take the day off if you need to.'

'No, I want to go in,' said Eve. She was already dressed. Her hip was too sore for fitted trousers, so she was wearing a pair of black sweatpants with a white shirt and her suit jacket. The heels would have to stay at home in favour of her silver New Balance trainers. Not ideal, but she looked presentable. 'Sitting at home will just make me feel worse.'

'You can't blame yourself, Eve. It wasn't your fault,' said Beverly. 'It sounds like a random attack, and you were just unlucky. It could've happened to anyone.'

Eve wished she could believe that.

Chapter Thirty-Two

She'd forgotten her security pass in her rush to leave the flat and was having a tough time convincing the sergeant manning the Lewisham front desk that she was authorised to access the Novus incident room. In the end, too worn out to argue, Eve asked him to summon DCS Strutton.

'Yes, that's right, sir,' said the sergeant when he called Strutton's extension. 'Says she's Eve Wren from the CPS.' He peered over the desk to take in her joggers and trainers. 'She doesn't look like she's from the CPS.'

Strutton appeared a minute or so later, his customary frown even more pronounced than usual. He beckoned her to one side, away from prying eyes and sharp ears. 'What are you doing here? I thought you'd have taken the day off after what happened.'

'You know about it?'

'Yeah, we heard. How's Horner?'

Eve repeated Beverly's prognosis of earlier. 'He should be discharged in a day or so.'

'What about you? How are you doing?'

Eve wanted to tell him how upset she was with Lees, but how would Strutton react if she told him about the made-up message? She had no idea how close they were, but Strutton had already lost a DO from the case – she doubted he'd welcome his OIC's ethics being called into question too.

'My hip's bruised, but otherwise I'm fine,' she said, forcing a smile. 'Sorry you had to come and get me, but I left my pass at home. Can you sign me in?'

Strutton batted away the request. 'You don't look fine. You look like you should be resting. Not being funny,' he said, nodding down at her casually attired lower half, 'but you're dressed for it.'

'My hip's sore from hitting the ground and these are the comfiest things I have to wear,' she said defensively.

'Eve, you don't have to pretend everything's normal. What you saw happen to Horner . . . it's alright not to be okay about it.'

Strutton's unexpected kindness made her feel awkward. She shifted her gaze to the front desk, where the sergeant was watching them. 'I'm fine. I just want to get on and finish the review.'

Without another word Strutton nodded and headed to the desk. He signed her in and she was issued with a temporary visitor's pass.

'Is DS Lees in today?' she asked when they were in the lift heading up to their floor. She tried to keep her voice casual.

'He's out and about this morning. Why?'

Eve conjured up an excuse about wanting to ask him about some unused material she already knew wasn't of any importance.

'Lees will know,' Strutton confirmed. 'But really, Eve, I mean it. If it gets too much today, go home.'

'I will, but with the trial ongoing, finishing the review is more important.'

'I understand,' he said.

The office was locked and on first appearances appeared exactly as Eve had left it when she rushed off to meet Horner the evening before. But as she sat down at her desk and pulled out the yellow legal pad from her bag to read over her notes from yesterday, something felt off. The pens and highlighters and folders she'd left on the desk's surface were too sharply presented, as though someone with a neatness compulsion had come along and straightened them in the night.

Then she noticed her keyboard had also moved. Rarely afflicted by a need to tidy herself, she'd shoved it to one side while she was packing up the day before, leaving it at an angle to the monitor. Now it was parallel to it.

Someone had been in again.

Eve knew it wasn't the cleaners. They'd been told to keep out by the building's facilities manager at her request, and had kept to the arrangement. The waste bin by her desk was now overflowing.

Her irritation mounting, she thumbed through the folders she'd left out on the desk to see if they contained anything contentious, but thankfully they didn't. She moved them to one side, placing them on top of the keyboard – and the screen on her monitor sprang to life.

All that appeared was the secure log-in landing page, but Eve was certain she'd turned the monitor off completely before she left. She always did. It rattled her to see that someone had turned it on, presumably to check if she'd been careless enough to leave it logged in.

Even though Strutton had let himself into the office on Monday when she'd gone to see Horner at court, Eve knew he wouldn't risk interfering with the review. Lees, on the other hand, she could see trying. If she had left anything sensitive out in the open, she could've got in trouble for it.

Suddenly she remembered the Post-it that Lees had given her. Where was it? It was the only proof she had that he'd set her up. After a few frantic seconds of searching, she found it on the floor beneath the desk, where it must've fallen while Lees was rifling through her stuff. Her anger piqued as she read the scrawled message. Setting her up like that with Horner was a shitty thing to do. It could've made things really awkward between them—

Eve shuddered as she contemplated again whether Lees had an ulterior motive for engineering the meeting between her and Horner. He was the only person who knew they'd be at the pub at that particular time . . . What if he had been behind the attack on them at the Tube station, because she'd worked out there might be an eighth person missing from the Bailey dock?

Thrown by the thought, she exhaled shakily. Lees certainly had motive for wanting to conceal the existence of the burner phone. As the OIC on Novus, it was his job to make sure every line of inquiry was followed up. The eighth man hadn't been properly pursued, so Lees was now trying to cover his tracks. It would explain his hostility from day one – he knew there was a chance she might uncover the truth about the burner phone because it had been recorded on COPA, so he'd tried to unsettle her. When that didn't work, and he'd guessed she'd shared her finding with Horner – or maybe he had somehow overheard them discussing it – he had tried to stop them both by having someone attack them last night.

The other explanation, which chilled her even more, was that Lees was a Decorous sympathiser. At some point he could've become aware that the burner phone pointed to a missing accomplice so he buried it in the unused pile to help that person elude justice. Eve knew Lees wouldn't be the first officer to take the side of the accused: there had been a recent case involving a Met officer who was kicked off the force for being a neo-Nazi alt-right sympathiser.

But how could she prove either theory? It was all circumstantial, and if she told anyone at the CPS, they'd probably say she was being paranoid. She had no evidence Lees was behind what happened at the Tube station other than the Post-it instructing her to meet Horner beforehand.

With trembling fingers Eve put it in her bag. She wasn't losing that again.

◆ ◆ ◆

After an hour of trying to work, Eve gave up. The pain in her hip was building, and sitting still wasn't helping. Her focus was also shot because she was distracted by worrying what she'd say to Lees when she saw him next, and wondering how long it would take Horner's Forensics contact to get back to them. It was frustrating to have to wait; she wanted to be doing more herself to confirm who had had the burner phone during the siege.

She went back over her conversation with Horner about whether Brendan Morgan could've dumped the burner phone in the foyer restroom when he had helped the hostages escape. An idea began to form. She could continue to plough through the data to cross-reference whether he had been less active on the encrypted app during the times the texts were being traded, but it would be less time-consuming to just talk to those hostages. As a CPS advocate, she was allowed to talk to witnesses to go over their statements, so what was to stop her asking if they had seen Morgan using a retro flip-lid Motorola phone like the device the CSIs found? It was a distinctive model and should've been noticeable.

Actually, protocol would stop her. The CPS had to go through the police if they wanted to speak to a witness about their statement. However, when she looked up the statements of the hostages helped by Morgan on COPA, Eve could see no mention of him using any phone, so technically, at a push, she wasn't asking them to go over what they'd already told the police. It was a blurred line she was willing to cross.

She decided to work through the witnesses alphabetically, starting with Luke Bishop. His contact details were recorded with his statement, so she called the number listed for him.

'Hi. I'm trying to locate Luke Bishop,' she said.

'This is he.'

'Great. Hi. My name is Eve Wren, and I'm a Crown advocate with the CPS. Do you have a minute, sir?'

'Is this about me giving evidence next week? Is it still happening? I've been bumped once already,' he said, sounding agitated.

'I'm not calling about that, sir. I'm calling about something else relating to the events of last April. It would be better if we spoke in person, though,' she said, deciding it was a good opportunity to escape the cubbyhole for a bit and maybe ease the stiffness in her hip. 'Are you free today to meet?'

'I guess. Can you tell me what it's about first?'

'It's just to go over your statement.' Not quite the truth, but not an outright lie either.

'Okay. Well, I'm free now, if that works for you.'

'It does, and I can come to you. Where are you based?' she asked Luke.

'Not far from London Bridge.'

She checked her watch. 'It's just gone ten. I can be there in half an hour.'

Luke seemed reluctant for her to come to his apartment, so they agreed to meet outside the main entrance to London Bridge station.

'How will I recognise you?' he asked.

'I know who you are – I'll find you first.'

Chapter Thirty-Three

LUKE

Now

The timing of Eve's call was serendipitous. Luke needed a distraction from pacing the streets, which he'd been doing since he left Madeleine's apartment at two in the morning, too wired to go home and sleep. He had been obsessing about her furious response to him saying the Morgan brothers deserved some understanding for being brainwashed. She was so angry, it had forced him to accept he was stupid and naive to think that she and the others might agree with him. Now he was worried about the impact it might have on Sebastian's family if he brought it up in court. They'd been so supportive this past year, despite dealing with their own grief, and he feared they would see it as a betrayal of Sebastian's memory. Yet Luke couldn't ignore his conscience and he was sure Sebastian wouldn't want him to either. Sebastian had always stood up for what he thought was right, which made it even more of a tragedy that he never felt able to stand up for himself and his sexuality.

It was no longer a secret now. His death and Luke's survival had made it headline news. Sebastian's parents were the ones who had shared it with the world, telling a reporter from their Missouri hometown paper. The young hack had knocked on their door to get a quote for an obituary and instead found himself with a worldwide scoop.

Like Luke, Sebastian's parents had never fully understood the fear that drove their son to keep his sexuality a secret, and they wanted him to be celebrated in death for who he truly was. It broke Luke that Sebastian never got to witness and revel in the huge out-pouring of love and support from his peers, the industry and fans that followed their relationship being revealed – knowing him, he'd have dined out on it for years.

Luke was heading for the entrance to London Bridge station, the towering Shard skyscraper next to it casting a deep, chilly shadow, when the group chat pinged with a message from Horatio. There were no accompanying words, just a link to an article from the *Evening Standard* about an accident last night involving a CPS lawyer who was part of the Novus prosecution team. Luke winced as he read that the man, who wasn't named, had fallen down an escalator at a Tube station and was now in hospital. That didn't sound good, and what did it mean for the trial? He got to the end of the article, where it was explained that a colleague from the CPS would assume his workload until the injured man was well enough to return to work. There was a quote from a legal commentator who said it should have no bearing on the continuation of justice being served because the CPS would replace him with someone also well versed in the case. Luke fretted for a moment. If that person was Eve Wren, why did she want to see him now?

But it was too late to back out of their meeting, he realised, looking up from his phone. Unless he was mistaken, the young woman with dark brown hair staring intently at him as he approached the entrance was her.

◆ ◆ ◆

Eve rejected his invitation to grab a coffee somewhere and suggested they walk along the waterfront instead. Luke didn't mind more walking, even though it was now overcast, the darkening clouds scudding across the grey skies like they too were rushing to get indoors before it rained.

As they walked towards Borough High Street to cut through to the Thames Path, Eve apologised for what she was wearing.

'I don't normally dress like this. I wasn't expecting to meet anyone today.'

Luke hadn't paid attention to her outfit, but now she'd pointed it out, the sweatpants and sneakers did seem a bit incongruous with the suit jacket and freshly laundered shirt.

'Looks fine to me. You said you wanted to talk about my statement?' he said.

'In a roundabout way. I'm currently reviewing some of the unused material from the Novus investigation to make sure it's all in order – that's evidence gathered by the police, but which isn't due to be presented in court. Sometimes these reviews take place when a trial has already started,' she said. 'I'm telling you this so you're clear about what I do.'

Luke nodded. Now he was even more intrigued about what she wanted from him.

'Let's go down to the Thames Path before we chat properly,' she said. 'It's a bit crowded here.'

They'd reached the flight of steps next to Southwark Cathedral that would take them down to the path. There was a bottleneck of tourists waiting to descend while another group made their way up, so they hung back until it was their turn. Then they followed the crowd along cobbled lanes, past the replica of Sir Francis Drake's

Golden Hinde galleon ship and the Clink Museum until, at last, the churning grey expanse of the River Thames opened out in front of them and the path widened enough to put some space between them and others walking it.

Eve re-started the conversation. 'I've read your account of how Brendan Morgan helped you and some others escape, and I'd like to talk to you more about his behaviour during the siege,' she said.

'Right,' Luke replied, struggling to hide how disconcerted he was. He'd just spent God knows how many hours walking the streets contemplating what to say in the witness box about Brendan, and now, all of a sudden, someone from the CPS was asking questions about him.

'You had quite a lot of interaction with him, didn't you?'

'You could say that.'

'Before your escape, did you see him communicating with the others much?'

Luke was confused. 'The others who escaped?'

'No, sorry, I meant his accomplices. Nye and the other followers.'

'Sure. He spoke to them a little. We were all told to sit quietly, but sometimes they talked or shouted to each another across the auditorium.'

'Did you see Brendan at any point using a mobile phone?'

The line of questioning wasn't what he had expected, but Luke did his best to answer.

'I guess once or twice I saw him on it. I didn't pay that much attention. Is this the phone they had the encrypted app on? I read about it,' said Luke sheepishly.

'It might've been. Do you remember what model it was?'

'I didn't see it close up.'

'Was it a flip phone by any chance?'

'No, definitely not.'

'Did he have just the one phone on him?'

Luke couldn't help himself. 'Why are you so interested in what kind of phone Brendan had?'

'I'm afraid I can't say. But if you did see him with more than one phone it would be helpful for us to know.'

Luke tried to think back but, fifteen months later, his memory of that night wasn't what it was. 'I think I only saw one.'

He could see she was disappointed with his answer.

'Sorry I can't be of more help.'

'That's okay.' She shrugged, but it didn't look okay to Luke. She came to a halt and stuck out her hand. 'Thanks for your time.'

Luke suddenly realised this was an opportune moment to ask the CPS whether he should mention the brainwashing when he gave evidence, to see if they thought it was a bad idea too.

'Before you go, can I ask you something about me giving evidence?'

She nodded. 'Of course.'

'I know I'll be asked about Brendan helping us, and I want to say that I don't think he would have got involved if he hadn't been indoctrinated by Patrick Nye. Same with his brother. That's how I feel. But I'm in this group, see, with some of the other survivors, and I think they'll be upset if I say that in court. Do you think I should?'

Eve considered it for a moment. 'First and foremost, you'll be asked to stick to the facts, although I can't imagine the defence will object to you sticking up for them. But what do you hope to achieve by sharing your feelings on it?'

Luke repeated what he'd said to Madeleine the previous evening, about learning lessons from what happened. 'Brendan was groomed and manipulated by Nye. Nye did everything he could to make Brendan feel like he was some kind of chosen one. He was even sworn in by Nye's second-in-command to officially join The

Decorous, like he was being anointed or something. It's no wonder Brendan got swept up in it all—'

Eve held up her hand to interrupt him. 'Wait. Nye had a second-in-command?'

'Um, yes. At least that's what Brendan said.'

'Did he say who it was?'

'Um, no, not exactly.'

'But he told you all this during the siege?'

Luke hesitated, realising he'd dug himself into a hole.

'Mr Bishop?' Eve said.

'I don't know if I should say anything else. Is this an official interview?'

Eve's taut expression broke into a smile. 'No, it's just a fact-finding mission. I'm curious to hear more about this swearing-in ceremony.'

'I don't think it was a ceremony exactly,' said Luke, relaxing a little. 'Brendan had to read and sign a declaration pledging his loyalty to The Decorous. Cal did the same a few months later.'

'But Patrick Nye didn't conduct Brendan's swearing-in, even though he was the leader?'

'No. Brendan only met the person who did his that one time, but he got the impression they were really involved and high up in the group.'

Eve's expression shifted and her eyes gleamed. 'Was anyone else present?'

'Not that I'm aware of.'

'It wasn't any of The Seven, like Barker or Woolmore? Or any of the followers who died in the blasts?'

'No. Once Brendan was officially part of The Decorous, he had a bunch of meetings with Nye and the others to plan the siege, but he only met this person once, at his swearing-in.'

'He didn't say if it was a man or woman?'

Luke hesitated, fearful of tripping himself up. 'He didn't.'

'Did Brendan mention where his swearing-in took place?'

'In Manchester.'

Eve looked lost in thought for a moment, staring into the distance. Coming up ahead was Southwark Bridge and rising into the London skyline across the river was the dome of St Paul's. Even against a backdrop of grey clouds it looked majestic. But Luke wasn't taking in the view, he was braced for what she might ask him next.

'I'm surprised to hear you say Manchester and not Bournemouth,' she said. 'It's common knowledge now that Nye ran The Decorous and plotted the siege from the hotel Edwin Barker owned there.'

'Well, Brendan lived in Stockport, and that's closer to Manchester, isn't it? Maybe Nye wasn't there because it was too risky for him to travel.'

For what felt like an excruciating length of time, Eve stared out across the river again, clearly thinking about what Luke had shared. He had a pretty good idea what was coming next, and he was right.

'That was quite some chat the two of you had while the siege was happening,' she said. 'I thought the hostages were made to sit in silence or risk being hurt.'

'We were, for the most part,' said Luke awkwardly, his heart hammering against his ribcage. He wished he'd never started this line of conversation now.

Eve shook her head. 'I don't believe you found all this out just from talking to Brendan that night. I think you've been getting your information from somewhere else, and I need to know where. Who else have you been talking to, Mr Bishop? Is it something to do with the group you're in?'

'God, no. They're all survivors like me. A man called Horatio who worked at the Novus set it up.' Luke reeled off a list of names Eve mostly recognised, a few of them famous.

'If it wasn't any of them, who else have you been talking to?'

Luke fell silent for a few moments, before making a decision.

'Okay, I'll tell you, but I don't want this person's name to go any further, because it will get them into trouble. Not from the authorities, but from the people who know them.'

'To be honest, I don't even know what any of this means yet, or whether it makes a difference to what we already know, so I'm not about to run to my bosses with it.'

Luke felt reassured. 'It was Brendan and Cal's sister, Caitlyn.'

'You know her?' asked Eve, clearly surprised.

'We, ah – well, we've spoken a few times.'

Her expression darkened. 'Luke, a prosecution witness shouldn't be in contact with a defendant's family ahead of giving evidence at their trial. Have the Morgan family been trying to intimidate you? If that's the case, the police can—'

'No, absolutely not. I contacted her, not the other way round.'

'But why?'

'I know this might not make sense to anyone else, but I wanted to tell Caitlyn how brave her brother was in helping me escape. It was important to me she knew that. Whatever else Brendan did that night, I owe him my life.'

Chapter Thirty-Four

EVE

Now

Eve's mind was racing. According to Luke, Nye's second-in-command had overseen Brendan Morgan's swearing-in but was absent from the subsequent meetings during which the siege was planned. Why would any of those involved have skipped them – unless it was to keep their distance from the others?

This had to be the eighth person whom Nye had sworn to protect.

'I want to go over everything Brendan told you about Nye's second-in-command,' she said, trying to dampen her excitement because she didn't want to rouse Luke's suspicion that something was up. 'But let's find somewhere to sit down first.'

There were no benches on that stretch of Thames Path, only a rough-hewn wall separating it from the river. Eve suggested they keep walking until they were on the other side of Southwark Bridge. They found a pub on the corner that had an outside seating area.

Luke went inside to buy them soft drinks while Eve settled herself at a table next to the riverbank with her back against the panoramic view. She was still on edge from Horner's fall, and it felt safer sitting where she could see people approaching. There was a moment near the *Golden Hinde* when a sightseer coming up behind them had brushed against her by accident and she'd nearly screamed.

She watched Luke cross the pathway between the pub and the seating area carrying two glasses of orange juice topped with ice. He showed little resemblance to the photographs she'd seen of him taken before the bombing. No longer clean-shaven and with his hair straggling past his collar, he'd lost a lot of weight, making his face appear gaunt and older than his thirty-one years. Eve considered his wanting to stand up for Brendan, and wondered how he squared that with his grief.

Once Luke was seated, she asked him to explain how his and Brendan's dialogue inside the Novus had begun.

'I guess it was after I told him a lie about Jimi being sick,' said Luke.

'Jimi Regan?'

'Yes. He was in the same group as me. I lied and told Brendan that Jimi was diabetic in the hope that he might give us some food, or at least some water. It must've been six hours in by then and people were starting to struggle,' he added. 'At first Brendan was hostile, because we were supposed to be sitting in silence, but then something happened, and he stopped. He went from yelling and hitting and threatening people to being apologetic for what we were going through.'

'What happened?'

'Brian Woolmore stabbed Ellison Moran right in front of us. Mr Moran didn't die straight away, and we weren't allowed to help him, so we had to sit there and watch the man bleed out. It really got to Brendan – like, the reality finally hit home and he wanted the siege to be over. He didn't want anyone else to die.'

'He knew the theatre was rigged with explosives though?' said Eve.

'That's why he decided to help as many of us escape as he could. He knew Nye was crazy enough to set them off.'

Again, Eve was struck by Luke's defence of Brendan. It took a remarkably forgiving person to see the good in someone complicit in so many deaths.

'Did any of the other hostages in your group hear what you and he were discussing?'

'Only Jimi and another man nearest to us; the rest of the group was spread out. But it doesn't matter what he heard. He's not here to repeat it.'

It took Eve a second to realise Luke meant the hostage was among the forty-three who hadn't survived.

'How did you get on to the subject of the swearing-in?'

'Brendan started getting upset because Nye refused to move Ellison's body. He said it had to stay where it was. After that, Brendan lost it and kept saying he wished he'd never answered Nye's call to arms or got his little brother involved. That's when I asked him how he met Nye and he told me it was online, via a website, and then he told me about the swearing-in. He kept calling himself an idiot for ever listening to Nye.'

'Why do you think Brendan became interested in The Decorous in the first place?'

'I think he was just tired of feeling disadvantaged. Nye preyed on that.'

Eve understood what Luke was referring to. Unlike Cal, who had done well at school, Brendan had dropped out with only one GCSE to his name and had a minimum-wage job hand-washing cars in their local supermarket's car park. He had little in the way of prospects, so when Nye had offered him the chance to take a stand against a group of people who had more money and opportunity than he could ever dream of, Brendan was easily seduced.

'Are you sure he said he was sworn into the group by someone other than Nye?' Eve asked, needing to be sure herself.

'Yes. I did ask if the person was in the theatre, but he wouldn't tell me. He got scared then, he thought he was saying too much. To be honest, it didn't cross my mind again until I spoke to Caitlyn. She also said how she wished her brothers had never met Nye, and that's when I remembered.'

'How did you contact her?'

'Through social media. I was honest about who I was, I didn't catfish her or anything,' he added hastily. 'I just wanted to tell her how brave Brendan was at the end and leave it at that. I didn't expect her to respond, but she did, and we talked. She told me she's estranged from their parents now because they're supporting Cal. She's sickened by what he did.'

'What about what Brendan did?' asked Eve. 'Doesn't that sicken her too?'

'She's conflicted. Cal's showing no remorse, whereas she believes Brendan didn't know what he was getting himself into.'

'With guns, knives and explosives?'

'All I can say is that after Ellison Moran was stabbed, Brendan was like a different person. It broke him. That's why he helped us get out.'

Eve took a beat. 'None of this is in your statement, and it should've been.'

'When I was interviewed, I wasn't really thinking about the men behind the bombing. All I could think about was the aftermath and losing Sebastian. I did tell the police how Brendan had helped us, but it was only months later, after speaking with Caitlyn, that I remembered him mentioning the swearing-in and I asked her if she knew anything about it. She told me it took place in

Manchester and that Brendan hadn't seen that person again at any of the meetings.'

'How would Caitlyn know about the swearing-in unless she knew what her brothers were planning?'

'She didn't know a thing. She was devastated when she heard her brothers were part of it. But she went to see Cal when he was first remanded, and he told her a little bit about how he and Brendan got involved. That was before he stopped showing remorse and she disowned him.' Luke paused. 'Why are you so interested in the swearing-in?'

'Just filling in gaps,' said Eve carefully. 'It's good background detail.'

'Right. Did you also know there are some people who think Nye didn't really mastermind the attack and that someone else did?'

'Who's been saying that?' Eve asked, taken aback.

'Some people I've been chatting to. People who know a lot about Nye and what happened when he was back in California. They're questioning his status as leader because this time it was actually Edwin Barker who resurrected The Decorous, not him. They think a lot of what happened doesn't add up.'

Eve stilled. 'How did you meet these people, Luke?'

'I did what made sense,' he said, his tone defiant. 'I joined a cult.'

Chapter Thirty-Five

FAYE

Now

Richard was sulking. Nearly three days had passed since he'd last spoken to Faye. Every attempt she'd made to strike up conversation had been rebuffed by sour looks and audible huffing. It had dawned on her as she fell asleep last night that instead of him taking her running away from the café on Monday as a personal slight, it would've been nice if he'd bothered to check she was okay. With that in mind, this morning she was returning his coolness like for like.

Freddy and Olivia had picked up on the atmosphere before they'd left for school but had presumed it was caused by Faye being up early for once and disrupting their dad's routine. While she'd been sleeping off her hangovers Richard had got into the habit of cooking them elaborate breakfasts, and he didn't like her pointing out, after she'd watched them pick at plates of scrambled eggs and smoked salmon out of politeness, that a hot meal was a bit heavy when they were rushing to get ready and they'd both be fine with a slice of toast. For that she'd received a scowl from Richard but a nudge of thanks under the table from Freddy.

She was up early because, for the first time in months, she hadn't touched a drop of alcohol the previous evening. The only reason Richard had wanted her to attend the survivors' group was because her excessive drinking made him think she wasn't coping; therefore, if she cut down, or even stopped, it would no longer be an issue. It was a sacrifice worth making to never go back to Stepney again.

She did need to make amends for running away though. Not with Richard, but with Samuel. Since Monday he'd left half a dozen voicemail messages asking her to call him, and at least as many texts. So, after a shower and a slice of toast, which she pointedly ate standing up by the kitchen island while Richard grumpily cleared the breakfast crockery from the table, she went up to her bedroom to call him back. When he picked up, she didn't give him a chance to speak before launching into her apology.

'I'm so sorry, Samuel,' she said. 'It was rude of me to rush off like that without an explanation.'

'You don't owe me anything of the sort. I just wanted to check you got home safely,' he said. 'You were clearly very distressed.'

Faye sank down on to the edge of her bed and her eyes swept over the mess that littered every surface: used glasses and plates, clean clothes she hadn't put away, dirty ones that hadn't made it to the laundry basket. How had she let her life come to this, skulking in a hovel of a bedroom while the rest of her house – and it was her house, with only her name on the deeds now – was overrun by the man who had broken her heart and almost financially ruined her?

You know why, a whiny voice in her head abruptly reminded her. *It's because of what you did at the Novus. Richard living with you is your penance.*

But today she wasn't prepared to listen to her inner nag. She was tired of wallowing in guilt about her actions on that night. Her behaviour wasn't wrong, it was opportunist: a way out had presented itself and she'd seized it with both hands. Anyone in her shoes would've done the same.

'Enough.'

'Pardon?' said Samuel.

Faye jumped. She hadn't realised she'd said it out loud. 'Oh, I meant I've just had enough of going over what happened, that's why I didn't stay. I know the group has helped Richard a lot, but I'm afraid it's not for me.'

'We must all do whatever feels right for us,' said Samuel. 'I would like to talk to you though, about Matthew.'

Panic swooped over her. Had Samuel found out what she'd done too?

'The FIDM has been in touch to suggest an exhibition of Cynthia's stage costumes. I think it's a wonderful idea – it will help remind people of what she achieved, instead of her being forever tied to the Novus. But Matthew is reluctant to give his consent because he thinks it's too soon, what with the trial,' said Samuel. 'I was wondering if you might talk to him – and also help curate it. We have so many things here at the house that I think would be lovely to include, but you more than anyone she worked with would know which costumes best represent her career.'

The Fashion Institute of Design and Merchandising Museum in Los Angeles was one of the most prestigious curators of costume in the world, and selecting items for the exhibition was an honour, no question. For the first time in a long time Faye felt a spark of excitement.

'I'd love to help curate it. But if Matthew won't listen to you, I doubt he'll take any notice of me,' she said.

'Won't you at least try? This would be such a marvellous thing to happen,' said Samuel, his voice quivering. 'Her legacy, everything she worked so hard to achieve for so many years, has been destroyed by what happened. I strongly believe this exhibition would go a little way towards addressing that. The FIDM does too. We just need to convince Matthew. I was thinking you could come here and we could talk to him together.'

Go to Hampstead in person? Out of the question.

'I can't – it wouldn't work,' said Faye anxiously. 'He won't change his mind.'

'I think there's a way we can make it impossible for him to say no,' said Samuel.

'How?'

'By using the few costumes stored here at the house. If you came over and helped me set up a display, we could show Matthew how even more wonderful a much bigger exhibition would be.'

Faye was torn. The opportunity to sift through Cynthia's stage wardrobe was not one she wanted to turn down. But to set foot in that house again, knowing what she did—

'Matthew's in Malmö now until next Friday,' Samuel interjected, 'so we could get it ready for his return.'

Faye could hear the keenness in the old man's voice and knew there was no excuse she could muster that would deter Samuel from badgering her until she agreed. 'Okay, I'll do it,' she said, the swell of fear in her chest expanding. If Samuel ever found out the cause of her trepidation, he'd never forgive her.

'That's wonderful. Thank you. Are you busy today? There's no time like the present,' he said, chuckling.

Faye glanced again at the mess of her bedroom. She had no plans for today and nothing to do. Maybe it was time to pull herself out of her rut.

'I'm not busy, no. I can come over in an hour or so.'

Samuel was thrilled, and said he'd rustle up some lunch for them himself, as he was the only one in the house today.

'Isn't Roddy there?'

'He's gone to watch some of the proceedings at the Old Bailey today. Apparently, there are long queues to get a seat in the public gallery so he left early to avoid missing out.'

'He can't watch the case if he's a witness,' said Faye. She'd been warned by one of the witness support officers that she could not step inside the courtroom until she was called.

'He's not giving evidence any more. He found out a few weeks ago.'

That caught her off guard. 'Why not?' she asked warily.

'He hasn't said. I don't think he minds. It means he can spend his days at the trial now.'

'I thought Matthew had kept him on to look after you?'

'I'm perfectly capable of seeing to myself for a few hours every day, I'm not an invalid,' said Samuel haughtily.

'Does Matthew know he's paying Roddy to sit in court?'

'It was his idea, my dear. While he's stuck working in Sweden, Matthew likes Roddy to call him every evening to talk him through the day's testimony. He prefers to hear it first-hand rather than reading the news.'

Faye's mind flitted back to that last conversation she'd had inside the Novus and the deal she'd made which had changed everything in a split second.

'Do you think Roddy tells him everything?' she asked.

Samuel sounded amused. 'Why wouldn't he?'

Faye hoped he didn't. If Roddy shared everything, what was to stop him from sharing the secret that could damn her?

Chapter Thirty-Six

FAYE

THEN

21 April, 1.46 a.m.

Matthew joining their group had caused consternation among Nye's followers. The young woman who'd been standing guard over them was now furiously whispering to a couple of others who'd joined her. Faye wondered what the problem was. Matthew was hardly being intrusive, sitting quietly on the floor next to his grandmother's chair, which he'd persuaded Nye to swap for the beer crate. He was holding Cynthia's hand, which can't have been comfortable, keeping his awkwardly raised to clasp hers. His focus was entirely on the elderly woman who for so long had been the centre of his world, and who was becoming increasingly confused the longer they were made to sit there. Watching Matthew now – his face wan and creased with worry – Faye could see the haunted little boy he'd been when she'd first met him all those years ago.

It was 1996 and Cynthia was undertaking her first acting job since her son and daughter-in-law had died three years previously. Faye was the set costumer but spent as much time being a sounding board for Cynthia, who had been finding filming stressful because she was concerned Matthew wouldn't cope with her working again. She took her responsibilities as her grandson's guardian very seriously, refusing to employ help and taking a career hiatus so she'd be there to take him to and from school herself. She'd only said yes to the role because it was more of a cameo, working with a director she'd long admired, and it only necessitated a three-week shoot that helpfully coincided with the school holidays, when Matthew was staying with his maternal grandparents in Sweden.

Then Matthew broke his arm slipping on wet tiles at the side of their swimming pool in Malmö. He was so upset he begged to return to the UK. Cynthia had sought permission to bring him on set for the rest of the shoot and Faye ended up keeping an eye on him. She found him to be a sweet-natured boy but shy and reserved and clearly affected by the loss of his parents. He wasn't remotely interested in the film-making process and spent all his time obsessively playing with a Tamagotchi and various other gadgets; Faye wasn't surprised in the least when, in adulthood, he turned his back on the family profession and instead went to work in tech, basing himself in Sweden.

Thinking back to that time, Faye suspected Cynthia's determination to do a good job of raising Matthew was to make up for having been an absent parent herself when his father was little. Saul Seymour had lived permanently with his father – husband number two in the marital running order – but during his custody visits to Cynthia she had an army of nannies to pick up the slack. Her opposite approach to Matthew had paid off, because they were now close in the way Faye hoped she'd be with Freddy and Olivia when they reached adulthood.

Matthew must've noticed Faye staring at him, because he turned round and raised his eyebrow quizzically.

'How's she doing?' she mouthed at him.

'Not great,' he mouthed back. 'I don't know what to do.'

'I'm sure the police will be here soon. This can't go on much longer.'

Matthew shook his head. Then he leaned forward again to whisper. 'Did you see where they went with Madeleine?'

'Somewhere backstage.'

It had been more than an hour since Madeleine Farmer was led away from the auditorium by one of Nye's male accomplices, and she hadn't been seen since. Faye hoped, fervently, that she was being made to record a message to air on social media, because their captors had already filmed footage of them sitting in their huddles to send out to the public. The alternative was too horrific to contemplate.

The young woman having the heated debate came over and stood between Faye and Matthew, the large sheath knife she carried a stark reminder that these people held all the cards. She'd stripped off the navy sweatshirt that acted as a kind of uniform for The Decorous and was down to a sleeveless black vest that showed off her pale, scrawny arms and unfettered armpit hair.

'What were you two whispering about?' she asked. Her accent was British, with a West Country twang.

'We're worried about my grandmother,' said Matthew. 'She's nearly ninety and very frail.'

'Not so frail she couldn't have a fancy party thrown for her though,' the young woman said astutely.

'Can she please have some water?' he asked.

'No, she can't—'

Nye suddenly appeared carrying a small paper cone filled to the brim with water. 'Back away, Millie.' He handed the cone to Matthew.

'This is just for your grandmother, no one else,' said Nye.

The young woman, presumably Millie, started to protest. Nye silenced her with a steely look.

Matthew thanked him. It must've stuck in his throat to be grateful to the man keeping them there, but Faye didn't blame him for being polite. They had no way of knowing how many more hours they'd be in this situation, and there was little point in antagonising him. Cynthia would need more than one small cup as time ticked on.

As Matthew held it up to his grandmother's lips and urged her to take a sip, Nye looked around. Faye realised he was doing a headcount.

'There's too many of you now. One of you needs to move.'

The surge of panic was palpable, because Faye clearly wasn't the only one in the group who had noticed how relatively mellow Millie was compared to her accomplices. Her aggression was purely vocal, so none of them wanted to give up their place with her standing over them. Nye waited a moment, then made it clear that if someone didn't volunteer, he'd choose for them. Faye held her breath and stared at the floor, praying it wouldn't be her.

'You.'

She looked up, and her heart sank when she saw he was pointing at her.

'Up.'

Reluctantly, she climbed to her feet, an ungainly manoeuvre in an unyielding dress and with limbs that were less flexible than they used to be, and from being made to sit still for so long. Nye smirked as she struggled but made no move to help her.

'Say goodbye to your pals.'

Fighting back tears, Faye turned to tell Cynthia not to worry and that she'd be back soon, but stopped. Something was wrong. Cynthia was slumped over in her seat, head lolled forward, and she was drooling.

'Matthew, what's wrong with her?'

His head spun round to check, then he let out a small moan. 'No, no, no.'

Not caring if Nye objected, Faye scrambled to his side. 'Is she breathing?'

Matthew delicately pressed his fingers against his grandmother's wrist to check for a pulse, then held his palm up against her mouth, hoping to feel the warmth of her breath against it. 'I think so.'

'What's wrong with her?' asked Nye with irritation.

Faye was no medical expert, but it looked to her as though Cynthia had suffered a stroke. The right side of her face was slack and when Matthew lifted and dropped her right hand it flopped like a piece of raw bacon slapped on a counter.

'I think it's a stroke,' said Faye, turning to Nye. 'She needs a doctor.'

His expression blanked. 'Can't help you with that.'

'Please,' begged Matthew. 'You can't just let her die.'

'I can do whatever I want,' he said evenly.

Faye couldn't stop herself. 'You monster! She's an elderly woman. She needs help.'

Nye grabbed her by the upper arm and dug his calloused fingertips in, causing her to cry out in pain. 'I don't like being called names,' he whispered right into her ear, his breath warm against it. 'Now say you're sorry and mean it, or I'll make my friend Snow White come over and make you sorry.'

Every fibre of Faye's being wanted to refuse and stand up to this brute, but her mind swam with images of Olivia and Freddy. For their sake she had to comply.

'I'm sorry. I shouldn't have shouted,' she said quietly. Satisfied, he released her arm.

'Anyone know first aid?' Millie quipped.

'Her carer does,' said Matthew. 'His name's Roddy. He was in the green room at the start of the event, but I think he's in one of the other groups now.'

'What's a green room?' Millie asked.

'Kind of like a waiting room,' said Nye. 'For this event it was a dumping ground for all the people who weren't important or rich enough to get a seat at the dinner table.' He then cupped his hands around his mouth and shouted, 'Someone bring me Roddy Jepson,' at the top of his voice. There was movement on the other side of the auditorium, then Faye watched as Roddy, in his teal carer's uniform, was frogmarched across the room to their group by another of Nye's flunkeys.

He looked terrified. His skin was flushed, his scalp glowing pink beneath his closely cropped blond hair. Faye didn't know his exact age, but Cynthia had once told her that Roddy had lived in London for twenty years since graduating in his native Denmark, so that put him in at least his forties, even though he looked far more youthful. When he clapped eyes on his employer, he let out a cry of shock.

'What did you do to her?'

Nye shrugged. 'I didn't do anything.'

Matthew and Faye stood back to let Roddy examine her. He tried to get her to speak, but Cynthia just stared at him blankly, and when he asked her to move her right arm she couldn't.

'Does she need more water?' Matthew asked him desperately.

'No, we shouldn't give her anything in case she's lost the ability to swallow. It looks like a stroke,' Roddy replied.

Matthew paled. 'Can you help her?'

'She needs to get to hospital.' Roddy looked round at Nye. 'Call an ambulance. Now.'

Nye threw back his head and laughed. 'I don't think so.' Then he leaned down and put his face close to Roddy's. 'You want her to live, *you* help her.'

Roddy glowered at him but didn't argue back. 'We need to lie her down. She should be on her side with her head and shoulders raised,' he instructed Matthew and Faye. 'We need a cushion or pillow.'

He looked at Nye again, who this time nodded. He ordered Millie to find one.

'Where?'

Nye sighed exasperatedly. 'Could you be any dumber? Check backstage.'

Embarrassed, Millie hurried off, but not before passing Nye her knife first.

Matthew and Roddy helped Cynthia to lie down. Their movements were slow and gentle, but Faye's concern grew as Cynthia's eyes rolled back while Matthew cradled her head in his hands.

'Wait, let me take this off first,' said Roddy. He reached around her neck to remove the choker she was still wearing and went to pass it to Faye to hold, but Nye intercepted it.

'I'll keep that,' he said, grinning. 'We wouldn't want something so valuable to get into the wrong hands.'

Faye felt a prick of satisfaction. He had no idea the choker was costume jewellery she'd sourced for Cynthia to wear tonight. Made from moissanite and lightweight enough for her to endure for an evening, the stones were worth far less than the diamonds they aped.

Millie returned, clutching a red velvet cushion. Faye heard her say in an undertone to Nye that there was some 'fucked up shit' going on backstage and that he needed to put a stop to it.

'Who?' Nye asked.

'Barker.'

Nye took the pillow and tossed it down on the floor beside Roddy. 'Make do with that. It's all you're getting.'

'For God's sake, she needs an ambulance,' Faye protested.

Nye turned on her, his dark brown eyes like pools of black in the dim light. Faye saw his grip tighten on the knife and she began to shake.

'You are really starting to piss me off, lady,' he said in that chilling half whisper he seemed accustomed to using.

Everyone around them tensed as Nye took another step towards her.

'I want you out of my sight before I can no longer be held responsible for my actions. Move her to another group,' he ordered Millie. Then he glanced down at Roddy, still tending to Cynthia. 'Actually, two of you need to move if he's staying here.'

Faye couldn't bear the thought of leaving Cynthia when she was so ill. She knew begging wouldn't persuade Nye to let her stay in the group, but what might? She looked around anxiously and her gaze fell upon Liberty, still huddled beneath a loaned dinner jacket and sitting next to the young theatre worker.

'Take those two instead,' she said in a rush, before she could talk herself out of it. She'd promised Richard she'd look after Liberty.

Nye laughed as he followed her gaze. 'That truce didn't last long. Not feeling as generous towards your husband's mistress now you've been stuck with her?'

'I can't stand to be around her, so you'd be doing me a favour,' said Faye very quietly, not untruthfully. 'Then I can do you one by staying here. I can help with Cynthia. We can look after her between us.'

He looked thoughtful for a moment. Liberty realised what was going on because she started to shake her head forcefully. 'No, no. Please no. I want to stay here. You can't make us move.'

It was the red flag to the bull.

'Tough,' said Nye. 'Get up, both of you.'

Liberty and the girl were hauled away, both sobbing in terror. Halfway across the auditorium, the dinner jacket slipped from

Liberty's shoulder to reveal the gossamer-slender strap of her gold dress. The air was filled with catcalls as Snow White reached out to paw her chest. Horrified, Faye turned away, unable to bear witness to what she'd just done. She'd sacrificed two young women to save herself and, if anything happened to them now, it would be on her.

Chapter Thirty-Seven

EVE

Now

Luke's confession that he'd joined a cult shook Eve to the core, until he explained he hadn't done so as himself but under a pseudonym. And even then, only so he could fish for information. Desperate to make sense of what had driven The Decorous to storm the Novus and kill dozens of people including Sebastian, his infiltration began with him reading as much background material on why people set up cults that he could lay his hands on. He wanted to know what Patrick Nye's true purpose was.

The cult itself was a bust. Its members were too obsessed with its core aim of preparing for an Earth-ending Big Bang to answer their new recruit's questions. Luke's search then led him to an organisation that helped former cult members struggling to deal with their experience and those still in one who wanted to escape. Luke pretended he was the latter, and it was in the organisation's website chatroom that Nye's standing as the mastermind of Novus was called into question. Among those posting were four former members of The Decorous from its California days, who'd lived at the Carpinteria compound. None of them believed Nye had it in him to plot and pull off the siege.

Eve's heart pounded as she listened intently. Luke had taken a huge risk – as a witness for the prosecution he shouldn't have had contact with anyone from The Decorous, past or present – but the information he'd gleaned was useful. She asked if the former Decorous members had shared their reasoning, given Nye had done a pretty good job of arming his compound to the hilt, so that when the FBI raided, it wasn't the easy target they thought it would be.

'They said he often left the logistics of running the compound to others far smarter than he was,' said Luke. 'It was like he wanted all the trappings that came with being the leader but none of the work.'

'Just because he didn't get his hands dirty with the day-to-day running doesn't mean he wasn't capable. We know he was, because of Novus,' said Eve. 'What else did they say?'

'They talked a lot about his girlfriend, Joan Beck. They said if anyone had it in them, it was her. They seemed to think she was the brains of the organisation.'

Eve's mind whirled. If that were true, it might explain why Joan had never spoken publicly about Nye and why she was in London now for the trial, even though she apparently had no intention of attending court. She couldn't stay away because Novus was her doing. Then she remembered what Strutton had told her.

'We know Joan Beck wasn't involved this time though,' she said doubtfully. 'That's been confirmed by our police and the FBI.'

'I'm just telling you what these people said in the chatrooms,' Luke replied testily.

Eve didn't want to upset him any further, so she decided to call their meeting to a close. She went to thank him for his time, but a speedboat roaring past on the river below drowned out her words, its life-jacketed passengers whooping and waving as it bounced along the choppy waves.

'We did that a couple of years ago when Sebastian was shooting another movie in town,' said Luke. 'We got a speedboat up to Greenwich and back, then had dinner at The Connaught. It was such an awesome day.'

His voice cracked, and Eve was about to say something consoling when she was interrupted again, this time by a commotion across the pathway. It looked as though a man had knocked into a woman as she left the pub carrying some drinks, and most of a glass of red wine was now spilled down her front. He briefly glanced in their table's direction and Eve gasped.

It was the man who'd shoved Horner down the escalator.

Chapter Thirty-Eight

Eve was sure it was him. She'd only caught a glimpse of his face at the Tube station, but he had the same blond hair, same build. He was also wearing the same coat, hood down this time, and had that same intense stare. Before she could consider the danger of what she was doing, she was on her feet and yelling that Horner was in hospital because of him. People stopped and turned to stare at her, while Luke appeared stunned. Eve then shouted that she was calling the police, but as she fumbled for her phone in her bag the man shot off in the direction of Southwark Cathedral.

'Who is he?' asked Luke, by now also on his feet.

'That's the man who pushed my colleague down the escalator last night,' Eve panted. 'I was there, I saw it. I know it's him.'

Luke reeled. 'Wait, you were there and saw him do it, and the next day he shows up outside a pub where you're having a drink? That's crazy.'

'I have to follow him,' she said, grabbing her bag from the table. 'I need to find out who he is.'

'Who do you think he might be?'

'I don't know.' She stopped short of saying it could be someone connected to the trial, her suspicion that Lees was behind it looming large in her mind. 'It may be someone from The Decorous. Did you recognise him?'

'I've never seen him before. Look, I'll come with you,' said Luke.

They set off in the same direction as the man, but it soon became apparent he'd outpaced them and had already turned off the path somewhere. Frustrated and in pain from her hip, Eve slowed down. 'He's gone.'

'You should call the police and tell them he's been following you, if you're sure it's him,' said Luke.

Eve wanted to say she was, but doubt crept in. 'I think so. He had the same jacket on, same build, same expression.'

She recalled Leah saying over breakfast that it could be someone with an axe to grind against them prosecuting The Seven, and knew she had to call the police. She rang the number she'd called first thing. This time Eve got through to the right department, but the officer who'd given her his card was off duty. She left another message asking him to ring her back.

'What about 999?' asked Luke.

'It's not an emergency,' said Eve.

'Do you think he has something to do with the trial?'

'No, it'll be something else,' she fibbed, suppressing a shudder. She didn't want Luke, a prosecution witness, to be rattled just because she was. 'I should probably get back now. Thanks for coming to meet me, I appreciate it.'

They shook hands, and Eve went to leave first, but Luke put out his hand again to stop her.

'Before you go, I need to say something. What I said about Cal and Brendan . . . I don't want you to think I don't want Cal to be punished at all,' he said plaintively. 'I do. He can't just get off scot-free. I just feel there's an opportunity to educate others at the same time. At least that's what I hope to do.'

Eve wasn't sure anyone involved in Novus would share that sentiment but kept it to herself.

They parted ways, with Luke heading back to London Bridge and Eve to Blackfriars station. On the way there, she decided that instead of going back to Lewisham she'd first catch the Tube to St James's Park, the closest station to Petty France. She wanted to see if Horner had left any clues on his desk about who his contact in Forensics might be. She wasn't expecting it to be as easy as finding a note scrawled with a reminder to ring Bob Smith at Lambeth Road, where the Met's forensic science lab was based, but there might be something else that hinted at who the contact was. After listening to what Luke had to say about the unknown second-in-command member, Eve was keener than ever to find out if the burner device itself could shed any light on its holder's identity.

But as she entered Blackfriars station an image of Horner falling backwards down the escalator ballooned in her mind and she was suddenly overcome with anxiety. It felt as though someone had punched the air from her lungs and she backpedalled out of the station to find a quiet corner to stand in to gulp down breaths. She couldn't quite catch them though, and her chest heaved in panic the more she tried. She was aware of a man approaching her and asking if she was alright, but that made her panic even more. She staggered away from him, hand up to stop him getting any closer, tears wetting her cheeks.

'I'm only trying to help, love,' he said, affronted.

But Eve couldn't see him now. Looming in her vision was the man in the hooded jacket, his arms outstretched, palms facing towards her, ready to push. Eve moaned and flailed her fists to stop him, but the only thing she struck was fresh air, and the vision dissolved as rapidly as it had appeared.

Chapter Thirty-Nine

LUKE

Now

It was Luke's turn to ask for an emergency session with the group. Walking back towards Borough Market, he fired off a message asking if anyone was free to meet right now. The conversation with Eve had unsettled him, and not just because of the way it had ended with her going crazy at that man in the hooded coat. He desperately wanted to discuss what they'd talked about with the others, to see if they had any theories as to why she was so keen to discuss Brendan's swearing-in ceremony. Eve hadn't asked him not to repeat their conversation to anyone else, and he trusted the group to keep it between them.

A growing sense of guilt was also behind his wanting to see them. While he stood by every word he'd said about Cal deserving some understanding, he wasn't immune to Eve's reaction. She hadn't looked impressed. He realised he had to warn the group about what he was planning to say in the witness box and explain his thinking behind it. For all he knew, a couple of them might feel the same but, like him, hadn't felt able to say it aloud.

Waiting for the others to message him back, he clicked on a link Caitlyn Morgan had emailed him a few weeks previously. It took him to one of those photo websites where people post private albums for a selected audience. The album she'd linked to was filled with pictures of Brendan, from babyhood to him having his first official pint in a pub with his dad on his eighteenth birthday. Caitlyn had shared the photos to show Luke that Brendan had been normal and happy before Nye got his hooks into him. Luke closed the album down. He wouldn't show it to the others.

His phone began to ping with confirmations that they were free to meet him. None of them was working, with the exception of Jimi, who did the early commuter shift at an outdoor juice bar near Liverpool Street station. It was poorly paid, Ruby confided in Luke, but since the bombings Jimi hadn't felt comfortable working anywhere indoors, not even in the café.

The next message to arrive was from Samuel, requesting a change of venue. Could the others come to Cynthia's house in Hampstead instead of meeting at the café for once? He was in the middle of doing something related to her films and he thought they might like to see it. Intrigued, Luke said he could and watched the blinking dots that indicated the others were compiling their replies. Within a minute, all the others bar Hilary, still in Scotland, said yes. Samuel replied by sending the address and a request that they arrive at 3 p.m.

Then Luke noticed that Madeleine hadn't responded. It wasn't unusual for her not to reply to a thread about meeting up when she was in LA, but given how upset she was that the last meeting had been derailed by Faye, he thought she might welcome another today. She'd been very drunk when he'd left her at 2 a.m. though, and it occurred to him that she hadn't replied when he had checked in that morning. Maybe she was still in bed sleeping off her hangover, or was in a meeting with her assistant, Gina. But something about the lack of reply bothered him, a fear he couldn't quite shake off. Madeleine was in a bad way, any fool could see that, and her experience in court last week had knocked her mentally. Perhaps he should've stayed last night, instead of putting her to bed then leaving.

He looked up and down the street. A black cab was trundling along the road in his direction, its orange light on. Luke stuck out his hand and the cab braked and swerved towards the kerb.

'Where to, mate?' asked the driver, his window wound down.

'Nottingham Street, Marylebone, please. Fast as you can.'

He wasn't the only person eager to check on Madeleine. When the cab pulled up outside the pizza restaurant below her apartment, Luke spied Gina standing outside the discreet navy door to the side of it, talking into the intercom.

They'd met once before, prior to Madeleine returning to LA after her initial release from hospital. Exiting the cab, Luke reintroduced himself, saying he had been with Madeleine last night when she was drunk, and he was worried about her.

'I am, too,' said Gina. 'She hasn't replied to any of my messages that *Vogue* and *Vanity Fair* are vying to do fronts with her. It's not like her.'

'They want to do what?'

'Put her on the cover. I know, it's amazing. What she said in court about the industry dropping her has really hit home, and now her manager and publicist are fielding all kinds of requests,' said Gina excitedly. 'Plus, you know, she looked great in the purple Dior. This could be the start of her comeback.'

'Is she not answering?' asked Luke, nodding at the intercom.

'No. I've been buzzing for a long time.'

'Do you have a key?'

Gina pulled a face. 'She doesn't like me letting myself in.'

Luke guessed why. Even as he had put Madeleine to bed last night, she'd insisted on waiting until he left the apartment before removing her wig and eye patch to go to sleep.

'I think we might have to if she's not responding.'

'You don't think—?' Gina looked troubled. 'She's said a couple of things recently that have worried me, like, once the trial is over, she wants to disappear for ever. I thought she meant she wanted to leave LA for good, and I thought, well, that's silly—'

'Give me your key,' said Luke firmly.

Gina let him go into the building first. The apartment Madeleine had rented was the only one accessible from the navy door on the street, but at the top of two narrow flights of stairs there was a second, interior door, painted white.

'I don't have the key for this one,' said Gina. 'She usually buzzes me in and it's open by the time I get up here.'

Luke rapped loudly with his knuckles. 'Madeleine? It's me, Luke. I'm here with Gina. Can you let us in?' His voice was so loud that Gina, squashed on the top step with him, winced.

There was no answer.

He knocked again, and this time shouted.

'Madeleine, open the door!'

'Why isn't she responding?' Gina fretted.

Luke didn't dare articulate the fear mounting inside him. Instead, he tried to stay focused on how they could get into the apartment.

'You definitely don't have a key for this door?'

'No. She made me take it off the set when we arrived.'

'Who did you pick up the keys from?'

'The owner, but they live on the other side of London. Hang on, though.' Gina lifted her phone and began frantically scrolling through emails. 'I think there was something about a spare key left downstairs.'

'At the pizza place?'

'Yes—'

Luke didn't wait for her to find the email; he was already running back down the two flights to the exterior door.

The pizza restaurant was called Durazzo. It was busy for the time of day, the lunchtime crowd lingering into the afternoon. The owner was in the back, but one of the waitresses fetched him when Luke asked and, to his relief, he confirmed that he did indeed have a spare key for upstairs.

'Can I borrow it? My friend's not answering the door and I'm worried about her,' said Luke.

'Is this the lady who's been on the news?' asked the heavily accented owner. 'The one who got hurt by the bomb? We have seen her go in and out.'

'Oh my God, you're Sebastian Waghorn's boyfriend!' exclaimed the young waitress. 'Aww, it's so sad what happened to him.' She plucked her phone from her pocket. 'Can I get a selfie?'

Luke flushed red. 'Not right now. Please, I need your help.'

The owner launched into a torrent of Italian that Luke, who had a rudimentary grasp of the language, translated as him berating the waitress 'for bothering the poor man for a stupid photograph'. He then went behind the polished counter where rows of glasses were stacked and, after fishing around in a drawer, found a clutch of keys. He isolated two and handed them to Luke.

'One is for main door, the other for inside. Don't know which.'

'I'll work it out, thank you.'

Luke raced back into the flat and upstairs to let himself and Gina in.

'You go first,' she said nervously.

There was no sign of Madeleine in any of the living spaces, so Luke headed to the bedroom where he'd last seen her when he helped her into bed. The room was still in darkness, thick and heavy black-out drapes blotting out the day. He groped on the wall by the door for the light switch and, as the room came into bright focus, Gina let out a strangled cry of shock.

Madeleine was on her back in bed, mismatched pyjamas covering her body. Her scalp and her face were exposed and they, like her other visible skin, were tinged blue. Luke tried to fight against it, but the empty eye socket and scarred flesh around it made him flinch. Exposed, Madeleine's injuries were far, far worse than he could ever have imagined. How could he not have realised their extent and the trauma she must be enduring every waking moment of every day?

Yet it wasn't being confronted by her boss's injuries that made Gina cry out. 'What's that on her mouth?'

'Vomit,' said Luke grimly. It caked Madeleine's mouth and chin and the sheet she lay on.

'Is she dead?' Gina stuttered.

Luke went over to the bed to check for a pulse, taking it as a good sign that Madeleine's skin was still warm to the touch. Then he felt it, the faint throb beneath his fingertips that told him she was breathing.

'She's alive.' He leaned forward and gently moved her into the recovery position. 'Hey, Madeleine, it's me, Luke,' he said softly. 'Can you hear me? Can you wake up?' She was unresponsive. 'Call an ambulance,' he ordered Gina.

She stared at him helplessly. 'I don't know the number here.'

'It's nine-nine-nine.'

'Shouldn't I call for a private ambulance though? She needs to go somewhere the press won't find her.'

'I don't think private hospitals have ERs in the UK. Plus, even if they did, there isn't time to find one that'll take her. She needs urgent medical attention.'

Gina nodded and dialled the number. As the call connected, Luke watched her finally take in the left side of Madeleine's face.

'I had no idea it was that bad,' she whispered.

'Me neither.'

She turned away then, snapping into practical mode to outline to the operator what the issue was and where the ambulance needed to be sent to.

'No, she's not conscious, but she is breathing. I know she was drinking heavily last night' – Gina shot Luke a look – 'and she's also on pain meds. Yes, medication. She must've mixed the two by mistake.'

Luke let go of Madeleine's hand and went to the side of the bed. There were three pill bottles with their lids off, and he checked the labels; they were heavy-duty pain relief prescribed by a doctor in Los Angeles. All three were almost empty.

He recited the labels to Gina for her to relay to the operator. Moments later she hung up. 'Paramedics should be here within ten minutes.'

Luke gently tried to wipe the vomit from Madeleine's chin with a tissue he plucked from a box beside her bed. 'Madeleine, it's Luke. Please wake up.'

Again, she didn't stir. His insides constricted with dread and he pulled the covers up over her body to keep her warm.

He turned to Gina. 'Do you know how many meds she had left in these bottles? Because they're virtually empty now,' he said.

'I don't know, I can't remember. But she's always careful when she takes them.' Gina's face fell. 'You don't think she took too many on purpose? I mean, she can't have. She's too strong to give up. And there's *Vogue* still . . . *Vanity Fair* . . .' She tailed off and clamped her hand over her mouth to stifle her sobs.

Pierced by guilt, Luke fought back his own tears as his gaze shifted from the empty pill bottles to Madeleine lying prone on the bed. He'd known she was in a bad way after testifying, knew she'd had too much to drink to think rationally, and yet still he selfishly chose last night to leave and clear his own head.

What if he was too late to save her now?

Chapter Forty

EVE

Now

Eve didn't want to go to hospital again, but the Brazilian tourists who scooped her up mid panic attack and gave her an empty paper sandwich bag to breathe into insisted upon it. The two young women hailed a taxi and accompanied her to the A&E department at St Thomas's. But they decided not to linger when they saw the five-hour-plus waiting time being broadcast in the reception area.

Eve swiftly reached the same conclusion. She gave it fifteen minutes until she could be sure the young women would be clear of the hospital grounds, then headed outside herself. She didn't need medical treatment or a second stint in hospital in twenty-four hours, she just needed to go home. Leah could check her over later if she started to feel unwell again.

Heading outside, however, the adrenaline surge triggered by the panic attack began to abate, leaving in its wake shaky limbs and a feeling of utter exhaustion. She stalled for a moment, leaning against a railing for support.

It took a few moments to register that Horner was being treated somewhere in the vast building beside her, and her pulse skipped again. What she'd give to be able to talk to him about what Luke had just shared with her.

Eve stared up at the building, scanning the countless windows and wondering which one Horner was behind. She doubted she could just stroll in to see him, but perhaps she could find out how he was doing while she was there?

Mind made up, she gingerly headed into the main building and went up to the information desk, which was staffed by a young man wearing a face mask. Eve had a disposable one stashed in her bag that she hadn't worn in ages and had to shake off bits of fluff and crumbs before putting it on.

'How can I help?' asked the man. He had friendly eyes, the corners of them crinkling in an otherwise hidden smile.

'I was hoping to check on a patient.'

'Are you a relative?'

'No. I'm a friend.' Not strictly true, but it sounded more genial than 'colleague'.

'Do you know which ward they're in?'

'I don't, sorry. His name is John Horner. He was brought in yesterday evening, and I was admitted to A&E at the same time. My name's Eve Wren.'

The man began to peck away at the keyboard in front of him, then peered at the accompanying screen. 'It says here he's on Sullivan Ward. Visiting hours are between 2 p.m. and 7.30 p.m., so you could go up now, but if there are other visitors already with him it might not be possible to stay.'

Eve hadn't expected it to be as straightforward. 'I can visit now?'

His eyes crinkled again. 'Yes, you can.'

She asked what floor, then thanked him for his help.

'No problem. I hope your friend is better soon.'

Arriving on the ward, Eve's hopes of seeing Horner were dashed by a nurse who told her that he had just been taken downstairs for another scan and she'd have to wait until he was brought back.

'His wife is in the visitors' room if you want to say hello,' the nurse added.

Eve's instinct was to flee – she wasn't sure she had the emotional wherewithal to answer Mrs Horner's questions about what had happened to her husband. But she also knew it would be selfish of her not to. Fighting her reluctance, she followed the nurse's directions to a room at the end of a long corridor and pushed open the door.

Horner's wife was, thankfully, alone. She was staring absently at the TV screen in the corner, which was silently tuned to a rolling news channel broadcasting that hour's headlines. Eve could tell she was one of those women who always looked well put together regardless of how dire the situation, chic in loafers, light blue cropped trousers and a crisp white shirt worn beneath an oatmeal-coloured cardigan with delicate gold chains layered around her neck. Mrs Horner's only concession to scruffiness was her hair, pulled off her face in a low bun and perhaps hastily done, because a thick strand had already escaped the band securing it.

'Mrs Horner?'

It took the woman a moment to realise Eve was addressing her. But when she did her head snapped round so quickly Eve feared she'd given herself whiplash. 'Is there news? Did the CT scan show anything?' She was on her feet before she'd finished her sentence.

'I'm not a doctor, Mrs Horner. I'm Eve Wren, I work with your husband.'

'Oh.'

Never had one tiny word sounded so loaded.

'I don't mean to intrude,' Eve floundered. 'I was nearby, and I thought I'd pop in to see how he was doing. If it's not convenient . . .'

Mrs Horner stared at her for a moment, then smiled. 'That's really kind of you. He'll appreciate you coming. They've told me he'll only be another ten minutes, so you're welcome to wait with me. If the scan's clear, he should be discharged later today.'

'Really? That's great news.'

'Yes, he was lucky.' Mrs Horner reclaimed her seat and patted the one next to her. 'Here, sit down. How are you feeling? John said you took quite a tumble too.'

'Nothing as bad as his,' said Eve. 'I'm fine, really.'

'I'm glad to hear it. Have the police spoken to you yet?'

'No, they haven't. They asked me to call them to arrange to give my statement and I've tried a couple of times, but I can't get through to the right person.'

'An officer came to visit John earlier, and he gave them hell about writing him up in the incident report as drunk.'

'He absolutely wasn't,' confirmed Eve. 'He had one pint of weak ale, so I don't know why the police stated otherwise.'

She had her suspicions though. If Lees was behind the attack, could he have put pressure on the transport police to say Horner was intoxicated?

'We were discussing the Novus case,' Eve then blurted out in a rush, anxious that Mrs Horner had misconstrued their after-hours meeting. 'I'm working out of Lewisham station at the moment, so it was easier to meet there than in the office.'

Mrs Horner smiled again. 'I know, he told me. If John had his way, he'd have every meeting in a pub.'

'I wish I could've stopped him from falling, but I couldn't get up fast enough,' said Eve morosely. 'I'm so sorry, Mrs Horner.'

'Please, call me Lizzy. You mustn't blame yourself,' she said reassuringly. 'You were assaulted too. Have you been to work today?'

'Yes.'

'They should've given you the day off,' said Lizzy reprovingly.

'They offered, but I'm reviewing the unused evidence in the Novus case and I just want to get it done.'

Lizzy rolled her eyes. 'If anything was going to put John in hospital, I'd have put money on it being that bloody trial. His workload has been ridiculous, and he's always stressed because there aren't enough hours in the day to get everything done. I can't wait for it to be over.'

They were interrupted by a nurse coming in to let them know Horner was back in his room. 'The consultant will be round in a bit to let you know the results of the scan,' he added.

Lizzy jumped to her feet. 'Come on, let's go and see how the grumpy sod is doing.'

Eve already liked her a lot.

Horner was sitting in an easy chair beside his bed, wearing a skinny-rib long-sleeved burgundy top and coordinating tartan pyjama trousers, a thick bandage encircling the top of his head. That wasn't why he looked strange to Eve though, and she couldn't put her finger on why until he reached for his glasses and put them on.

'This is a nice surprise,' he said, on seeing Eve walk in alongside his wife. He dismissed her apology for turning up empty-handed when she saw his bedside cabinet was overflowing with cards and chocolate.

'I didn't plan to visit,' she said. 'I had, um, something to do nearby.'

Horner's eyes narrowed. 'That's quite a detour from Lewisham. DCS Strutton messaged me earlier to see how I was, and he said you were there this morning.'

'Change of plan,' said Eve cautiously, uncertain how much she should say in front of Lizzy. 'I had a meeting with someone.'

Lizzy must've caught the frown on her husband's face because she rose to her feet. 'Why don't I leave you two to talk business for a bit while I go downstairs to get us some coffees? Eve, would you like one?'

Eve nodded gratefully. 'A latte would be great, thanks.'

Lizzy touched her husband's hand briefly then strolled away from his bedside, the leather soles of her loafers squeaking like a mouse in distress against the linoleum floor. Horner watched her go, eyes brimming with affection behind the thick lenses of his glasses. Then, remembering Eve was still there, he shrugged bashfully. 'What can I say, my wife is bloody amazing. Twenty-seven years we've been together. I still don't know what I've done to deserve her.'

Eve found Horner's proclamation of love touching. It seemed a million miles away from how she'd felt about Nick.

'How are you doing after yesterday?' he asked her, dragging his gaze from the doorway his wife had just disappeared through.

'My hip's a bit sore, but I'm fine,' she said. Then she paused. 'Do you think we were deliberately targeted because of the trial?'

'By one of Nye's supporters? It's crossed my mind, and I did raise the possibility with the police. We have had some threats sent to the office. But it's been low-level stuff, nothing like what happened to us last night.'

'I think I saw him again.'

Horner looked shocked. 'When?'

'Just now.' She told him about the man being on the river path and how he had scarpered when she spotted him.

'Did you call the police?' asked Horner.

'I tried to get hold of the BTP officer handling our case, but he's not got back to me.'

'I have his mobile number. I'll message him after this and ask him to call you.' He gave her a piercing look. 'Are you sure you're okay?'

'I am now.'

He didn't look convinced but didn't press her for anything further. 'Tell me about this meeting of yours then. I assume it was something to do with the review?'

'Are you sure? I don't want to burden you about work when you should be resting.'

'I'm bored out of my mind already. Tell me everything, but make it quick before Lizzy gets back and tells us to stop.'

'I met with Luke Bishop.'

Horner raised his eyebrows in surprise. 'How did that happen?'

'I called him,' she admitted. 'I wanted to be proactive while we were waiting to hear from your Forensics contact and I was thinking about what you said about Brendan Morgan possibly dumping the phone in the restroom after he released those hostages. So' – she sucked in a deep breath, uncertain what his reaction might be – 'I thought it might speed things up if I just asked those witnesses if they saw Brendan with the Motorola, starting with Luke. I just left him, in fact.' She decided to omit the bit about having a panic attack afterwards and being taken to A&E again.

'Did he remember?'

Eve was relieved Horner didn't seem bothered by her bending the rules.

'No, but he did tell me something interesting about Brendan's swearing-in ceremony when he joined The Decorous.'

She talked, Horner listened, and as she finished Lizzy returned with their coffees.

'Are you two done?'

'We need to call Victoria,' Horner told her. He caught Eve's quizzical look. 'Victoria is a friend of Lizzy's from uni. She's my contact at Lambeth Road. She's a lab technician there. Can you ring her so I can talk to her?' he asked his wife.

Just then, the consultant stalked into the room with a number of junior medics in tow and made a beeline for Horner's bed.

'I'll wait outside,' said Eve.

Horner thought for a second. 'Lizzy, if you give Victoria's number to Eve, she could call her while we talk to the doctor.'

'John, I don't think—'

'Please, love. I wouldn't ask if it wasn't important.'

Lizzy gave in, opening her contacts and bringing up her friend's number.

'You can call her from my phone, but please apologise for the imposition,' she said. 'I wouldn't normally do this without checking with her first.'

Eve nodded and left the ward. She made the call from the corridor outside. Victoria picked up after a few rings and expressed surprise not to be hearing her friend's voice. Eve quickly explained who she was, why she had Lizzy's phone and passed on the apology from Lizzy.

Victoria seemed satisfied by the explanation. 'How's John doing?'

'He seems on the mend. The consultant's with him now and they're hoping he'll be discharged later today.'

'That's great news. Please pass on my best wishes,' said Victoria. 'So, the Motorola. I've checked, and it was examined here, and a partial print was found. I was going to let John know once he was out of hospital.'

Eve's pulse leapt. 'Were there any database matches for the print?'

'No.'

'Not for any of the defendants or the accomplices who died in the bombing?'

'No match for the accused. Alive or otherwise,' said Victoria brusquely. 'Whoever had hold of that phone, it wasn't one of them.'

Chapter Forty-One

Ignoring the pain in her hip and a cry of 'slow down!' from a nurse she nearly collided with, Eve sprinted back to Horner's bedside. He and Lizzy were chatting quietly as she skidded awkwardly to a halt beside them, the consultant and his shadows now with the patient in the next bed.

'It's not any of them,' she blurted out, but she was panting so heavily, having run along the corridor, that it came out in a nonsensical torrent.

'Do you want to take another run at that?' Horner chuckled.

'Victoria said Forensics did find a partial print,' she said again, handing Lizzy her phone back. 'But it wasn't a match for any of The Decorous – not the ones in the dock or the ones who died.'

Horner paled. 'Christ.'

'What's going on?' Lizzy asked her husband.

'CSIs found a pay-as-you-go phone in a waste bin inside the men's toilet at the Novus. It was dismissed as unimportant in the investigation, but Eve worked out someone was using it to text Nye throughout the siege.'

Eve leapt in. 'Every time the two of them traded messages, something else kicked off, like a hostage would be killed or footage would be uploaded to social media,' she explained. 'We assumed it was one of the others, but the print means it can't have been.'

'Victoria's sure there's no match?' Horner asked again.

'Certain. It's none of Nye's known accomplices.'

'You mean someone else was involved and had the phone that night,' breathed Lizzy, her eyes wide with shock.

Horner nodded grimly. 'It looks that way. Someone who must've been inside the theatre that night along with everyone else.' He turned to Eve. 'You were right from the start. Good call.'

Eve batted away the praise, too busy trying to work out who the insider was.

'There were a hundred and twenty guests in attendance, thirty theatre employees and two dozen catering contractors. It could be any one of them, but for all we know the eighth person could've died along with the other victims,' she pointed out.

'Didn't the police look at all possible links between the attendees and The Decorous though?' asked Lizzy.

'Yes, and none came to light,' her husband replied.

'Can you check the attendees' prints?'

'Prints were taken from the deceased during the post-mortems, so we know it can't have been one of them if there's been no match. The survivors weren't asked to provide dabs, however, so the missing accomplice has to be among them,' said Horner.

'What I don't get,' said Eve, 'is why the DO didn't list the discovery of the print on the MG form. It should've been recorded, and it wasn't.'

'It's time we talked to Strutton. He needs to know about this,' said Horner.

'We don't,' said Lizzy sharply. 'You heard what the consultant said. No work for a few days. They're discharging him, but he still needs to take it easy,' she said in an aside to Eve.

'I can still make calls while I'm resting at home, love.'

'No. Let Eve handle it and she can keep you updated.'

'I'm happy to do that.' Eve nodded.

'Fine. I want regular briefings though, I'm still the senior advocate here,' he said officiously, which made his wife's mouth twitch in amusement. 'Once you've spoken to Strutton, we'll let everyone at Petty France know so we can work out how to handle it with the defence. It's a bloody nightmare though. Someone in the investigation team cocked up by failing to disclose the existence of the print, either the officer tasked with getting the forensic results back in the first place or the DO when he incorrectly filled out the MG form. Legally, it's an abuse of process.'

'What does that mean?' Lizzy asked.

'The defence can argue that The Seven are being denied a fair trial because the police have withheld significant evidence that suggests someone yet to be identified was calling the shots with Nye that night – that's the abuse of process. If the judge agrees with them, this trial could be over before it's barely begun.'

Chapter Forty-Two

Eve rang ahead to ensure Strutton was there to meet her when she returned to Lewisham. This was a conversation to be had in person. She kept her tone light during the call, telling him she needed to run something by him.

It was only as the train pulled away from the platform at Blackfriars that Eve realised how bone-achingly fatigued she was. Her eyes stung and her skin felt itchy. She wished she could nap but she was worried she'd miss her stop.

Strutton's reaction was better than she'd feared. They were in Eve's tiny workspace, she in the swivel chair and him leaning against the windowsill, the glass behind him streaked with rain from another downpour. He listened without interruption to Eve's explanation of how she'd stumbled across the burner phone and the steps she and Horner had taken to clarify whether it had been forensically examined, taking care to conceal Victoria's identity as their source.

'Why didn't you just ask me or DS Lees whether Forensics looked at it?' he asked when she'd finished.

'I wanted to be sure I wasn't reading more into it. John wasn't as convinced as I was by the timing of the texts. Also,' Eve took a deep breath, 'I wasn't sure I could trust DS Lees to bring this straight to him.'

'Why not?' asked Strutton sharply.

Her voice faltering, Eve told him how Lees had given her the message to meet Horner, setting them up as a prank. 'If he hadn't done that, John would've gone home to his family as usual, and we wouldn't have been anywhere near that escalator—'

Strutton reacted fiercely. 'That's out of order. I know Gary can be a bit of a dick sometimes, but you can't blame him for what happened.'

'I'm just telling you why I was reluctant to involve him,' she said flatly.

Strutton put his hands on his waist and dug his fingers in like he was trying to ease a stitch. 'I don't know where to start with this. I mean, what you're saying, if what you think is true—' He broke off and his fingers dug deeper.

'It's all true,' said Eve. 'Did you really not know about the print?'

'No, I had no idea. The phone wasn't found until some weeks after the bombing because those toilets were pretty much flattened by the first explosion. I did know Forensics looked at it when it was recovered, but I was told they'd come up blank and there was nothing of note in the data recovered from it.'

'Didn't the fact it was found inside a waste bin seem suspicious?'

'Not necessarily. In a blast like that, stuff gets thrown everywhere. We found all sorts of things in odd places. It could've been inside the bin before the explosion, or it could have ended up there.' Strutton sighed frustratedly. 'The data on it didn't merit being disclosed in court because there was nothing relevant to the investigation.'

'Except you didn't look at the data yourself, did you? You took someone else's word for it that it wasn't worth pursuing.' Eve rifled on her desk for the document she'd made that matched the time-stamps of the texts to the timeline of the siege. She handed it to him. 'This is why I thought it was relevant when I checked the data on Cellebrite.'

Strutton's face was impassive as he began to read but by the time he'd reached the last text, it had flushed to the shade of a poppy in bloom. She waited until he raised his eyes to meet hers.

'Which officer entered the phone into evidence?' she asked.

'I don't remember,' said Strutton, but she could see that was a lie. 'There were thousands of pieces of evidence we had to sift through. I can't remember who handled every piece.'

'As far as John and I am concerned, a phone recovered from a bin, when every guest had theirs taken from them at the beginning of the event and stashed in a security pouch, warranted further investigation.'

Strutton's face mottled further. 'Where are you going with this, Eve?'

'Our contact in Forensics confirmed an hour ago that the partial print doesn't match any of The Decorous on trial, or any of The Decorous killed alongside the guests and employees when the bombs went off.'

Strutton's face contorted. 'That can't be right.'

'It is, we've checked. Patrick Nye was trading messages throughout the siege with whoever had hold of this phone, but it wasn't any of his known accomplices. Do you understand what I'm saying, DCS Strutton?' asked Eve, as he stared blankly at her. 'The print doesn't match any of Nye's followers inside the Novus that night, which means someone else there was helping him. We don't know who they are yet, but it's pretty obvious they should be on trial with The Seven as well.'

Chapter Forty-Three

FAYE

Now

Stepping into Dame Cynthia's home on the edge of Hampstead Heath was like stepping into a hug. Every furnishing was stuffed and cosy, every surface adorned with knick-knacks and souvenirs accumulated over a lifetime that had spanned nearly ten decades and two continents. There were a lot of rooms to fill inside the four-storey house, but Cynthia had managed it. Yet to Faye it never felt cluttered. It was a house that was tangled and chaotic yet restful and comforting. Even the wallpaper was velvety to the touch. It felt like a home.

That was not how Faye found it that morning, however. From the moment Samuel opened the front door it was evident that significant changes had been made to the interior since she was last there. Peering over his shoulder into the flagstone-floored entrance hall as she went to greet him, she saw that the long console table and bench seat previously pushed against one wall had both disappeared, along with the ornate mirror and two Old Masters replicas that had hung above them. The walls themselves had been stripped to bare plaster.

'What's going on?' she asked, stepping fully inside as Samuel shut the front door behind her with a dull thud. 'Is Matthew redecorating?'

'I'm afraid so,' said Samuel balefully. 'He's having the entire house painted white from top to bottom before it goes on the market. He thinks he'll get higher offers if the decor is more neutral and minimalist.'

How much more money does one man need? thought Faye incredulously. The media had estimated Cynthia's net worth as £25 million, even without taking the Hampstead house into account. Faye didn't know if that figure was correct, but she suspected it wasn't far off. Matthew had inherited the entire estate on top of the trust fund he'd already received from his late parents on turning twenty-one.

The rooms leading from the entrance hall had been similarly pillaged of furnishings and features, while the staircase was covered in dust sheets. It upset Faye greatly to see Cynthia's home stripped back to nothing. There was ugliness in its bareness now, any sense of warmth brutally displaced.

'Has he put everything into storage?' she asked.

'No. It's all going to auction.' Samuel caught Faye's expression. 'I know, I feel the same. But it belongs to Matthew now, it's up to him what he does with it.'

'When you say all, do you mean her awards?' Cynthia's Oscars were displayed in a glass cabinet in a screening room in the basement of the property, along with the myriad of other acting trophies she'd received over the decades.

'No, he's keeping those. Same with her costumes, which is why I'm so glad you're here to help me with them, my dear.'

Matthew hanging on to his grandmother's awards was something, Faye supposed, but it did little to quell her upset at his stripping the house back. She followed Samuel along the sweeping hall and into the kitchen. She'd sought and found solace inside

Cynthia's home many times since she and the children had settled permanently back in London after the divorce, even staying here alone at her friend's behest when Richard had flown in from LA to spend time with Olivia and Freddy at the Dulwich address for convenience.

'Lunch is laid out in the breakfast room,' said Samuel as he gingerly crossed the kitchen. From his awkward gait, Faye wondered if he was in pain.

She was taken aback to see the extended table in the breakfast room heaving with platters of food. She counted eight different types of salad and three cheese boards, along with an array of cold cuts and six batons of crusty French bread that filled the room with a delicious fresh-baked smell.

'I think you might have overestimated my appetite, Samuel,' she said with a laugh. 'There's so much food here.'

'Ah, yes, about that. It's not all for us. The others are coming as well.'

Faye was rooted to the spot. 'The others?'

'The support group. We were due to meet later, but I realised it was going to be tricky for me to get to Stepney with Roddy out for the day. So I asked everyone to come here instead. The plan is for you and me to look through Cynthia's outfits, then after the others arrive we can show them what you've curated while we have a late lunch. I thought it would be nice for us to do something uplifting for a change.'

Faye's heart sank. Had she known this was Samuel's intention she would never have agreed to come.

'I didn't think you'd mind,' he said. 'Didn't Richard mention it? I did say to.'

Richard was still sulking and hadn't responded when Faye had told him she was going out, much less inquire where to. 'No, he didn't.'

'Are you hungry now? We can eat if you are. I'm sure the others won't mind if we start before them.'

Faye's appetite had deserted her, replaced by a leaden sense of dread. 'I'm fine to wait.'

'In that case, shall we go straight up to Cynthia's dressing room—' Samuel paused. 'Was that the front door?'

It did indeed sound like someone had just let themselves in. Faye tensed. 'Is it Matthew?'

'It can't be, he's in Sweden. It must be Roddy. I wonder why he's back so early.'

It was Roddy, back from court. He must have heard their voices and came straight to the breakfast room, his thick-soled ankle boots clunking against the flagstones on his approach. Faye had never seen him on his day off before and it was odd to see him dressed casually, in jeans, shirt and a blazer. Cynthia had always insisted he wore a carer's uniform while on duty. Teal, her favourite colour. Roddy acknowledged Faye's presence with a nod, and she felt her cheeks burn.

'I thought you were going to be out all day,' remarked Samuel.

'I got bored. They kept sending the jury out. One of the prosecution lawyers fell down a Tube escalator yesterday and is in hospital and the defence was arguing they shouldn't proceed without him,' said Roddy, his Danish accent more pronounced than Faye ever remembered.

'That's awful,' she exclaimed, her awkwardness at seeing Roddy evaporating. 'Is he seriously injured?'

'They didn't tell us. I suppose it's no one else's business.'

He stared at her unflinchingly. In that moment she wasn't sure she'd ever disliked anyone more in her life.

The three of them jumped when the doorbell rang. Samuel frowned. 'It's a bit early for the others and I'm not expecting anyone else.'

'Shall I get it?' offered Faye, desperate to step away from Roddy's laser-like stare.

'No bother, I'll go. I need to keep active,' said Samuel, and off he went in a slightly lopsided shuffle.

That left just the two of them. Faye couldn't hold back a second longer.

'I can't go on pretending. We have to say something,' she hissed, keeping her voice low so it didn't carry.

'Say what, exactly?' Roddy challenged her. 'And to who?'

'The police. We need to tell them what we know.'

A fissure appeared in Roddy's calm exterior. 'Are you mad?' he said, frowning. 'We can't do that.'

'Are you worried about keeping your job, is that it? You walked into this one; you'll walk into another,' said Faye dismissively.

She'd heard the story about how Roddy came to work at the house a hundred times, because Cynthia had found it all so serendipitous and had loved to repeat in company. The same day her previous carer's visa was unaccountably revoked and she was given notice to return to Latvia, Samuel was in a bakery in Hampstead Village when he overheard a pleasant-looking man with blond hair lamenting to someone on the phone that his current contract as a private carer was coming to an end and he needed to find a new position. Samuel had waited until Roddy hung up then struck up a conversation that resulted in the two men travelling back to Greenhill Gardens to meet Cynthia. She had offered Roddy a job on the spot.

'I won't be getting any jobs if I'm convicted of perverting the course of justice,' said Roddy. 'That's the minimum they'll charge us with for keeping quiet for this long.'

Faye's eyes filled with tears. It was the threat of going to prison that had assured her silence this past year.

'The time to say something was April last year,' Roddy added darkly. 'But you didn't because you put yourself first.'

'I put my children first,' Faye cried. 'They needed both their parents.'

Roddy took a step closer towards her and Faye shrank back. He intimidated her as much now as he had that night.

'They still need you, don't they? Because if you tell—'

His sentence was punctuated prematurely by Samuel returning to the breakfast room. He wasn't alone. With him was a tall, angular man with a pinched face. He nodded curtly to Roddy, who introduced him to Faye as Horatio, the Novus assistant manager who'd set up their survivors' group. Also with them was a young woman Samuel introduced as Annie, but she paid no heed to Faye, who was blinking back tears, because she was too busy shedding her own into a scrunched-up tissue. Faye turned to Samuel and saw he too had tears streaking his cheeks.

'What's happened?' she asked him, alarmed.

'Madeleine's in hospital,' he said despairingly. 'She overdosed last night. Luke found her this morning and managed to call for help, but it's touch and go.'

'She tried to kill herself?' asked Faye, aghast.

'I don't think she could cope any longer,' said Horatio. 'Her injuries, the memories of what happened – it's been a living death for her.'

His comment hit Faye like a stinging blow to the head and she started to shake violently. She had to say something. It was time.

But before she could, Roddy grabbed her hand and pulled her from the room, telling the others they'd give them a minute alone to talk. Outside in the hallway, he flung Faye round to face him so forcibly she almost toppled over. 'If you say something we're both done for,' he said, his voice laced with panic.

'Forty-four,' Faye whimpered back at him. 'Forty-four.'

'What are you talking about?'

She grabbed him by the lapels. 'If Madeleine dies, that'll be the forty-fourth death we're partly responsible for. Forty-four deaths we might've been able to prevent but didn't.'

Chapter Forty-Four

FAYE

Then

21 April, 4.07 a.m.

Dame Cynthia Seymour passed away in the early hours when the auditorium was at its quietest. Nye had relented and allowed the hostages to lie down to rest, where they generally oscillated between fitful sleep or motionless stupor. Only his followers remained alert, taking it in turns to stand guard over the groups and escort those who needed the toilet to the makeshift restroom in the centre of the auditorium.

It wasn't until Millie had returned from a break to resume her watch that Cynthia's demise was noticed. Faye had drifted off and hadn't witnessed the slowing of Cynthia's breathing as she lay beside her.

'The old lady's dead,' Millie announced loudly, rousing the group as one.

Faye, befuddled by sleep, asked her what she meant.

'Exactly what I said. The old lady's dead. Look.' Millie reached down and gently shook Cynthia's arm. The motion caused the old woman to flop on to her back, making it indisputably obvious she was dead.

Faye covered her mouth in shock. How could Cynthia have died right next to her, and she hadn't noticed?

She went to turn to Matthew, but he wasn't in his spot on the other side of his grandmother. Roddy was nowhere to be seen either.

'The two men that were with her, where are they?' she asked. 'One's her grandson.'

'Loo, probably,' said Millie. 'Right. We need to move her. She can't stay there. When someone dies all sorts of shit gets released, and I'm not clearing it up.'

'Move her where?' asked the male guest who'd earlier given Liberty his dinner jacket.

'I don't know. But she's not staying here.'

Millie's proclamation of Cynthia's death caused a ripple effect around the room. Faye could hear people breaking down as word spread. Cynthia had been the reason they'd gathered here tonight. What was meant to be a celebration of her life had killed her.

Faye felt a hand on her shoulder and looked round to find Roddy behind her. 'She's gone,' she said, breaking down herself.

'I know, it happened just as I was getting up to use the bathroom. She didn't suffer, it was very peaceful,' he said.

Despite her distress, Faye was hit by a lucid thought: Roddy had watched Cynthia take her last breath then gone to the toilet before bothering to tell anyone else? Who did that? She looked at him, bewildered.

'Was Matthew with you?' she asked. 'I don't know where he is.'

'He, um . . . yes. In the queue.'

She assumed he meant for the toilet. Did that mean Matthew also knew his grandmother had died but didn't say anything? Roddy she could just about understand – Cynthia was his employer, not a loved one – but Matthew behaving indifferently to her death made no sense. Then again, maybe he was in shock.

'They want to move her,' said Faye, as she was forced to step aside to let some of the other captors join Millie in standing over Cynthia's body. The tone of their chatter was upbeat, and it infuriated her. 'We can't let them do that until Matthew's seen her.'

Roddy nodded. 'I agree.'

Without any thought to his personal space and how he might react, Faye buried herself against Roddy's side and began to sob. She desperately needed to be comforted, for someone to hug her and tell her everything was going to be okay and that she would see Olivia and Freddy again. After a few awkward moments, Roddy raised his arm and placed it high around her shoulders.

Then something odd occurred. As she cried, something vibrated against her leg. Twice. She raised her head, tears streaking her cheeks – only for it to happen again. A vibration against her leg, two times. Stunned, she pulled herself away from Roddy, who by the look on his face knew exactly why. Very quickly he raised a finger to his lips then mouthed, 'Be quiet.'

'You have a phone on you,' she mouthed back silently, unable to hide her shock. 'How?'

'It's not mine. It's Matthew's. He slipped it to me in the toilet,' he mouthed back.

Faye was astounded. All this time, Matthew had a phone in his possession, and he'd done nothing to help them? Done nothing to help his grandmother?

'Why hasn't he called the police?' she mouthed.

Roddy shrugged helplessly, eyes flickering towards the followers standing over Cynthia's body. None of them had noticed their silent conversation because they were too busy debating what to do with it. Millie wanted it moved. The others didn't want to touch it.

'You call them then,' Faye silently urged.

'The phone is locked. I don't know the PIN.'

Faye stared at him, incredulous. Then she held her palm out. 'Give it to me.'

'I can't. Matthew won't like that.'

Faye almost let out a squeak as she exclaimed noiselessly, 'I don't care what he thinks. We need to call for help. People are dying in here.'

'If we try to use it, he'll go mad.'

'But why?' Faye's jaw dropped as he stared at her plaintively. 'No way. You don't think Matthew—'

'The rest of us had to give up our phones,' Roddy mouthed frantically. 'Why does he still have one unless they let him keep it because he's in on it?'

Disbelievingly, Faye shook her head. 'No, Matthew can't be involved. Look, just give it to me—'

Roddy reached into his pocket and Faye's spirits lifted, thinking she'd convinced him to hand it over. Instead, he fiddled with it for a moment.

'What are you doing?' she angrily mouthed.

'Turning it off. If they hear it' – Roddy jerked his head towards their captors – 'they'll kill us.'

Faye opened her mouth to protest but was cut short by Matthew's return. He was escorted by the youngest of Nye's accomplices, the teenage boy. On seeing his grandmother surrounded, Matthew demanded to know what was going on.

'She died,' said Nye, who had also suddenly materialised. 'It must've been from the stroke.' Then, to Faye's surprise, he added, 'Sorry for your loss.'

Matthew acted as though he hadn't heard him, barrelling past everyone and pushing through the circle to reach his grandmother's body. Dropping to his knees beside her, he let out a low, guttural wail that ricocheted through the auditorium, prompting an audible fresh wave of collective grief. Faye didn't join in though. She couldn't. She was too confused. Matthew's reaction now, distraught as he knelt over Cynthia's body, didn't align with him having a phone that he could've tried to use at any point to summon help. Faye knew it might've been risky to try where they were sitting, but he could've tried to use it in the makeshift restroom. Instead, he had given it to Roddy. Why?

With Nye and his followers preoccupied with watching Matthew and the noise building in the auditorium as the other guests cried with him, Roddy pulled Faye to one side.

'I know how we can get out of here,' he whispered. 'When I was waiting in the green room while you were being seated for dinner, I saw an emergency exit at the end of the corridor. If I create a diversion, you could make a run for it and call for help.'

'Me? That's crazy. I can't run.'

'Walk fast then. I'll think of something to give you plenty of time.'

'Why me?'

'Because they're less likely to notice you've gone.'

Faye bristled. 'Because I'm a middle-aged woman?'

'No, because I stand out in this ridiculous uniform,' he said. 'It's better if it's you.'

'I can't.'

'Why not?' Roddy whispered angrily. 'Don't you want to get out of here?'

'Of course. But what about Richard? I can't just leave him here.'

Roddy scoffed. 'You honestly care what happens to your ex after the way he's treated you?'

'He's the father of my children,' she whimpered. 'I don't expect you to understand.'

'You're right, I don't.' He sighed frustratedly. 'Okay. What if I found a way to get you both out? Would you try then?'

'But how can we possibly make a run for it? They have guns and knives. We'll never make it. Just use the phone.'

'I've told you, it's too risky.'

'But me making a run for it isn't?'

Roddy looked down at Matthew, still sobbing over Cynthia's body.

'We have to try something. If we don't, we'll all end up dead like her.'

Chapter Forty-Five

EVE

Now

Strutton wheeled through an encyclopaedia's worth of excuses to try to justify how the partial print had ended up on the burner phone. A mistake in the lab. Cross-contamination. A guest had handled it. Anything to detract from the obvious: evidence existed that someone previously not identified as one of The Decorous was working for Nye from inside the theatre, and Strutton and his team had failed to identify that fact.

Eventually he ran out of steam. He stopped pacing the room and slumped heavily against the wall for support, sliding his back down until he was sitting on his haunches. Eve took his expression of defeat as her cue to speak.

'Which officer entered the phone into evidence?' she asked. 'I'm not talking about the DO, I'm talking about the detective you assigned to investigate it once it was recovered by the CSIs.'

Strutton couldn't meet her stare.

'I get you want to protect a colleague,' she said. 'I can understand that—'

'Can you?' Strutton snapped. 'You didn't understand when it was your colleague making the mistake. You went over his head.'

'My colleague's actions could've resulted in a wrongful conviction for his client,' she said. 'I couldn't stay quiet. And neither should you. It's our duty.'

Eve's heated retort did the trick and a heartbeat later Strutton confirmed what she'd been suspecting the moment he'd stopped meeting her eye.

'It was DS Lees,' he said heavily, his face masked in misery. First his DO, now his OIC. Their mistakes were his now. 'He dealt with the phone. He was the one who told me there was nothing of note in the texts.'

'Do you think it's possible he failed to flag the print on purpose?'

'No, I bloody well don't. It was an oversight, because he was swamped with too much work and knackered from pulling double shifts. Whatever you think of Gary, he's a good copper.'

'There is another possible explanation,' said Eve, aware how incendiary her next comment would be, but knowing she had to still say it. 'DS Lees could be a Decorous sympathiser. No, wait, hear me out,' she said, as Strutton threw up his hands in anger. 'He wouldn't be the first officer to get caught up in a movement he was investigating, and he could've decided not to enter the phone into evidence to help this eighth person elude justice.'

Strutton was appalled. 'No. Christ, no. That's not Gary. You're barking up the wrong tree. This was an oversight, nothing more.'

He peeled himself off the floor and paced the room again, his bulk filling the tiny space, hemming Eve in behind her desk.

'We'd have known if there was someone else involved. We examined every aspect of their lives going back years – especially Nye – including who they associated with. We cross-matched them against everyone else inside the Novus that night and there were no links. The ones in the dock and the ones who died are the only ones responsible.'

'But you don't know where Nye had been for twenty years, so you can't be certain you traced everyone he was associating with. We can't ignore the fingerprint either,' said Eve matter-of-factly. 'It shows there's another accomplice still at large and there should be eight in that dock.'

Strutton stopped his pacing. He was right beside Eve's chair now, his legs almost touching hers. Her impulse was to recoil, but she was impeded by her desk and panic began to climb up her throat.

'I know,' he said. 'I'm not arguing with you.'

Her mind flooded with images of Horner falling, Eve couldn't speak. Strutton was too close . . . She couldn't get away from him . . .

He suddenly noticed her discomfort and stepped back. 'Are you okay?'

Eve exhaled shakily. 'I – I'm just . . . yes, I'm fine.' She hid her distress by making a show of straightening the pile of documents on her desk. 'Oversight or not, this needs to be investigated further. We are also obligated to let The Seven's defence team know.'

'Can you give me some time before you do that?' Strutton pleaded. 'I want to personally go over everything relating to this, including looking into the device that Nye was using to text the burner phone. That one was never recovered.'

Eve was torn. She wanted to be accommodating and allow Strutton to make his own checks, but she didn't feel it was her place to say yes. 'I'll have to talk to John Horner,' she said. 'I can't make that decision alone.'

'I thought he was in hospital?'

'He is, but I'm still reporting to him.'

'Fine. Call him now. And while you're doing that, I'll start double-checking everything my end.'

That felt like a decent compromise, so Eve agreed. In the meantime, she could get on with the review. There weren't many boxes left to go through and her initial checks indicated they mostly contained admin documents relating to the investigation, such as invoices and delivery notes. She wasn't expecting to find anything as remotely contentious as the burner phone data.

'Who else at the CPS knows about this?' Strutton asked.

'So far just me and Horner.'

'What about your contact in Forensics?'

'They were simply asked to clarify the results. As far as they're aware they didn't tell us anything we didn't already know,' said Eve.

'Have you thought about what this is going to mean for the trial? The judge could rule our failure to investigate and disclose means it can't continue,' said Strutton, his voice tightening. 'The defence could make an application to have it tossed out. We'd obviously push for a retrial, but the victims' families and survivors are going to be devastated to have to go through it twice. Can you live with that?'

Eve didn't like where Strutton was going with this.

'I'm aware of the implications, but that's the nature of disclosure in our legal system. "Fair disclosure to the accused is an inseparable part of a fair trial,"' she said, quoting the Attorney General's guidelines on disclosure in criminal proceedings. 'Like it or not, the defence needs to know about this, and soon.'

'It changes nothing as far as Patrick Nye and the others are concerned,' he pointed out. 'They still did what they did.'

'That shouldn't mean the mystery texter gets to go unpunished.'

'We could just leave it in the unused pile.'

Eve stared at the detective in open-mouthed disbelief. 'You're not actually serious? We can't wilfully ignore evidence like this.'

When he didn't answer she grew even more alarmed. 'Is that what you're asking me to do, DCS Strutton? Ignore what I've found? I'm sorry, but we both know I can't. I have a professional responsibility to make sure this line of inquiry is now properly investigated. I can't believe I need to spell that out to an officer of your rank.'

'Of course you don't,' said Strutton, unconvincingly. 'But do I want to risk Nye getting off? No, I don't. It infuriates me that we'll be handing him a get-out clause on a silver platter.'

'We don't know that. Even if the defence makes an application to dismiss, there's a good chance the judge will decide the mountains of other evidence still make the trial viable,' said Eve. 'Or he'll agree to a retrial.'

'Your faith is touching, but I don't share it. From day one Nye has milked being the mastermind of Novus, and now he might get away with mass murder on a technicality.'

'It's a bit more than a technicality though,' said Eve. 'A person involved in killing forty-three people is still out there and for all we know could be planning another attack. You want to risk that happening? I don't.'

They both knew he couldn't argue against that logic. Seconds later he confirmed it by wordlessly leaving her office and slamming the door behind him.

Chapter Forty-Six

LUKE

Now

Luke was lost. Paddington wasn't an area of London he knew at all, and in the hour he'd been wandering around aimlessly since leaving Madeleine's bedside at St Mary's he'd lost his bearings entirely. He'd walked down the street he was on at least three times already, yet he couldn't bring himself to turn on his phone to check where he was. He didn't want to be deluged by messages and missed calls from people scrabbling for news. Just thinking about it stressed him out even more.

The news wasn't all bad though. Madeleine was, by some miracle, clinging to life. The doctor treating her believed she hadn't ingested any tablets until late that morning, not too long before Luke and Gina had found her. The medical school of thought was that Madeleine had awoken in pain and taken a few pills, not realising how much alcohol was still in her bloodstream. This had brought Luke some comfort, and Gina relief; an accidental overdose due to the pain of her injuries made for far better headlines than Madeleine deliberately trying to take her own life.

The damage the drugs had done to Madeleine's organs remained to be seen, however. The doctor told Luke and Gina that an opiate overdose of the kind she had suffered had slowed her breathing until the lack of oxygen put her body into a state called cyanosis, when it started to turn blue. Her heart and lungs were also affected by the diminished oxygen supply, which was why Madeleine was now on a ventilator to help her breathe. All they could do now was wait to see if she was strong enough to pull through.

Luke reached the corner of the street and a maze-like garden called Norfolk Square. It was the sort of old-school London setting that Sebastian had loved, with tall white stucco buildings that back in the day had been filled with aristocrats and servants. Luke found a seat on a bench inside the garden, close to the giant chessboard, then pulled out his phone. He couldn't ignore people for ever. As he began to scroll through his messages, he saw that everyone in the survivors' group was frantic for news and he felt bad for leaving them hanging.

He sent a response detailing Madeleine's condition. Then he noticed Richard's ex-wife, Faye, had sent him a message too. He was surprised; he wasn't aware she even had his number.

> *I need to talk to you urgently about Matthew Seymour. Please don't tell the others. Best, Faye.*

Luke frowned. Why would she want to talk to him about Matthew? And why couldn't the others know?

> *Of course*, he messaged back. *I'm free now if you want to call me.*

He watched as the little dots blinked to indicate Faye was responding immediately to his reply.

Can you come to Cynthia's house in Hampstead? We're all here now with Samuel. F.

The thought of going to Hampstead drained Luke of his last drop of energy. He couldn't face talking to anyone right now, not even his friends. He just wanted to go home, curl up and go to sleep.

Before he could make up an excuse not to go, more dots appeared.

Please come. F.

Luke toyed with ignoring her, but he couldn't bring himself to. Faye reaching out to him, someone she barely knew, suggested that whatever she wanted to talk to him about must be serious. He couldn't imagine what though. With a sigh, he typed out a reply.

On my way.

The atmosphere at Cynthia's house was already too funereal for Luke's liking and it put him on edge the moment he walked through the door. For reasons Luke didn't have the energy to query, Samuel had decided to cater for the meeting as though he was expecting dozens more people to arrive. Luke's appetite remained resolutely suppressed despite the table heaving with platters of food and the fact he couldn't remember the last time he'd eaten anything. It was well before he had met Eve Wren on the South Bank yesterday, which already felt like a lifetime ago.

Samuel did insist he have something to drink though. Between sips of sweet tea, Luke expanded on the text he'd sent updating them on Madeleine's condition. He also told them about how he and Gina had come to find her. Jimi sat close to him as he talked, a sign he was struggling with his emotions. When he was really low, Jimi craved physical proximity and Luke was his chosen ballast. Normally Luke didn't mind, but today it felt smothering. He scraped his chair sideways to put some space between them, only for Jimi to move his closer again.

As he talked, Luke kept glancing towards Faye. She hadn't acknowledged his arrival at the house in a way that suggested she needed to talk to him urgently, but now, as their eyes met sporadically across the kitchen, he could see she was worked up about something. He assumed she'd wait until they were alone to talk to him, but he couldn't see how they'd manage to escape the others.

'When will the doctors know if Madeleine's out of the woods?' asked Horatio, who was still wearing his jacket indoors and standing stiffly at the side of the room.

'They're hoping later today. They flushed the drugs out of her system and now it's a case of seeing if there's any lasting damage,' he said. 'Gina wants to have her flown back to the States for treatment, but I said it might be too risky. Hopefully the doctors agree.'

'That's a decision for Madeleine's family to make, not Gina,' said Horatio crossly.

Luke shrugged. 'I'm not sure her parents give a damn. We called them, and they were pretty disinterested.'

'Poor Madeleine,' said Samuel, who looked to Luke like he'd aged another decade since he'd last seen him, the curve of his shoulders more pronounced and his hands continuously trembling, even though they were clasped together in his lap. 'When will we be able to visit her?'

'I don't know. Gina said she'd keep me updated.'

'You've been up all night and look worn out, dear boy. Would you like to take a nap?' asked Samuel. 'There are plenty of spare beds.'

'I'm fine.' Then Luke caught Faye's gaze again and the unspoken plea behind it. 'But I could do with freshening up. Would it be an imposition to take a shower? I'd love to wash the hospital smell off me.'

'Of course it wouldn't,' said Samuel. 'You can use the guest room on the second floor, it has a lovely en suite. It's the door on the left as you go up the stairs. There are fresh towels laid out.'

'Thanks.' Getting to his feet, Luke asked Samuel why he'd asked for everyone to come to Hampstead instead of going to Ruby's.

'A design museum in Los Angeles wants to do an exhibition on Cynthia's film costumes, and there are quite a few things here at the house. Faye's kindly going to help me curate them and I thought it might be nice if, for a change, we did something uplifting as a group. I was going to show you all the costumes before we pack them up.'

Luke was touched by the old man's sentiment. 'That's a lovely idea, Samuel. Let me freshen up, then I'll be ready for the fashion show. I mean, I'm assuming someone's going to be modelling the costumes, right?'

He affected a twirl and laughter broke out, lifting the room's oppressive mood. The one person who didn't join in, Luke noted as he left the room, was Faye.

◆ ◆ ◆

Ten minutes later, freshly showered, he was buttoning his shirt when he heard a knock on the guest-room door. He wasn't in the least bit surprised to find Faye on the other side. She darted inside without waiting to be invited and closed the door behind her. But he was shocked when she deadbolted it too.

'What's this about, Faye?'

She raised her finger to her lips then gestured for him to follow her into the bathroom, which was still fogged from his shower. Puzzled, Luke did as she asked. Again, she shut and locked the door behind them. Then she reached into the shower cubicle and turned the water back on.

'This is a little much, don't you think?' said Luke, bemused.

'Keep your voice down. I don't want anyone listening.'

Luke didn't think there was much chance of that behind two locked doors and the hiss of the shower drowning out all other sound, but he decided to humour her.

'Okay, so what's all this cloak and dagger got to do with Matthew?' he asked.

'It's about what he did during the siege. Do you remember seeing him when you escaped?'

Luke floundered, taken aback by the question and its echoes of what Eve Wren from the CPS had asked him about Brendan Morgan. 'What do you mean?'

'I mean his behaviour, how he was acting,' whispered Faye impatiently, as though Luke was being deliberately dense.

'I – I don't remember. What are you saying he did?'

Faye's eyes filled with tears. She began to shake. Luke realised she was scared witless, and it shocked him to see.

'I should've said something at the time,' she cried, 'but I didn't because I wouldn't have got out of that building, and I had to, I had to for my kids—'

'Faye, just tell me what he did.'

'Matthew had a phone on him the entire time,' she said hoarsely.

Luke's stomach flipped. 'He what?'

'He had a phone. He could've called for help the moment the siege started, but he didn't.'

'You knew this?'

'Not at first. It was after Cynthia died that I found out.'

Faye's tears gave way to heaving sobs and Luke was suddenly grateful for the shower being on to drown them out.

'Cynthia died long before the siege ended though,' he said.

'I know. I feel so guilty because I should've said something, and then when the bombs went off—' Releasing another sob, she grabbed Luke's shoulders, digging with her fingers. 'You have to believe me. I thought that if I said anything and Nye found out about the phone, he'd kill us all. So I kept quiet and made a run for it instead. I need to know, Luke, is that why you escaped as well? Did you know about the phone too?'

Luke's mind was reeling. How could Matthew have had a phone on him the entire time and not raised the alarm?

'Did you know?' Faye pressed again.

'No, I didn't,' he stuttered. Dizzy with shock, he pulled away to lean against the sink unit for support, his legs barely keeping him upright. 'How could you have known all this time and not said anything?'

'I know it was selfish, but I was only thinking about my children and getting to safety so I could see them again. Nye knew where we lived, he threatened to send people after Olivia and Freddy if I said anything.'

Her excuses repulsed him. Did she really expect him to make her feel better about her decision not to say anything? Matthew could've used the phone at any point to call for help. He did nothing. And then Faye did nothing and people died because of it.

Sebastian was killed because of it.

'Why are you telling me this now?' he yelled, not caring if he was heard.

Stricken, she flapped her hands as though to shush him. 'I keep going over and over why Matthew had the phone on him, and I keep coming back to the same thing,' she said. 'I think he was in on it. I think he knew the siege was going to happen and that's why he did nothing to stop it.'

Chapter Forty-Seven

FAYE

THEN

21 April, 10.14 a.m.

Six hours had dragged by since Faye had discovered Matthew had kept hold of his phone, and her anger had built to the point that she could barely contain it. She wanted to call him out in front of everyone, but Roddy had counselled her that she'd wreck their chances of getting out if she did. If she provoked a scene with Matthew, Nye and his men would want to know what it was about, or worse still, they'd punish her for it. It was better to say nothing and focus on trying to escape.

Faye thought Roddy was crazy to think they could make a run for it and not be spotted. Nye was watching the hostages like a hawk from the stage. He'd stepped down briefly when Cynthia died and again when a woman had a panic attack that triggered a Mexican wave of hysterical crying in her group – he'd struck the woman hard across the face with the back of his hand to shut her up and ordered his followers to do the same to anyone else crying.

The rest of the time he'd remained on his perch though, silently observing the room.

Roddy was sitting next to Faye on the floor. He was murmuring under his breath to a male guest slumped on the other side of him. The man, in his fifties, had his head in his hands. The whispering scared her because she knew it might set their captors off. She couldn't hear what Roddy was saying but, worryingly, the man was becoming more agitated instead of calming down. He started kicking his legs out in front of him as though aiming at a target and, instead of trying to pacify him, she could hear Roddy urging him to 'do it'.

'What are you saying to him?' Faye hissed at him fearfully.

'I'm getting us out of here.'

'What? How?'

'Wait and see.'

She didn't have to wait long. Less than a minute later the man was on his feet, screaming to be let out. People in their group urged him to sit down, but he was too hyped up, grabbing at his dinner-jacket sleeves as though he was trying to pull them up, readying for a fight.

That was when he ran.

Millie, the flunkey guarding their group, tried to grab him, but the guest was too quick and escaped her outstretched hands. He laughed at her manically, which was when Faye realised the stress and panic of being held captive must've tipped him over the edge.

Before she could react, Roddy had hold of her hand and was pulling her to her feet. 'Come on, we need to go, now.'

Faye was petrified but hurried with him towards the rear of the auditorium – past the makeshift restroom, to a door in the corner marked 'Staff Only'. Behind them there was shouting as the man continued to taunt his captors. She realised with a start that Roddy had wound him up to cause a diversion.

'They'll kill him,' she cried.

'They're going to kill us all if we don't try to get help,' said Roddy hoarsely. 'The theatre's been rigged with bombs.'

Terror squeezed the breath from Faye's lungs. 'Bombs?' she gasped.

'That's what I heard. Now hurry up.'

The commotion behind them was getting louder. Screams began to ricochet around the theatre while their captors shouted. Faye glanced behind her and saw that a few hostages were on their feet and the guards were aiming their rifles right at them. Then a gunshot rang out and the screams became deafening.

Faye let out a sob. That poor man.

'Come on, we need to hurry,' urged Roddy, pushing the door open and pulling her through it.

The door took them into a corridor with a staircase leading downwards at the other end.

'This is our way out,' said Roddy. 'The stairs go down to the basement and we can cut through there.'

Faye grabbed his arm. 'Wait. How do you know all this?'

'While you and the other guests were all sitting down for dinner, I was stuck waiting in the green room and got chatting to one of the theatre managers. He was telling me about the renovations and mentioned there was a way out through the basement.'

Faye began to weep with relief.

They were getting out of here. She would see her children again.

Suddenly the door behind them opened and Faye cowered in terror again, thinking Nye had noticed they'd made a run for it and sent his acolytes after them. But, to her surprise, it was Richard. Once he was clear of the doorway Roddy shut it quickly behind him.

'I can't believe you did it,' Richard said to Roddy. 'You're a genius.'

Faye stared at her ex, bewildered.

'We were queuing for the toilet at the same time earlier and Roddy told me he was planning to create a diversion and that when it kicked off I should make a run for this door,' Richard explained, panting slightly.

'You said you wanted him to come with us,' said Roddy.

Faye was overcome with gratitude, but Roddy shrugged off her thanks.

'Save it for later. We need to get out of here before they notice we've gone.'

'What about Liberty?' asked Richard. 'I can't leave her behind.'

Faye was stung.

'There isn't time,' said Roddy, 'but as soon as we're free we can tell the police everything we know. They'll storm the building and rescue everyone else. You'll see her soon.' He pointed to the stairs. 'The way out is down there. You go first.'

Richard flew down the stairs like he was worried Roddy might change his mind. Faye was about to follow, but Roddy grabbed her wrist and held her back. 'Do not say a word to him about Matthew having the phone,' he whispered.

'Why not? People should know how selfish he's been.'

'Right now, it's not important. We'll deal with Matthew afterwards. We just need to get out of here.'

Faye followed him down the stairs. From there the three of them ran along a corridor that wound through the bowels of the building, turning a corner to see a sign marked 'Emergency Exit' looming. She finally allowed herself to think they'd made it, until a door on the left opened – and Nye stepped into the corridor, armed with a handgun.

'Well, well, well. Where do you think you're all going?' he smirked.

Faye screamed and tried to turn back, but Nye raised his gun. 'Be quiet.' Then he stepped forward and pushed the barrel against Richard's temple. Faye felt her ex-husband quake beside her.

'I said, where you do you think you're going?'

Richard tried to answer but failed. 'I – we, we—'

'We want to see our children,' cried Faye. 'They'll be terrified, wondering what's happened to us. You can't keep everyone here for ever.'

Nye stared at her unflinchingly. Then, to her astonishment, he lowered the gun.

'This is your lucky day. The cops are outside and have been for hours. They've been trying to negotiate with us to release some hostages, so I'm willing to let you go as a goodwill gesture, since you got this far.' He turned to Roddy. 'You seem like one of the good guys, even if you're a fool working for a bunch of rich assholes. Do yourself a favour and get a job looking after decent folk.'

Roddy, who was trembling like Richard, nodded.

Then Nye turned his cold blue eyes on Faye. 'I'm only letting you and your ex go because you're with him, so you'd better be grateful. We've got a lot of supporters out there who'll be watching what you say about us after this is over. Say the wrong thing and you might get a visit to your house when your kids are at home.'

Faye recoiled.

'We will be grateful, I swear,' she said, tears streaking her cheeks.

'Good. Now leave, before I change my mind.' He reached over and pushed down the bar on the emergency exit to open it. The burst of cool air from outside made Faye shiver. 'Well, what are you waiting for?'

Roddy went first, then Richard took Faye's hand and together they went through the door. She turned back briefly as Nye pulled it shut behind them.

'Eleven Argyll Street, Dulwich,' he said, with a malicious grin. 'I never forget an address.'

Chapter Forty-Eight

EVE

Now

Eve called Horner to tell him about her confrontation with Strutton, but he didn't pick up, so she left a message saying she urgently needed to talk to him. She was on edge now, wondering whether she should have outright denied the detective's request for more time.

She understood why Strutton wanted to double-check everything himself before The Seven's legal team was informed. He had to be sure, because the fallout was going to land firmly at his feet – it had been his officers, working under his command, who'd overlooked evidence showing another suspect was still at large. Even accounting for the somewhat obscure nature of the texts and the fact they were among thousands of pieces of evidence that had to be sifted through, a fundamental error had been made. There might even be an inquiry into his handling of the investigation, which could spell disaster for his career.

His comments about the trial collapsing weighed heavily on her. The idea that The Seven could use what she'd unearthed to argue they weren't getting a fair trial sickened her. There was even a tiny part of her that thought maybe Strutton was right; they should just leave it in the unused pile and people would be none the wiser. The Seven should still be convicted – did it really matter if an eighth one got away with it? But of course it did. There was a risk that person could commit further crimes and Eve could never consciously conceal evidence. She'd rather quit law all together than let herself be put in that position.

With so many what-ifs rattling through her head she found it difficult to concentrate. Her hip ached from sitting down, so she decided to head out for a coffee. To her surprise, the incident room was empty when she passed through it. No Strutton, no Lees – thank God – but no other officers either. Strutton had meant what he said about personally corroborating everything she'd told him. She imagined he'd gone to Lambeth Road to talk to Forensics himself about the print.

She walked down to the reception area as fast as her hip would allow. The pain was worsening as the day progressed and she wondered if there was a pharmacy nearby where she could buy pain-killers to ease it. She swiped out of the building and headed for the exit, her phone open on a map app to search for one. It was only as she lifted her gaze from her screen that she spotted DCS Strutton across the street, talking to a man who had his back to the slow-moving traffic. A car horn sounded nearby. The man turned his head slightly to the side, making his profile visible to Eve. She stumbled backwards in shock.

It was the man who'd pushed her and Horner in the station. The same man who'd followed her when she was with Luke.

What the hell was Strutton doing with him?

A double-decker bus slowed to a halt in front of her, blocking them from view, so Eve retreated back inside reception. She hovered by the entrance for a moment, unsure what to do. When the bus passed, she could see that Strutton and the man were still deep in conversation. The DCS's expression was tense but their rapport appeared otherwise comfortable. They didn't look like strangers.

'What are you doing?' a voice suddenly rang in her ear.

Eve almost jumped out of her skin. Lurking at her shoulder was the desk sergeant who'd earlier questioned her ID. He followed her gaze across the street.

'Why are you spying on DCS Strutton?'

'I'm not,' she said. 'I'm waiting for him, but I – I didn't want to interrupt him. Do you know who he's talking to?'

'Looks like DC Colgan.'

'Are you sure?' Eve gasped.

The sergeant peered intently through the window. 'Yep. That's him.'

DC Colgan was the disclosure officer who'd sparked the CPS review. He was the one who'd attacked her and Horner.

Eve was floored – and also terrified. Her instinct was to get away from Lewisham as quickly as possible. But first she needed to get her bag, which she'd left upstairs. Without another word, she swiped back inside and hurried to the bank of lifts, ignoring the shooting pain in her hip. She couldn't ease up now, she had to get out of there.

The incident room was thankfully still empty. Eve unlocked the door to her office with trembling fingers, hobbled inside then grabbed her bag and her yellow legal pad, which was on the desk. Then, almost as an afterthought, she rifled in her bag to double-check she still had the Post-it note DC Lees had given her. Colgan might be the one who had pushed her and Horner, but Lees was the one who set it up. He was behind all this. The minute the review was triggered he must've realised he'd made a terrible error in failing to flag the phone data to Strutton and started plotting to cover his tracks. Colgan, the DO who reported to Lees, would've been a helpful stooge to conspire with, because his career would probably not survive another of his mistakes being exposed. So they schemed to get her and Horner to be in the same place that day – them going to the Tube station together afterwards was just luck on their part. If Colgan hadn't been able to attack them there, it would've been somewhere else.

The question was, had Strutton just inadvertently put her in even more danger by telling Colgan outside what the CPS had uncovered in their review?

Eve wasn't waiting around to find out. She wanted to get back to the safety of Petty France, where she could get help. But first she needed to warn Horner. As the lift descended to the ground floor, she tried him again, but it went to voicemail.

'You need to call me. I know who pushed us and why,' she said, then hung up.

Leaving the building, she inched towards the exit. Strutton and Colgan were no longer across the street. Eve, now shaking with fear, went outside, hoping a black cab would come along for her to flag. She couldn't see any though, so she set off for the train station – only to stop dead in the middle of the pavement a few paces later.

DS Lees was coming towards her.

'Where are you off to?' he called out.

Eve backed away from him, frantically looking to the road in the hope that a cab had suddenly materialised. Out of luck, she turned on her heel, clenched her teeth against the pain in her hip, then ran.

Chapter Forty-Nine

Eve didn't get far before the pain slowed her to a stagger. Her only consolation was that Lees hadn't followed her, confirmed by her anxiously checking over her shoulder as she bolted into the next street.

Knowing he hadn't didn't make Eve feel any safer though. He was probably in the incident room now, telling Strutton he'd seen her run off. Perhaps Colgan was with them too, a thought that chilled her to the bone. She had to believe Strutton didn't know his officers had conspired to cover up their mistake, but how could she convince him of what they'd done? She knew it was too much for her to tackle alone, especially with Horner still at the hospital. Continuing her slow shuffle up Belmont Hill, from where she could catch a bus to Blackheath train station, she called Beverly – only to learn that her boss had been on the verge of calling Eve herself.

'We need to talk about what's been going on at Lewisham,' she said.

For a moment Eve's spirits lifted. Horner must've called Beverly to tell her about the discovery of the burner phone. But what Beverly had to say next sent them plummeting again.

'I've just got off the phone with the DPP and he's not happy. DCS Strutton has made a complaint against you.'

'He's done what?' Eve's exclamation was so loud it attracted the stares of passers-by. She stopped walking and moved away from the kerb, next to a shopfront. 'What's the complaint?'

'He says you've made a serious and unsubstantiated allegation that DS Lees deliberately hid the evidence to assist the defence because he sympathises with Nye's cause. DCS Strutton thinks you cannot objectively continue working on the review. He's asked that you be removed from the case.'

The blood rushed to Eve's ears, muting the sounds around her of people chatting as they walked past, of buses straining to make the gradient of the hill, of the cars revving impatiently behind them. This couldn't be happening to her again. She'd done nothing wrong.

'That's not what happened. We were discussing the reasons the phone could've been overlooked and I said it wasn't unheard of for officers to hide their beliefs, but DCS Strutton put me straight and said Lees wasn't that kind of officer, and that was it. I never made a specific allegation of wrongdoing against DS Lees,' said Eve, fighting to stay calm.

'But you did raise it.'

'Only as a hypothetical. Look, let me talk to DCS Strutton, I'm sure we can sort this out.'

'You can't. Sol has agreed with DCS Strutton that you shouldn't continue with the review because there's been a breakdown of trust.'

'But the review's nearly finished,' Eve protested.

'Sorry, but you're off Novus as of now,' said Beverly. 'I'm not going to lie, Eve. It doesn't look good and Sol's not happy.'

'This isn't fair. I'm being scapegoated to distract from their mistake. DS Lees was the officer who entered the phone into evidence in the first place, so he knew the print found on it didn't belong to any of The Decorous. He must've got DC Colgan to file the MG form incorrectly and put it in the unused pile, but then we

291

came along and he realised our review might uncover it. He's been trying ever since to stop us finding out. Strutton's just trying to protect himself by making it about me now. There's something else you should know,' Eve added angrily. 'It was Colgan who attacked me and John Horner. I saw him talking to Strutton just now – I recognised him as the person who pushed us.'

'That's another very serious accusation, Eve,' said Beverly sternly. 'Do you have proof it was DC Colgan?'

'There'll be CCTV from inside the Tube station. That should prove it.' Eve's eyes pricked with hot tears. 'What's going to happen with the phone and finding the eighth accomplice now?'

'DCS Strutton wants to look at all the evidence himself before any next steps are decided.'

'What about me? What should I do?'

'You need to come back here. Sol wants to see you. Where are you now?'

Eve couldn't return to Petty France, not yet. This was no longer just about them proving there was an eighth person missing from the dock – this was about saving her career as well. If Strutton's complaint was upheld, it could ruin her prospects of staying at the CPS, let alone getting a job anywhere else. She had one disciplinary strike against her already – she wouldn't recover from another.

'I'm in Lewisham. I'll be back soon. I – I need to do something first.'

'No, you need to come back now. Don't make matters worse for yourself.'

'I have to do this one thing, to tie up the review before it gets passed on to someone else. Please, Beverly, I just need a couple of hours.' Eve was painfully aware she was begging like Strutton had only a short while earlier when he'd asked her for more time to investigate. She could barely get her head around the speed at which the tables had turned.

'Fine. I'll make an excuse and hold Sol off for now. Two hours, that's all, though. It's ten past three now and I want you back here in my office just after five,' said Beverly firmly. 'What is it you need to do?'

'I'll tell you when I see you,' said Eve, but the truth was she didn't know where to start. Returning to Lewisham was out of the question. She'd bought herself some time but didn't know what to do with it. 'I'll be back in two hours, I promise.'

'Make sure you are,' said Beverly, hanging up.

Staying where she was, Eve called Horner. He didn't pick up, so she kept trying. On her fourth attempt, Lizzy answered.

'Eve, now's not a good time,' she said tetchily. 'We've just got home from the hospital and John's resting.'

'I'm sorry for disturbing him, but I really need to talk to him. I wouldn't ask if I wasn't desperate.'

'I know you are. Sol called him as we were leaving the hospital.'

Eve was gripped with dread. The DPP had called Horner himself to tell him about Strutton's complaint? 'The police are trying to make this about me. If I could just talk to John—'

'He doesn't think you did anything wrong, Eve, but Sol said you're off the review now so it's out of his hands,' said Lizzy. 'He's put everything into Novus for more than a year and that has to come first.'

'I know, that's what I'm doing too. Putting the case first,' said Eve. 'Lizzy, I really need to speak to your husband. There's someone else out there who helped kill all those people and they're getting away with it.'

'I'm sorry, Eve, but it's a no. John needs to rest.'

Although frustrated, Eve couldn't be angry at Lizzy. She was simply being protective. Her loyalty was always going to be to the man she loved—

Eve stopped. That was it. Loyalty. She knew what she should do.

Seized by certainty, she said goodbye to Lizzy and hung up, then opened the search engine on her phone. It didn't take long to find the address she needed – every aspect of the case was being reported online and this detail was no exception. Better still, it was only a seven-minute walk from the Bailey. She hobbled on.

Chapter Fifty

The hotel across the road from Eve was a national chain that prided itself on the comfiness of its beds. This particular branch was on the north side of the River Thames, close to Blackfriars. Staying there, according to the various online reports, was Joan Beck, Patrick Nye's girlfriend before he did his vanishing act from California twenty years ago. She had a health condition that prohibited her from being in court every day – so there was a good chance she was inside the hotel now, biding her time.

If Eve's hunch was correct, Joan Beck might be able to confirm, unwittingly or otherwise, who the eighth person was.

It was Lizzy Horner who'd triggered Eve's train of thought. A woman's fierce loyalty to the man she loved. Joan Beck hadn't publicly shown loyalty to Patrick Nye since his arrest, but she'd told FBI investigators she'd forgiven him for faking his death and leaving her behind. Eve was hoping – praying – that her presence in London meant there were still some feelings in play and that they were now in regular contact. Joan might've been in the States when Novus happened, but Nye could have confided in her since; if there was a slim chance he'd told her about the mystery person he'd sworn to keep secret from the others, Eve had to ask. She certainly didn't trust that Strutton was going to rush to review the evidence like he had assured the DPP he would.

The only reason Eve wasn't inside the hotel talking to Joan Beck already was because she didn't have a clue how best to approach her, much less get her to open up. Obviously, she couldn't hide that she was from the CPS, but nor did she want to wade in with that as her opening line and risk Joan clamming up. After twelve years behind bars, it wasn't a leap to assume she might be wary of talking to anyone involved in criminal justice.

Eve checked her watch. Forty minutes had passed already since she'd spoken to Beverly – she needed to get a move on. Chin jutted, she crossed the road and walked into the reception area – only to find it was set up as self-check-in. Eve swore under her breath. Now what? Looking around, she saw there was a garishly decorated restaurant through a doorway with only a smattering of people inside, so she went in and sat down at a free table. It was a good five minutes before a member of staff came over to see if she wanted to order, but in that time she still hadn't come up with a way of finding out which room Joan Beck was staying in.

'What can I get you?' asked the server, a young man with a rosy complexion that clashed with his purple dyed hair.

'Um, a pot of tea, please.'

'Anything to eat?'

Eve scanned the menu, but nothing jumped out to spark her appetite. She was too wound up. 'Can you give me a minute?'

'Sure.'

He sloped off and, as he did, Eve, with her back to him, heard him say a cheery hello to someone who'd just walked in. She couldn't believe her luck when he followed it up with, 'Usual for you, Joan?'

'Yes, please. Gammon steak, plain with salad.'

'No pineapple, no eggs, no chips. Gotcha.'

'Thanks, sweetheart,' she replied in a Californian drawl. 'I'll be over by the window.'

The window was next to where Eve was sitting, and she froze when a few moments later Joan Beck entered her peripheral vision, recognisable from the few photos Eve had seen of her online, taken after the Carpinteria raid. Then, Joan had long blonde hair and was slim and graceful in build, like a dancer. Now in her fifties like Nye, her hair was still bright blonde but cut short, in a pixie style, but her back appeared out of alignment, with one shoulder noticeably higher than the other.

Eve pretended to be reading something on her phone but watched surreptitiously as Joan made her way to a table three feet away from hers. Even though she was staying in the hotel, she'd put on a short navy raincoat to come downstairs to eat and was wearing it over a pair of light denim jeans and a floral top, her feet in trainers. When she sat down at a table facing Eve's direction it was with an audible wince and a pained expression.

The server returned to Eve's table with her pot of tea, and she became aware of Joan glancing her way as she poured a cup. Still Eve didn't know what her opening gambit should be. What would Horner advise? *Actually, scratch that*, she thought – he'd tell her to get the hell out of there. But that was easy for him to say when his career wasn't on the line. Again.

She was about to sip her tea when her phone suddenly leapt to life, its shrill tone cutting through the relative silence of the restaurant. It was her mum. Eve scrabbled to silence the call, but then it rang again and she knew if she didn't answer her mum would worry and keep trying. They'd only traded texts since the weekend, and Eve knew she still owed her parents a conversation about not going back to celebrate their anniversary.

'Hi, Mum,' she said, trying not to talk loudly but aware Joan Beck could still hear her. 'I know why you're calling, and I'm so sorry, I wish I hadn't missed the pa—'

Her mum cut across her. 'There's no need to apologise, love. I'm very upset with your sister. She had no right, having a go at you. Of course we'd have loved to have seen you, but your dad and I understand you had to work. Between you and me, I could've done without the fuss of a party and just gone out for a curry, the two of us, instead. But Emma got it into her head we had to celebrate properly, and you know what she's like.'

Eve was touched by how understanding her mum was being. Fuelled by Emma's outburst, she'd built it up in her head that her parents were angry with her when it wasn't the case at all.

'Did you have a good time though?' she asked.

'Yes, but your Auntie Marie drank too much as usual and had to be carried home. Nick popped in and it was nice to see him. He asked after you.'

'How was he?'

'Oh, fine. He talked about cycling a lot though,' said her mum, referencing Nick's new hobby, which he'd taken up after their split. 'He does go on a bit, doesn't he? I can see why you got bored now. There's only so long you can nod politely when someone's talking about spoke size.'

Eve giggled. It felt good to be talking to her mum like this. In the next beat, without over-thinking it, she said she'd had to work at the weekend because she had a new job. It was about time she told them.

'New job? Since when?' asked her mum, sounding shocked.

'Not long. I've been meaning to tell you, but it all happened quickly, and I've been so busy since starting. I'm working on a really big case.'

'Is it in the City still?'

'No. It's a long story and I'll tell you all about it when I see you next. It's a great job though, and I'm really enjoying the work, Mum.'

She meant it too. Working at the CPS had turned out to be far more rewarding than she could ever have imagined. The thought that her position there might be in jeopardy because of Lees and Colgan incensed her.

'That's wonderful,' said her mum. 'As long as you are happy. That's all me and your dad care about.'

'I am happy. I'd better go now. I promise that as soon as I'm done with this case I'll come home for the weekend and I'll take you and Dad out for that curry. Don't tell Emma though.'

Eve's mum laughed. 'I'll hold you to that. Love you, sweetheart.'

'Love you, too.'

Eve smiled as she hung up. She put her phone back in her bag, then looked up to see Joan Beck staring at her. Shit. She'd mentioned to her mum she was working on a big case without thinking. Then Joan broke into a broad smile.

'It's always nice to hear young people being kind to their moms,' she said loudly, so her voice carried to Eve's table.

'I'm lucky to have her,' replied Eve, her pulse cranking up a notch. Was this her moment to approach the woman?

'She not local?'

Eve shook her head. 'No, she's in the Midlands. That's where I'm from.'

'I have no idea where that is.' Joan laughed. 'I'm just here on vacation.'

'That's nice. Where are you from?'

'The States.'

Eve took a deep breath. 'Are you waiting for someone?'

'No, not right now.'

'Mind if I join you? I hate eating alone.'

Joan beamed and patted the surface of the table across from her. 'Same here. Bring your tea over.'

Eve endured a few minutes of idle chit-chat about the hotel and why Joan liked to eat dinner early – 'I'm on medication that means I can't eat anything after five p.m., or it screws with my digestion and I can't sleep' – before she asked Joan which landmarks she'd visited so far. The woman pulled a face. 'Not as many as I'd like. I had an accident years ago that messed up my spine and I can't walk far.'

Eve felt wretched. She liked Joan, and now she was going to upset her. She leaned across the table and lowered her voice.

'I know who you are, Joan. I actually came here today to talk to you.'

Joan's expression shifted again. She looked angry. 'Are you a damn reporter? I've already said I'm not doing any interviews.'

'I'm not,' said Eve hurriedly. 'I'm a lawyer for the Crown Prosecution Service.'

Joan's eyes narrowed. 'Isn't that like the DA's office?'

'Yes, it is. My name is Eve Wren. I work at the CPS headquarters at Petty France in Victoria.' She slid her business card across the table. Joan viewed it like it was giving off a bad smell.

'What do you want from me?' she snapped.

Eve knew she had to tread carefully now. If Joan was in regular contact with Nye, as she suspected, she mustn't reveal anything specific about the burner phone that Joan could pass on to him. But she had an idea that might get her to open up.

'I'm part of the team that's prosecuting Patrick Nye and the others. My job involves reviewing evidence relating to the case and I've been asked to clarify a detail with you personally, because you are one of the only people who will know the answer,' she said, aware of how nervous she sounded.

'What detail?'

'Specifically whether Patrick held swearing-in ceremonies for new members when The Decorous was at the compound in Carpinteria.'

Joan reacted with surprise. 'That's what you came here to ask me?'

'Yes. So, did he?'

Clearly bemused, Joan nodded. 'Sure he did. Patrick wanted people to feel special when they joined us. He'd say a few words, and then they'd swear their allegiance and afterwards we'd all party. Why do you want to know?'

'Was it always Patrick who conducted the welcome ceremonies?'

'Mostly. Sometimes I'd do them if he was busy.'

'You were his second-in-command, right?'

'I sure was,' replied Joan, with more than a hint of pride. 'But I didn't have anything to do with what happened at that theatre, if that's what you're asking. I didn't even know he was alive until after it happened and he'd been arrested.'

'We know you didn't,' said Eve quickly. 'The FBI confirmed you were in the States and that you had no contact with him prior to his arrest. We're just curious which of his new followers was Patrick's second-in-command this time round.'

Joan's face fell. She'd walked right into it without realising. Eve's hunch was right.

She knew.

Chapter Fifty-One

Joan Beck quickly corrected herself.

'Don't go asking me stuff like that. I told you, what happened at that theatre had nothing to do with me.'

'I know it didn't, and I'm not here to cause trouble for you,' said Eve. 'But it looks like someone else stepped in for Patrick to conduct at least one swearing-in this time round too, and I think you might know who that was.'

Joan glowered at her. 'You're asking the wrong person, lady.'

The server came over with Joan's gammon steak and salad and put the plate down in front of her, oblivious to the tension between the two women. The food looked unappetising, the salad leaves wilting and slimy and a thick line of fat dissecting the bright pink meat like a crack in a pavement.

'I'm hungry,' said Joan dully, after the server walked away. 'I need to eat.'

Eve felt torn. If she pushed too hard, Joan could go running to Nye and all hell would break loose. But she couldn't give up just yet.

'Maybe it was one of the girls on trial with Patrick, Millie Tinkler or Jenna Sandwell. It would make sense for him to pick a trusted girlfriend to be his second-in-command again.'

Joan's mouth twitched angrily, but she held off replying.

'My money's on Jenna,' said Eve, trying to sound casual. 'She's got long blonde hair just like you used to have. Patrick must have a type.'

The dam burst. 'He never dated either one of those bitches.'

'How can you be so sure? You weren't there, you had no idea what he was up to.'

'Because he told me he didn't, and I believe him.'

'Believe him? After he left you behind at the compound? How can you trust a word he says?' Then, looking at Joan's lopsided shoulders, a thought struck her. 'How did you hurt your spine?'

Joan's knuckles blanched as she gripped her knife and fork. 'I was attacked in prison by another inmate,' she said quietly.

'A prison you wouldn't have been in if Patrick had kept his word and taken you with him when he disappeared.'

Joan flinched, and Eve knew she was getting through to her. She leaned across the table and dropped her voice to a whisper. 'The person who was Patrick's second-in-command before the Novus attack is still out there. I know you know that. Patrick told you after his arrest, didn't he? You're in touch with him again. That's why you're in London now. Have you visited him while he's been on remand?'

Joan wouldn't meet her eyes.

'I need to know who it is, Joan. Anything you tell me I will treat in the strictest confidence. People will never know we talked.'

'What does it matter? Patrick and the rest of them are going down for this, we all know that. The victims will get their justice,' said Joan wretchedly.

'What about the next victims? This person could be planning another attack, for all we know. Do you want more innocent people to die? Forty-three families lost their loved ones at the Novus. How many more families do you want to suffer like they are?'

Joan turned her head to stare out of the window, food forgotten. Eve could see she was wrestling with a reply and held her breath expectantly.

Finally she turned back.

'Patrick didn't tell me his name. He just said he was from the north of England and he was up there while Patrick and the others were in Bournemouth.'

Eve fought to hide her excitement. Now they knew for certain it was a man.

'Patrick said he'd known him for a while. They met when Patrick first came to Europe.'

Now they had some idea where Nye had been for the past twenty years.

'To England?'

'No. Somewhere else in Europe, but not anywhere like France or Germany. Patrick's not stupid. This guy was living there at the same time as Patrick. I think he's English. But that's all I know.'

Joan looked like she was telling the truth. Eve thought for a moment. 'Is there anything else you know that might help? Like why Patrick wanted to keep this man a secret from the others?'

'Because it could've blown his cover. Patrick said the man was right under everyone's noses the whole time and he still is.'

'Still is? You mean he's in London now?'

'I don't know,' said Joan waspishly. 'That's for you to find out.'

It was like the shutters had come down, and Eve knew she wouldn't get anything else from her. She got to her feet.

'Thank you. You've been really helpful.'

'I'm only telling you what I know because I don't want anyone else to get hurt. I want my name kept out of it, like you promised. If this gets back to Patrick, he will never forgive me.'

And there it was. The blind loyalty that twenty years apart couldn't dilute.

'I won't tell anyone, I swear.'

Eve didn't know how she'd manage to keep her out of it, but she would. She left the restaurant just as Joan Beck picked up her knife and fork and began to eat.

Chapter Fifty-Two

LUKE

Now

Even with the extractor fan at full pelt, the bathroom had become uncomfortably humid with the shower running. Luke couldn't think straight with the heat, noise and Faye tearfully begging for absolution for what she'd covered up. He threw open the door between the en suite and the bedroom and fell gratefully into the cooler space, Faye hot on his heels.

'What do you think, then?' Her voice was still lowered and, when Luke frowned, she cupped her ear then pointed to the door to remind him that they risked being overheard still. 'What should we do? Tell the police before it's too late and the trial's over?'

The 'we' needled him. He hadn't asked to be a part of any conspiracy.

'It's on your conscience. You have to decide,' he replied, exhausted, lowering himself down on to the edge of the fastidiously made bed. 'But are you absolutely sure Matthew had the phone? Did you see him give it to Roddy?'

'No. Roddy told me Matthew gave it to him.'

Luke rubbed his brow. Despite showering, he felt grimy again. 'Here's the thing I don't get. Why would Matthew be involved in a plot to terrorise his grandmother and her guests? Nye's motive for wanting to take out a roomful of rich liberals, while reprehensible, at least makes some sort of twisted sense. But Matthew is one of the very people Nye despises, and now he's even richer after inheriting Cynthia's estate.'

'Matthew hates the film industry because of the way his parents died. He blames his dad's addiction on the fact he was an actor,' said Faye, groping for an explanation. 'Maybe it was revenge for their deaths, and he recruited Nye and his followers as a cover so no one would suspect him?'

Luke managed a smile. 'You should be writing movie scripts yourself. Sorry, but I can't see Matthew hurting innocent people like the theatre staff who died, and especially not his grandmother. Wasn't it you who told Richard how upset he was when Cynthia died? He told us at one of our meetings. Also, how could Matthew have known Nye was still alive to recruit him in the first place?'

'Why did he have a phone then?'

'Well, presumably because he was one of the organisers of the event. There must've been a bunch of stuff going on behind the scenes that he needed to be on call for. He didn't have to abide by the rules of the event because he set them.'

'That still doesn't explain why he didn't use it to call for help when it all started,' said Faye, flopping down on the hard-backed chair next to the vanity table.

'No, it doesn't. The same for Roddy though. If someone had handed me a phone, I'd have used it.'

Faye flushed scarlet. 'He couldn't unlock it. He didn't know the PIN.'

'You don't need a PIN to make an emergency call.'

'He might not have known that. Not everyone does,' said Faye lamely.

There was a rap on the bedroom door, which made them both jump.

'Who is it?' asked Luke.

'It's us,' Horatio's voice rang out. 'Me and Jimi. We wanted to check you were okay because you've been gone for a while.'

Luke threw a quizzical look in Faye's direction. She nodded. Then he got up and padded across the thick-pile carpet to unlock the door.

'Are you – oh, you're not alone,' said Horatio somewhat sharply. Jimi looked worried. 'Sorry, we didn't mean to intrude.'

'You're not. We were just chatting.'

Horatio bowed his head fractionally in acknowledgement but didn't shift from the doorway. Jimi, on the other hand, simply pushed past into the room.

'Is it Madeleine? Have you heard from the hospital?' he asked.

'No, nothing yet.' Luke gestured to Horatio. 'Come in too. We were just talking about how the siege ended and how Faye managed to escape with Richard and Roddy. She's not really had the chance to talk about it before.'

Faye picked up the distortion and ran with it. 'Luke's been helping me understand my guilt. We were so lucky to get out when we did, and I feel bad we didn't take others with us.'

'Anyone would've done the same in your position,' said Horatio, standing stiffly just inside the threshold. 'Luke and Jimi did the same thing.'

'Our departure was slightly different,' said Luke, resuming his perch on the edge of the bed. Jimi immediately sat down beside him. 'We had a gun, for one thing.'

It had been Brendan's idea. He'd said they should pretend Luke had wrestled the rifle from him and was going to shoot Brendan if he didn't let him into the foyer along with Jimi and whoever else they could persuade to make a run for it. It was a risk, but Brendan thought it might be their only chance to escape and so they'd seized their moment when the male guest in Faye's group lost control. With the members of The Decorous trying to restrain the guest while others screamed the place down in fear, the pandemonium proved the perfect diversion.

'The point I'm trying to make is that Faye shouldn't judge herself for what she did or didn't do that night,' said Horatio.

As Luke listened, something stirred in the back of his mind, a memory he'd suppressed and forgotten about, shaken loose by his conversation with Eve Wren yesterday and now the mention of them escaping. It came back in snatches – him and Jimi and the others fleeing once he had hold of Brendan's rifle . . . them running through the foyer in a panic . . . Brendan too, trying to keep up the pretence that he was their hostage now . . . then someone else was there, unexpectedly, and Brendan reacted to their presence like he was frightened . . .

Luke bolted upright, white as a sheet. He remembered.

Chapter Fifty-Three

EVE

Now

Eve didn't notice the black sedan with the darkened windows parked across the street from the hotel. She was hunched over her phone, typing out a message to Horner. Lizzy was fielding his calls, but Eve hoped he might still read his texts. She didn't say she'd met with Joan Beck – she was determined to keep the woman's name out of it, as she'd promised – but she said she'd uncovered solid information that the eighth accomplice was a male who had lived in the north of England in the run-up to the bombings and who had first met Patrick Nye abroad. Typing it out made her realise how thin on detail it was, but she was hoping it might ring some bells with Horner, given his exhaustive knowledge of the case.

Within seconds her phone pinged with a reply.

Eve, half the guests lived abroad.

She cringed. She should've thought of that and been clearer in her message.

Source says it was in a European country that wasn't France or Germany.

Instead of texting his next reply, Horner rang her. 'How good is your source?' he asked, forgoing any preamble.

'I'm confident they were telling me the truth.'

'A country in Europe that isn't France or Germany hardly narrows it down,' said Horner grumpily. 'There were quite a few guests at the event with European nationality, including Samuel Fraise, Dame Cynthia's personal assistant, who is French by birth. Plus, there might have been workers from EU nations. It'll take me a while to come up with a list—'

Eve heard a voice ring out in the background and then muffled sounds, as though Horner had put his hand over the receiver. 'That was Lizzy telling me off,' he said, when he resumed the call. 'She's annoyed because I'm meant to be resting.'

'I'm sorry, I shouldn't have texted you.'

It was then, turning on the spot, that her gaze was drawn to the blacked-out vehicle across the road. An uneasy feeling spread through her. She couldn't see the car's occupants from the angle she was at, but it felt like she was being watched.

'I'm glad you did,' said Horner, his voice distinctly quieter for a moment. 'I don't like sitting around doing nothing.' His voice rose. 'Yes, love, I'm hanging up now,' he called out to Lizzy, who was presumably still hovering nearby. 'Eve, I'll text you the list when I can. And don't worry, I know all about Strutton's complaint and I'm going to make sure Sol knows I have absolute faith in you.'

Eve should've been happy to hear that, but her focus was still on the car. Then, as though in slow motion, the passenger door swung open – and DC Colgan climbed out. Moments later, Lees emerged from the driver's side.

Eve's breath stuck in her throat. They'd come after her. She started backing away, eyes darting from side to side, desperate for an escape route but finding none.

Lees reached the pavement a footstep behind Colgan. 'Eve, we need to talk to you,' he said.

'I don't want to hear it,' she said hoarsely, still backing away. She pointed at Colgan. 'Don't you come any closer.'

He shot Lees a look, then stepped forward. 'It's not what you—'

The rest of his sentence was drowned out by Eve's scream. 'Help!' she shrieked. 'They're trying to rob me! Someone help!'

She heard Horner's voice, tiny and distant, echo from her phone. 'Eve? Eve? Are you okay? What's going on?' She cut the call and yelled again for help.

There was a flurry of footsteps as two young men who'd been walking past laughing and chatting came running back at full pelt to Eve's aid. 'Get away from her,' one of them shouted, squaring up to Colgan. His friend did the same to Lees, effectively putting a barrier between them and Eve.

She knew she had a matter of seconds to act before Lees and Colgan revealed they were police officers and the narrative changed. She darted past the four of them into the road, forcing a van driver to slam on his brakes, then dashed round the corner, where the street intersected with a main road choked with traffic. She couldn't see Lees or Colgan behind her and assumed they were being held back by her rescuers. Directly in front of her was a cab with its light on, so Eve jumped in the back and slid down low in the seat so her head wasn't visible through the window.

'You okay?' asked the driver.

'I've hurt my hip,' said Eve. 'It's more comfortable sitting like this.' It wasn't a lie. Her damaged hip throbbed from running, and being almost horizontal made it hurt a fraction less.

'Where to?'

There was only one place right now where Eve would be safe. 'The Old Bailey, please.'

Chapter Fifty-Four

The journey to court felt like the longest drive of Eve's life. She couldn't risk peeking out of the taxi's rear window to see if Colgan and Lees were following, but her gut told her they were somewhere close behind. She'd seen the looks on their faces. They meant to stop her. Colgan had already proved how far he was prepared to go to do that when he'd pushed Horner down the escalator.

The taxi eventually began to slow. Eve's pulse juddered in fear. She made sure the doors were locked so they couldn't be yanked open from outside, but still she couldn't shake off the fear that the moment she exited the vehicle, Colgan and Lees would be there to grab her.

'It's snarled up around the court. It must be that crowd shutting the road off again because of that trial,' said the driver, speaking through the gap in the Perspex divide between the front and back of the cab. 'It might be quicker if you walked the rest.'

'Where are we?' she asked, her head still below window level.

'Halfway along Fleet Street. Reckon it's a four-minute walk to the court, maybe five with a dodgy hip.'

Fleet Street was a busy thoroughfare between the City and the Strand. Lees and Colgan couldn't attack her there, not without drawing attention to themselves.

'Is there a car behind us?'

The driver swivelled round in his seat and stared down at her lying prone on his back seat. 'The road is full of traffic, love,' he deadpanned.

'I meant one specifically. Dark sedan, tinted side windows. Two men in the front, both fair-haired.'

He raised his gaze from her to the rear window. 'No. There's a van behind us. The driver has no hair at all.'

'Can you see behind the van?'

''Fraid I left my X-ray specs at home today,' said the driver with a laugh, which calmed Eve a bit. She was starting to sound ridiculous. 'Would you like me to pull over?' he asked.

'Yes, please.' Cautiously, she raised herself up in the seat and looked intently out of the windows in every direction. She couldn't see Lees and Colgan anywhere, but that didn't mean they weren't nearby. Then she noticed a café a few doors down from where the cab had pulled in. It was one of those organic/vegan/no additives eateries that had proliferated in the City in recent years and which Eve – an affirmed meat lover – never patronised. Well, there was a first time for everything. She settled the fare and, drawing a deep breath, made a run for it.

The young woman behind the counter was startled when Eve came bursting through the door as though she were on fire. There were no other customers in the place, though, so she sheepishly slowed her pace.

'Table for one,' she said.

'Take your pick.'

'Thanks. Um, is there a back way out of here?'

The server laughed. 'Only if you don't mind climbing the bins into next door's yard.'

Eve chose a table towards the rear of the café that still had a view of the front window. If Lees and Colgan had followed her, she would see them before they saw her. She wondered how her sore hip would take to climbing.

The server brought a menu over and said she'd give Eve a minute to choose. Eve waited for ten before looking at it, her gaze not budging from the front window. Twice the young woman came over and twice Eve politely batted her away.

When the ten minutes were up, Eve began to unclench. If they knew where she was, they'd have come inside by now. Catching the expectant look of the server, she picked up the menu and began to browse. She hadn't been planning to eat anything, but the dishes sounded more appetising than she'd anticipated, so she ordered mushrooms on sourdough with vegan scrambled eggs. Then, while she waited for her order to be prepared, she checked her phone. Horner had messaged her a bunch of times asking what the hell was going on, had she been mugged, was she hurt, while Beverly had sent just one: *YOU'RE LATE.*

Eve groaned. It was twenty past five – she'd missed Beverly's deadline for her to return to Petty France. Knowing there was little she could do to change that now, she left the text unanswered. She also realised with a start that the Bailey would've closed for the day too; its doors shut at 5 p.m.

Horner. She tried him, but it went to voicemail.

'It's me, Eve,' she said, after the tone signalled for her to leave a message. 'I'm sorry about earlier. I thought someone was trying to grab my bag. I'm fine now.' She faltered, close to tears. 'But I really need to talk to you. I can't do this on my own.'

She hung up and wiped her eyes with a bamboo napkin from the dispenser on the table. It felt as rough as sandpaper.

Her plate was scraped clean by the time Horner returned her call. She'd surprised herself both with how hungry she was, and how delicious she found the food. She was now enjoying a slice of carrot cake washed down with green tea. She couldn't see herself ever giving up bacon sandwiches, but she at least vowed to be less judgemental about vegan food going forward.

'Thanks for calling back,' she said, hastily swallowing the mouthful she'd shovelled in just as her phone went.

'You should've called or messaged me straight back,' he said. 'Don't ever leave me hanging like that again. I thought you were hurt.'

Eve was shocked by how stern his admonishment was, but knew she deserved it for letting him worry. 'I'm really sorry. I should've let you know I was okay. The thing is, it was DS Lees and DC Colgan I was yelling at. They must've followed me from Lewisham and came after me in the street.'

'You what?'

She told him everything, from her conversation with Strutton, when he had asked for more time to investigate, to Beverly telling her about his complaint to the DPP, to seeing Strutton outside Lewisham Police Station talking to Colgan and then him and DS Lees coming for her in the street outside the hotel in Blackfriars, which was when Horner cut her off.

'Why were you at a hotel in Blackfriars?' he asked.

Eve kicked herself for mentioning it. She'd promised Joan Beck she'd leave her out of it.

'I stopped off to use their toilets,' she said. 'It was on the way to the Bailey.'

'Is that where you were headed? Why?'

'I don't know. I thought I'd be safe there. You weren't picking up your calls and you said you'd send me that list.'

'I couldn't talk,' he said. 'I was underground.'

Eve paused. 'You've been on the Tube?'

'Yes. I decided to come into town because I was worried about you and I think we should talk about what to do next in person. Lizzy's furious, but I'll smooth it over with her later. Now, where are you? I'm outside Monument station.'

Eve gave him the address of the café.

'I'll get a cab. See you in a bit.'

Fifteen minutes later the door to the café opened and Eve sagged with relief when she saw Horner walk in. He was dressed casually in beige cargo trousers, trainers and a pale pink polo shirt and his dark green jacket was slung over his forearm. His hair was more unkempt than usual, but he wasn't wearing the bandage any longer. He looked tired though, which made Eve feel guilty because he should've been at home resting like Lizzy wanted.

'What happened to the bandage?' asked Eve when he reached her table.

'They glued the wound closed, so I don't need one.'

'That's good. Um, are you going to sit down?' He wasn't moving from his position standing next to the table.

'I will, in a minute.'

Eve felt a prick of alarm. 'What's up? Why are you looking at me like that?'

'I don't want you to be scared, Eve,' said Horner gravely. 'It's going to be alright. We're going to sort this out.'

'What do you mean?'

The café door opened again and Lees and Colgan walked in.

Chapter Fifty-Five

Eve turned on Horner, horrified. She could barely get her words out, and her voice sounded strangled to her ears. 'Why did you tell them where I was?'

'I told them because you need to listen to what they've got to say,' said Horner matter-of-factly. Then he sat down in the chair next to her, hemming her in. Lees and Colgan crossed the café floor, calling out to the server on the way that they'd like two coffees, please, white, no sugar. They sat down in the chairs across from her and Horner. Colgan stared at her impassively while Lees kept an eye on the young woman behind the counter. Eve felt tears begin to build again. She'd trusted Horner, and all this time he was in on whatever this was.

But then he startled her again.

'DS Lees called me after they saw you outside the hotel. He realised you had the wrong impression of him and DC Colgan, so he asked me to intervene and talk to you before this whole thing blows up.'

Although upset and scared, Eve felt the beginnings of anger too. 'You think you can get me on board to hide their shitty secret? I am not covering up for their mistake. I can't believe you're in on this – you're meant to be one of the good guys,' she said accusingly.

'We're not asking you to cover up anything,' said Lees. 'We're all good guys here.'

'He's not,' Eve shot back, pointing at Colgan, who was diagonal to her. 'You know he's the one who pushed us, right?' she said to Horner. 'I know it was him.'

Colgan seemed genuinely shocked by the accusation. 'I did no such thing. For Christ's sake, John, you said she was reasonable.'

'Eve, Frank didn't attack us. I know he didn't.'

'How do you know?'

'He and I had several meetings when the Novus investigation started. I would've recognised him. The person who pushed us was someone else.'

She was having a tough time believing anything Horner said right now.

'You followed me again though,' she said to Colgan, 'when I met Luke Bishop on the South Bank yesterday lunchtime.'

Colgan shook his head. 'That wasn't me either. I was at Charing Cross nick yesterday. I've been put on desk duty pending my disciplinary, if you want to check.'

'I think this is a case of mistaken identity, Eve,' said Horner gently. 'Whoever attacked us, for whatever reason, I can tell you it wasn't either of these two.'

'It's someone else you know then; that you arranged,' Eve spat at Lees. 'You set us up. We wouldn't have been anywhere near the Tube station if you hadn't tricked us into meeting.'

'That wasn't me either,' said Lees evenly.

The three of them were patently trying to humour her, and she was infuriated. She heaved her bag on to the table and burrowed in its depths until her fingers grasped the piece of paper she was looking for. She pulled it out and slapped it down on the table in front of Lees with a resounding smack. It was the yellow Post-it note with his message about meeting Horner in the pub.

'This is a work of fiction,' she said.

Lees took a beat, then slid it back across the table.

'It is . . . But I didn't write it.'

'But you gave it to me,' she said. 'You said you were passing on a message and you gave me the note.'

'I did, that's right. But I didn't take the message or write it down, I was just asked to give it to you.'

'Who by?'

'DCS Strutton.'

Eve pulled a face. 'Why would he fake a message and ask you to deliver it?'

'Because he wanted you out of the way. I didn't know that when he asked me to bring that to you,' said Lees, gesturing to the Post-it note, 'but it's pretty obvious now that's why he did it.'

'Why would he want me out of the way?' asked Eve, nonplussed.

Colgan rolled his eyes. 'Haven't you worked it out yet? He was worried you'd find his fuck-up during the review and he wanted to get to it before you did. So he got you out of the station to have a look at what you were working on.'

Eve's mind zipped back to finding the office door unlocked and Strutton waiting for her at her desk.

'But he was too late because you'd already found it,' Colgan went on.

'You mean . . . ?'

'It wasn't either of us who messed up and stopped the burner phone being properly investigated,' said Lees. 'It was Strutton.'

Chapter Fifty-Six

Eve fell into a stunned silence that was only punctured when the young woman manning the café appeared at their table and clattered down the coffees the detectives had ordered. All four of them sat stiffly while she cleared away the remnants of Eve's cake and asked if they wanted anything else.

'No,' was the resounding collective reply. The server beat a hasty retreat.

Eve turned to Horner. 'Do you believe them?'

He nodded. 'I do. You will too when you listen to what they have to say.'

She levelled her gaze at Lees and searched his expression for signs that he was spinning another line, and for the thinly veiled arrogance he usually displayed whenever they spoke. But she saw no trace of either. Instead, he appeared dispirited and drained, the tiny blue veins mapping his alabaster skin even more pronounced than usual.

'Tell me,' she said.

◆ ◆ ◆

The Motorola flip phone had been recovered around five weeks into the investigation, by experts from the Defence Science and

Technology Laboratory's Forensic Explosives team. They were the ones tasked with combing through the bomb site fragment by fragment. The phone was inside an integrated metal waste container set into the long basin unit and therefore largely shielded from the blast. The men's restrooms and the rest of the foyer had been severely damaged, but the waste container was pretty much intact under the rubble.

By this point in the investigation, The Seven had already been arrested and charged. While they offered no comment during their interviews – no doubt mindful of mentioning anything that could harm their defence when they went to court – the evidence amassed by Forensics and the investigation team was more than enough for the CPS to agree that charges could be brought.

It could be argued that as the SIO orchestrating the response, DCS Strutton had a relatively straightforward task, Lees told Eve. He had the culprits banged up awaiting the start of the legal process, so his job then was to just make sure every line of investigation was followed up and the evidence duly recorded. To build a secure case.

'I think, like the rest of us, he was relieved it wasn't going to be a complicated investigation, for the sake of the victims' families and the survivors,' said Lees, who was talking quietly so the server couldn't hear them. 'Nye had left a trail that would put Hansel and Gretel to shame – we even recovered a file on his laptop that we seized from the hotel in Bournemouth with the names, addresses and phone numbers of every current Decorous member. My four-year-old would've done a better job of being a criminal mastermind.'

Lees said the burner phone was brought to Strutton's attention by a junior officer, at which point Eve, who'd been hanging off his every word, interrupted.

'Wait, he told me he'd given it to you to investigate.'

323

'That was after. The DC in question was tasked with looking into Mark Cleaver's burner phones and had quickly established they were for his girls on the side. The third burner phone was originally lumped in with them, until this DC, like you did, had another look and thought there was something a bit iffy about the messages. Cleaver's data reads like badly written soft porn, the texts are pure filth, but these ones are clinical and not remotely raunchy. So, he takes it to Strutton, who asks me to have a look,' said Lees. 'I do, and I agree with the DC – those aren't sexts and we shouldn't be dismissing them as such.

'I get nowhere with tracing the phone itself – it was bought for cash and the SIM's unregistered. But given it's been dumped in the loo when every guest and worker had their phone removed from them, I thought there was a possibility it belonged to one of the suspects and we should do some more digging on it,' Lees went on. 'I tell this to Strutton and say I think we should look into the other number too, the one ringing and texting it, but he says to leave it for now, he doesn't think it's relevant. Then he makes me OIC, and after that I'm as busy as shit following up a million other things, so it slips my mind.' He side-eyed Colgan. 'Which is where you come in.'

'It doesn't matter that the guv doesn't want the burner phone followed up, I still have to enter it into disclosure, so the CPS and defence are aware of it,' said Colgan. 'It's already logged on HOLMES, so it's not like he can just chuck it away and pretend it never existed.'

Every line of inquiry in an investigation went through the Home Office Large Major Enquiry System before it was actioned. If it wasn't on HOLMES first, it didn't get done.

'The CPS knew about it fairly early on,' Horner interjected, 'but because of the information we were given regarding its provenance, we agreed it was one for the unused pile.'

'Strutton told you to leave it, he didn't say to dismiss it entirely,' Eve remarked to Lees. 'The investigation could've come back to it at some point.'

Colgan nodded. 'It did. The DC comes to find me one day and says he was concerned it is being overlooked. He also thinks there might be something in the timing of when the texts were sent. I follow the correct chain of command and inform Gary as OIC and we both flag it up again to Strutton, who says he'll make sure it's looked into. About a week later he appears at my desk and orders me to write up the MG form saying the messages are obviously sexts between two people having an illicit relationship and the data's not worth disclosing to present in court and I'm to stick it in with the rest of the unused material.'

'He specifically told you to write that on the form?' asked Horner.

'He practically dictated it,' said Colgan morosely. 'Later on, I saw the DC and he said Strutton had told him the same thing.'

'The DC didn't question why the phone wasn't returned to him to investigate further?' Eve asked.

'Strutton had given him bigger things to do. The kid's now a DS.'

'That wasn't the end of it though,' said Lees. 'Frank then spoke to me about how Strutton had made him write up the MG form. He was concerned.'

'The guv is a brilliant detective, the best SIO I've ever worked for, but I think he got a bit cocky that we had Nye and the rest charged and on remand by then. I don't think he wanted to contemplate another person being involved,' said Colgan.

'Plus the texts weren't conclusive, as you know, Eve,' Lees added. 'There was enough doubt to make him think it wasn't worth the aggro.'

She nodded. 'No, they aren't. It was pure luck I spotted the correlation between the timestamps and the timeline of the siege.

But Strutton was far more aware of the phone's significance than he's let on, because at some point the handset was sent to Forensics and they recovered a partial print that doesn't match any of the Decorous members present that night. We think Nye had someone else helping him inside the Novus that the others didn't know about.'

Eve then explained she'd found a text from a year previously where Nye had promised to keep the person's identity a secret.

Lees turned even paler, as Colgan dropped his face into his hands and swore.

'Strutton knew that?' said Lees, his voice hoarse.

'I think he must have, and that it was after the print was flagged to him that he got Colgan to write up the MG form to rule the phone out.' Eve hesitated. What she was about to say would hurt Lees and, despite her initial impression of him, she was starting to believe he was the good copper Strutton had said he was. 'He's blaming you for the failure to thoroughly investigate it.'

Lees swore loudly, causing the young woman behind the counter to glance nervously in their direction. Horner placatingly asked her for four more coffees.

'I should've known something was up when your review was ordered,' Lees replied miserably. 'He went off on one, saying it was outrageous that our work was being called into question. I can't believe he's trying to pin this on me though.'

Colgan tried to reassure him. 'But he can't now, not now the four of us know what's really gone on. I made an error on that rape trial, and I own that. I'll take whatever the disciplinary outcome is, but neither of us messed up on Novus and we won't be taking the blame.'

'We will make sure of it,' said Horner, nodding.

'I've been meaning to ask,' Eve addressed Colgan. 'Why were you moved off the case?'

'I don't know. One minute my work's fine, the next thing I'm being told it isn't up to scratch and I'm off the case.'

'I bet the guv was worried you'd go back to the phone at some point and bug him about it, so it was easier to just get you out of the way,' said Lees.

'Then I came along and blew his plan,' said Eve.

The four of them sat in silence for a few moments, each absorbing the gravity of the situation they were now mired in.

'It's one thing to overlook a line of investigation that could lead to the arrest of another suspect, it's quite another to knowingly suppress evidence,' said Horner heavily. 'I need to inform the DPP.'

'What will it mean for the trial?' asked Lees, almost panicked.

'I don't know. We could try to persuade the judge it's not a serious enough breach of evidentiary process in the grand scheme of things, and that it doesn't undermine the case against The Seven,' said Horner. 'But the defence will probably argue that Strutton's cover-up is an abuse of process and denies them a fair trial.'

The two detectives looked broken. 'He can't have been thinking straight,' said Colgan. 'He'd never have deliberately jeopardised the trial. He's put everything into the investigation.'

Eve thought back to Strutton's emotional response to his wall of headshots in the incident room and knew Colgan was right. His suppressing the evidence sounded like a misguided attempt to avoid any delay in securing justice against The Seven. He must've panicked when he realised her review might unearth the burner phone he hoped had been forgotten about, and that the defence could use his abuse of process to their advantage in court.

'This missing eighth man needs to be in the dock with them though,' she said. 'We know he was texting Nye during the siege and yet he's still out there, free as a bird, possibly even planning another atrocity. He's a mass murderer and should be on trial.'

It was Horner's turn to slap a piece of paper down on the table, making them all jump. 'Here's a list of everyone who attended or worked at the event who either comes from a European nation or has significant ties to one,' he said.

Both Lees and Colgan were bewildered.

'What's this about?' asked Lees, picking up the paper and scanning it. 'Why is Matthew Seymour's name at the top?'

Horner and Eve shared a knowing look.

'Okay. Now it's your turn to listen to me,' she said.

Chapter Fifty-Seven

By the time Eve had finished telling them what Luke Bishop knew about Nye's second-in-command swearing in Brendan Morgan, and Joan Beck telling her how Nye had met this person abroad – taking care to refer to Joan only as 'a credible source' – Lees and Colgan were alert and upright in their chairs, primed for action. It might be too late to prevent the current trial having to be abandoned, but tracking down and arresting this other suspect could go some way towards repairing the damage caused by Strutton suppressing evidence. The Seven could stand trial again with their accomplice in the dock beside them.

'Matthew Seymour's not your man though,' said Lees, handing the list back to Horner.

'How can you be so sure?' said Horner. 'He's on the list because for a large part of the year he lives in Malmö, the Swedish city his late mother was from and where he spent summers with his maternal grandparents.'

'He was treated as a suspect initially. As the organiser of the event and the guest of honour's grandson who stood to inherit millions, we needed to be sure Matthew wasn't involved. The security services and Counterterrorism did a deep dive and found nothing. There wasn't a corner of his life that wasn't investigated.'

Eve took a pen from her bag and drew a line through Matthew's name.

'Next is Samuel Fraise, Dame Cynthia's French personal assistant.'

'He's also about ninety himself and hasn't lived in France since the sixties. I think we can safely cross him off,' said Lees, trying to subdue a smile.

Eve hitched an eyebrow. 'You're certain?'

'He's right,' said Horner. 'Cynthia was practically housebound and Samuel never left her side. He hasn't lived in France for decades.'

Lees ruled out a few more names as having been thoroughly investigated at the time. They included some theatre employees and catering staff who were EU nationals and a few of the higher-profile guests Horner had recalled from their statements would travel to Europe for work.

'The next one is an interesting one,' said Lees. 'Nye let go three hostages he caught trying to escape through the basement. They were Richard and Faye Winter and this guy.'

'Roddy Jepson,' Eve read aloud. 'Dame Cynthia's live-in carer.'

'He's from Denmark originally, so that could fit. We would need to check if he was abroad in the year before the siege,' said Horner.

Suddenly Eve gasped. 'Hang on, I think I know how we can work out who it is.'

The three men stared at her, wide-eyed.

'It was something the source said when they told me Nye had met this person in Europe. They said it wasn't anywhere like Germany or France because Patrick's not stupid.' She stared back at them, a grin slowly spreading across her face. 'Which countries in Europe don't have extradition treaties with the US?'

Lees and Colgan's expressions contorted, while Horner thumped the table jubilantly.

'Of course! Patrick Nye wasn't going to risk being caught and sent back to California to stand trial for what happened at the compound. He'd have picked somewhere he knew wouldn't cooperate with the States. Well done, Eve,' he crowed.

Lees had his phone out. 'According to this, the only European nations without extradition treaties with the US are Ukraine and Moldova.'

Horner's face fell. 'There's no one on the list of either nationality.'

While he, Lees and Colgan debated how easy it would be to find out whether any on the list had lived in Ukraine or Moldova, Eve had another idea. She took out her own phone and opened the search engine, then tapped in a few specific words. A few seconds later she had her answer.

'I've got it. It's Switzerland,' she said.

'How do you know?' asked Colgan.

'Because I've just googled if any European nations have ever refused an extradition order from the States, and Switzerland came up. Not only that, but there's a direct connection to Nye.' She held her phone up for them to see. 'In 2010, the Swiss refused a request to extradite Roman Polanski back to the US after he was convicted of unlawful sex with a minor because it was felt due process hadn't been followed. Polanski was declared a free man by the Swiss justice minister at the time and the US was told it couldn't appeal.'

Horner breathed out heavily. 'The same Roman Polanski whose wife's murder by the Manson Family kickstarted Nye's obsession with being a cult leader?'

'The very same,' said Eve. 'Switzerland provided a safe haven for Polanski, and that wouldn't have been lost on Nye.'

The three men sat back in stunned silence. 'Fucking hell,' said Lees, speaking for them all.

Eve grabbed the list from Horner. 'So, come on, which of these names has a connection to Switzerland?'

'Just one. Him.' Horner pointed to a name second from the bottom. 'Born in Switzerland but moved to the UK in 2018.'

'Guest or employee?'

'He was the theatre's assistant manager,' said Lees.

Horatio Moser.

'Oh my God. Luke Bishop mentioned his name to me yesterday,' said Eve excitedly. 'Apparently Horatio has set up a survivors' group with him, Luke, Samuel Fraise, Richard Winter, Annie Moran and a few others.'

The others looked shocked.

'The two of them must've met while Nye was in hiding in Switzerland. But if Moser plotted the bombings with him, why would he then want to help their victims?' asked Colgan.

'He wouldn't be the first murderer to hide in plain sight,' said Eve prosaically. 'He could've had a sick urge to witness first-hand the damage his actions had inflicted. He couldn't return to the scene of the crime, so he chose the best alternative – wheedling his way in with survivors who got together to share their trauma.'

The four of them exchanged looks.

'Luke might be able to help,' she added. 'He must know Moser well. I could ask him to tell us what he knows.'

'Call him,' urged Horner. 'Do it now.'

The three of them watched her as she located Luke's number in her contacts and rang it. He picked up after six rings.

'Luke, it's Eve Wren from the CPS again. Do you have a minute to chat?'

The call had connected, but Luke didn't respond to her greeting. She could hear voices in the background, but none of them were his.

'Luke, can you hear me? I need to talk to you urgently about Horatio Moser.'

Still no reply. Then a woman's voice, a mumble.

'Luke, can you hear me?' Eve repeated, louder this time. 'I'm calling about Horatio Moser.' She suddenly paused, casting the others a worried look. 'Are you with him now? Is that why you can't talk?'

Finally Luke replied. 'Yes.'

'He's with him now,' she whispered to the others. Lees jumped to his feet and began punching numbers into his phone. 'Find out where he is,' he instructed.

'Luke, where are you?' Eve asked.

This time he answered clearly, almost a shout. 'Greenhill Gardens.'

Then the line went dead.

Chapter Fifty-Eight

LUKE

THEN

21 April, 10.23 a.m.

Luke had never handled a gun before, let alone a rifle with a magazine clip full of ammunition. But there was no time for him to question his inexperience as Brendan thrust the rifle into his lap and told him to make a run for it.

'Go, now, before they catch you,' he urged.

The diversion they'd been waiting for had kicked off moments earlier, when one of the male guests from another group had started running around the theatre like he'd taken leave of his senses. Now other hostages were matching his screams as he pushed over chairs and tables and Nye's followers were fighting a losing battle to maintain control.

'For fuck's sake, Luke, go,' Brendan hissed again.

Luke pulled Jimi to his feet and told the hostages within earshot to follow them. Then, at the very last second, he grabbed the back of Brendan's collar and yanked him up too.

'You're coming with us. I'll make it look like you're our hostage now and I'll tell the police what you did to help us. I'll make sure they know you saved us.'

Brendan nodded tearfully. 'Let's get out of here first though.'

The group of five ran through the double doors into the foyer. Luke went last, holding the rifle, while Jimi dragged a stumbling Brendan by the collar to keep up the pretence. Keeping the doors slightly ajar, Luke frantically scanned the room for Sebastian but couldn't see him. He wanted to take him with them, but also knew if he delayed much longer, they could all be killed.

Then he was spotted. The one called Snow White gestured and yelled at him to stop. Instinctively Luke raised his rifle and aimed it squarely at the man's chest.

'Stay back or I'll shoot,' he shouted. 'I mean it. Stay back!'

Snow White faltered for a minute, then lowered his own weapon. Luke backed away into the foyer, keeping the rifle trained until the doors swung closed behind him. Then he stopped, dazzled by the brightness of the foyer after sitting in near-darkness for so many hours.

'Can't we lock the doors?' asked one of the other escapees, who looked as petrified as Luke felt. Inside the auditorium a gunshot rang out and the screams grew louder. 'Or put something in front to block them?'

'You want to lock all the hostages inside? If we do that they won't be able to get out,' said Brendan. 'Leave it.'

Luke could see the police gathered outside and knew he needed to put down the rifle in case they mistook him for one of the hostage takers. He couldn't wait to: it felt heavy and alien in his hands and he loathed everything it represented.

Suddenly a man's voice screeched across the foyer. 'Wait!'

Luke swung round, rifle raised. The man who'd called out was standing in the bar area and dressed in the all-black uniform worn by theatre staff. He was tall and held himself confidently, but when he saw Luke was holding a gun, his hands sprung up in surrender.

'Please don't shoot me,' he said in an even tone. 'I only work here.'

Brendan, who was standing beside Luke, let out a strangled cry.

'We cannot take him with us,' he told Luke, clearly panicked. 'Let's just get out of here.'

Jimi let go of Brendan's collar. 'It's fine, I know him, his name is Horatio. He's one of the managers. He can come with us.'

'No, you mustn't take him with you,' said Brendan, vehemently.

Luke could see how frightened Brendan was and tried to reassure him. 'He's one of us. We can't just leave him—'

The door next to the bar abruptly opened and they all froze. It was Patrick Nye. He came through holding a hefty-looking handgun in his right hand and raised it when he saw Luke was armed.

'How the hell did you let this happen?' he asked Brendan, who shook violently.

'He's our hostage now. We're going to walk out of here with him and you're going to let us go,' said Luke forcibly.

Nye looked amused. 'Am I now? You decided that, did you?'

'Yes. You can't hold us here for ever,' said Luke.

It was then that Horatio lowered his hands. He appeared admirably calm as Nye stared at him for a moment, then turned back to address Luke again.

'The rest of you can go. He stays,' he said, pointing to Brendan.

'No, he's coming with us.'

'Either he stays or I kill some more hostages,' said Nye.

Luke went to protest, but Brendan begged him to be quiet. 'Do what he says. I'll be okay. Please, just go.'

'What will he do to you?' asked Luke, casting a wary look at Nye.

'It doesn't matter. I deserve it. Go. Save yourselves.'

Jimi, Luke and the other two escapees walked backwards towards the floor-to-ceiling glass entrance, keeping Nye in their sights the entire time.

'What about him?' Luke asked Nye, nodding to Horatio by the bar.

'He's not going anywhere either.'

'Let us take him,' Jimi begged. 'He's not done anything to you.'

Horatio smiled benignly. 'It's okay, Jimi. You go. I'll be fine.'

'I'm sorry,' Luke mouthed at him.

Once they had reached the entrance, Luke had the presence of mind to turn and shout to the police that they were hostages and being let go. He then waited until Jimi and the two others were safely outside the theatre and sprinting towards the cordon before slowly crouching down and placing the rifle on the floor.

Then he caught Brendan's eye and silently nodded his thanks.

It was the last time he ever saw him.

Chapter Fifty-Nine

FAYE

Now

The shift in atmosphere inside the guest room frightened Faye. Something had triggered Luke. His eyes blazed with fury and he was so tense the veins in his neck stood out like strands of rope beneath the skin. Was it that call he'd answered moments ago, when his phone had rung but he'd barely said a word? A female voice, tinny and distant, talking a lot, but Luke weirdly not replying, so Faye had asked him what was wrong. Luke then blurted out, 'Greenhill Gardens,' and hung up, and Faye was now afraid for herself and the others.

She could tell by Horatio's expression that he'd sensed the shift, too. He drew himself up to his full height, a few inches over six feet, and squared his shoulders. 'I think we should go downstairs to eat. Who's hungry?'

Luke erupted, leaping to his feet. 'We spilled our guts out to you,' he howled at Horatio. 'You encouraged us to share our grief and pretended you'd been affected too, but it was all lies! All this time you've been laughing at us.'

Horatio said nothing. Faye was confused and Jimi looked scared.

'Why would Horatio be laughing at you?' she asked.

Luke ignored the question and turned to Jimi. 'He was in on it all along. That's why he was in the foyer with Nye and that's why Nye made him stay behind,' he croaked. 'He's been using us to cover his tracks.'

Jimi's mouth fell open. Spots of colour appeared on his cheeks. 'No. No way,' he said, getting to his feet too. 'He wouldn't. You're wrong, Luke. Horatio, tell him he's wrong.'

But Horatio wouldn't meet his gaze, and Jimi gasped.

'Will someone please tell me what's going on?' Faye begged.

Again, Horatio said nothing. He pulled his shoulders back a little more.

'It's him. He's the one that Brendan told me about, the one he met in Manchester. I didn't make the connection when we were in the foyer, but I should've done,' said Luke, his chest heaving as he ranted to Jimi, who was now pacing the room. 'Brendan looked terrified when he saw Horatio. He was adamant we shouldn't take him with us. I thought it was because he thought that bastard Nye and his lot would catch up with us if we delayed, but looking back, I realise it was because he knew Horatio was really one of them. Do you remember how Horatio was when Nye said he couldn't go with us? Cool as a fucking cucumber.'

He spun on the spot and addressed Horatio directly. 'I remember it all now. You put your hands up in surrender when you saw me pointing Brendan's rifle, but when Nye walked in waving his gun you dropped them again. You knew you were safe with him.'

Faye was bewildered. Having never attended the group's meetings, she had no knowledge of who Horatio was other than he'd worked at the theatre. She looked over at him and saw his stare was fixed on Jimi. It was as though he wasn't listening to a word Luke was saying.

'Jimi, you know me,' he said. 'You know this isn't true.'

The young man shook his head forcefully. 'I don't believe you. Luke's right. We saw you in that foyer. You didn't give a shit that Nye wouldn't let you escape with us.' His voice broke. 'You knew the theatre inside out. You . . . you were on duty that night. You used what you knew to help Nye pull off the siege.'

Shock slammed through Faye and she rounded on Horatio. 'Is that true?'

'Luke and Jimi are confused about what they remember. It's been a terrible day with Madeleine in hospital, we're all upset,' Horatio replied. He tugged at the cuffs of his thin cotton bomber jacket, worn with a white shirt and jeans. 'I suggest we put an end to this nonsense and join the others downstairs.'

Luke lunged at him. 'You killed all those people and then you encouraged us to mourn them with you, you sick, sick bastard.'

Horatio managed to sidestep Luke, whose tears streamed down his gaunt cheeks. Jimi rushed to grab Luke before he fell to the ground.

'Please stop this now, Luke, before it goes too far,' Horatio said.

'We're going to make sure everyone knows it was you,' Jimi shouted at him.

Faye didn't know what to believe. 'Why on earth would Horatio be involved?' she asked them.

'Because he believes Nye's bullshit conspiracies about the rich being too rich, or whatever the crap it is he stands for. It was you, wasn't it? You were Nye's second-in-command for Brendan's swearing-in.' Luke broke off for a moment, then, to Faye's surprise, he smiled at Horatio through his tears. 'You're done for. Someone else has been asking questions about you.'

'Who?' Horatio demanded sharply.

'The person who just called me. She works for the CPS. I met her and told her all about Brendan's meeting in Manchester, and now she knows you're here. She's on her way now. Probably with the police.'

Horatio's veneer of calm slipped so suddenly it terrified Faye.

'You think you're so clever,' he shouted at Luke. 'You're pathetic. You all are. Whining about everything, when you've got more than most people could ever dream of having.' He whipped his hand underneath the back of his jacket and pulled a small handgun from the waistband of his trousers. Faye screamed and Jimi let out a terrified yelp.

'Shut up, both of you.' Horatio grabbed Faye by the arm and thrust her towards Luke and Jimi. 'Stand over there with them.'

She did as she was told, trembling uncontrollably as Horatio aimed the gun at them. 'I don't want to hurt any of you,' he said, his forehead glistening with sweat and his breathing laboured.

'Why did you do it?' Jimi asked.

'I would've thought that was obvious,' said Horatio testily. 'You know what The Decorous stand for.'

'No, I mean our group. Why would you spend all that time helping us if you hate us so much?'

Horatio's expression flickered. 'What can I say? You make a great alibi. Why would the police suspect someone so traumatised by what he'd experienced that he set up a survivors' group to cope with it?'

'You sick bastard,' Luke repeated with a groan. 'We shared stuff with you we couldn't bear to tell anyone else. The stuff we saw during the siege, everything that happened in the aftermath. I told you about me and Sebastian, how we'd fought that night, and do you remember what you said? You told me not to feel guilty and that he'd have known I loved him at the end. That comforted me, it really did. How could you have been so fucking cruel, knowing it's yours and Nye's fault he died?'

Faye watched Horatio intently while Luke spoke. Was that a tinge of regret she saw in his eyes?

'You must've seen some terrible things too after the bombs went off,' she cut in. 'I mean, that part wasn't planned, was it? Everyone knows Nye changed his mind at the last minute and decided to detonate them but didn't tell his followers. He let half of them walk into the path of the second bomb too, knowing they'd be killed or seriously injured. Those were your friends he did that to.'

Horatio slowly blinked at her. His grip on the gun remained firm. 'They weren't my friends. I didn't know them. I'd never met them.'

'But we're your friends now,' said Jimi. 'Samuel, Annie, me, Richard . . .'

Faye let out a sob as Jimi said her ex's name. Richard must've arrived at the house by now and was probably downstairs with the others, unaware their lives were in danger again.

'I don't believe you've just been using us to hide from the police,' Jimi added. 'I think our group means something to you.'

Horatio blinked again. 'You don't know what you're talking about, Jimi.'

But Jimi did, and so did Luke, also picking up the theme.

'You've cried with us so many times, Horatio, and we've held your hand and hugged you just as much as you comforted us. You talked to us about how you tried to help some of the victims as they lay dying from their injuries – at least you told us that's what you did.'

Faye shot Luke a warning look. They could be getting somewhere – *don't antagonise him.*

'I don't believe you've been faking your grief,' Luke added quietly. 'You feel guilt for surviving, like we all do.'

His words hit a nerve. Horatio's face contorted then straightened again.

'He's right,' said Jimi. 'You're one of us now.'

'One of you? Never!' Horatio shouted, the last vestige of his control evaporating. 'Why do you think I joined The Decorous? Because I'm not one of you. You have no idea what it's like to have to scrimp for every penny to survive,' he spat. 'I grew up in a country where people are offensively wealthy, so I know what I'm talking about. The rich just get richer while everyone else suffers.'

Luke let out a hollow laugh. 'Surely you know by now that even Nye didn't believe in what he said. Did you not see the footage from inside the theatre of him saying he was going prove everyone wrong, and that he wasn't a loser? He wasn't there on some mission to rebalance society and redistribute the world's wealth, he just wanted to be famous again.'

Jimi nodded. 'You want to talk about being poor? I earned minimum wage working at the theatre, but I know you didn't as a manager.' His voice cracked again. 'I really thought you were my friend. You said to me you'd always be here for us. You lied.'

Tears rolled down Faye's face, but she knew her distress was nothing compared to Luke's and Jimi's devastation. This man they had trusted had betrayed them in the cruellest way.

'I wasn't lying about that, Jimi,' said Horatio. 'I might have been pretending at first, but when I said I was your friend I meant it.' For a moment he floundered, his poise deserting him. 'When I first heard what The Decorous stood for, it made sense. It felt important. Then I met Nye in person, and he said the Novus was our mission and that we were helping everyone who was tired of having nothing when the rich had everything. I – I never thought he'd set the bombs off. He said they were just to get the hostages to take us seriously and obey our instructions.' Then, his voice so hushed Faye had to strain to hear him, he added, 'I'm sorry.'

With that he lowered his gun. But as Luke reached out to take the weapon from him, they heard police sirens approaching outside and Horatio panicked. He clasped the grip again and flicked the safety catch off, but Luke was too quick and barged into him, knocking the gun from his hand and sending it flying across the carpet. Then, with all his strength, like a man possessed, Luke pushed Horatio into the en suite bathroom, shoved the door shut and put his full weight against it. After a second's hesitation, Jimi added his to it.

'Grab that chair,' Luke yelled to Faye, nodding at the upright chair next to the vanity. She dragged it across the floor and Luke jammed the back of the frame under the handle. Horatio hollered and banged on the door, begging to be let out, but Luke ignored him. Jimi slumped back down on the bed and sobbed.

'Go downstairs and get the police,' Luke instructed Faye.

She didn't need telling twice.

Chapter Sixty

EVE

Now

The news that a Met Police armed response unit had stormed the Hampstead home of the late Dame Cynthia Seymour led every bulletin throughout the evening, and was still the main headline in the early hours when Eve finally fell into bed. Sleep eluded her though, despite her best efforts, and when she got up at seven-thirty it felt like she'd managed to shut her eyes for ten minutes at most.

After two strong coffees and a conversation with Leah in which she couldn't answer her flatmate's many questions about her involvement in the biggest news story of the past twenty-four hours, she got herself ready for work.

Beverly had arranged for a car to be sent to take her in. Partly for security reasons and partly because Eve was struggling to walk even more than she had yesterday. The bruise that had flowered on her hip was an intense shade of purple and painful to the touch. But still she forced her legs into her suit trousers and slipped her feet into heels, because this morning, more than any other, she needed to look the part.

As per Beverly's instructions, the car also stopped outside Monument underground station to collect Horner. The bags under his eyes matched Eve's in size and shadow and he confirmed he'd had little sleep either.

'We worked until gone midnight trying to get this submission polished, and then I was too wound up to relax. There's a lot riding on this.'

The car was taking them not to Petty France but to the Old Bailey, where in half an hour there would be an emergency closed session in front of His Honour Allardyce Ritchie. No jury, no defendants, no members of the public or press, just Darius Philbin KC arguing for the prosecution why the trial should not be thrown out despite the abuse of process by DCS Seth Strutton that had come to light as the result of the CPS's review of the unused evidence. Peter Cheney KC would be responding for the defence.

'Any word from the defence yet?' she asked.

'No, nothing. Cheney wants to keep his powder dry until we're before the judge. But we're pretty sure he'll be asking for a retrial.'

'Has there been any update about DCS Strutton?'

'He's suspended pending an IOPC investigation.'

Entering Courtroom Number Two, Eve's gaze fell upon counsel's row, the deep, worn benches from where Philbin and Cheney had presented and argued their cases for the past few weeks. Both men were already in place, appropriately attired in gown and wigs despite the closed hearing, and deep in conversation with their respective juniors. Eve's throat felt more parched the closer they got, but Horner, sensing her nerves, gave her a reassuring smile. Sitting in the row behind the KCs was the CPS case information manager. Next to her was the DPP himself, Sol Archer, who greeted Horner with a handshake before doing the same with Eve.

'You've done a fantastic job on this review,' he said to her. 'Well done.'

Philbin rose to shake their hands too. 'It's good news. The defence is prepared to support our motion that the abuse of power isn't egregious enough to ask for a dismissal.'

Horner and Eve both reacted with a mixture of surprise and relief, having feared the worst. Peter Cheney nodded from his side of counsel's row. 'I've been instructed by my clients that they do not wish to contest the motion. They want the trial to continue.' He shrugged. 'They say Moser's arrest makes no odds to them.'

In other words, Nye wasn't going to let anyone steal his thunder.

Horatio Moser was currently in a police cell at Kentish Town and cooperating with detectives. According to the update DS Lees had given Eve and Horner late last night, he had fully admitted his involvement in the Novus bombings in an interview that had started yesterday evening and would resume this morning. He confirmed he was a member of The Decorous and had met Nye in 2010 while the latter was in hiding in Switzerland. Horatio, then in his early thirties, had been posting on a forum in support of the cult, and Nye – using an alias – began directly messaging him. Once Nye felt he could trust Horatio, he confided who he really was and how he wanted to execute the kind of atrocity he'd planned in LA before the FBI raid.

Bowled over by his idol's trust in him, Horatio set to work making it happen, spending the next few years working in hospitality in Geneva to gain the necessary experience he'd need to infiltrate their target venue. Both men were happy to play the long game, knowing they'd need to be patient to succeed with Nye's plan.

After Nye made contact with Edwin Barker, both men came to the UK. Horatio went to stay in Manchester because Nye wanted to keep him a secret from the others in Bournemouth, viewing him as The Decorous' secret weapon. The only time he surfaced was as Nye's stand-in on the day Brendan Morgan was inducted into The Decorous. Brendan had been showing signs of backing out, so, rather than make him travel to Bournemouth, Nye decided the ceremony should be held closer to his hometown of Stockport to win him over. Horatio told the detectives interviewing him that he wasn't surprised by Brendan's change of heart during the siege, because he had clearly harboured doubts about what they were doing.

Horatio also confirmed he had been in possession of the Motorola burner phone throughout the siege, texting Nye to synchronise events from his vantage point roaming around the foyer, basement and backstage. Nye had explained Horatio's autonomy to the other followers by claiming they needed someone from the theatre to facilitate access to different parts of the building.

Unsurprisingly, Horatio's fingerprint matched the partial found on the burner. When asked why he and Nye had used devices separate from the encrypted app, Horatio confirmed it was to maintain his anonymity as their inside man at the Novus. Even though he had attended that one meeting in Manchester with Brendan, none of the others had ever been aware of his true involvement.

It was DS Lees who'd arranged for the armed response unit to be despatched to Dame Cynthia's house after he, Colgan, Eve and Horner had realised Luke was warning her that something was wrong when he'd shouted 'Greenhill Gardens' down the phone. In his update last night, Lees also revealed that Horatio had indicated his intention to plead guilty and accept his sentence at the earliest possible hearing. Once in police custody he had repeatedly expressed his concern for the rest of the survivors' group and wanted them to know the grief he'd shown in their meetings had been genuine and that he was sorry for the part he'd played in causing theirs.

Eve hadn't spoken to Luke in person yet to see how he was faring after Horatio's arrest, but he did text her the good news late last night that Madeleine Farmer had regained consciousness and was expected to make a full recovery. Without Luke's help, Eve might never have been able to connect the dots.

The clerk called the near-empty court to order. They rose as one as the judge came in, sat down, then peered at them from his bench. Eve's stomach knotted.

His Honour cleared his throat. 'Shall we begin?'

Epilogue

Six Months Later

Luke ran his finger between his neck and his collar. It was the first time in a long time that he'd worn a suit of any kind, let alone black tie, and the bow tie's snugness was making him feel like his throat was closing up.

Madeleine reached over and gently pulled his hand away. 'Stop messing with it,' she said. 'You look great.'

'So do you,' he said, and she did, in a silver custom-made Oscar de la Renta gown that brought out the blue in her right eye and matched the patch covering the left side. The gown's skirt was so voluminous Luke had spent the journey squashed up against the door on his side of the limousine to avoid creasing it.

'You don't think I've gone overboard with the dress, do you?' she asked him.

'Absolutely.' He laughed. 'But it's what Matthew wanted. "All out" is what he said the dress code was.'

Madeleine puffed out her cheeks, which were flushed despite the thick layer of make-up covering them. Her scars had faded a little more over the last few months with treatment and the worst of them were less vivid than they had been. 'I feel so nervous,' she said.

'Me too. But it's going to be fine. The others will be there.'

Jimi and his mum Ruby had left the hotel moments after them and were in the car behind theirs now. Jimi had been texting throughout the journey and Luke was pleased to note there was no trace of anxiety in his messages, only excitement. It was Jimi's first trip to the States, and he was loving every moment so far, although Luke knew his experience as Matthew's all-expenses-covered guest was a far cry from the usual tourist trip. Ruby, meanwhile, was resplendent in a gown Madeleine's stylist had sourced for her, and she'd adored having her make-up and hair professionally done in Madeleine's suite. The worry patch she had rubbed bare on her scalp was now artfully hidden beneath the swept-up style they'd given her, much to her delight.

'Not all of us,' said Madeleine mournfully. 'It won't be the same without Samuel. It's not fair, especially after all the work he put in to making the exhibition happen.'

Samuel's cancer diagnosis had been caught early by his doctors, but the treatment he was now undergoing was so debilitating he couldn't fly to Los Angeles to join the others. They were devastated he wouldn't be there, but they had a plan to make sure he was still very much a part of tonight's preview showing of Dame Cynthia's costumes at the FIDM.

The museum was in downtown LA, a half-hour drive from the Sunset Marquis Hotel, where the rest of the group were staying on Matthew's tab. Except for Richard, who'd finally moved back to LA a month previously and was now living in his old home in Holmby Hills. After everything that had happened in his grandmother's Hampstead mansion, which he'd now sold, Matthew couldn't do enough for the group.

'How much further?' asked Luke.

Madeleine peered out of the limo's window to get her bearings. 'I think it's on the next block.'

He pulled at his collar again.

There was none of the usual fanfare as their limousine pulled up in the side street next to the museum. No photographers, no red carpet, no assistants with clipboards waiting to direct them to where they needed to go. Just Matthew, waiting by the open fire exit, decked in black tie himself, as had always been the plan. Tonight was just for them, the survivors' group, and no one else.

Luke helped Madeleine out of the limo and held her hand as they crossed the pavement, her gown rustling heavily as she walked. She no longer relied on a stick to support herself, and she had also managed to reduce her pain meds intake to a minimum, following months of intensive physio. Luke still had no idea whether her overdose was accidental or not, Madeleine wouldn't discuss the subject, but almost dying was enough of a scare to convince her she did still have a life worth living. A career too, as a producer, with her first film set to go into production in the spring. She'd turned down the offers from *Vanity Fair* and *Vogue*.

She'd offered Luke any job he wanted on the production, but he'd declined. He wasn't sure if the film industry was for him any more, but he wasn't sure what he wanted to do instead. For now, he was still living in London.

The car bringing Jimi and Ruby pulled up moments later and they joined Luke and Madeleine in greeting Matthew. 'Faye just messaged to say she's already here,' said Jimi.

'She is. And Richard and Annie too. Hilary's going to be last to arrive, but she's only a few minutes away,' said Matthew, after disentangling himself from Ruby's enthusiastic embrace. 'Shall we go in?'

Matthew had fitted seamlessly into the group. There was a time after Horatio's arrest when it looked like they might never meet again; the trauma of discovering his betrayal almost too much for them to bear collectively. It was Jimi who drew them back together, refusing to take no for an answer until, almost two months after the incident in Hampstead, they had assembled once again in the back room of Ruby's café and talked it through. There were tears, anger and regret, but no recriminations. Not even for Matthew, who admitted he'd had a phone on him during the siege but had been too terrified to use it in case Nye saw. He lived daily with the guilt that more lives might've been saved had he tried to raise the alarm, but the group was helping him deal with it. None of them could ever have guessed the secret Horatio was hiding from them.

Luke had come to realise that Jimi had a remarkable capacity for empathy and forgiveness. So, with his and the others' encouragement and Matthew offering to cover his student fees, Jimi was applying to college to train to become a counsellor. But there was something he wasn't being honest about, something Ruby had confided in Luke because she was worried about her son. Tonight they all needed to deal with it.

The exhibit hall was empty except for them. They all agreed they couldn't face attending the actual opening night – a red-carpet event would be far too triggering – but this way they still got to dress up to celebrate the incredible job Faye had done in working with the FIDM to curate Cynthia's costumes. As he walked past the exhibits, marvelling at the intricacies and familiarity of the designs that delineated her most successful roles, Luke found he was moved to tears. This was how Dame Cynthia deserved to be remembered.

Minutes later, Matthew called him over. He was holding a tablet. 'Ready?'

With the others crowded behind him, Matthew made the call. The screen sprang to life and there was Samuel, his upper half in black tie, his lower half tucked beneath the blankets on his bed. Sitting on one side of him was Roddy, bow tie worn comically over his carer's uniform, and on the other was Eve Wren, who'd become a good friend to the group since her work on the evidence review had led to Horatio's arrest. She was wearing a sparkly top beneath a black suit jacket and was clutching a glass of something fizzy.

'What time is it there?' asked Matthew.

'Almost midnight,' said Samuel. 'But it's so lovely to see your faces that it's worth staying up late. Although this one was still working until ten minutes ago,' he added, tilting his head towards Eve.

'The CPS is working me even harder now I'm permanent,' she said, smiling. 'So, are you going to show us this exhibition or not?'

'Follow us,' said Matthew, and together the group walked through the room again, with the other three watching from London.

After the viewing, the video call at an end, the group was served champagne and canapés by a waiter Luke knew had been vetted by Matthew's personal security. The fear that someone might try to repeat Novus would never leave him.

It was as they were standing in a circle that Luke decided to bring up what Ruby had told him with Jimi. He knew Jimi wouldn't mind the public airing – there was nothing they hadn't shared in the group, and this was pertinent to them all.

'Your mum told me you've been sent another visiting order,' he said.

Richard, to Luke's left, swore softly under his breath, while Annie and Hilary both shook their heads in frustration.

'Yeah, it arrived the day before we flew out,' said Jimi.

Horatio had been begging Jimi to visit him in prison ever since he'd received a life sentence for his involvement in the Novus bombings. The Seven's trial had continued at the Old Bailey despite the police's failure to investigate Horatio – they were all found guilty by a unanimous vote and handed down the maximum sentences.

Luke gave evidence eventually, and he had defended the Morgan brothers on the stand, just as he'd vowed. He spoke in particular of Brendan's bravery in the foyer when he must've realised Horatio had overheard him saying the doors to the theatre should remain unlocked to help the other hostages flee. That was the moment when it became obvious Brendan was helping Luke and the others to escape and his fate was sealed. Once Nye was made aware of Brendan's betrayal, he forced him to lead the second group through the basement and into the path of the second bomb, condemning him to certain death.

Nye, it sickened them to see, had become even more of a cult figure after his imprisonment. The media gave more coverage to his first interview from behind bars than they ever did to the victims' families' reaction to his conviction. Joan Beck, meanwhile, had finally broken her silence to say she hoped to marry him now, but Lisanne Durand had countered with an interview of her own saying he was hers.

Sebastian's parents had ceased contact with Luke after the trial, unable to reconcile themselves to the fact he'd spoken up publicly for the Morgans. Other victims' families condemned Luke too. But not the group. After the way Horatio had tricked them into thinking he was someone he wasn't, they could appreciate how easily Nye had been able to brainwash Brendan and his brother.

True to his word, Horatio admitted all charges to avoid the survivors being dragged through more court proceedings. He'd been sending Jimi visitor orders because he wanted to apologise in person, prompted by Jimi's outburst that day in Hampstead when he'd expressed his sense of betrayal. In the letter that accompanied the first order he sent to him, Horatio confirmed the group had genuinely helped him and that he wanted to make amends. Luke suspected he was trying to chip away at Jimi, the youngest of them and at times the most vulnerable, because he knew the others wouldn't be as easily convinced.

'What did you do with the order?' asked Annie.

Jimi shrugged. 'I threw it away like all the rest.'

ACKNOWLEDGEMENTS

The actual writing of a novel is an incredibly solitary task. It's just the author, sitting alone at their desk for months on end, trying to marshal ideas, scattergun thoughts and bursts of imagination into readable prose. Getting the finished novel into readers' hands requires far more than just the author's input, however. It takes a huge team to publish a book – and mine is the best there is.

My agent Marilia Savvides, a million thank yous and more for your unshakeable faith in me and my writing, and for your forensic attention to detail. You are a superstar. Likewise, the team at 42MP, especially Alex Bloch, and also Alexandra Cliff and Charlotte Bowerman at RMI.

My editor, Victoria Haslam, you've shown such mind-blowing enthusiasm for *The Seven* from day one, I will be forever grateful. To everyone at Thomas & Mercer and Amazon Publishing, thank you for the warm welcome, it's great to be here! Special shout-outs to Russel McLean, Sadie Mayne, Freya Ward-Lowery and Sarah Day for working so hard on the edits to make *The Seven* the thriller it is, and Dan Mogford for the cover design.

Julie Seddon, I couldn't have written Eve's story without your brilliant insight into the workings of the CPS. I am indebted. Thanks also to Alison Bailey and Jo Jhanji for the early feedback and to Duncan McGarry, Harriet Tyce, Neil Lancaster, Merilyn

Davies and Imran Mahmood for answering my police and legal queries. It goes without saying that any errors in procedure are mine alone! I must also acknowledge Vincent Bugliosi and Curt Gentry's compulsive and brilliantly researched *Helter Skelter: The True Story of the Manson Murders* for inspiring Patrick Nye's backstory.

My dear family and friends, especially my parents, Elaine and Mick, your support is everything. Likewise, my crime author friends. You know who you are. If you hadn't urged me to stay put and hold my nerve, I might have given up my seat on the roller coaster long ago.

Finally, Rory and Sophie. Thank you for your endless patience and good humour during the many months I zoned out to write *The Seven*. I couldn't do any of this without you. Love you more than Arsenal.

ABOUT THE AUTHOR

Robyn Delvey is a pseudonym for critically acclaimed and award-winning writer Michelle Davies. She is the author of several previously published novels and has worked for some of the most successful brands in UK magazine publishing, including *Grazia* and *Stylist*. She trained in journalism and for a period was court reporter on an award-winning weekly newspaper in Buckinghamshire, covering trials at both magistrates' and Crown court. She now lives in north London with her partner and their daughter.

Follow the Author on Amazon

If you enjoyed this book, follow Robyn Delvey on Amazon to be notified when the author releases a new book!

To do this, please follow these instructions:

Desktop:

1) Search for the author's name on Amazon or in the Amazon App.
2) Click on the author's name to arrive on their Amazon page.
3) Click the 'Follow' button.

Mobile and Tablet:

1) Search for the author's name on Amazon or in the Amazon App.
2) Click on one of the author's books.
3) Click on the author's name to arrive on their Amazon page.
4) Click the 'Follow' button.

Kindle eReader and Kindle App:

If you enjoyed this book on a Kindle eReader or in the Kindle App, you will find the author 'Follow' button after the last page.